THE AMBASSADOR AND THE SPY

THE AMBASSADOR AND THE SPY

A Novel by

Vincent Brome

CROWN PUBLISHERS, INC., NEW YORK

Inquiries should be addressed to Crown Publishers, Inc., 419 Park Avenue South, New York, N.Y. 10016.

Library of Congress Catalog Card Number: 73-84254
ISBN: 0-517-511150

Printed in the United States of America

Published simultaneously in Canada by General Publishing Company Limited

Designed by Michael Perpich

For Maire

THE
AMBASSADOR
AND
THE SPY

CHAPTER 1

He was almost a travesty of a hunted man, with sweat gleaming on his face, his breath coming fiercely, and he called in a kind of shrill whisper: "Quick! Quick! Open up!"

Inside the embassy the security guard behind the reception desk woke abruptly, went to the door, looked out, and walked swiftly across the courtyard. Peering through the iron bars he said, "Who the hell are you?"

"British subject," the man gasped and thrust an unmistakable blue and gold passport through the bars. "For Chrissake, quick—they'll be here."

The road stretched behind him wet from recent rain, echoing empty. The expectant hush before dawn had settled over everything.

"I don't see anyone," Thompson said.

"For God's sake, hurry."

"Or hear anyone."

"Asylum—I want asylum!"

Herbert Thompson carried the passport back to the old-fashioned brass lamp with its pool of pale yellow light over the arched doorway, and scrutinized it as a kind of frenzy overtook the stranger. He threw himself against the bars like a caged animal and dropped his caution and bellowed, "Open up, you dumb bastard!"

His words echoed round the cobblestoned courtyard, and were picked up by the baroque façade of the embassy to be thrown back into the night.

"Quiet!"

But now the man saw his advantage and a torrent of abuse in three languages echoed round the courtyard as his trapped figure leaped up and down almost maniacal in its desire to break out of—reality—into the safety of the embassy compound.

Away up on the second floor in the duty room the duty officer allowed a small grimace to pass across his face. Why in God's name did some lunatic have to arrive in the middle of the night and create a scene when the subtleties of Proust's sophisticated world had just reabsorbed him. And tomorrow was Bag Day of all days. . . .

1

Far off in the last of six rooms on the third floor of the left wing of the embassy the ambassador turned over in his four-poster bed, listened a moment for a fresh outburst, sat up, and discreetly switched on the small table lamp on his side of the bed. Sleep no longer came easily and it was far too precious to be disturbed by any casual stranger breaking open the night. In the dim light of the table lamp his wife lay inert beside him, her hair in curlers, the signs of a double chin emphasized by the position of her head on the pillow.

The voices beat up again from the courtyard. They were shrilly abandoned now and four people in the sleeping hulk of the embassy came half awake to listen. The ambassador found himself trying to pick out words against his will because he knew now that short of taking another sleeping pill he was doomed to stay awake for at least two hours.

He heard the old-fashioned iron key grate in the lock as clearly as if he had turned it himself, and before it happened he saw the big iron gate rumble back on its thick hinges. Who in God's name could Thompson be admitting at this time of night? Bag Day tomorrow, a whole sequence of telegrams unresolved, and at least ten people to receive in—so to say— audience—before trying to deal with that formidable character, Joseph Kalogh.

Outside in the wet yard Herbert Thompson stayed close as he escorted the man to the main entrance through the big mahogany door and took his place behind the reception desk.

"Sit down," Thompson said and his eye ran carefully over a man who continued to shiver and sweat. He had the long, leaning bleached look of a tree that had been struck by lightning and survived. Thompson noticed that his old overcoat had a velvet collar.

"Your name?" he said, and the stranger thrust his passport at him again. "I want to see the ambassador."

"Not at this time of night you won't . . . Peter Robinsohn . . . That's an odd way to spell Robinson."

"I must see him now—before the police arrive—don't you understand?"

He was still breathing heavily.

"Understand what?"

"I want asylum—now before they come."

Thompson turned to the duty book. "Mr. Hargreaves is the duty officer tonight," he said. "He's working in the cipher room—and said he wasn't to be disturbed."

Specially trained in diplomatic security, Thompson knew, as in everything diplomatic, the first law must be to remain unruffled. In his small way he had taken to aping what he regarded as ambassadorial calm.

The stranger came to his feet abruptly and a transformation overtook him. He ceased to shiver and his frame seemed to swell visibly into that of

2

a person of authority. A new and deep voice boomed across the reception room.

"Get your Mr. Hargreaves on the phone at once."

Thompson sat back before the sheer force of the new personality. "You—er—know him?" he said.

The stranger strode up close to the reception desk and stared straight at Thompson, his face ruthless. "At once—do you hear—"

Idiotically in the middle of the night Thompson began the patter which had preceded hundreds of daytime visitors.

"You need to have an appointment to see . . ."

They heard the roar of motors, the scream of tires, and almost as the cars ground to a halt the doorbell echoed through the reception room.

In one dive the stranger leaped through the inner door into the corridor, raced along past the typists' room, through the swing door across information and out toward the lift to find the gate padlocked. Thompson rushed after him, almost grabbed him, but missed as he dashed up the stairs, turned along the corridor, hurled himself through the door marked chancery, and there at the far end was the cipher room. Swiftly grabbing the handle he found the door locked and hammered on it.

The steel trap at its center swung up and there was the pink smooth face of the perfect Englishman, Franklin Hargreaves, first secretary to H.M. embassy at Veralian. The stranger thrust his passport at him.

"I have an English passport—I want asylum."

Hargreaves had perfected the art of saying nothing in unexpected situations, and he took the passport to glance at it in silence before allowing the steel trap to fall back into place again. Behind its protection he scrutinized the photograph closely, opened the steel trap again, compared the face with the photograph and said, "Right—I'll come out."

As he emerged from the cipher room the night bell rang furiously and long. "Stall them while you check," the stranger said with the same dash of authority that made Hargreaves look at him sharply.

"You've timed your arrival badly," Hargreaves said and led the way downstairs toward the reception room again. He stopped abruptly at the door. "Your passport says businessman—is that true?"

"Yes," the man said.

"Can you prove that?"

"You can check in your files—"

The doorbell filled the room with its ringing and now Hargreaves walked swiftly to the door microphone.

"Hallo," he said, and a cool high voice spoke into the external microphone in vigorous Veralian.

"You have taken in a criminal we apprehended—please return him."

In equally fluent Veralian Hargreaves replied: "He's a British subject. We will check in the morning."

"We want him now."

"Let's not play games," Hargreaves said. "You know the laws of diplomatic immunity." Through the side window he could see that they were not big broad-shouldered men in raincoats with their hands buried in gun pockets but chunky men wearing the ABVO uniform who stood as if in a prearranged group, their faces missing in the gray night light.

"He is criminal and comes under our law," the high voice said.

"We will check in the morning."

"I demand to see the ambassador."

"In the morning I will tell him."

"You are refusing to turn over a criminal we arrested."

"I do not know whether he is a criminal."

"You make a very big mistake. There will be trouble."

"We will see," Hargreaves said.

"Yes . . . We will see . . . we will see," the voice echoed.

Hargreaves expected the cars to drive away but they remained outside the courtyard and he watched through the side window as the men piled back into them and simply sat there waiting. They made a black silhouette of silence and Hargreaves felt a nerve twitch somewhere far down his back as he turned and examined the stranger more closely.

"You've chosen a helluva time to arrive," he said. "It's Bag Day tomorrow. What sort of business are you in?"

"I suppose you would call it Intelligence."

"Intelligence?"

"Counterintelligence, if you like."

"You'd better come up to the duty room."

The stranger said, "Do you have any coffee?"

Somewhere far back, buried in the words, Hargreaves detected the faintest possible echo of someone not completely English, the echo of an accent which only a very literate Englishman would be able to pick out.

"How about it, Thompson?" Hargreaves said and Thompson looked very disgruntled. "It's very late for coffee in an English embassy," Hargreaves said blandly. "It's like the English licensing laws. Risk it, Thompson—break the law and be damned to H.E."

When he turned round again the stranger was taking off his overcoat and something on his inner sleeve riveted Hargreaves's attention. There was a stain. "You—er—wouldn't be hurt, would you?" Hargreaves said lightly.

"A scratch," the stranger said.

"Perhaps we'd better have a look at it. . . . Come upstairs . . . I'm sorry about the lift—it's been out of order for a week. Don't forget—two lumps for me, Thompson."

Looking out on the peace of the morning from the bathroom window Henry Gilroy Malvern reflected how he sometimes hated sunshine. It

4

burned his fair skin, it pained his eyes, it emphasized the wrinkles, and re-vealed in the scene outside the window matters that he occasionally regarded as diabolic.

Three times the old-fashioned razor went over the sensitive skin until not a trace of anything resembling hair remained. Then he massaged the deeply rutted bags under his eyes with the special cream the skin specialist in London had recommended. Still in his braces as he carefully powdered the skin, he was aware in the long mirror that all his efforts had not stopped his stomach's threatening to become a bulge. Collarless, tieless, in his red braces with a vest showing through the unbuttoned shirt, he smiled wryly as he thought that anyone might have taken him for a workingman if he were out walking like that in the street. Except perhaps for the contradiction of the face. Peering into the mirror at the wrinkling craters of skin that had formed around his eyes, he thought how lucky he was not to need glasses yet. The bold nose redeemed the oversensitive mouth and there was an impressive sweep of forehead, but somehow, on this early morning after a disturbed night, the ambassador had a terrible sense that one day—not so very far off—he would wake to find the decaying lines and deepening wrinkles suddenly collapsing upon themselves into the cadaver of an old man. For the moment with his slanting, hooded eyes and drooping chaps, he knew that his enemies were delighted to compare him to a slightly degenerate overbred Saint Bernard.

Slowly out of what he regarded as the partial ruin of his body, face, and person, he continued to refurbish the public image of the ambassador. Other men were sometimes vain enough to dye their hair as it lost its natural coloring but if Henry Malvern resisted vanity carried to that pitch, he still made concessions to it, which distressed him. But he always managed to console himself with the thought that it was all part of the interminable and elaborate night and day charade of being one of Her Majesty's ambassadors in an age when rank and good family no longer brought their natural rewards. In any case, with him the silvered hair looked distinguished.

When the teeth were cleaned he massaged the gums, another part of the night and morning ritual to hold at bay that final horror constantly threatening him—false teeth.

Before the silk shirt went over the torso and stomach, he carefully fitted and tightened an inner cummerbund made of white cotton elastic which flattened the threatening bulge and converted him to uneasy slimness. Then the plain silk tie perfectly knotted, the cuff links, the Kilgour and French tailored jacket, and the silk handkerchief at the breast pocket. Always at the end of the ritual came the sigh—a substitute for announcing the resurrection of His Excellency Henry Gilroy Malvern, Her Majesty's ambassador to this benighted country Veralia where alien materialists talked of nothing but Five-Year Plans and the proletariat.

5

Satisfied at last with his image, he went to the window, opened it, leaned out, and drew a deep breath of pine-scented air. There were the tree-lined avenues, the trolley trams, and the terraces rising from the other side of the river with the expensive villas reserved for the Party cadres. The cream-and-white taxis were already moving around the streets with the jerky ferocity of badly made toys. The serene river made a division of the classes no less distinct in this East-European country than those of England. Stretching away up on the beautiful terraces were the pink and yellow houses of the new technocrats, managers, party members, with the thirteenth-century Gothic castle thrust up on a gnarled fist of land as if the past were brandishing its glory among all these contemporary bureaucrats.

The magnificent six-lane Stalin Boulevard swung down from the castle, through the villas, to cross the river, carried on a suspension bridge whose engineering stresses forced a kind of grace into its steel utility. Once across the river, the bridge entered the industrial complex with its towering blocks of modern workers' flats and concrete forest of offices. There, at its heart, day and night glowed the crimson signal of the now state-owned prize possession—the huge iron and steel works once run for private profit by an old-world family but now proletarianized.

Henry Gilroy Malvern came from a very old-world family, with roots stretching back into sixteenth-century England but nowadays, under the new dispensation, he exercised some of his more cunning diplomacy in concealing the fact.

Now as he stood there staring out of the window, he became aware of someone brushing a hair from his immaculate shoulder and in the mirror he saw his wife, her haggard face expressionless as she slowly turned him round and ran her expert eye over him. "Very good," she said as a smile tried to break through the carefully controlled features. She kissed him gently on the cheek and he said, "Something happened at three—did you hear it?"

"No—I had a pill—two in fact."

"We weren't due for a Q.M. last night were we?"

"No."

She was always sure among the uncertainties of his much more subtle mind, and she never made a mistake about Queen's messengers.

"It couldn't have been anyway—I heard police cars," he said.

"You don't think Mason's in trouble again, do you?"

"No—it wasn't Mason." The green telephone beside the bed rang its specially subdued note as if its very presence in a bedroom was an intrusion.

"I'll take it," she said.

The voice of the first secretary said, "I'm sorry to intrude so early, Mrs. Malvern, and I do hope I did not wake you up."

"You missed that chance by five minutes," she said.

6

"I do apologize, but something very urgent has cropped up and we need His Excellency's advice."

"Is it about last night?" she said. Franklin Lionel Hargreaves heard the question with immense distaste and wondered all over again why the old man allowed his wife to ask indiscreet questions about professional matters which should not concern her.

"Perhaps—if it's convenient," he said, "I could speak to His Excellency a moment."

"Is it convenient?" she said so that both could hear, and the ambassador knew that what she meant to say was—put this man in his place, tell him it's not convenient, and let me deal with it. The number of small matters which stretched him on the rack of pleasing his wife and not upsetting his professional colleagues was long beyond counting. He adopted the usual compromise.

"Tell him I'll ring back," he said, but when she gave the message to Franklin Hargreaves he persisted.

"It is very urgent," he said.

She took her chance with calm certainty.

"Perhaps," she said in her deep voice, "if you told us what it concerns we might admit the urgency."

Franklin Hargreaves thought—so she's in that mood, is she—well—we will see about that. "I'm sorry to seem difficult, Mrs. Malvern, but for various reasons perhaps I had better wait for him to ring me back."

As she replaced the receiver Penelope Malvern said, "I sometimes think your Mr. Hargreaves comes close to being rude."

"He doesn't mean to be."

"I should say that is precisely what he aims at, but hasn't quite the courage to carry through." She frowned and added, "Oh, my God, there are two more receptions tonight, aren't there?"

"Three."

"Three? What's the other one?"

"The Germans."

"Do you mean to say we're meeting the new French ambassador, the American consul, and the German first secretary all in one night?"

"Wasn't that your doing?"

"Now don't try to foist it on me . . ."

"Caroline told me you wanted to get rid of all three at one go."

"Well, Caroline misinformed you. I certainly said I would *like* to—which is very different. Isn't it about time you found yourself a new private secretary?"

"You want me to get a man instead of a woman, don't you?"

"They're more efficient."

"And less pleasant."

"I would hardly call Caroline pleasant."

"She is to me."

The telephone rang softly again and a woman's voice said, "Have you anything more for the bag, sir?"

"Of course I have. Hold it until nine, will you."

As he replaced the receiver he said, "I must go down to the office . . ."

"Shall we be having lunch?"

"I doubt it—what with mysterious strangers out of the night, undecipherable telegrams, and someone leaking confidential information. . . ."

The embassy had come alive. Typewriters, briefings, telephones, cipher machines, teleprinters made their own background blur of noise as the ambassador walked down the creaking corridor with its threadbare carpet, nodding to the chaplain typing in his cubicle, and opened the big door to the chancery. Greeting the two secretaries in the outer office he said, "Where's Mr. Hargreaves?"

"In the registry, sir."

He walked across to registry and Hargreaves opened the door to greet him—"Good morning, sir."

"Good morning, Franklin."

They understood each other. Bred in the same schools, sharing the same politics, each could predict the other's reactions in most situations. The empty pipe, the Rugby tie, the urbanity were as much part of Hargreaves's cultivated persona as quizzical irony was part of His Excellency's.

"What was all the trouble about last night?"

"That's what I wanted to talk to you about. A man called Robinsohn, sir—English passport—asking for asylum—he spells it OHN—says he's of Jewish extraction."

"Where is he?"

"Asleep in the guest room."

"Have you checked?"

"I was just running through the personality stuff in the files, sir. But there's nothing."

"What's his story?"

"Says he's in business."

"Might mean anything. Didn't you press him?"

"He was very exhausted—and wounded."

"Good Lord! Wounded?"

"Not badly. The police were after him. Shot him—superficially—a flesh wound in the forearm. We've been waiting four hours for a doctor. They're very busy trying *not* to send one."

"They seem to want him pretty badly."

8

"He says they'd like him dead or alive. Odd thing is—he appears to know the layout of this place."

"You mean . . ."

"He said I could check in the blue files."

"The blue files! How on earth would a stranger—He *is* a stranger, isn't he?"

"To me, yes. Do you happen to have your key to the strong room?"

"Yes—but I can't stop now. Here, take it and see what you find."

"Kalogh's personal secretary telephoned at eight this morning. That's why I rang you. He's demanding an interview with you about Robinsohn today—this afternoon. He suggests three o'clock. She wanted me to ring back at once."

"Impossible. It's Bag Day—and I must finalize half a dozen telegrams. Tell him I'll see him tomorrow."

"He came on the line himself then, and was very insistent."

"So am I."

"He said he didn't want to jeopardize the good relations we had achieved."

"And you told him that kind of bluff was rather threadbare."

"I don't think it was bluff this time—"

"Well, for heaven's sake let's find out at once why this man is so important to them. Can't we wake him up?"

"He said it's all in the files, sir—the blue files."

"I can't remember anyone with that name in blue. I must be going." As H.E. moved toward the door he said, "Let me know when you've checked."

As he went past information he nodded to the big redheaded information officer who was talking fast on the telephone, with the door wide open.

The registry girls were busy handing in and collecting telegrams from the cipher room, its steel trapdoor crashing up and down, the machines seeming noisier than ever this morning. Five thousand telegrams a year. . . . If only the outside world knew how much the Foreign Office spent on telegrams and how many were superfluous verbiage.

His secretary was waiting for him at the door of his office. "The minister of the interior phoned five minutes ago, sir. He said it's very urgent." She was tall and angular to the point where the typists swore she must be a man dressed as a woman. Hygiene ranked so high, according to the information officer, that she had destroyed her sweat glands. Every day her clothes were bandbox new, elegant, bright-colored—almost transvestite in their determination to impose femininity on the flat chest and square shoulders. The private office called her The Icicle.

"Make an appointment for three tomorrow."

"But, sir . . ."

"And can I have the first draft telegram."

"Which one, sir?"

"Now, Caroline, surely you know which one."

"Approximately twenty were typed last night, sir."

"The one about chromium."

"Oh—yes, sir."

"And the file please."

Everything in the room deliberately preserved the atmosphere of another century. The faded carpets, the heavy mahogany furniture, and the ancient swivel chair in which he now sat. Once he was settled in his office, some of the mechanical crudities of the modern world were put at a distance. The days of Queen Victoria's Corps Diplomatic relaxed in the room along with crimson plush curtains. As he lit his morning cigar the ambassador glanced through the file again. There was that first idiotic telegram, nearly a month old now.

"In approaching the Veralian Government concerning the possibility of the chromium deal you should urge them to agree to stop the hostile propaganda about Gibraltar, the sale of arms to South Africa, and our implicit support of American policies in Vietnam. Above all we desire to stop the circulation of the clever rumors emanating from sources clearly traceable to Veralia which make us exclusively the allies of the Israelites in the Egyptian-Israeli struggle.

"This should be continuously pressed, for at least a month, as the only grounds on which the supply of chromium can eventually be arranged.

"If they finally refuse to cooperate in some such quid pro quo, the details of which are open to your negotiation, you are authorized to offer the following alternative: that the value of the chromium exports shall precisely be matched by the value of imports which they are prepared to buy from us.

"In no circumstances, however, can H.M. Government agree to the negotiations for the supply of chromium being publicly acknowledged for a period of one year."

It was his wife who had devised a simple technique for coping with Foreign Office telegrams which revealed London's inability to absorb small but important details of the briefings regularly sent from Veralia. Being on the spot and dealing with actual personalities gave a nuance to certain information which could easily be misread by an Olympian authority in far-off detached Whitehall. Thus, when over the dinner table one night Penelope skillfully extracted from her husband the details of the chromium telegram, she at once said: "Kalogh will never swallow that."

"I quite agree."

10

"You could even draft a reply to it *before* you see him about it."

"I suppose I could."

"Try it."

"What's the advantage?"

"Well, to begin with, we shouldn't have all that last-minute rush on Bag Day, should we?"

Whether he ever asked his wife what she would say in reply to the chromium telegram Malvern could not clearly remember, but she was very skilled at not appearing to interfere. She had casually inquired what line he would take and then a blur of ambiguity descended on question and answer in which he was never quite sure who had sown what seeds in whose mind. It was pleasant to know that she took such an interest, but every few months an odd feeling overtook him that perhaps in some infinitely subtle way there were situations, problems where she gently—*manipulated* was too blunt a word—*advised?*—too informal—*beguiled?*—too feminine—well, left some sort of vague impression on him of having hinted at one particular solution as against another.

After receiving the chromium telegram he had made an appointment with Kalogh for a week ahead but then—following Penelope's suggestion—he had sat down at once in his office to draft a reply to the Foreign Office telegram before seeing Kalogh. The ghost of his wife's words somewhere haunted it:

"I took action today and saw the Minister of the Interior concerning your telegram number 14 dated 16th July 1970. I regret to report that the Minister could not agree to your first proposal because the foreign policy toward all the territories you mention has—as we know—been carefully coordinated among Eastern European states. I do not need to say that this reply was really a euphemistic way of stating that he receives his foreign propaganda directives from Moscow, not from London.

"On the second alternative—that of matching exports with imports—I received the reply that his government had little hope of meeting such a condition since the class of manufactured goods involved are either in high demand domestically or, if a surplus occurs, exported to Russia.

"I therefore made discreet overtures about a third possibility which had occurred to me after reflecting on the rejection of the previous two. In so doing I of course made it very plain that I was speaking personally and not in my official role as ambassador, underlining the fact that I would need your approval before confirming or denying the proposal.

"It consisted simply in the suggestion that we might sell the requisite chromium if they were prepared to remove certain trade

11

barriers and allow our agents to compete in areas so far forbidden which our commercial attaché enumerates to you in a separate note sent by this day's bag.

"Assuming that you agree with this third proposal I will confirm the details to the minister of production and he will then consult his fellow members of the Central Committee but I should be grateful for early instructions because the committee is due to meet toward the end of next month."

So there it was. The complacency of head office forced one into diplomatic duplicity and one spent part of one's time anticipating events and not carrying out instructions quite as the foreign office expected. You wrote telegrams about interviews with the ministers of the interior before you had actually had such interviews, rejected F.O. tactics before they were heard by the other side, and tailored new solutions to a proper interpretation of the detailed facts. Worse still, the commercial attaché forced you to deal with sordid business details which he had bungled and caused your finest skills to suffer a certain degradation. You were even liable to forget in the elaboration of the exchanges that perhaps it was your wife who had devised the technique.

In the chancery registry, Hargreaves turned the personal biography files with cynical swiftness, cursing Robinsohn for interfering with his day's routine. Normally the girls would have combed the biographies for him but this came—heavily—under confidential. Being head of chancery made you something of a dog's body. You had the double function of chief of staff and executive officer and the interruptions in both capacities were sometimes worse because they often clashed. Matters were particularly pressing at the moment because a mysterious Veralian bug kept attacking different members of the staff and you never knew who would be the next victim. His administration officer would normally deal with staff queries, but he had been sent home for a month's sick leave. Secretaries, decoders, Queen's messengers, service attachés, all—even down to security guards— had the right to put inane queries. There were many assistants and secretaries to protect you but there were also those who had perfected ways and means of penetrating those defenses for the sheer pleasure of doing so. The regulations governing communications up and down the hierarchy were open to fascinating manipulation once they had been mastered in detail.

Hargreaves paused at a very short sharp scathing note on the personal secretary to the minister of the interior. Who wrote that? Probably the information officer. He had a nice turn of sardonic wit when challenged. "Ivan Dabrowski can be relied upon, if presented with off-the-record information, to be completely indiscreet within a matter of twenty-four hours."

12

Hargreaves spun the last file through his fingers as if shuffling a pack of cards but there was no sign of any reference to a person called Robinsohn. Could the man conceivably have been right in the first place? Was he really is that holy of holies, the final classified absolutely secret blue files? And if so, why . . .

He glanced at his watch. Ten thirty and all that stuff waiting for the bag. God damn and blast all Robinsohns. Swiftly he turned the combinations of the safe, his mind automatically spelling out the sequence. H.E. made a point of never trusting the combination to anything but memory and his own personal diary, although one of these days, Hargreaves reflected for the hundredth time, they would be caught out with memory lost and the personal diary missing.

The heavy door swung open and there on the lower shelf was the dispatch box which H.E.'s small elegant key opened. Hargreaves took out the three blue files and settled down at the steel side desk. Number one. Confidential minutes of unofficial exchanges between His Excellency and members of the Veralian Government. That was at least one week's fascinating reading. Number two looked as if it had not been opened for some time and as he turned its alphabetical index almost at once his eye jumped to the name Robinsohn.

"Peter Robinsohn," he read, "aged thirty-five, alias Pierre Regnier, alias Anton Vladomiticz. Son of Russian lawyer and English mother. His father came to England and set up in practice having repassed his law examinations in 1930. Peter Robinsohn, his son, speaks English, Russian, French, and Veralian with very little trace of an accent. Began career as an actor. Recruited M.I.5, 1955. Reliable—unmarried—and not homosexual."

Security classifications ranged from private through confidential to top secret and this one was stamped top secret.

So they had taken in a bloody spy. Hargreaves hated spies. The word was old-fashioned, he knew; spies now were more to keep our end up in a computerized game than to yield any useful information. But whether they were useless or not, he hated them. They deliberately broke all the canons by which he lived.

Swiftly relocking the dispatch box and the safe, he hurried from the strong room down to H.E.'s office. As he went into the outer private office he said to Caroline Masters, "Is he alone?"

She nodded.

He strode in to find the ambassador using the green scrambled telephone.

"Sorry," Hargreaves said and was about to back out of the room again but His Excellency gestured to a chair and went on talking. "No . . . we have not checked yet . . . But we have no evidence whatever that he is a criminal . . . Charge sheet? Yes, that is what we call it in

13

England. Yes, I see . . . But, Kronowitcz, you would not expect us to accept the evidence of your charge sheet as absolute truth, would you . . . Oh, come . . . We've known each other long enough not to deal in naïvetés . . . No . . . I'm sorry if I sound short . . . But you must know what Bag Day means at an embassy . . . As I said before, tomorrow at three . . . Well, that's very accommodating of you . . . Oh, but before you go—those men in the embassy courtyard here—they're a bit of an eyesore. Could you have them removed, do you think? . . . But, Kronowitcz, they make my staff uneasy . . . You do realize that *legally* they should be *outside,* not *inside* the courtyard . . . No—no, I'm sorry, it just won't do. If they are going to stay, I must ask you to remove them *outside* the courtyard . . . No difference! But that's absurd. You know better than I do it's the difference between civilian and diplomatic immunity . . . Oh—come now—it would be an act of total supererogation for me to try to instruct you in the laws of diplomatic immunity . . . I'm sorry. It's an absurd English word meaning—overdoing your duty. My duty . . . You have no need to remind me of that . . ."

Listening, Hargreaves remarked what a deceptive man Malvern could be. The image of the stuffed dummy of Her Majesty's government mouthing ventriloquist phrases from the Foreign Office vanished when someone roused in him a person of implacable determination. The second secretary, Paul Rostand, called it pigheadedness, arguing that he stuck to a point beyond its true validity. Strength like that became a weakness. Hargreaves saw it otherwise. Once again a grudging admiration of the Old Man broke through as Malvern took the initiative to wind up what threatened to become an interminable conversation. "Well—if they are not outside the gate by midday I'm afraid there will be serious trouble . . ."

As he put the receiver down, Hargreaves handed him the file with the red marker at Robinsohn, and Malvern read it swiftly.

"That's going to complicate life," he said. "Is he up yet?"

"Shall I check?"

"Don't bother. I will." H.E. deflected the switch of his desk microphone. "Caroline, find out whether a Mr. Robinsohn who stayed in one of the guest rooms last night is available yet—will you?" He sat back in his chair. "How in God's name can this fellow know about the contents of the blue files?"

While they talked on, the traffic in the private office increased until the military attaché arrived with half a dozen telegrams which Caroline discreetly added to the pile on the ambassador's desk without interrupting him. While he talked on to Hargreaves he took up his ancient fountain pen, and without reading more than the first and last lines automatically initialed one telegram after another. He had perfected decentralization in some areas. In the outer private office the two telephones rang continuously, but Caroline stalled all calls.

The desk microphone made its small atmospheric signal and Caroline's voice said, "Mr. Robinsohn is here."

"Send him in, will you."

He came in, leaning to one side, watchful, monosyllabic with something in the bones of his face denying the word English.

The ambassador greeted him with enough restraint to indicate his uneasiness, and Hargreaves completely masked his distaste for anyone connected with M.I.5.

Seated in the red leather visitor's chair Robinsohn kept his face professionally expressionless. Presently the ambassador said, "We were much impressed by your knowledge of our confidential files."

Robinsohn nodded.

"You wouldn't in the first place care to tell us how you came by that knowledge?"

"Six years ago I was a clerk in the registry."

"Here in this embassy!"

"Yes."

"That must have been under Rosenberg."

"It was."

"Why a clerk in the registry?"

"A cover job."

"You have been an agent for six years."

"More."

"You liked Rosenberg."

"Ambassadors come and go."

His English was flawless and his expressionless face managed to convey a—was it a vacancy?—as if he were in another place listening simultaneously to a quite different and much more profound conversation.

"But a registry clerk. That wouldn't give you access to classified information."

"No—I reclassified myself."

"How did you manage that?"

"It wasn't difficult to get access late at night."

"And you probed into confidential files."

"I needed practice—the cover job was boring. I had to wait until the Veralians accepted me as a real registry clerk before I could begin operation. It took too long. I had to do something in my own line to stop my boredom."

"But—today—how did you know about the blue files? The blue system was only instituted three years ago."

"You have people here who talk too much."

15

The ambassador shifted in his chair and with the most elaborate smile said, "I don't want to appear blunt, but would you care to identify them?"

"Not now—no."

"You refuse?"

"I refuse."

"And I suppose you have been regularly reading the contents of the blue files once a week in whatever hotel room you inhabited?"

"Not quite, no."

"Have you had access to them?"

"No."

"Then how did you know we would find your details there?"

Robinsohn sighed. "Do you mind if I smoke," he said, taking out a cigarette case. It was delivered with the perfect diffidence of the middle-class English practicing their polite rituals.

"Not at all—"

"Would you care to . . ." He gestured with the case.

"No, thanks. I don't know about Mr. Hargreaves."

Hargreaves shook his head and Robinsohn lit his cigarette, which gave off the unmistakable odor of a Gauloise. He drew deeply on it, holding the smoke in his lungs, but still he did not speak.

"I don't wish," the ambassador said, "to appear to rush you, but since you know so much about the inner workings of the embassy, you must know that Bag Day is a very busy day. How did you know we would find your details in the blue files?"

"It was anybody's guess, wasn't it. Since I was to report to you in the end—I thought they would forewarn you."

"With your name and identity?"

"Yes."

"And that would go into the blue files?"

"Yes."

"And I suppose if we asked you what was the subject of our lead telegram today you could tell us."

For the first time the vacant eyes came alive and a flash resembling amusement went across them.

"One of them will certainly concern me."

The ambassador rose.

"Well, I don't need to tell you your arrival seems to have upset six months' careful work with the Ministry of the Interior and I don't know yet exactly what we are going to do about that or you. Tell me, Mr. Robinsohn, why are you so important to them?"

"I wouldn't know."

Halfway to the door the ambassador said: "But your mission—it would be hopelessly indiscreet to ask what you hope to find in this country."

"Not at all."

"I understood agents never talked."

"Everyone knows what I am after."

"Everyone—except Her Majesty's embassy."

"It would surprise me if you didn't know."

"Why would it?" ·

"Because we are both working on the same project."

The ambassador stopped with his hand on the ornate brass handle of the door.

"You know, Mr. Robinsohn," he said ponderously, "your omniscience almost embarrasses me. Pray—what project do we share?"

"I understood you were trying to discover which way Veralia would jump if a traditional war broke out between Eastern and Western Europe."

"Such a war is remote."

"The Russians find it more and more difficult to hold down certain satellites."

"But what can you hope to discover?"

"It's romantic, isn't it—one man against all your diplomatic machinery. But there is a document."

"What document?"

Robinsohn at last allowed a smile to spread from his eyes over the whole face, but something in the taut lines of the mouth refused to relax and it stopped there. "You don't know about the document?"

"You must forgive my ignorance."

"Isn't the number 435 bracket (a) bracket (top secret) familiar to you?"

"What," the ambassador said with theatrical patience, "does this document concern?"

"You are in a much better position to tell me than I am you," Robinsohn said.

The ambassador had opened the door now for Robinsohn and as he stood back, a quick frown went across his face.

"Your arm," he said, "I completely forgot to ask about your arm. How is it? Did the doctor come?"

"No. But it's nothing . . ."

"English understatement is dangerous with damaged arms. You must see a doctor."

"They refuse to send one."

"I trust it is not too painful."

"No. When do we meet again?"

"At dinner, this evening."

Hargreaves's total immobility broke immediately the door closed behind Robinsohn.

"If you wanted to put up a detailed alibi, his would be word perfect," he said.

"You don't believe his story?"

"He's too pat—too smooth."

"Draft a telegram to London for me will you, Franklin. You know what to ask—should he be here, is his story accurate—and ask for instructions."

"You don't think they engineered the whole thing?"

"I can think of reasons why they might have done something like it."

"So can I."

"But," the ambassador said, a kind of glassy distaste clouding his features, "you are not familiar with 435 bracket (a) bracket (top secret)?"

"No," Hargreaves said. "I am not quite as well informed as you are."

The ambassador's face broke into a beaming smile. "Thank you, Franklin. Thank you for your moral support—I'm all at sea with spies."

"I wonder," Hargreaves said, "whether I made my meaning quite clear."

"Clear, Franklin? In what way?"

"What I meant was—that the Veralians had probably engineered the whole thing."

The ambassador's face slowly emptied of all expression.

"Yes," he said, "I understood. Given him a forged passport, scratched his arm, chased him into the embassy, demanded his return at once—all in order to get him safely in here to rifle everything."

"You remember how they placed the bugging device last year in the registry."

"My God, don't remind me."

Pressing the microphone switch down, the ambassador said: "Caroline, get hold of Thompson and tell him to stay with our visitor, Mr. Robinsohn, will you? He's to keep him company everywhere—and Robinsohn's to have access to nothing—you understand—absolutely nothing. . . ."

CHAPTER 2

The frictions which arose and sometimes grew into vendettas because of last-minute inclusions in the bag made the registry a dangerous place to visit on Bag Day.

Checking, initialing, rechecking, answering the ceaseless chatter of telephones, and coping with the traffic of visitors from every section of the embassy made the chief clerk's life what he described as 'a torture chamber' for forty-eight hours. Twice a week he laid plans to outwit the stragglers, the late-comers, and those—like H.E. himself—who never missed a chance to have the bag reopened, even when the seals had gone into place, but it was useless. He had long ago accepted the fact that the call—"Closing now"—meant absolutely nothing to even the most menial member of the staff.

The Queen's messenger sauntered in, adjusted the black leather pouch over his regimental blazer, sat down, and sucked an empty pipe.

Prodding the not very clean white canvas sack labeled O.H.M.S. he said, "Five minutes, forty-five seconds to go."

A retired naval commander, he carefully economized with words. The chief clerk looked at him cynically. "I estimate you will miss your plane by anything up to—ten weeks."

"Someone will go to the gallows," the Queen's messenger said.

"It won't be me," the chief clerk replied.

It was then that Robinsohn walked in with his steps so quick and light he seemed to materialize into the room before anyone knew he was there, and Thompson came clumping after him.

Robinsohn went straight to the open sack and was thrusting in a long blue envelope when the chief clerk said, "For God's sake—do you realize you've committed treason."

Robinsohn did not speak but simply looked a question.

"No one tampers with the sack without my permission."

"I simply put in a letter to London."

The chief clerk stood back, rested his hands on his massive hips, and ran a scathing eye over Robinsohn.

"Perhaps you wouldn't mind telling me who you are?"

Thompson came forward and clumsily explained. "But that doesn't authorize you to use the bag," the chief clerk said.

"I think," Robinsohn said, "it might be better if you didn't make unnecessary difficulties."

"And you'd better get someone to authorize you."

Robinsohn simply turned on his heel and was walking out of the room when the chief clerk pulled the envelope from the bag, strode after him, caught him by the arm, and said, "I believe this is yours."

Once again a lightning metamorphosis overtook Robinsohn. The cheeks paled, the absent eyes blazed with fury, and the concentrated malevolence in the look drove the chief clerk back a pace. Snatching the envelope, Robinsohn strode off down the corridor.

"Phew!" the chief clerk said. "Boris Karloff in person."

The Queen's messenger said, "Three minutes to go."

"Look," the chief clerk countered: "I know you're a great traveler, but you're not going to the moon. We don't want a bloody countdown."

Betty Carstairs at her small typing desk relit the old-fashioned red candle and began warming the massive stick of sealing wax. She loved the smell of sealing wax and dimly knew that the soft lava that melted from the red shaft had sensual undertones that always made her wriggle slightly on her seat. She dripped sealing wax on the desk, on her fingers, and on the big bronze seal, and oversealed everything.

"One minute to go," the Queen's messenger said.

"You must be crazy if you think you're going to catch that plane," the chief clerk said.

The Queen's messenger began his final check of all his papers from the special red passport and first-class tickets to the silver greyhound badge that he no longer wore and put carefully back in his blazer pocket.

Hargreaves came striding in with two envelopes, one a long blue one. "Just made it," he said, slightly breathless. He pushed them into the bag and without another word strode out of the room again.

"And to think," the chief clerk said, "I don't believe in miracles. We're going to make it on time for once."

Carefully closing the bag he held it while Betty went through her ritual of pouring the red libation on the dead body and pressing the seal home with the finality of an obsequy.

The rambling hulk of the embassy had two small wings extending from the main façade with a mansard roof and sufficient ornate decoration to mark its period clearly. A four-story building with a beautiful main staircase, its proportions had been vulgarized by the introduction of a lift and some serious interior reconstruction in the interests of safety and efficiency. Selected as an embassy by Malvern's predecessor, it lacked what Malvern much preferred—a separate ambassador's residence—but the new cost-efficiency experts with the Foreign Office financial division still found its upkeep too expensive. The ambassador's suite of rooms in the west wing had its own special approach corridor, but he never really felt aloof from the remainder of the building—a fact which pleased one side of his nature and displeased another.

Under the chandeliers in the big dining room with the Bristol glasses gleaming in the candlelight, the silver throwing back every highlight, and the oval table flawlessly arranged, the ambassador always felt, as he slid into his chair at the head, that he was momentarily back in the world to which he really belonged. It was a world of set values, where everyone had his place, a world where elegance took precedence over efficiency, and noblesse oblige replaced the mistaken attempts to mix the classes. A powerful conflict continued in his personality. Externally he seemed to have made the concessions necessary to the new diplomacy, but the battle was continuous. Only Penelope knew what a strain it had been to keep in place the impression that he belonged to the modern world. She had proved much more adaptable than he, and he admired the ease with which she accepted their son Raoul's long hair and their daughter Vanessa's new bohemianism.

In this dining room, very occasionally, he would reconstruct the old-world atmosphere right down to a hired butler and silver candlesnuffers. London was constantly pressuring him to get out of this ancient house which was too big and badly designed to make an efficient embassy. Cost coefficients—the creed by which the new world lived—demanded it, but Malvern would rather dig into his own private pocket occasionally than abandon it.

Four people stood by the big fireplace tonight—the first and second secretaries and the ambassador and his wife, all drinking sherry as they waited for Robinsohn.

"I thought agents were a punctual breed," Penelope said.

"The question is, Paul," the ambassador said, "what are we going to do with him?"

Paul Rostand was a new recruit to the Foreign Service, representing the modern image that no longer insisted on public school, well-connected young men with the right accent and overdeveloped charm. Paul came from a Northumberland miner's family and had graduated on scholarships from a grammar school to Oxford, but the working-class accent that almost disappeared at Oxford still left Northumberland undertones in his speech. They struck a rugged note among the refinements of this room and the public-school voices of the other members of the group. Already Paul had a reputation for the kind of sharp efficiency

21

from which men like Hargreaves recoiled. In Hargreaves's view, if efficiency meant a loss of graciousness, then efficiency must be modified. A touch of uneasiness remained from Paul Rostand's lowly beginnings. He had never quite mastered the art of feeling superior and it annoyed him that with a better brain and a dash of real originality, he still felt twinges of inferiority when the implacable confidence of smooth-talking people like Hargreaves implied a certain disdain for his—person?—no—Hargreaves concealed that by concentrating on his methods. It would be too crude of Hargreaves to object to a man as a man.

The ambassador reframed his question. "Has anyone any ideas what to do with Robinsohn?"

"It shouldn't be difficult," Paul said, "to smuggle him out of the back door again one dark night."

Languidly Hargreaves replied: "Every crevice of this place is crawling with ABVO agents."

"Thompson tells me," the ambassador said, "they've posted men at every exit. We must find out tonight why he is so important to them. I have to face Kalogh tomorrow."

"I must say," Penelope said, "it would be very tedious if we had to keep him for long."

Tedious was a favorite word of hers combining a certain aristocratic boredom with graciousness.

"Perhaps we could advertise in the local press," Hargreaves said, " 'Spy found. Medium height, sober-sided. Owner apply British Embassy.' "

It was always a challenge to Paul Rostand. One of the ways by which the upper middle class displayed its superiority was in being witty.

"It suggests a *New Statesman* competition, doesn't it," he said, preserving a face as expressionless as Hargreaves's.

"What competition?" the ambassador said, knowing he was inciting rivalry.

"Advertisements They Wouldn't Take."

At that moment the door opened and there was Robinsohn, still escorted by Thompson, and still so light on his feet that his approach across the room seemed almost soundless.

"Ah, Robinsohn," the ambassador said, moving over to greet him. "How is the arm?"

"All right."

"Good. This is my wife . . . and this is Mr. Rostand, our second secretary. You know Mr. Hargreaves, of course." They all formally shook hands. "You must be getting quite used to this place by now," the ambassador continued as Penelope escorted everyone to the table and said, "Perhaps, Mr. Robinsohn, you'd sit next to me."

22

"Thank you," he said. His face had a kind of waxen intensity and his voice was hoarse as if he had not spoken for a long time.

As Penelope rang the tiny handbell on the table, Paul Rostand shrank into himself. This survival from another age always embarrassed him. Summoning servants from the kitchen with handbells belonged for him to the days of serfs—and his own father had been close to a serf.

"I don't know what kind of food you like," Penelope said, "but tonight we've made it as near English as we can. If you stay with us long enough we'll get around to the Russian."

Robinsohn sat there immobile without responding. Penelope wore the long turquoise frock she used for difficult receptions, but Robinsohn was oblivious to the implied compliment. Elegant, sophisticated, with her tall figure and with her flaxen hair piled high, she seemed to tower over the table.

A local girl came in and clumsily served the cold consommé, without a word since she spoke no English. In the next fifteen minutes each person round the table tried one conversational gambit after another but failed to draw Robinsohn beyond monosyllables. Under one guise or another they each observed him closely, and presently Hargreaves and Penelope exchanged glances that said—What a dull little man.

Paul Rostand found himself admiring Robinsohn's indifference to the faded splendors of the room, the sophisticated company, the elaborate dinner rituals, and the attempts to draw him out. His suit was so obviously a ready-made factory job and he looked so out of place beside Penelope, but his impassive face showed nothing. His wide black eyes directed an uncompromising stare from one member of the dinner party to another, and conversation grew steadily more difficult.

At last the ambassador said: "You must know Joseph Kalogh?"

Robinsohn nodded.

"I never understood why they made him minister of the interior, do you?"

"Yes, I think I do," Robinsohn said but did not elaborate.

"Would you be prepared to enlighten us?"

"It's simple," Robinsohn said. "He can lie so convincingly."

Everyone laughed.

"But seriously . . . isn't he too impulsive a man to carry such a job?"

"There is another reason," Robinsohn said.

Again he waited to be asked to elaborate. When Hargreaves prompted him, he said: "He knows when to make concessions to the proletariat— like the English ruling class in the past."

"Does Kalogh ever really make concessions?"

"He may have to make some pretty soon now."

23

"What makes you think that?"

Robinsohn simply left the question in the air without answering it.

There was a long uneasy pause as the steak-and-kidney pie came steaming from the kitchen.

"How long is it since you left England?" Penelope asked as she cut and served deftly.

"Six weeks."

"How was the old country?"

"A man called Wilson causing some minor trouble."

"They say," Hargreaves said, "he is an undercover socialist on the run."

"But badly trained," Robinsohn said.

The ambassador changed the conversation abruptly, and decided to take a strong line. "I must, I'm afraid, come to the point," he said. "I have to see the minister tomorrow—he's very angry about you. He wants to arrest you as a common criminal."

"Yes, I know," Robinsohn said.

"Can you put me a little more in the picture?"

"Well . . ." Robinsohn said, and stopped to direct a very obvious stare at Mrs. Malvern.

Penelope laughed an easy, experienced laugh. "I don't think you need worry about me," she said. When he did not answer she looked at her husband. "Perhaps you would prefer to wait until after dinner?"

Turning away from the table, she managed a half-grimace with the side of her face toward her husband, which he rapidly decoded. "Not at all—my dear," he said. "I think we can talk quite freely in this company." He carefully avoided Hargreaves's face as he spoke.

"What do you want to know?" Robinsohn said. It was phrased so bluntly that the ambassador had to conceal a flash of distaste.

"Well—since you are so direct, Mr. Robinsohn—how did the police come to shoot at you?"

"They wanted to kill me."

The ambassador laughed uncomfortably.

"But—er—why would they want to kill you? I've always understood a live agent is better than a dead one."

"I was getting dangerously close to what I wanted."

"And what—exactly—did you want?"

"I told you before—the document."

"And that document concerns . . . ?"

Again Robinsohn looked first at Penelope and then round the table.

"Some other time," he said and now for the first time he gave a certain force to his words.

"I—er—appreciate your discretion," the ambassador said. "Perhaps,"

24

he added, "you could just tell us the—so to say physical—details of how they came to shoot at you?"

But it was not until the wine had flowed freely, the cognac had been replenished twice, and Robinsohn had accepted and begun smoking a cigar with the skill of a London clubman that he at last said: "I was meeting a contact man—a clerk from the records office of the Ministry of Propaganda. They shot him down before I could reach him—I ran for it . . ."

"You think he was dead?"

"Very dead."

"I must have a better brief than that for tomorrow," the ambassador said. "Have you ever broken any of the laws of this country?"

The ghost of a smile relieved Robinsohn's waxen features.

"That, of course, is my job."

"Would you describe yourself as a common criminal?"

"Not common—no."

"But have you—er—stolen any money, attacked anyone—possibly—er—used a firearm?"

"I never carry firearms."

"What I mean is very simple. Can they pin any ordinary, so to say civilian, crime on you?"

"No."

"That's good—" the ambassador said. "Very good. I should like to get this all on record."

"I don't want anything on paper," Robinsohn said.

"You don't trust us?"

There was a long pause, but Robinsohn said nothing.

"Perhaps," the ambassador said, "when you have finished your cigar you will come down to my office with me if the others will excuse us . . ."

CHAPTER 3

Drawing the heavy curtains, the ambassador paused a moment to glance out of the window at the silhouette of a burly man wearing the green ABVO uniform.

"You see what I mean?" he said, and stood aside for Robinsohn to look.

Robinsohn nodded.

"I lived with them for weeks," he said.

"This is the most comfortable chair," the ambassador said, pushing forward the yellow-brocaded survival from the eighteenth century. "Another cigar?"

"Thanks." As Robinsohn lit his cigar, the ambassador went on:

"Your passport says sales executive. Does the cover briefing touch on chromium?"

"It is part of the brief, yes."

"In that case you can be very helpful to me. But I must get something else straight for tomorrow. You have twice mentioned the—er—document. Can you tell me what this document concerns?"

"I thought you knew."

"It has something to do with subversive forces in Veralia—that's all I know."

"I don't think I can go beyond that myself."

"Look, Mr. Robinsohn, if I'm to protect you I must be sure of what I'm protecting."

"You've telegraphed London?"

"Yes."

"Why not wait for a reply?"

"It may not arrive in time."

"You can stall Kalogh."

"I've stalled him so often."

26

They sat measuring each other for several minutes in silence, and at last Robinsohn said:

"Have you ever heard of Grundel's Café?"

"Somewhere off the north end of Stalin Boulevard."

"You know its reputation?"

"Rebellious students, an occasional prostitute—all very innocent."

"You think so?"

"What else?"

"It's a haunt of a man called Dabrowski. Is that a familiar name?"

"He's in the Ministry of the Interior. He's also an intelligence officer in the political branch of the army."

"He's also part of a complicated subdivision of the self-spying liaison system—the military watches the secret police, the secret police watch the politicians, and the politicians employ military intelligence to watch the army."

Whether it was the privacy or the drink, Robinsohn was talking much more freely.

"Does Dabrowski have the document?" the ambassador asked.

"I don't know."

"And its contents?"

"As you say—subversive."

"Do you think there's much resistance in this country to Kalogh?"

"How would you answer that question yourself?" Robinsohn countered.

"I don't think there is."

Robinsohn shook his head.

"You're not romantic enough," the ambassador said, "to believe the Grundel cell carries much force?"

"How much do you know about Grundel?"

The ambassador carefully lit his second cigar, and stared at Robinsohn, scrutinizing him afresh. The man baffled him.

"Look, Mr. Robinsohn—we've had a very heavy day—and I was hoping to get to bed at a reasonable hour. I need to know about you— not you about me. So supposing you tell me what you know about Grundel."

"Those student meetings are not innocent," Robinsohn said. "Sophisticated counterrevolutionaries work behind the front. They are ruthless revolutionaries, not bleating children. I was on the point of infiltrating their meetings when I had to run for it."

"You almost make it sound as if they seriously threaten the government."

"Not yet."

"But you take them seriously as a political force?"

"Very seriously."

"I cannot agree with you."

"Have you seen this?" Robinsohn drew from his inner jacket pocket a crumpled, crudely printed leaflet which the ambassador read:

IMMEDIATE AIMS

1. The removal of Premier Constantine Berlowski by assassination if necessary.
2. A national policy independent of Russian dominance based on the principles of socialism.
3. Fifty percent of executive jobs in the factories to be taken over by the workers.
4. The present humiliating system of wages, norms, and social security conditions to be completely revolutionized.
5. A total reorganization of the structure of the party, its relations to the state and the leadership.
6. No more secret police. The ABVO to be forcibly disbanded.

The ambassador threw the pamphlet down on his desk. "How long did you say you have been operating in this country?"

"On this mission, six months."

"I've been here three years. I've seen half a dozen pamphlets like that. Students breed them like lice."

"There is one difference."

"And that?"

"I think that leaflet was written by a highly placed member of the present government."

"Are you suggesting he is also a member of Grundel?"

"Yes."

They talked on for another hour before the ambassador at last felt that he knew enough to face Kalogh with confidence the following afternoon.

But as he said good-night and slowly made his way up the stairs to his bedroom, it occurred to him that an agent planted in the embassy by Kalogh would have all the details he had just heard imprinted on his memory for reproduction whenever required.

In the hot summer night Penelope lay naked on the sumptuous bed reading Angus Wilson's *Such Darling Dodos*. As her husband came in, she glanced at her watch. "That was a long session," she said. "Did it yield anything?"

"Far too much," he said and began undressing. Penelope picked up a silver hand mirror from the bedside table, peered closely at her face, and went to work on a minute blackhead.

"Oh, Lord," she said, "I add another wrinkle every day." She put down the mirror and turned to scrutinize her stomach. "Just look at that, wrinkled like a tree."

"You have got two grown-up children," he said.

"Grow*ing* up," she corrected.

"That's not their view," he said. As he went through the elaborate ritual of dismantling the public image once more, she picked up the book again and pretended to read, but she was eying him carefully, trying to interpret his impassive face. At last he put the question she was waiting for.

"Well, what did you think of him?"

"He looks mediocre and isn't. He talks frankly and isn't. He looks trustworthy and isn't. He has the appearance of . . ."

"My God," the ambassador interrupted, "didn't you always say one shouldn't damn people on first meeting? You don't like him, I gather."

"He's a challenge."

"In what way?"

"I don't understand how he ever came to be what he is."

"Well, he seems to be pretty good at it."

"What makes you think that?"

"If I start talking now, my dear, I don't stand a chance of getting to sleep—and I must reserve the pill for when I wake in the middle of the night."

"That alibi wears a bit thin," she said and snapped her book shut and turned over huffily. She never came by professional information easily and the conflict of her curiosity and his diplomatic discretion went on ceaselessly.

Moving over to the window, he pulled the curtain aside and glanced out. The ABVO man was quite openly marching up and down like a sentry on duty.

"God knows how we'll ever get Robinsohn out of here," he said.

"Maybe he'll add some variety to the dreary social round," she said.

The embassy had settled down for the night with the chancery in darkness, and only the registry lit by a night-light where Rostand sat trying to kill time by reading the confidential biographies of well-known personalities in Veralia. God! What an array. Years of work from the commercial people, the military attaché, the press and information boys, which produced results highly embarrassing to some of the people involved. But they would never know. Or would they? Look at that: Istvan Bolsover, aged thirty-three, Secretary of the Central Committee, a known womanizer and secret drinker.

Suddenly Rostand heard the faint click-click of a hidden mechanism . . . The teleprinter in information . . . or was it the radio . . .

God damn it, if the radio had started up at this hour of night he would have to ring the radio officer. For some reason His Excellency had put the place on a crisis schedule—it couldn't simply be on account of Robinsohn. They would need the night cipher clerk too and that made life impossible because once roused from his bed Wilson never stopped talking. And then the light on his desk flickered—he knew it was the radio—and wondered what on earth could be worth sending at three A.M. in the morning in the current diplomatic climate. Cursing softly he dialed Jamieson, the radio officer's number, and a dazed voice answered.

"Sorry to break in on you," Rostand said, and explained why. The voice at the other end gave a groan. "Look, old man," it said, "I've picked up this damn Veralian bug. I've got a temperature of 103°. Do you think you can possibly manage on your own?" Rostand strongly resisted the idea at first. He knew Jamieson might be taking advantage of the fact that once at the very outset of his career Rostand had tried radio counterintelligence work and found it hopelessly alien. It was Jamieson's voice fading away into a kind of whisper which finally convinced Rostand that he was too ill to venture out. He then checked on a number of technical points, repeated back procedures, agreed to try, and hung up.

Frank Wilson, the cipher clerk, also woke uneasily out of sleep and mumbled that he would be round at the embassy in ten minutes. As he again replaced the receiver Rostand thought—why did they have to keep the radio key at reception and why concentrate all those keys in the safe under the counter into one big temptation for the most pure-minded patriot? (Just to have the means of finding out what the Old Man had written in confidential memoes about oneself back to the red, white, and blue elephant in Whitehall was temptation enough.)

Rostand went softly down the stairs, found Thompson missing from his desk, and reflected that he must be on his rounds. He opened the safe under the counter, selected the radio key, and climbed up again past the other three floors to the very top of the house. As he entered the low-raftered room with three sets of instruments placed on heavy trestles along one wall, a green light winked on and off from the central machine. Rostand's confidence suffered a severe setback when confronted by mechanisms or machines. Inanimate objects were malignant enough in failing to respond to his touch, but when they took on an electrical life of their own, such as belonged to this radio receiver, they became straightforwardly vindictive. Gloomily he picked up the headphones, placed them on his head, and looked at the dials marked "Recording." Now what had Jamieson said—turn the unscrambler on immediately, or wait until he heard that damned bleating signal coming all across Europe from the crumbling block in Earl's Court?

As he turned the switch—left—and pressed the button marked "Record," the tape, to his relief, began turning slowly and then he heard the bland voice repeating endlessly it seemed: "The night is calm. The night is calm."

There followed the mad gobbledegook which results when the speed of a tape is increased and voices run together hysterically. Once he had it on the recorder he relaxed. It was easy routine from now on. Slow down the tape, space out the words and scribble them down on paper. Five minutes later he made his way down to the cipher room. He remembered as he went what had happened to a message sent by code years ago when one of his forebears commanded a battalion on a major field exercise and found himself in desperate straits: "Enemy advance on right send me reinforcements," had become at the hands of the witty decoder: "Going to a dance tonight lend me three and fourpence."

A tired and still sleepy Wilson was already seated at his desk with Code Book Three open. Exchanging a few cynical comments on F.O. night life, Wilson went to work at once converting the letters of the message into figures. Then he moved over to the small computer, unlocked it, fed the figures in and now some were selected at irregular intervals by the computer and converted back into letters. At last it began to make sense:

"Your Telegram 384 Information Incorrect." The final safeguard meant reversing the meaning of the words decoded and Wilson now scribbled down the message: "Your Telegram 384 Information Correct."

"There you are," he said. "I hope it's worth it."

"Won't you stay for a drink?" Rostand said.

"No—thanks—I'm so damned tired I could die." He went then with a touch of churlishness. What the hell was 384 about? Rostand wondered as he made his way toward the registry, switched on the light, selected the current telegram file and turned to Number 384. It read: "Peter Robinsohn asked asylum embassy. Claims to be British Agent? Confirm."

So Mr. Robinsohn was genuine after all. At that moment somewhere in the silence of the big old house—in the corridor, on the floor above in information—Rostand heard the faintest hint of footsteps. He slipped silently out into the corridor, switched on the light, stopped and listened. Nothing . . . nobody . . . the sound had ceased. He went swiftly through chancery, down the stairs, and opened one door after another. Information empty too but ghostly from a streetlamp; the private office in darkness, H.E.'s office locked. At the far end he tried the door marked Military and Naval Attaché and it too was locked. He listened carefully. But no one moved inside. Knocking softly even the gentle knock echoed down the corridor. It was correct that it should be locked.

Turning right he took the short corridor on the left and there was the pool of light representing reception. As he entered Thompson started up from half-sleep.

"You haven't seen anyone about, have you?"

"No sir—not a soul."

"I thought I heard something up in the cipher room just now."

"Did you, sir? Well, I've heard nothing."

"I wish that damned lift could be used after midnight. The way people sleep in this place nothing would disturb them. Are our ghouls still outside?"

"Ghouls sir? Oh, you mean the Raincoat Boys. Yes, they're still there."

"Don't you think," Rostand said, *"we* should keep a closer check on *them?* After all, someone happily got himself the free run of the place six months ago."

"Yes, sir. I'll do my best. But they are at the back door too, you know."

Rostand made his way far up to the north wing of the third floor again and walked silently down the corridor to the guest rooms. Slowly, very slowly, he turned the handle of Number Three and at once a voice said, "Who's that?"

Rostand laughed lightly. "Sorry to disturb you—it's me—"

"You're not disturbing me. What do you want?"

Rostand shriveled a little and said on the spur of the moment, "I thought you'd be interested to know they've cleared you from London."

"It doesn't interest me," Robinsohn said and added, "If you want to know whether that door is locked, it is . . ."

"Well, I hope you manage to sleep," Rostand said, and when he got no more than a grunt in reply he moved away down toward the duty room again. On the way he thought, Lord! What a fool I am. I shouldn't have told him that.

CHAPTER 4

he ambassador set out in the Rolls-Royce to keep his appointment with the minister of the interior. It was a vintage Rolls with wire wheels, high wings, and two huge brass headlights like the lamps on an old-fashioned gig. It purred mellifluously and might have been driven in its near soundlessness by sheer personality. Anything so vulgar as internal combustion could not—obviously—take place under its aristocratic bonnet and one expected not electric bulbs in its ornate lighting but candles. The wooden fitments were of polished mahogany, the seats deep and engulfing and the smell of real leather permeated its salon. The windows were curtained in pale yellow silk and an interior ceiling light diffused when necessary a glow which matched the curtains. Once the doors were shut and the curtains drawn an elegant salon on wheels was offered to any traveler and his voyage would be almost equivalent to the soaring of a bird.

The building at which the Rolls finally drew up was in total contradiction, and the functionalism of the steel and concrete room on the sixth floor was relieved by a blaze of crimson carpet with a hammer and sickle burned hugely into its center.

Joseph Kalogh was such a short man he seemed to come up from underneath his big desk to greet the ambassador. Thick-set, with sculptured features and a bald head, he prided himself on his resemblance to Lenin, and he certainly had some of Lenin's quicksilver life. Now his handshake was extravagant, his gestures elaborate, and his words fluent.

"You are so punctual, Mr. Malvern," he said. "It is not our strong point . . . Try this chair—the sun will not trouble you in this chair."

The room at the top of the huge rectangular block that housed the Ministry of the Interior had one complete wall of bulletproof plate glass through which the morning sun poured.

"It's a beautiful day—yes." His syntax was almost flawless, but he accented the words oddly.

"Yes, beautiful," the ambassador said.

"Did I ever tell you," Kalogh said, "I was in England for three years in the war?"

"You did tell me."

"I'm sorry. Would you like some coffee?"

"No, thanks."

"Well now, Your Excellency. I propose coming straight to the point."

"I would like that."

"When are you going to—how say you—over turn this man to us?"

"Turn over this man."

Kalogh laughed and gestured. "My English! But the question—how do you answer the question?"

"Not, I'm afraid, in the er—foreseeable future."

"But why is that? Let me show you some of the documents."

He undid a green cord, opened what seemed to be a big dossier, selected three photographs, and pushed them across to the ambassador. One showed Robinsohn with his hand raised as if about to strike a second pudgy little man wearing a heavy overcoat. The second showed the pudgy man lying on the pavement with blood pouring away from his head, and the third a quite transformed Robinsohn, his head ducked down trying to leap across a road full of traffic. The third picture was blurred but enough of the features appeared to reveal a man in terror for his life.

Kalogh had been talking while the ambassador examined the pictures. ". . . and the photographs completely substantiate the charge."

"I'm sorry—what charge?"

"You would call it in England—robbery with violence. Mr. Robinsohn attacked the man in the first photograph, knocked him down, and fractured his skull."

"And you—were able to photograph him just at the right moment when he was doing it."

Kalogh's smile was as remote as a flash of refracted light. "Our police too are sometimes wonderful."

"You said robbery—what did he steal?"

"A key ring with a number of keys."

"I see . . . Well, Mr. Kalogh, I regret to have to inform you that your account of Mr. Robinsohn's activities does not coincide with ours. He denies having broken any of the laws of your country. He is a genuine businessman discussing the chromium deal with your technical experts. He does not understand why he was shot at and as you might expect greatly resents anyone taking such a liberty with him."

Kalogh laughed and now his whole face was alight with amusement. "You English," he said, "are amazing. Someone shoots at you and you call it taking a liberty. But, Your Excellency—let us get to more important matters. I wanted to ask you about the keys."

"I know nothing about any keys," the ambassador said.

34

"Mr. Robinsohn made no reference?"

"None."

"Well, let us get the legal situation clear. We have what you would call a warrant for this man's arrest. He is a criminal. You must turn him over to us."

"Mr. Kalogh—we have, as you would expect, checked with London and they confirm that he is a businessman of the highest possible integrity."

"We do not believe those two things can go together, Your Excellency. But seriously, why do we have to play these games? You must know the real nature of this man."

"I do not believe he is a criminal."

"He is a criminal or something more."

"I do not understand."

"I'm sure you do, Your Excellency."

The ambassador shrugged his shoulders. "Sometimes, Mr. Kalogh, you are too clever for me."

"You have been asking us, Your Excellency, to modify our propaganda policies."

The ambassador nodded.

"You are also very interested to close the chromium deal if you can."

"Yes."

"Now I must tell you that there is an unfortunate connection between these matters and Mr. Robinsohn."

It was one of the remarkable skills of Kalogh that he could always adapt himself to the jargon of the person with whom he negotiated. The ambassador reflected that he might almost have formulated that last sentence himself and all over again he reflected on the fascination of Kalogh's personality. How anyone so human, so capable of spontaneous outbursts, with irony flickering just beneath the surface of half his remarks could subscribe to Marxist dogma so unswervingly was one of the mysteries of the modern world beyond the comprehension of a traditionalist like His Excellency.

"I don't see the connection."

"The fact is, Your Excellency, that our propaganda line will not change and the chromium deal will not come off unless you surrender Mr. Robinsohn to us."

"Forgive me," the ambassador said, "but Mr. Robinsohn seems more important to you than anyone should in his station in life. Why is that?"

"You know very well why."

"Not unless you tell me."

"I don't propose boring you with what you already know."

"Are you seriously suggesting that you will break off the chromium negotiations, and refuse to modify your propaganda all because a casual English businessman asks for asylum in the embassy?"

Suddenly the chunky figure unfolded its legs and arms like the leaves of a vegetable and came out of its chair with hands thrust deep in the pockets of its baggy trousers to perform a few steps round the desk.

"It's no good, Your Excellency. These games are out of date. You know as well as I do—diplomacy has entered a quite new phase—maneuvering of this kind is meaningless. I have no more to say. I have told you the facts and I simply say—we give you a week. If you do not turn Robinsohn over to us by then, our relations with Britain will—how say you—suffer a severe setback, a decline. I do not know, but they will certainly suffer—and that won't do any of us any good, will it?"

As always, a meeting on one specific issue presently led onto many side issues. For nearly forty-five minutes, they fenced, evaded, came into small collisions, made concessions, and felt their way nearer to what His Excellency described as a modified understanding.

As he listened to this man concealing the iron determination of his purpose under a certain air of—could it be called gaiety?—the ambassador remembered that he was a protégé of the Khrushchev regime. Life had begun for Kalogh as a miner's son, but he wore his origins lightly.

"The trouble down in the south," the ambassador said, "is it serious?"

"Trouble?" Kalogh said. "What trouble?"

"I understood there had been some—er—disturbance."

"You have been listening too much to your BBC radio."

"It was another source."

"We have no trouble in the south."

"But the new higher prices for basic foods—I understood they were being resisted."

"Of course—inside the Party—not outside."

"I am glad all is calm," the ambassador said. As he watched the bald man's face come alight, smiling, he wondered for the tenth time how such a man with such genuine warmth could possibly have ordered the troops to shoot down some of his own working class and how all those catacombs beneath this cold-blooded building carried on such unpleasant practices at his orders. Or was it his orders? Did he really have effective control over the ABVO? After all, Colonel Ladislav Miches was titular head of the ABVO. But the political prisoners were prisoners at Kalogh's orders and when he went home at night to his second wife and the two much-publicized children, did he draw a shutter down dividing off areas of his mind which might infect the political sphere with too much feeling? Or was he as ruthless at home as here in this soulless concrete box? Or was the ambassador, in his absurdly outdated way, asking questions quite irrelevant to such a man and such a scene?

As the ambassador prepared to leave, a curious hope arose in his mind—it was a hope that Colonel Miches and not Kalogh really controlled the ABVO's work. At last the ambassador came slowly to his feet, took up his hat, and said, "I will consult my government about Robinsohn."

Kalogh's smile broadened. "Your Excellency," he said, as he rose to escort Malvern to the door, "there is no need to. I think they will be prepared to surrender Robinsohn."

"I wonder," the ambassador said.

"It is romantic," Kalogh said, "to value one individual above the good relations between two such countries as ours."

"It depends how you look at it," the ambassador said, "but I can only consult my government."

"I am glad to tell you," Kalogh said, "that we shall win."

"I trust," the ambassador said, "it may not prove to be a Pyrrhic victory."

Kalogh stopped in his tracks. "That word," he said, "I do not know it. Pirrick?"

"It doesn't matter," the ambassador said and moved toward the heavily curtained door.

"By the way," Kalogh said as he opened the door, "there was a phrase I learned in the blitz in London—something about spiriting people away—it would not work of course with Robinsohn."

"Of course not," the ambassador said.

"You will be coming to the reception on August the twentieth?"

"It will be my pleasure."

"And your wife?"

"I trust she will come too."

"My regards to her."

As he drove back in the ancient Rolls, the ambassador tried to find a better explanation for liking some small part of this man's character. It was not merely his humanity or his civilized awareness of irony. There were times when Kalogh seemed almost to come to the point of appreciating—or was it too big a word?—what Britain was trying to do in certain parts of the world, but that, on reflection, would not do either. Somewhere at a deeper level the ambassador had an odd feeling that given a different world situation, with political contradictions modified, Kalogh might communicate with him in a quite new sense, and at once the implicit idea that somewhere deep down he and Kalogh had something in common made him shudder. That was impossible.

CHAPTER 5

Robinsohn quickly became an all too familiar figure to the embassy staff. He seldom left the guest room until ten o'clock in the morning but he preserved it, to Penelope's surprise, in immaculate order. As he tried to settle down to the routine life of the embassy a discipline became apparent in his personal life. He insisted on having a clean shirt from the laundry every day and Penelope sent out to try to buy him a supply of shirts that fitted his narrow neckline. They were not easily available and without consulting her husband she found herself driven to persuade her personal assistant to use the black market.

It seemed to irritate Robinsohn abnormally when he had to wear the same shirt two days running and he threatened to wreck the ancient heating apparatus by having too many baths. The preoccupation with hygiene extended down to his fingernails, and he borrowed a manicure set to give detailed attention to his hands. They were stubby powerful hands. For the first two days he had chain-smoked cigarettes and then abruptly he gave it up. Now no ash was spilled over the bed and carpet, his shoes shone, and he made several inquiries whether anyone on the staff understood the art of barbering. The same discipline was apparent in the regular ritual he followed: rise at nine, breakfast at nine thirty, read the local press until ten, begin his inquiry into the workings of the embassy, lunch in the canteen with one or other embassy group, retire to his room at three o'clock, lock the door and stay there until six. What he did in those three hours remained a mystery in the first weeks.

It was his wandering about the rooms and corridors and his elaborate questioning that caused the early frictions. Thompson admitted defeat early in the battle. It was impossible to shadow Robinsohn all the time. Instead as a countersafeguard Hargreaves issued a general directive to the whole staff that he should not be given access to information in any form. Now that he was cleared in London, there seemed no point in pressing security beyond that.

Thus Robinsohn's light-footed figure continued to come quietly down the stairs and go systematically from room to room on the second floor making little attempt to modify the sheer watchfulness of his presence. First he simply observed people at work and then after a time he would begin to ask a whole series of interrelated questions. The chief clerk regarded himself as an imperturbable Yorkshireman, but when Robinsohn began with the simple question: "How does the filing system work?" and followed it with a string of specific inquiries, each one more penetrating than the last, he said one day: "You wouldn't be trying to take over the job, would you?"

"Not at all," Robinsohn said with perfect English politeness.

"I don't think my union would like that. It's a bit of a closed shop here."

"I just wondered," Robinsohn said, "how you can go on and on filing things away without destroying some of the old stuff. It seems to me the whole embassy should be overwhelmed by now—"

"I must say," the chief clerk said, "you're really on the ball. You've put your finger on my biggest bugbear. But I'll have to get clearance before I can talk." When the chief clerk consulted his immediate boss, he saw no reason why Robinsohn shouldn't be told about the mad status-ridden battles that produced the crazy filing system in registry, providing he was given no access whatever to those files. And three days later as Robinsohn stood there leaning against the steel filing cabinets, the chief clerk said: "Let me tell you what happened when I tried to clean up Air Affairs. It's one of the big files with twelve separate volumes, the earliest falling to bits. No one had opened it for twenty years. Do you know what I found? Details of German planes in the First World War—sixty years ago—out-of-date, hopeless stuff. I had to get to the fourth volume before anything up to date. There was a whole file on pets, another on nuclear warheads, and masses of ballistic missile stuff. File number five—copies of secret air coordination agreements between Russia and Veralia—details of disarmament discussions with America and England, and so on. I decided to see whether there were any cross-references in other files. And do you know what I found? It turned out that half the stuff in Air Affairs was duplicated in at least three other files: Disarmament, Ballistic Missiles, and Treaties. So I tried to get clearance for destroying duplicates and immediately ran into trouble. Air Affairs got all angry and said, 'The 1914 stuff is of the utmost historical importance.' The disarmament boys said, 'We must have a cross-reference in Air Affairs.' The ledger clerk said, 'But I'll have to remove all the entries from my ledgers,' and Miss Caperson, who keeps the card index, wailed, 'All my numbering will be wrong if I take the cards out.' And finally the library really had me in front of the firing squad. 'Original copies of anything must not be destroyed. . . .' I ask you—*original copies* —What the hell does that mean?"

The chief clerk paused. "At the moment," he said, "that's the state of the game—and if you do happen to want this job, all I can say is you're welcome to it."

Within three days it was Caroline who first said to the ambassador one morning that Robinsohn constantly stared at her in the rudest possible manner. The ambassador simply replied that the man was clearly unaccustomed to living in such close contact with attractive females. Robinsohn for his part began to make discreet inquiries about Caroline. Over lunch one day in the refectory reserved for higher grades he brought up her name with the first secretary.

"Married?" Hargreaves said. "Good heavens, no—she's not married."

"You make it sound as unlikely as Armageddon."

"It is."

"A lover perhaps."

"Good Lord, Robinsohn, for one in your trade your questions are bloody indiscreet."

"I'm sorry."

"What she does outside of this place I've no idea."

"I understand the typists have a nickname for her."

"Yes—The Icicle. If you think you can melt her, why not try?" Hargreaves said.

Robinsohn visited the private office several times after that. He would walk in at coffee time and hope to be invited to join the closely integrated couple—Caroline Masters, the private secretary, and Joanna Fairweather, the buxom typist. Since they were old friends from the days when they once shared a Bloomsbury flat, the inevitable Lesbian rumors had circulated. On the second day, without consulting Caroline, Joanna made the mistake of offering Robinsohn coffee, and he remained talking for nearly half an hour with Caroline becoming colder and more monosyllabic every minute. When he had at last gone, she blasted hell out of Joanna so vigorously that the sound even penetrated the double door and thick curtains of the ambassador's office. It was when His Excellency called Caroline in that she complained about Robinsohn. "There's an easy remedy," he said. "Tell him to stay away from the private office."

After that Robinsohn made three attempts to make appointments with His Excellency, but he was overwhelmed by visitors, consultations, exchanges with air and military attachés, Veralian contacts, external dinner parties, and a round of embassy receptions.

And then one morning Robinsohn waited outside the door of the private office and walked along beside Caroline as she came out. "I can't invite you to dinner," he said, "because I can't get out of here—but have lunch with me in the canteen."

She simply did not answer but quickened her pace. "You interest me," he said. "Perhaps a cup of coffee after office hours?"

She stopped then, turned, and stared down at him as if he were a pigmy freak in a circus. "And where," she said in a voice cold as steel, "would this cup of coffee take place?"

"You could come to the guest room," he said.

"For God's sake," she said, "has no one ever told you English girls do not go to the bedrooms of strangers for cups of coffee?"

"Strangers?" he began, but she cut across him.

"Mr. Robinsohn, I must ask you to leave me alone."

He smiled then, his intense inward-looking smile.

"I fear," he said, "I am in this place for quite a long time."

She reacted in the formula manner, stamping her heel, whisking round, and storming back toward the private office. Robinsohn remained there leaning languidly against the wall for some minutes after she had disappeared.

Then, hands in pockets, frowning at the threadbare carpet, he walked on and very slowly climbed the stairs back toward the guest room.

As he approached, he heard someone moving inside. Immediately his tread became even lighter, he slowed his pace, and all his training went into action. He stood against the wall outside, listening, but the sounds of movements inside had ceased. Very carefully he began turning the handle of the door, flung it suddenly open, and stood back.

Penelope Malvern sat beside the small writing desk with a black diary in her hand, and as the door crashed open she swung round and dropped the diary on the desk.

"Ah, it's you, Mr. Robinsohn," she said, regaining her self-possession with astonishing speed. "You must forgive me appearing to intrude on your room like this—but the charlady is ill this morning—and I thought I would just tidy up for you."

"Which includes," Robinsohn said "reading my diary."

"I picked it up to dust the desk," she said.

"And read it," he pressed.

"No," she said, "just picked it up."

Robinsohn moved slowly into the room. "You can reconcile reading people's private diaries with some sort of diplomatic privilege," Robinsohn said ironically.

"No," she said and now two strong personalities were challenging each other and she felt afresh a force in him which his everyday self concealed.

"Let me be frank," she went on. "I find you and your way of life very interesting. I would like to know much more about you."

"So you came in here under the pretext of . . ."

"There was no pretext," she interrupted. "The charlady is stricken with the flu. Tell me, Mr. Robinsohn, have you ever read the private diary of a stranger without his permission?"

"It is my trade. It isn't yours."

She smiled then. "You really believe I read it, don't you?" she said.
"Of course."

"You believe in expediency," she said.

"I don't believe in anything," he said, "but sometimes expediency is forced on me. I must ask you to leave now."

She rose without any sign of resentment.

"Of course," she said. At the door she said: "Some other time, perhaps, we can talk at greater length."

It was seven o'clock in the evening, with few members of the day staff still remaining on duty, when Robinsohn paused outside the door with the stenciled words Paul Rostand, Second Secretary. The night-lights were on in the corridor and he had to peer closely to read the message typed on a piece of embassy-headed paper. "At lunch—phone extension 14 for anything urgent."

As he read the message he heard footsteps behind him and there was Paul Rostand hurrying along with a bulging briefcase. "Hallo," he said, "I've just finished one of those marathon Veralian lunches."

"I understood you wanted to see me," Robinsohn said.

"Good heavens, yes. I'd forgotten. I'm sorry—it's been so rushed today."

Rostand unlocked the door, flung his briefcase down, and drew up a functional armchair. Robinsohn felt the different atmosphere in this office that, despite its spaciousness and blue carpet, had no unnecessary decorations, no flowers, no traditional reproductions from classical paintings.

"A hair of the dog that bit you—you know that phrase," Rostand said.

Robinsohn nodded. "You'll have one too?"

"Thanks."

"It's cognac."

Rostand unlocked the lowest drawer of his steel desk, drew out a flask of brandy, went over to a concealed cabinet and came back with two glasses. Filling them he spilled some cognac on a pile of telegrams.

"Mustn't send them drunken telegrams," he said, and mopped up the stains.

As Robinsohn settled down and sipped his brandy Rostand said without preliminary and quite abruptly: "Tell me—why did you ever go into a trade like yours—it must be hell."

"Being second secretary would be hell for me."

"The case can be made," Rostand said. "It's a naïve question, I know," Rostand went on, "but it must be a very special brand of satisfaction you get out of your work."

For the first fifteen minutes Robinsohn did not yield one detail, one piece of relevant information about his past or present, but by the time they had finished another glass of cognac, both men were beginning to communicate at a different level. Robinsohn suggested moving up to the guest room where he had a bottle of brandy presented by the ambassador, and Rostand said, "I suppose this can come under the heading of work—I have been asked to give a detailed briefing on you."

"Never a wasted moment," Robinsohn said.

"You're beginning to interest me for other reasons," Rostand said. He turned back to his desk, selected a slim buff file, and put it under his arm.

Five minutes later, settled in the faded crimson armchair in the guest room, with a third glass of cognac in his hand, Rostand said: "Shall I read you what it says about you in the blue file?"

"Okay."

" 'Peter Robinsohn, thirty-five, alias Pierre Regnier, alias Anton Vladomiticz, son of Russian lawyer and English mother. His father came to England and set up in practice, having repassed his law examinations. Peter Robinsohn, his son, speaks English, Russian, French, and Veralian with very little trace of an accent. . . .' "

When Rostand came to his career as an actor, and his reliability because he was not homosexual, Robinsohn sighed.

"As if," he said, "heterosexuals were not just as vulnerable. But perhaps I had better put you right on a point or two."

"Excellent," Rostand said.

"Tell me, Mr. Rostand, if you were playing the English game of placing people, what class would you say I came from?"

"Middle class."

"But there you are wrong."

"Your father was a lawyer."

"I'm afraid," Robinsohn said, "all that stuff about my father is a pack of lies—a form of double cover. Control knows about it."

"Control?"

"M.I.5."

"But it says here . . ."

"That report was replaced by another. You should have a copy in the file."

Rostand spun the pages through his fingers. "No replacement here."

"Someone's slipped up."

"Supposing you give me the facts."

"All right. My father was a Russian cobbler—an anarchist—they jailed him—but not before the anarchist message was passed on to me. My mother was a laundry woman. It is true my father came as a refugee to England, but he knew nothing about the law."

"My God, we are in confusion, aren't we? Go on."

"What else do you want to know, Mr. Rostand?"

"Any others in the family?"

"Yes, I had a younger brother."

"Did he come to England too?"

Robinsohn stiffened visibly at the question. "I don't see the relevance," he said.

He emptied his glass at a gulp, and added, "As a matter of fact, he is dead." He leaned forward, offered Rostand the bottle, and when he refused, carefully refilled his own glass.

"Look, Mr. Rostand," he said. "You interest me as much as I interest you—can we strike a bargain?"

"What sort of bargain?"

"If I tell you about myself, will you tell me about yourself?"

Rostand thought a long moment. There were a number of incidents in his life he had no desire to recall or talk about, least of all to a stranger like Robinsohn and he saw no reason why he should agree to such an absurd bargain.

"My job is to find out about you," he said.

"But if I make this a condition?"

"I am unimportant," Rostand said.

"Modesty, not flagellation, is the English vice," Robinsohn said.

Rostand sighed and emptied his glass.

"Can we get back to the brief?"

"Not unless you agree."

"You're serious about this then?"

"Quite serious."

"And you won't talk unless . . ."

"That is so."

"Well, what does it matter—I'll agree on the understanding that we talk about you first." He glanced at his watch. "It's seven o'clock and I have a dinner date at eight."

"How about smuggling me out with you?" Robinsohn said.

"If only I could."

"One day soon I'll go bursting through that front door with a machine gun."

"Claustrophobia already?"

"You wouldn't understand."

Rostand saw him clasp his fingers tightly round the brandy glass. Now as they talked on, the picture that slowly built up of a man called Peter Robinsohn, alias, became steadily more absorbing to Rostand. A skeptical Marxist-Freudian, he looked for one or another motivation behind any man's character, and here it all was with a detailed vengeance. A man born to a father who had been on the run half his life, brought up in poor circumstances to rebel against authority in any form. A mother soft, loving, kind, who recoiled from her husband and hated the way the child fought her. The boy's cleverness failing to realize itself in the framework of school and examinations, his poor roots constantly crippling his performance, but surviving splendidly to overcome the early menial jobs, to fight through self-education with his father's help into an isolated, tough, self-reliant person.

By now Rostand had warmed to a number of similarities in his own life. Half an hour later when Robinsohn interrupted his flow of questions with: "Isn't it your turn now—I've told you enough," he found he didn't mind any longer filling in some details. Working-class roots, family feuds, a self-educated struggle to break out of crippling family limitations. The errand boy who used to steal the early morning milk. The hopeless primary school pupil who suddenly blossomed out with a scholarship to higher things. The class intimidation at Cambridge that stunted his performance and the Upper Second that just scraped him into the new Foreign Service.

After which, the interchange between them deepened. Their minds appeared to work in a similar way. Rostand forgot the time in the fascination of trying to probe deeper into the psychology beneath all these external simplicities. When he referred twice to Freud, Robinsohn said: "You sound as if you believe all that stuff."

"It has its points," Rostand said. By now he was aware of the dangerous overconfidence in his manner, which came from drink. This near camaraderie, this readiness to open out and psychologically embrace someone was, he knew, a synthetic product, but it seemed to be working its way with Robinsohn too.

"As a matter of fact," Robinsohn said, "I'm the psychoanalyst's dream. I'm the living justification of all that crap—but I don't believe a word of it."

"I don't believe it," Rostand said, "but it has its uses. It's one model to apply . . . I know several."

"You're too intellectual for me."

"You were lucky with your mother anyway—"

"Hated her," Robinsohn said. "Didn't miss a Freudian trick. Just got my cues a bit mixed up. Loved my father, hated my mother. And as for my brother . . ."

He seemed to cut himself so short it fixed Rostand's attention.

"Your brother?" he said and he spoke softly as if he knew the word was charged with special meaning for Robinsohn.

"Yes, my brother," Robinsohn repeated and his voice fell away as he spoke. He continued in a monotone.

"You know this stuff the head-shrinkers talk about—murder your father and marry your mother—rubbish—no one really does it. My brother was more important." He stopped himself again and now as

Rostand tried to press the point he saw the strain in Robinsohn's face and changed the subject. Robinsohn suddenly said: "I've drunk too much. I must go."

"But this is your room," Rostand reminded him.

"Of course it is," he said and slumped down in his chair. "This place is getting me down."

"I'm the one that must go," Rostand said. "Shall I see you in the morning?"

"I fear so." Robinsohn closed his eyes as if he were falling asleep. He made no gesture of farewell and did not open his eyes again as Rostand left the room.

CHAPTER 6

ajor Theodore Jackson Rivers, Military Attaché, the stenciled notice said on the door and Robinsohn was reading off the decorations which followed when a burly man with a claret face opened the door from the inside and stood staring down from his considerable height.

"Ah," he said after a brief silence. "You must be the asylum chap."

"That could be misunderstood," Robinsohn said.

"I'm sorry . . . I didn't mean . . ."

"They asked me," Robinsohn interrupted, "to come and see you."

"The funny thing is I was just this minute coming up to see you," Major Rivers said. "Come in."

There were maps of Veralia on the wall with flags and three colored stars marking specific boundaries, and on the glass-topped desk a photograph of a pleasant middle-aged woman.

"Sit down," Major Rivers said.

"You don't mind if I stand," Robinsohn said.

"Stand—but—"

"I'll just move around as we talk."

"Ah, yes," the major said, "I gathered this place was getting on your nerves. How long is it now?"

"Ten days."

"I must say if I were shut in here for ten days . . ." He gestured. "Have a drink?"

"No thanks."

"Smoke?"

"No thanks."

"You don't mind if I do."

"Not at all."

"To come to the point. His Excellency has asked me to find some way of getting you out of here—he must have told you."

Robinsohn was quietly pacing to and fro in front of the military attaché's desk and Rivers found it disturbing. He had spent eighteen months in a Jap prisoner-of-war camp where he had paced—for centuries it seemed—just like that.

"There are half a dozen possibilities," he said. "Do you have any ideas?"

"Tell me yours," Robinsohn said.

"Well, there's the simple method of patience—wait until they take their bloodhounds off our gates."

Robinsohn shook his head. "They won't."

"They're bound to tire of it in time."

"How long?"

"Six weeks."

"You're not seriously asking me to wait six weeks?" He stopped in front of Major Rivers's desk, frowning heavily.

"Alternatively," Major Rivers said quickly, "there are forms of disguise."

Robinsohn began pacing again. "What forms?"

"I haven't worked them out—I wanted to get your reaction."

"Anything else?" Robinsohn said.

"What I think we should begin with is something quite different. In my experience there's always a point where night guards begin to get lax, but you have to pick the right night. Now if you were watching and ready to move—"

"You suggest I should stay up and watch every night?"

"And sleep in the day."

Some dash of arrogance in Robinsohn's manner was beginning to irritate Major Rivers.

"Any other ideas?" Robinsohn asked.

"We might swap you for someone they hold."

"But they don't hold anyone, do they?"

"They do—but we'd have to find someone—so to say—your own political weight." There was a long pause.

Major Rivers had maneuvered carefully toward this point. Now was the time deftly to drop hints of quite another kind. "The Egyptians once tried a trick I don't recommend," he said.

"What's that?"

"How tall are you, Mr. Robinsohn?"

"Five feet ten."

"Doubled up, say four feet?"

"Doubled up?"

"The boot of His Excellency's Rolls is four feet with a depth of eighteen inches."

48

"I see. How far does diplomatic immunity stretch?"

"It includes the boot of His Excellency's car. But it's no good discussing it. He would never agree."

"Need he know?" Robinsohn said.

Major Rivers smiled. Long before he met Robinsohn, he had planned this conversation in considerable detail. If it was to work, the initiative to deceive the ambassador had to come from Robinsohn. Major Rivers himself could have no part in it. "I warn you flatly," he said, "you must not try it. I did not mean you to take me seriously. I was only joking."

"Where do they keep the car?"

"There's a converted outbuilding in the back garden."

"Who has the key?"

"I'm simply not prepared to tell you."

"Come on," Robinsohn said, "who is it?"

"I want no part of it."

"Can I have a schedule of His Excellency's engagements?"

"Before we go any further, there's one thing we must get absolutely clear," Rivers said with emphasis.

"What's that?"

"If you seriously think of trying such a crazy idea, remember you carried it out yourself. It's nothing to do with me. And I want absolutely nothing to do with it."

When Robinsohn said nothing, Rivers sat back on his chair and looked ostentatiously reflective. "Mr. Robinsohn, you are in a profession where breaking undertakings are part of the stock in trade. But if you want me to help you, you must first of all give me your assurance now that you won't try to implicate me in anything you try to do entirely on your own bat."

"Of course."

Major Rivers sat forward again and stubbed out his cigarette with thick sausage fingers.

"In any case," he said, "I should deny the whole thing."

"I don't understand why you are making so much fuss about all this," Robinsohn said.

"You don't understand H.E. He's a stickler for correct behavior."

"In a country like this?"

"He believes it's more important because of the way they behave here."

Robinsohn grunted.

"I repeat," Rivers said. "Just forget H.E.'s car. Give me another forty-eight hours and I'll come up with something quite different and safe. I'll arrange for Thompson to keep watch on their bloodhounds. If any one of them does relax enough, be ready to try your luck. If that fails, don't worry, we'll find something pretty soon. Just forget about H.E.'s car, that's all."

"I'll give it a week," Robinsohn said and without another word strode out of Rivers's office. He never saw the pleased smile that broke over the major's face.

In the next week Robinsohn became a fresh irritation to one member of the staff after another. It was tolerable when he asked a few questions about their work; it was less tolerable when he pressed home detailed queries; but when the man became a kind of morose ghost who simply stood or sat there observing every detail of what took place, the sense of being watched by an outsider without the necessary training in embassy etiquette generated quite new frictions. He was definitely not one of them. Deviations in behavior patterns revealed that all too clearly. By the second Wednesday two separate complaints arrived on His Excellency's desk and he summoned Caroline from the outer office: "For heaven's sake, tell Robinsohn to stop prowling about the place and if he must prowl not to interfere." When Caroline issued the warning personally to Robinsohn with some pleasure, he acknowledged it by a casual nod of the head and continued his daily routine quite unchanged.

The nights also became steadily more difficult for him. Pacing his room at two in the morning, chain-smoking, unable to sleep, he was quite unaware that in the big bedroom down the hall, the ambassador frequently reached out for his middle-of-the-night sleeping pill. Presently Robinsohn's concern for order in his room broke down and a quite new phase began. One morning the local cleaning woman arrived to find the room in chaos, with half the bedclothes on the floor, cigarette ends stubbed out everywhere, newspapers scattered, and a terrible fug compounded of coffee, scraps of food, cigarettes, and brandy. She complained to the ambassador's wife who passed on the message to Robinsohn, adding her own particular edge to it. But nothing changed, night or day. His daily wanderings on the floors below, the aimless walking of corridors, the collisions with the archivist, the chief clerk, Caroline, Hargreaves, and once with His Excellency himself continued to generate the sense of a foreign body in their midst creating a kind of inflammation which occasionally drove people into quite irrational outbursts. Caroline took to looking over her shoulder to see if he were following her, Hargreaves made elaborate detours to avoid meeting him, and when one day Robinsohn concentrated on the typing pool, Miss Hallows, the enthroned queen on her slightly raised dais, swiveled her eye to follow his every movement. Two typists were checking stencils, another was taking dictation, and Miss Hallows was scrutinizing finished work to enter the results in her log book. Under the pretext of examining the big duplicator, he made a quick survey of the typing staff. One had a soft, sad, pretty face and at a glance he felt she was possibly the kind of girl who might surrender out of a combination of sheer generosity and lack of willpower, but he had no desire to get tangled up in such a situation. Miss Hallows, the supervisor, followed his every movement and presently she said in her harsh man's voice:

"We need some help," obviously not expecting to get any.

"What kind of help?" Robinsohn said.

"Five hundred copies of this," she said, handing him a stenciled circular. To her surprise he asked how the duplicator worked, and settled down for twenty minutes, pouring off copies with great facility. In that time Annabel Harding, the girl with the soft sad face, managed to stare at him hard and once—very timidly—half turned a welcoming smile.

Later that day she deliberately sat opposite him in the canteen and he spoke to her. The conversation plowed heavily through banalities, and as he stood up to leave he said out of sheer politeness, "Perhaps we'll meet again."

Annabel Harding followed him out of the canteen, a frightened and excited girl. She had come from England to this job in a country where she did not speak the language in search of—adventure?—romance?—reassurance?—she did not know which, but one reason stood out above others. Men went for her body alone in London. She had become a sexual object and they made no bones about it. Her body was voluptuous, but the face and mind that went with her flesh were pretty and empty. She had devastating memories of all those "one-night stands" when she had been completely abandoned by the man the very next day. She had reasoned it out that perhaps in Veralia, in Her Majesty's embassy, she would meet a different type of man, someone with whom she could achieve a real relationship. Instead, this small microcosm of the English class system concentrated its worst features and insisted that even to talk to Annabel Harding was to lose caste. She had all over again become a sex symbol to half the staff, but no one took her out to dinner, no one lowered himself even to sleep with her, and many a night she had been reduced to weeping insomnia in her functional room in the plywood hostel. Now this man had treated her like a human being and had suggested that they might meet again.

Back in his room Robinsohn reflected that there were certain prescribed prerequisites with lower-middle-class English girls that had to be gone through before sex became respectable. Two drinking evenings, one luncheon, and possibly with the more conventional—one dinner—and they never dreamed as they climbed into bed that they had accepted payment for their services. He had no intention of going through with the dreary rigmarole. He knew too well his own reactions—the small lust for a pretty girl's body, the ritual invitations and exchanges, the drinks, dinner . . . and then the terrible collapse into boredom. It had never really worked with anyone for him. If he had to find some new distraction in this embassy prison, it would have to be something very different. He had begun to know every twist and cranny, every detail of routine, all the machinery and personalities, and they were becoming like the figures of an endlessly repeated mime who spoke soundlessly with movements and gestures only, and it was as if somewhere binding them together there was the ghost of a growing collective threat.

He went to the window and drew back the curtains. The same impermeable figure draped against the wall, seemingly so much part of it he could no longer move of his own volition. They knew how well they had him trapped, and it could go on for months.

His eye lifted away to the sleeping villas up on the terraces across the smooth bland river and he wondered which one was Kalogh's and whether at this precise moment he enjoyed deep and undisturbed sleep. Did all that weight of secret knowledge of plotting and counterplotting with the memory of so many ruthless purges reducing men to emaciated animals crouching in stone catacombs ever keep him—for a fleeting moment—awake? Guilt! Such a naïve experience exclusively reserved for the bourgeois young. A luxury, an indulgence. He hated his own guilt. He loathed the weakness that sometimes beat up from the past and allowed adolescent sentiment to invade a sleepless night.

He lit a new cigarette from the stub of the last and began his pacing again. How crazily inadequate their information was, and how little Rostand had dragged out of him despite his drunkenness. All that flummery of classified information, all those registry keys, strong rooms, combination locks penetrating to the blue files that knew precisely nothing about him. Or if not nothing, a few surface details like a tube-train map of London that failed to show what flowed under and over the arteries, what hidden slums and inspirations, guilts and horrors made the whole city a teeming, stupid, self-contained macrocosm.

His brother—yes—his brother. The pale poetic face came up in his mind as vividly as ever. All these years of trying to suppress that image had done no more than reconcile him to its survival. What would Rostand say if he knew what was missing from his precious blue file. What would the immaculate Hargreaves or—above all—the man they so pompously called His Excellency, think of him. His Excellency! For God's sake! He might be back with the British Raj in India—the newly appointed high commissioner lumbering down streets reeking of malnutrition and poverty on his own bejeweled elephant.

Murder? How many thousands of times had he put the question mark after the word and then rejected both? Of course it wasn't murder, but what would His Excellency think of his trapped animal if he knew he was a man capable of pushing his own brother off a windowsill by an accidental stumble that sent him crashing to a mess of broken neck, bones, and features, and all because that illiterate hag they called his mother had dared to perform that worn-out dreary Freudian cliché of diverting her attention exclusively to him.

If only they knew. . . . But that was only the beginning. The man in Russia with the classical complaint of knowing too much had—on orders—to be eliminated and the man who would have killed him ten seconds later had to be killed first. It was no more than part of a stock in trade, but they were different from his brother—in an odd sense they were alibis for it. And beyond even that there was his wife—oh, God— yes—his wife.

They knew nothing, precisely nothing. All that stuff about neglecting his mother. Never going to see the old lady. They would never know what caused the heart attack and nor would he, but what was wrong with dying all alone? It was better than parading your terror and helplessness to the outside world—to the public—to your family—or even to your son. And that tremendous farce the English called a funeral. They knew about these things in England and they could make the going down of a stupid old witch of a woman as grand and moving as the death of a statesman, with all those flowers, prayers, and bare-headed people listening to the rich voice of a dog-collared gentleman who should have known better than to deceive with his falsified poetry. Thank God he, Robinsohn, had never witnessed it. Thank God the job came before everything—including the death of his mother and even her funeral. Because he might have revealed the worst weakness of all if he had gone, the weakness of sentimentality about the stupid old woman who happened by a crazy accident of lust to have given him birth.

He threw the cigarette-end down, crushed it out, and moved to the window again. Still there, still hunched in almost the same position but— Robinsohn pressed his face against the windowpane—could he possibly be . . . asleep—standing up asleep? He had done the same thing himself on one occasion and he knew that given enough training it was easy to sleep standing up . . . But how to test it?

Swiftly he went out of the door along the corridor toward the back garden where there was an iron spiral staircase used as a fire escape leading directly to the back door. Almost soundlessly he slipped down the stairs to the heavy iron grille over the frosted glass door through which nothing was visible. Folded to one side, almost hidden away, was a steel lattice riot gate seven feet high. Internally the door gave on a wide entrance hall and that in turn opened on the big parquet-floored room used for multiple purposes—library, exhibition room, personnel work, and, when cleared, official receptions. The windows were half-curtained and Robinsohn pulled a chair over soundlessly, climbed on it, and saw the sleeping figure within fifteen feet . . . or was he sleeping? Robinsohn held his breath as he scrutinized the dark shadow under the hat, trying to detect the slightest movement, and then the figure not merely moved, it coughed, and Robinsohn turned away in disgust. He might have known. Heaven help the Veralian agent who slept on duty. The penalties were too high.

Slowly he made his way back up the steel stairs, paused outside his room with his hand on the doorknob, and turned away again, shuddering. In the silence and emptiness of the room the echo might come back again. He needed company, something to do, some form of action. He walked on down the unlit corridor and as he walked an idea occurred to him which crowded out the tensions, the claustrophobia. If the duty officer was safe in bed with the alarm telephone beside him, Robinsohn had the free run of the embassy. What else did those blue files contain? Who else was misrepresented with a few details artificially extracted from official reports, newspapers, and superficial interviews? Did they not almost certainly contain details that would help him with his mission?

The night-lights were always burning on the first floor and as he moved past the chancery, he felt as if someone were following him. He stopped and slid back against the wall. The light was too dim to penetrate far, but there was no one there and nothing moved. Silence. Just the faintest whisper of water moving along pipes. Nothing new in the experience at all. The same old hint of paranoia, of feeling that he was being shadowed. Perhaps it was the old familiar trick he played on himself. He moved on again, slipped soundlessly into the registry, and stopped. There was a light on in the strong room and as he stopped, he heard the faintest sound of movement within. Creeping over to the massive door, he listened and could just pick up the chick-chick, chick-chick of counters being moved. Someone was busy on the combination lock of the safe. It was one of those moments when he regretted his iron rule never to be armed, but now suddenly he swung open the door and there to his astonishment was—the military attaché—frowning over the lock and clumsily manipulating it. Momentarily he looked startled, but went on manipulating and said: "What's the matter, old man, couldn't you sleep?"

"Nor, it seems, could you," Robinsohn said.

"I remembered," Major Rivers said, "that tomorrow was Bag Day and there's a special telegram I have to send. It needs about four cross-references to get it right. But I can't begin to get at any of them until I get the codicil to an agreement which Veralia signed with the Russians. It was all very hush-hush stuff. It's in here. Normally I would get H.E.'s key, but not at this time of night. They began duplicating safe controls last year—key or combination."

"You often work in the middle of the night?"

"Not unless I'm driven. God dammit!" He kicked the iron door of the safe. "I'll have to wait till morning. You like prowling about this place at night?"

"It's the first time I've tried—it seems to yield interesting returns."

54

Rivers moved over to the registry door, opened it, and ushered Robinsohn through. "I've thought up another scheme for getting you out of here," he said. "I'm glad you never did anything about H.E.'s car."

Robinsohn smiled and said nothing. He had all the details he required now, right down to who held the garage key and precisely when His Excellency was due to go to a late dinner party at the French Embassy on the outskirts of the town. It was the perfect occasion—three days away—

"What scheme is that?" he said.

"Would you like a drink?" Rivers said.

"Sure."

Settled in the military attaché's office, Robinsohn said, "I don't quite understand—you're billeted out, aren't you?"

Rivers said, "Yes—I've only got whisky."

"That's fine—but if you're billeted out, did you come all the way back to the embassy in the middle of the night?"

Rivers laughed his quick snorting laugh. "I'm duty officer tonight," he said. "Didn't you know?"

"I see," Robinsohn said. It could all be checked, of course. Rivers knew that. He could not be lying.

"What's this scheme?"

"Well, quite frankly I haven't got the details right yet and we need some outside collaboration. But it won't be long now. I wanted to ask you, Robinsohn . . . I know your work is confidential . . . but what in heaven's name did you ever hope to achieve in a godforsaken country like this?"

Robinsohn sat very upright in his chair, drank his whisky in a gulp, came to his feet, and said, "I'd better warn you, Rivers . . . I'm not staying here much longer. Either you get me out of here or I get myself out."

He left then, abruptly.

CHAPTER 7

As the ambassador opened wide the ornate doors of the wardrobe, the immense cluster of suits—from lounge to morning, from full evening to dinner jacket, from lightweight ceremonial to that final garment worn for presenting letters of credence to heads of state, a confection of light blue with gold embellishments—reminded him of the faded glory of the British Empire. He thought of the days when the Queen's Regulations and Admiralty Instructions laid down the number of gun salutes—nineteen for an ambassador, twenty-one for a governor-general—to be fired with special saluting guns which did not split the eardrums. He remembered half a dozen other similar regulations and smiled wryly. Childish rituals of another age, but they embodied a respect which ambassadors no longer commanded. Why waste time looking over these suits?

What he would wear tonight was a foregone conclusion. He knew that Hargreaves, like himself, would certainly wear a dinner jacket, but Rostand made a cult of occasionally flaunting the old conventions and Robinsohn still insisted on wearing the navy blue suit in which he had arrived. Several forays in the town had yielded suits from Veralian tailors but he complained about their cut. Rivers, too, could be relied upon to wear his dining-out uniform and Penelope—well, he could not remember the last time when she had failed to dress for dinner.

The ambassador frowned at his image in the long wardrobe mirror but his frown reflected more than a distaste for his own stomach line. Once a week he made a habit of calling for the file of outgoing telegrams since he could not hope to keep tabs on them all in the rush of day-to-day business. There, yesterday, as he turned the file, almost at the end he had suddenly read something that startled him. In plain English typed on the blue telegram copy form were the words: "For God's sake get me out of here 43026 (a)." Robinsohn must have slipped it into the bag at the last moment and God knows how old Bellincourt in the Foreign Office would react to such effrontery. Perhaps he simply wouldn't understand. Nothing so unorthodox had ever passed out of this embassy before under the guise of diplomatic immunity.

Half an hour later the ambassador descended to the drawing room to find Penelope already deep in conversation with Rostand and Hargreaves. For a woman who made no bones about her South Kensington code, she had developed a remarkable flexibility when dealing with entirely alien values. Rostand should have been her *bête noir,* but she appreciated his mercurial brain and found a common ground in his wit. Certainly in public no one would have known what she sometimes dared to say in the privacy of her bedroom. She never stooped to the vulgarity of the phrase, "a common little man," but there remained a distaste for a lack of elegance, of old-world graciousness in Rostand that she characterized with the slightest wrinkle of her nose and the diffident private comment, "Unfortunate."

As the ambassador entered the room and saw her talking, he reflected for the hundredth time how much better she was than he at adapting to the modern world. Major Rivers stood at the far side of the room, staring out of the big double windows, and as he exchanged greetings with everyone the ambassador moved toward him. Quickly and briefly he told Major Rivers the contents of the telegram. "Good heavens," Rivers said. "Why did he do a thing like that? . . . I must say I'm sorry . . . I feel partly responsible. But I've worked out a scheme for getting him out at last—and I think it will work."

"I hope it will," the ambassador said, "he's upsetting everyone. He's taken to prowling about the embassy at night—and I must say he looks in pretty bad shape. You'd imagine a prolonged rest in a sort of hotel with everything found might appeal to him, but it obviously doesn't."

"He's a man of action in a very special way," Rivers said. "He's afraid of getting soft. Inside a place like this you could quickly get soft."

"Yes," the ambassador said. "I know one or two people who have gone very soft already. What is this plan of yours?"

Before Rivers could answer, the door opened and Robinsohn came in, as soft-footed as ever, but looking very different from the last time he had arrived for a semiofficial dinner. There were bruised shadows under his eyes, and Penelope noticed that one eyelid had developed the smallest quiver, which might, she felt, easily become a tic. The cigarette between the nicotine-stained fingers went swiftly to and from his lips and he merely nodded at the assembled company, taking the glass of sherry and drinking it straight off. There was an uneasy lull in the conversation and it looked for a moment as if it would develop into an embarrassing silence, but Penelope came in at once.

"Well, perhaps we could all sit where we sat before," she said and led the way into the dining room. "You remember your place, Mr. Robinsohn?"

He nodded and went quickly to the chair next to the head of the table between Penelope and her husband. As they all settled down, Penelope switched off the electric light in the big chandeliers, and the Bristol glasses gleamed in the soft candlelight, the silver throwing back its usual highlights. She directed a swift look at her husband and he broke the silence at once.

"I was reading Talleyrand last night," he said, looking directly at Robinsohn. "Have you ever read Talleyrand?"

Robinsohn simply shook his head and the ambassador continued smoothly. "My favorite quotation comes from Talleyrand—'One ought never to be obstinate except when one ought to be and then one should be unshakable.' Would you agree with that?"

Robinsohn directed an extraordinary look at the ambassador that might almost have combined elements of pity and distaste. "I suppose I would," he said. Rostand saw that the ambassador needed help and came in at once.

"There is another Talleyrand I like very much—'There's nothing a determined diplomat cannot accomplish if he will allow others to take the credit for what he has done.'"

It was a slightly better quote and the ambassador—misunderstanding the motive—thought, How like the new breed of second secretaries. When he was a second secretary, even if he had a better quote he would have suppressed it in the interests of recognizing His Excellency's primacy. But primacy was a very dubious matter nowadays.

Penelope suddenly cut across the conversation, "Why, Mr. Robinsohn, you're not eating."

"Sorry. I have no appetite."

"Well, I'm afraid it's roast beef to follow. I hope that's not too heavy for you."

"Leave me out, will you," he said and now, without asking anyone's permission, in between courses he was actually lighting another cigarette. It was too much for the ambassador. "I hope, my dear," he said addressing his wife, "the smoke won't trouble you."

"I'm sorry," Robinsohn said and began stubbing out his cigarette. Conversation ran on desultorily until the ambassador said, "What do you think the chances are of another Russian satellite defecting, Mr. Robinsohn?"

"Like Yugoslavia?"

"Yes."

"It's possible."

"Which one would it be?"

"I'm not sure yet."

58

The ambassador risked a much more personal question: "You are not concerned in that particular field, I suppose."

Robinsohn shook his head.

"Of course the Russians fondly hope to get one of the NATO people to defect. Does that strike you as realistic?"

"No."

"But I understand finances between the East and West are loosening up."

"Yes—there may be a loan."

"You know about the loan?"

"Which loan do you mean?"

"The Veralian loan."

"I think there will be a loan."

The ambassador turned to Hargreaves. "It's extraordinary, Franklin, I only had the details yesterday. Veralia has applied to London bankers to raise a long-term loan—think of that—communism asks for a loan on the Western capitalist market."

He turned back to Robinsohn.

"You probably know the terms."

"Some of them."

"As I understand it, it will be a straight Eurobond issue of one million dollars repayable over five years."

"Do you know who's underwriting it in London?" Hargreaves said.

"There are three underwriters—unnamed."

"I noticed," Rostand said, "the *Economist* hinted that Warburton and Starbuck were interested in Veralian finance."

Robinsohn had been drinking steadily ever since he sat down and as the meal progressed to the final stage he relaxed visibly.

"There's an indiscreet question which keeps coming to the tip of my tongue," the ambassador said as he finished his creme caramel.

"You—don't mind indiscreet questions, do you, Mr. Robinsohn?" Penelope said.

"What is the question?"

"Do you have any politics?"

Robinsohn shrugged and emptied his glass and Penelope refilled it from the third bottle of vintage Châteauneuf-du-Pape.

"I'm against all politics," he said. "I'm an individualist."

"Carried far enough, people sometimes call that anarchism?" Hargreaves said.

"No—I'm an individualist."

Penelope laughed the soft smooth-flowing laugh that she always used when about to say something open to misunderstanding.

"That doesn't, of course, mean you don't mind whose side you are on—"

"No," Robinsohn said without responding to her smile, "it doesn't."

"I'm glad," Penelope said, artificially prolonging her smile. "But how do you make a choice?"

"I work for the side that tolerates me," he said.

There suddenly opened up for the ambassador an infinite perspective of speciousness, of opportunism and lack of values that made him inwardly shudder. "That could mean either side," he said.

"No—only the British would tolerate me," Robinsohn said.

"But you're not seriously suggesting that if the Russians tolerated you—you—would—"

"No," Robinsohn said. "They do not believe in individualism. They would never tolerate me."

The ambassador smiled and changed the subject.

"Who," he said, "really has the power in Veralia, do you think— Bolsover, secretary of the Central Committee, or our friend Kalogh?"

"Power in this country," Robinsohn said, "shifts its emphasis every week."

"You believe there is an internal struggle going on?"

"Yes."

"Are we in for a change of policy?"

"I don't know yet."

The ambassador sat back in his chair. "I must say," he said, "it would be the crowning satisfaction of my time working in this embassy if we minimally contributed toward Veralia's defection from the Eastern bloc." No one seemed to want to risk any comment, and the ambassador once again changed the direction of the conversation.

"I so frequently find in modern politics that men wear the semblance of power without being able to do what they want. There are too many checks and balances. It certainly applies to diplomacy. The primacy of an ambassador—even in his own embassy—is a polite fiction."

"I like power," Robinsohn said unexpectedly. "I've been trying to get power all my life."

"With any degree of success?" Penelope said.

"A little," he said, "a very little."

"You have power now?" Rostand said.

"In one sense possibly."

"What sense?"

"Knowing too much."

The ambassador had the strongest feeling that, once drawn out of the elaborate defense system behind which he now lived, Robinsohn might become eloquent on the most unexpected subjects.

"Do you think one ever really escapes from the power one's father has over one?" Rostand said to the table at large.

60

"Oh, certainly," Hargreaves said, and Robinsohn simultaneously shook his head.

Penelope smiled. "I was rather glad not to escape," she said.

"Well, there's no escaping a Rugby headmaster," the ambassador said. "One only hopes not to remain too much like him . . ." He broke off and added: "I suppose, Mr. Robinsohn, the reasons why people take up your profession are so varied, there's no one common factor."

"As far as I'm concerned I just like making the decisions myself."

"But *do* you make the decisions?"

"Once I'm away from London, yes."

"I suppose you come as near to running your own life as anyone can in modern society," Hargreaves said.

"No one runs his own life," Robinsohn said.

"But there must be something that sustains a man in your way of life. You couldn't possibly be religious?"

Robinsohn shook his head.

"Or patriotic?"

"No."

"Or a martyr to democracy?"

Robinsohn did not bother to answer the last question. He was thinking how crazily formal it was of these nice correct clean-living people to try to understand a psyche so tormented that it seldom yielded very much even to his own prolonged and painful prying.

"You must have some kind of credo," Penelope said.

"Well—yes."

"And that?"

"Never do anything you wouldn't like photographed."

They all laughed and Penelope's smiling eyes were warm with response. The man had wit—that was enough for her.

"Is that the only—principle?"

"There is one other."

"And that?"

"Learn to cooperate with the inevitable."

Once again they all smiled. Robinsohn had become distinctly more entertaining and interesting. Ten minutes later the ambassador said:

"Well, time's getting on and there is something I must talk to you about privately, Mr. Robinsohn. Will you join me for coffee in my study." He rose. "If," he said to his wife, "you'll excuse us, my dear."

Settled at last in front of his red leather desk, the ambassador began talking about the rule that required embassy guests to recognize the internal codes of the embassy if they hoped to remain welcome guests. Toward the end, a force entered his words that surprised Robinsohn. He had come to regard the ambassador as a soft, kindly, old-world gentleman whose self-assertion would always stop short at a certain point. Now His Excellency concluded: "So you see you must either stop abusing the privileges of this place or we'll have to restrict your movements. You'd better make a choice. You seem to have caused friction everywhere. And that telegram was outrageous. You make it sound as if we are doing absolutely nothing about getting you out of here."

The homily lasted a full five minutes, and Robinsohn left the ambassador's study holding him in a new respect. It also reinforced his determination to carry through his own plan.

CHAPTER 8

The following evening Robinsohn wandered down to the reception desk at a carefully prepared time when he knew that Ambleforth took over from Thompson for the night security round.

Tonight Thompson sat behind the desk cursing quietly. Ambleforth was late again. A big lumbering Yorkshireman, Ambleforth did not have too good a sense of time, and seven fifteen always seemed to him a reasonable interpretation of seven o'clock. What Thompson did not know was that Robinsohn had deliberately arranged to hold Ambleforth in his billet with a long series of invented telephone queries to add another ten minutes to the fifteen-minute delay he had already created himself.

Robinsohn now listened patiently to Thompson fuming and cursing and then quite casually he said, "There's no need for you to wait. I'll be here—if anything crops up—it never does."

Thompson hesitated. He hated this place. It had become a routine coffin that he entered every day to a kind of death. He didn't get on with H.E., he had no particular love for Hargreaves or that female icicle Caroline, and to come under the final authority of a man from the working classes like Rostand seemed to him a savage twist of fate. He had applied for a transfer three months ago, but three months to the Foreign Office constituted just another day.

"I solemnly swear," Robinsohn said, "to sit tight in your chair and shoot any unwanted intruder on sight. Go on . . . leave it to me . . . there's no risk."

Thompson glanced at his watch and back at Robinsohn. The Foreign Office in London had given him clearance, he had been told to stop shadowing him, and by now he was almost accepted as an itinerant member of the staff, an unacknowledged antidote to boredom. The key safe under the counter was carefully locked and Robinsohn obviously did not know the combination. "Give him another ten minutes," Thompson said at last. Goddam you English, Robinsohn thought savagely, why do you have to have such a sense of duty.

At the end of ten minutes, Thompson left with a small flurry of service invective, but time was now cut very short. Hanging on a separate hook under the counter quite unprotected was the bronze key that opened the garage door in the back garden. Snatching it up, Robinsohn slipped into the central corridor and was walking swiftly toward the rear garden when Hargreaves came out of the information office with Alfred Beddoes, the information officer, talking at the top of his voice.

"Still on the prowl," Hargreaves said, and Robinsohn nodded, smiled, and passed on. He dared not pick up the small holdall with those two in the corridor. Turning the corner, he waited out of sight and then with the corridor empty again hurried back to the cubbyhole used by the embassy chaplain, pulled out the holdall, and hurried on toward the back garden. At the glass door with its iron grille he took the big hoop handle and tried to turn it slowly and silently. It began to groan. Locked. Goddam it—why should that be? Thompson had assured him that they never locked the back door until seven forty-five and it was still only seven thirty.

Then he saw the tip of a big iron key, peeping out from the side curtain of the window, which looked like a medieval jailer's key. He pulled it out carefully, inserted the key, and—the lock yielded. Outside it was almost night. He made one swift, certain dive like an unseen shadow across the garden to the garage door. Pressed against the black wall, momentarily he merged with it and waited. Then he inserted the key, and opening the door a mere four inches, slipped round to the boot of the big Rolls to find it—thank God—unlocked. Push the holdall in and back again across the garden in a flash. Swiftly down the central corridor—no one in reception—behind the desk, the key back on its hook, and sitting waiting as Ambleforth arrived almost at once, breathless, sweating, full of apologies and explanations. "But where's Thompson?" he said.

"I took over," Robinsohn said.

"Did you now," Ambleforth said, "and on whose authority?"

"Thompson's."

"He has no right . . ." Ambleforth began and Robinsohn cut him short.

"I shouldn't push your luck too far," he said. "You were damned late—this place could have been looted."

Without waiting for a reply, Robinsohn hurried off through the half-glass swing doors and made a gesture of turning left toward the lift, but doubled back instead beneath the level of view from the swing door and hurried on down the central corridor. No one had relocked the back door. A momentary pause and then he flashed across to the garage again.

Now for the worst part. It was a big roomy boot but beside his holdall, a big leather case sprawled across its center. Wherever Robinsohn tried to shift the case it took up too much room. Haul it out completely, hide it behind a pile of tarpaulins and gasoline cans and climb into the boot. . . . The famous foetal position, curled up, knees almost touching the chin—it just about worked. There was a small grille at the bottom of the panel dividing the interior of the car from the boot. Air or gas fumes would pour through that grille but asphyxiation was a better death than some.

Time? His luminous watch showed seven forty-five P.M. Ten minutes before the ambassador was due to leave. Richards, chauffeur and handyman, a Devon-born countryman, would be putting on that green uniform and peaked cap that reminded Robinsohn uncomfortably of the green Vopos of Eastern Germany. If he tried to open the boot Robinsohn would simply jam the catch.

Final check. The sandwiches and whisky in the holdall, the fifty pounds of local currency stolen from Hargreaves's wallet, the traveller's cheques he had brought from England, the passport, fake business papers, and the capsule in its ordinary matchbox. He shook the box and the lethal pill gave off its appropriate death rattle. At the right moment, if this plan worked, he would transfer the pill to his anus.

Ten minutes later he heard Richards's footsteps coming down the garden path toward the garage and caught a glint of his swinging torch. The chauffeur began whistling "The Yeomen of England" and made a swift check of the engine, adjusted the silk pennant on its silver staff, and without further preliminaries started the car and drove round to the front entrance. Almost at once, with clockwork precision the ambassador and Penelope emerged, exchanged greetings with Richards, and were ushered into the big plush sedanlike interior.

"Would you like the light, sir?" Richards inquired as he pulled away a traveling rug encumbering their feet.

"Thank you, Richards."

The soft yellow glow of a silk-shaded lamp converted the salon into a private world of its own.

"You did check the route this time," the ambassador said.

"Yes, sir," Richards said. "I'm sorry about last time."

Before they even started, a strange mixture of smells began to flow through the grating to Robinsohn and he successfully induced an immediate if slight difficulty in breathing. It had nothing to do with lack of oxygen but was simply the expected sense of claustrophobia. The smells mixed petrol with oil and expensive scent with cigar smoke, and suddenly Robinsohn heard Penelope exclaim, the words barely audible, "Damn—I've left my cigarettes."

"There'll be plenty there," the ambassador said.

"Not those seaweed substitutes," she said. "Richards—would you mind—I left them on my dressing table."

"We're already late," the ambassador began and Penelope interrupted: "We're not going to the German Embassy you know—not everyone is such a maniac for punctuality. The French positively enjoy being late."

The murmur of the idling engine was scarcely audible, but the small accumulation of fumes seemed to Robinsohn to be increasing already. Supposing the exhaust pipe had the slightest flaw. . . . Supposing. . . .

By now Richards had obviously entered the embassy again. Three minutes slipped away and Robinsohn felt the sweat begin to form under his armpits.

The murmur of desultory conversation came through the grating to him until he heard the ambassador snap: "What in God's name is Richards doing? Ambleforth!" he called sharply.

Ambleforth came hurrying up.

"Yes, sir."

"For heaven's sake, check what's happened to Richards."

It was already getting uncomfortably hot in the boot, but once they were away it was a mere ten-minute drive and the movement would create a draught of fresh air—or so Robinsohn hoped. Suddenly he stiffened as he heard his name.

"You must get rid of Robinsohn," Penelope said. "I'm beginning to like him."

"But if you're beginning to like him. . . ."

"I shall miss him the more I like him."

"Miss him? You make it sound as if . . ."

"Oh, come on, darling—he's wonderful light relief to the ark."

In facetious mood she always described the embassy as the ark.

"Well, I can't believe anyone else thinks of Robinsohn as light relief."

There was a flurry of footsteps and Richards came panting up to say breathlessly: "They were under some clothes, Madame—I'm sorry—but they weren't—where you said—I—"

"Let's get going." The ambassador cut him short.

As they moved smoothly away, within a few seconds Robinsohn felt a tremendous kick of excitement release his frozen pulse. He had held his breath, crouched paralyzed, stiffened himself like a corpse, but now in one swoop everything burst to life again as they went through the gate, and he felt—almost vicariously because of the boot—free at last from the embassy.

For the first few minutes the powerful surge of the car moved over the road with hardly a bump, and then Robinsohn slowly became aware above the soft, well-bred purring of this very English car of a harsher note as of another quite different engine or series of engines. He tried to pick out the note clearly among the many minor sounds blending in the boot. The note did not vary as of cars passing or overtaking them but remained constant.

66

Then like a spasm of asthma the claustrophobia intensified and he had regressed right back forty-two years to the flooding shores of a circular world where the sky pressed round him like a warm pink envelope and a mysterious pump sent a gentle tide of warmth, food, and reassurance through every cell of his unformed body as one cell divided from the other, and the struggle for identity was no longer a struggle but a surrender to the cool message of genetic coding . . . and part of the message said that nothing could stop it now: nothing could prevent this mindless, sightless embryo from inheriting all those forty-two years of suffering with devilish certainty.

But now, a fully grown adult, thrust back into his foetal cave, a sudden sense of panic seized him and he felt he would have to get out or suffocate. He curled into a tight ball, his fists clenched, fighting the impulse that drove him to kick at the metal wall.

And then he heard the ambassador's voice again and he strained to pick out the words. "Richards! Richards!" He must be using the old-fashioned speaking tube to call the chauffeur. At first Robinsohn could not be sure he heard aright and then the sentence was repeated and it shriveled him into himself. "We are being followed Richards—draw in slowly and stop."

The note of the engine dwindled, and as the car slowed, the other harsher note rose higher and came closer. What did it mean? A routine check? But this car was immune. A traffic offense—invented or real—but why? They could not conceivably know what lay hidden in the boot. Impossible. No one knew—only—he, Robinsohn, knew.

The engines were clearly motorcycle engines as they roared up to the stationary car and stopped, and there was no doubt about their being police. The ambassador was winding down the window.

"What does this mean?" his rich voice demanded. "Why are you following us?"

A voice with a thick accent said in broken English. "Your car—zees part—" Robinsohn recoiled as if someone had hit him personally when a fist punched the boot—"It 'as a man."

"What absolute nonsense," the ambassador said. "I am the British ambassador and you have no right to interfere with my car."

The authority in his voice once again surprised Robinsohn. This was a very different, very strong-minded man, but now Robinsohn was shaken with a stab of real fear. If they opened the boot, arrested him, and carried him down to those cold, stone, bloodless cells again. . . . Shout now through the grating or wait to see if sheer strength of personality and diplomatic immunity would defeat the police, but this was no ordinary policeman either. Clearly they must be dealing with an ABVO man.

"Your papers, pliss."

"My papers!" The ambassador could not stop the note of total scorn in his voice. It was the final indignity to be asked for his papers. "That pennant—this car—are my papers. Have you ever seen a British flag before?"

"Must ask you to open," the voice said firmly.

"I'll do nothing of the sort."

"There is no way forward."

"What do you mean?"

"If there is no man there, why not you open?"

"Because I claim diplomatic immunity. Richards, drive on."

The voice said simply, "We shall follow."

"I shall report this to the Minister of the Interior," the ambassador said.

"Yes—pliss," the voice said. "But I must ask you—open—"

"Drive on," the ambassador said and the car surged away again as the motorcyclists kicked their starters and the coarse-grained roar drowned out the engine of the Rolls. They were following, if not surrounding the car, immutable outriders. Robinsohn knew the type of machine all too well. Big, glossy, chromium-plated, in a state of shining perfection, but they could cruise at ninety miles an hour using half their power.

Robinsohn knew also what they would do. Wait until the ambassador arrived at the French embassy and parked his car; break open the boot—no diplomatic immunity protected Robinsohn—drag him out and carry him away in ruthless kidnap. One course of action remained possible. Throw himself on the ambassador's mercy. Now . . . at once . . . before it was too late.

He kicked viciously at the grating with his shoes but the cramped space modified his kick. There was no response. Then he shouted—a sudden big shout—and Penelope said, "My God, what's that?"

The ambassador said: "Great Heavens—there *is* someone there."

Penelope was calling now, bending down, her face close to the grating, and calling, "It's you, Robinsohn, isn't it?"

The ambassador made an explosive noise as Penelope half chuckled. "God, what a nerve!"

"What in the hell do you mean," the ambassador was saying and then he cut himself short. "We'd better turn back—at once—I cannot afford to be caught with him in the boot. My God! What a fool! Richards! do you hear me? I want you to slow down and turn back as soon as possible—without stopping."

"Back, sir, but—"

"Don't argue—get back as soon as you can—without stopping."

Richards took a great sweeping curve at the next crossroad and accelerated swiftly as he came into the straight once more. Simultaneously the police swung across his path and stopped him.

"This is going to be very tricky," the ambassador said to Penelope.

He rolled down the window again as the gaunt young man with his peaked cap drove up and said, "We must ask again—you open."

"I claim diplomatic immunity."

"You have broken immunity," the man said.

"Nonsense. Now look, I'm going to order my chauffeur to drive on —if you choose to get in the way so much the worse for you."

A moment of uncertainty overtook the young man and he turned to his radio. Speaking at high speed he made a number of exchanges with the very guttural voice which answered him, and then abruptly switched off.

He kicked his starter.

"We come back too," he said, and with that stood astride the machine, waiting.

"Go ahead," the ambassador said to Richards, and Robinsohn became aware that he was shivering and sweating from a sudden intensification of fear.

The moment of confrontation in the ambassador's study ten minutes later was the more devastating because so icily controlled. The ambassador spoke with the withering scorn of someone unaccustomed to having his presence soiled by idiotic mountebanks. He wanted no truck with such a person.

And then his voice and manner changed. Slowly he became eloquently vituperative. "You break in on us in the middle of the night—you ask for sanctuary—you are taken in—you are given the protection of Her Majesty's Embassy—you disturb our way of life—you upset the staff—you take advantage of all our privileges—and you reward us by the most reckless and cheap-jack conspiracy of a cloak and dagger kind which might at its worst have withdrawn my letters of credence and at best will confront me with the intolerable superiority of a man I despise almost as much as I have come to despise you—Kalogh!"

Robinsohn sat there chain-smoking, saying nothing.

"You deserve to be pushed out into the jungle to take your chance, but I cannot do that. Besides, I have my instructions. There is, however, one thing I insist on—in future you will remain in your room under lock and key from seven o'clock in the evening, until we have found a means of getting you out of here. I'm seeing Rivers tomorrow morning. It shouldn't be more than a few days. That's all I've got to say."

The ambassador rose as if an audience were over but Robinsohn made no move to go. Instead he began pacing round the room talking fast. "I'm sorry—I thought it would come off—no one would know—least of all you—but you've overlooked something. You've overlooked the biggest thing of all. You've overlooked the *reason* why it went wrong. Someone must have leaked my plan to them."

The ambassador had walked to the door and stood there with his hand on the handle. "I've nothing more to say."

"Don't be crazy," Robinsohn said. "You don't understand what I'm saying—someone inside here is leaking information to the ABVO. I want to know who gave me away."

The ambassador thought for a moment and hesitated with the door half open. He had allowed his anger to cloud his thinking. Robinsohn was right. How did they know about his escape attempt and how were they able to follow him exactly to the minute? Slowly he walked back to his desk again. "You told no one about your plan?" he said.

"No one."

"Do you suspect anyone."

"There is one man."

"Who's that?"

"Can I speak in complete confidence?"

"Why—yes."

"I need more than a yes. I need your absolute assurance to treat this in confidence."

The ambassador sank back in his chair, his face crumpled into a kind of confused disdain. "You're not," he said, very softly, "proposing to become a man of principle all of a sudden."

"I don't understand," Robinsohn said.

"No," the ambassador said. "You wouldn't understand. Having just broken trust with me, you still talk in terms of trust—I don't trust you anymore, Robinsohn. But if you have something to say, say it now."

"In that case I'll say nothing," Robinsohn said, and unexpectedly he simply strode out of the room.

CHAPTER 9

It was going to be a very heavy morning, Caroline informed the ambassador as he entered his office. There were three staff interviews, the Queen's birthday party list to be okayed, two ministerial and three party interviewees coming from different parts of the Veralian bureaucracy, twenty-two complicated telegrams to be read and initialed, Kalogh phoning at midday, the lunch with the American ambassador beginning at twelve thirty, and Major Rivers insisting that he had priority over everyone for reasons he refused to disclose to anyone but the ambassador.

"He did have priority," the ambassador said, "but not now. Caroline, I want you to put everything back half an hour. Phone everyone, will you, and tell the American Embassy I'll be late. Then ask Mr. Hargreaves if he will kindly drop everything and come to my office."

Within a few minutes the first secretary arrived and the ambassador carefully closed the second green baize door behind the first mahogany one.' He flipped down the microphone: "Keep everything quiet for the next half hour, Caroline—please."

"Sorry to break in on your routine, Franklin," he said turning to Hargreaves. "I don't want to waste anyone's time this morning—so I'll plunge straight in. You must know all the details of yesterday's little farce. But something much more important lies behind it. When I saw Robinsohn after the whole unfortunate business, he said something which surprised me. He said someone in this embassy had leaked the details of his plan to the ABVO. But only one man knew about that plan. I'm trying to discover who that man is."

"Shouldn't we ask Robinsohn?"

"He's due in here in ten minutes—I wanted you to hear what he has to say. But there's something else, rather more important, linking in with this which he doesn't know. In fact, no one knows. There have been two other important leaks from this embassy recently. On two occasions I have discovered that Kalogh's ministry knew the contents of two of our top classified documents."

"From the blue files?"

"One from blue—one from telegrams. They carefully concealed that they did know, but Kalogh let slip a detail of the chromium deal one day —a detail known only to the Foreign Office and myself. On the second occasion he as good as warned me of the idiocy of anyone contacting underground forces in Veralia. That—as you know better than I do—is top secret classified. Now what I wanted to ask you was this—if you were looking for a leak in this place, where would you begin?"

"It's classic to begin at the bottom and go up," Hargreaves said, "but I can't see anyone in our typing pool having the drive and cunning to get at the blue files undetected."

"Supposing," the ambassador said, "we're looking at it from the wrong end. I must say I have never quite believed in Robinsohn. There's something unreal about everything he does: arriving in the middle of the night, asking for asylum, upsetting everyone, *not* escaping in the boot of a car. It's all too elaborate a trail. Has it—could it possibly—all have been laid on theatrically as an alibi?"

The ambassador paused but Hargreaves said nothing.

"Supposing," he went on, "the Veralians wanted to plant an agent in the middle of this embassy—what more cunning and convincing method than to have a man with flawless English and an English passport asking for asylum in the middle of the night. What even better alibi than to frustrate him while trying to escape. After all, they could have stopped us and taken him—why didn't they?"

Hargreaves concealed his amazement. Much of this had been suggested two weeks ago but here His Excellency was putting it forward as though it were his own brand-new insight into a complicated pattern of deception instead of Hargreaves's already expressed theory. Play along with him, Hargreaves thought; don't disillusion him; his memory must be less good than it was. After all, he would never deliberately lift another man's interpretation without acknowledgment: his code simply would not permit it. "But wait a minute," Hargreaves said, "we have to remember that they shot a man down in the process of getting him here."

"Robinsohn *said* they shot him down. It too could have been faked."

"That at least was original."

"And his own wound could have been self-inflicted. It was very superficial."

"They are, of course, ruthless and perfectionist."

"What about the confirmation from the Foreign Office?"

"The Foreign Office also cleared Philby on two classic occasions."

"There's nothing to stop Robinsohn being a double agent, I suppose, but we have absolutely no evidence against him."

"Except the coincidence of his arrival—and three separate leaks occurring . . ."

72

"And all that night prowling." Hargreaves found himself warming to the theme against all rational inclination. "Rivers told me he found him wandering round the registry once at three in the morning."

They talked on for another five minutes and then Caroline announced Robinsohn's arrival. He came in with a nervy self-confidence and after the briefest preliminaries the ambassador said: "You asked for an undertaking of complete confidence yesterday—I'm prepared to give that now. Nothing said in this room will be passed on to anyone else."

"I'd rather see you alone," Robinsohn said.

"I must play it my way," the ambassador said. "Now I believe you were about to tell me something yesterday?"

"Yes."

"What was it?"

"Nothing more than a coincidence."

"What coincidence?"

"Rivers is the only man who knew about my plan."

"Major Rivers?"

"Yes."

"You draw some conclusion from that?"

"No, but I thought you might."

"You're not seriously suggesting that Major Rivers, military attaché for five years to this embassy, would bother himself to pass onto the Veralian police details of your crazy escape plan."

"He was the only man who knew."

"I take it *you* conceived this plan—not him."

"Yes," Robinsohn lied, "but when I told him he made me swear not to try it."

"But you did."

"Yes."

"If he made you swear not to try it, how could he anticipate that you would?"

"If I were trying to persuade someone in my position to do something unorthodox, I should tell him *not* to try it at any cost."

"I see," the ambassador said.

"Was there absolutely no one else in the plot?" the ambassador continued.

Robinsohn seemed to hesitate a fraction of a second. "I used Annabel Harding as a decoy."

He explained the prolonged telephone queries to delay Ambleforth.

"She made them for you?"

"Yes."

"But she did not know the actual escape plan?"

"No."

"What is this girl to you?"

"Nothing."

"We are seeing Major Rivers in a few minutes," the ambassador said. "Would you care to remain with us?"

"No, thanks," Robinsohn said. "But I rely on your undertaking."

"Of course," the ambassador said.

Robinsohn seemed relieved to go.

Rivers was all that one would expect of a military attaché that morning as he came into the ambassador's office: freshly shaved, immaculately dressed, walking with military precision, but somehow the ambassador felt that he was having to make an effort to keep the act coordinated. The blotches on the cheeks could come from his heart condition or drink, and the bruised pits under his eyes from insomnia, or living it up, but where in the Veralian capital could an Englishman live it up to any serious extent.

"I don't think we need to go into any elaborate preliminaries, Theodore, do we?"

"I shouldn't think so."

"You know what it's all about?"

"Of course."

"Now can you just tell us—did you know anything of Robinsohn's plan to conceal himself in my car?"

"Is this an inquiry?"

"Well, hardly—we're just trying to clear up certain details."

"It has no official status?"

"None—nothing is being recorded."

"Well, I'd better tell you right away—I not only knew—I actually thought the whole thing up myself."

It was in the true-blue-clean-breast manner of what a service man would regard as real integrity.

"*You* thought it up?

"You seem surprised at that."

"Well, we had reason to believe Robinsohn thought it up."

"If he said that, I admire him."

"I didn't say he said that."

"You see," Rivers said, "the fact of the matter is that in a very mistaken mad moment, jokingly, I said to Robinsohn: 'You could always try the Hollywood trick of the boot of H.E.'s car.' When I realized he was taking me seriously I was horrified. I did my damndest to persuade him out of it. I thought I had persuaded him—but just as a safeguard I made him swear to keep my name out of it if he were ever crazy enough to try."

"So you accept full responsibility for the whole idea," the ambassador said.

"For its conception—not its execution."

74

"Well—that's frank of you—but why didn't you report the matter to me?"

"I never thought he'd be mad enough to try."

"Surely you realize we are dealing with someone very different from ourselves."

"Yes, of course."

"I must say I would never have believed you could be so foolish. I don't need to tell you—we haven't heard the last of the repercussions from this. Have you seen the local press?"

Rivers nodded. The ambassador picked up the Veralian *Zodium* from a pile of newspapers on his desk—"Ambassador Smuggles Spy," he read aloud. "The European press will have snapped it up by now and reprinted the story all over England and America. Nothing so juicy has come their way for months—and I am going to have to do some rapid, efficient, and very convincing explaining. Just how embarrassing—more than embarrassing—it will be I don't need to tell you."

"I am sorry, sir," Rivers said. "Very sorry indeed. It all began as a joke, and if only I had known."

"I want you," the ambassador said, "to write me a short succinct report of exactly how it all came about. I would like it by this afternoon—perhaps you could drop everything else . . ."

"Yes, sir."

"Before you go—I understood you had another plan for getting Robinsohn out of here. I trust it has nothing to do with my car or my person."

"No, sir."

"What is the plan?"

Major Rivers shifted uneasily and took out of his breast pocket an old-fashioned silver cigarette case. "Do you mind if I smoke?"

The ambassador glanced at his watch. "Look, this is a very heavy morning. You have landed us in the most terrible mess. I would like to go straight to the details."

The microphone buzzed. The ambassador deflected the switch and began: "I told you, Caroline— What's that? Kalogh—Yes—I see—No—I can't talk to him now. Tell him I'll ring back in half an hour. And, Caroline, come and collect these telegrams, will you—I shan't be able to deal with them this morning." He turned back to Major Rivers. "You were saying," he said.

"I don't know whether you've noticed, but Thompson and Robinsohn are roughly the same build," Rivers began. "Ambleforth comes in at six thirty to take over from Thompson and Thompson goes home. Supposing we wait for a dark rainy evening, dress Robinsohn in Thompson's uniform and cap and let him walk out in place of Thompson."

Caroline came in, took up the pile of telegrams, and left again. They remained silent while she was in the room and then the ambassador said: "It certainly has the virtue of simplicity. What do you think, Franklin?" He turned to Hargreaves.

"It might work," Hargreaves said, "but you'd have to fill in the fine detail."

"What fine detail?"

"Well, the way Thompson walks—that funny little attaché case he sticks to—the angle of his hat. But surely one man's clothes are not going to fit another well enough not to look odd."

"That's where I hope Caroline comes in," Rivers said.

"Caroline?" the ambassador frowned. "The fewer people who know about this the better. Why does she have to come into it?"

"Believe it or not she can work a sewing machine."

"Caroline?" the ambassador said. "I don't believe it."

"I've checked," Rivers said. "Well enough to shorten trousers anyway—and that's the main problem. Robinsohn is an inch shorter than Thompson in the leg. I believe that . . ."

The ambassador interrupted with a sweep of his hand . . . "I take it you've spoken to Robinsohn?"

"No sir."

The ambassador laughed drily. "He's the last man to consult, of course," he said. "Well, let's think our way carefully through this one for a few days. And in the meantime clamp down on everything. Do nothing until I give the final okay. Thank you for being so frank—and can I have that report around three o'clock this afternoon?"

When Rivers had gone the ambassador said to Hargreaves: "The question is—who shall we get to investigate these leaks. Bruce Canning isn't coming back for at least another month."

Canning, the resident security officer, had picked up the Veralian bug so badly that it had affected his heart and he was back in England on six weeks' sick leave.

"Let's get a wire off to London and ask for instructions."

"Isn't there something else we should decide first?"

"I can't seriously entertain the idea that Rivers leaked anything to the ABVO."

"Nor can I."

"His new plan will test his trustworthiness anyway . . . if they anticipate it this time."

It was twenty-four hours before the Foreign Office replied:

"Sending substitute security man." Twelve hours later a second telegram arrived: "Security substitute unavailable next two weeks. Proceed with preliminary inquiries yourselves."

The ambassador called Hargreaves into his office again and read the telegram to him. "It's a great relief to me. I can't stand these bloodhounds nosing into everything. I simply don't like have them hanging around the place. But who's the man for the preliminary inquiry?"

The two men looked at each other for a long minute. "Perhaps you'd like me to look into it," Hargreaves said as casually as possible.

"I hoped you'd say that," the ambassador said. "You're one of the few I can really trust." If only Rostand were there to hear that, Hargreaves thought, but another much more complex reason made him smile. Perhaps he shouldn't have had that twinge of anxiety after all when he first heard about these leaks.

"You'd better move cautiously," the ambassador said. "One can run into nasty legal implications with this kind of thing. And remember we alone know about the blue file leaks. Above all we must continue keeping check on everything Robinsohn does in this place. I loathe the idea of a nest of spies, but there's no alternative for the time being."

Caroline worked very late that evening because Joanna, the private office typist, was ill, and Caroline pounded out one telegram after another in a fury, each vindictive finger beating the image of Miss Fairweather's voluptuous body. At seven thirty, with the embassy empty of day staff and the night-lights on, she pulled the last telegram out of the typewriter. Then she made a swift survey of the private office, went to the door, checked the empty corridor, and moved back again through the double door of H.E.'s office. Once inside she dialed swiftly on the green scrambled private telephone.

"Is that you, Leon? Listen, I don't think we should meet tonight . . . Don't press me . . . I can't talk here . . . No . . . There are very urgent reasons . . . You are leaving town? . . . When did you say? . . . I see. Well, look, make it half an hour later—and somewhere quite different—not the club at any cost . . Your flat? All right. I'll take a taxi."

Caroline went back to the private office, snatched up the big glossy-black portmanteau handbag, and hurried down the corridor to the ladies'. There she stripped off her frock, pants, and bra and washed every crevice of her body. She did not love this man, but he knew how to extract the last drop of physical pleasure from her and she had a horror that some natural sweat or smell might remain to render the act too animal. Animal? As the word occurred to her she had begun the elaborate ritual of making up her face, and her cool eyes lit up. A shiver of anticipation went through her. Three long weeks since she had seen Leon . . . but now. She frowned at the image of her pouting lips in the mirror. What did all this security check mean? What did they know? What were they after? That ghastly man Hargreaves with his fancy accent and condescending manner. . . . What sort of fool would ever employ a tailor's dummy like that to investigate anything? He should be treated with contempt. She obviously had nothing to fear.

Leon's flat was on the tenth floor of a modern block on the north side of the river. Ironically, the wide window in its main room looked back over the river toward the British Embassy and from it Leon Schneisler could almost see the window of the private office. He received Caroline with that kind of tenderness that she had come to realize was theatrical. Veralians were like some Italians. They could make a pretense of love look and sound genuine for as long as it took to get what they wanted. She did not respond to his kiss.

The drinks were already poured and she knew how lethal they could be. She had long, long ago learned the lesson—"The superego is soluble in alcohol." But for that night two months ago when she took and drank the third Veralian cocktail, she would not have this haunting new fear surrounding her, the fear that drove her to agree to this meeting tonight.

Leon Schneisler was immensely tall, easily overtopping her six feet, and their whole relationship had begun because of his height. Among many other complicated desires behind Caroline's cool, logical façade, she craved one thing: a man to dominate her physically and mentally. Mentally she found most men anaemic, and physically she could not bear a man to have to reach upward to kiss her. The kiss had to be delivered from a dominating height and any man who tried to make love to her must have a dash of heightened masculinity—even ruthlessness.

It was in Leon's face marked by two deep furrows reaching from the nostrils to the corners of the mouth and beyond. The mouth was set in a firm, almost cruel line, and Caroline found a delicious frisson in remembering how close to cruelty this man could come. She also admired him for his double role of journalist and intelligence man.

As she sipped her way through that first powerful Veralian brandy, he spread his six foot three inches along the sofa opposite her armchair and ran his eye almost insolently from the tips of her immaculate shoes to the glossy crown of her ash-blond hair.

"You worry too much," he said in his thickly accented but grammatically perfect English. Voices mattered almost as much as height to Caroline and she could feel the most intimate parts of her body responding to what she called forest voices—like Leon's.

"You don't know what I'm worried about," she said.

"Didn't you say there was some security check going on?"

"No—I didn't."

"Well, if there's no security check."

"I didn't say that either."

Suddenly he swung up from the sofa and in one long stride reached her armchair. He sank down before her knees and began stroking her thighs. She shrank away, but even as she did so she felt the surge as if a spring had been released in her dried-up body.

"Why waste time?" he said. "It seems like centuries . . ."

"Good God," she said, "you're phoney."

He frowned slightly but his subtle caresses increased their intimacy and range. She sprang out of the chair almost pushing him aside and striding round the room said, "This is our last meeting—I mean it this time—I've been a complete fool."

He lay back on the rich green carpet, putting his hands under his head and followed her movements with a hint of insolence in his smile.

"Why have you been a complete fool?"

"I should never have come here—never have slept with you—never have talked."

"But I assure you," he said, "you said practically nothing."

She came and stood over him, her hands on her hips, looking down with an arrogance equivalent to his. That was another reason why she sometimes found him so attractive—they were, at so many different levels, equally matched.

"I'll make a bargain with you," she said. "You tell me what I told you when I was drunk last time—and I'll agree to go on sleeping with you."

"But you said nothing—nothing I couldn't have got from other sources."

"Then why do you go on inviting me? Why do you go on cultivating me?"

"Because," he said, reaching up and allowing his hands to slip under her skirt, "I want to make love to you." She shrank away from his touch.

"For God's sake stop pawing me. Why won't you tell me what I said?"

"Because it is better you should not know."

That was the strength of his position. She knew she had become so fuddled with drink and sex over the whole of that fateful weekend; she knew that he had subtly disentangled from her talk something that she had quoted from confidential papers in the registry; and he claimed that he had already used information drunkenly provided by her; but was he simply bluffing in order to blackmail her into bigger and better revelations? Because that was what had become explicit in his attitude—cold-blooded blackmail.

"Why do you go on inviting me here?" she repeated coldly. "To blackmail me?"

"Who on earth ever said anything so outrageous?" he said in his perfect English. "I want to go on seeing you—for your own sake."

He reached up and tried to grab her again, but she evaded him.

"Listen," she said, "I'll tell you this much. There *is* a security check on. They'll be coming to me along with everyone else soon. You—you bastard—have succeeded in making me feel guilty. So let's get it clear—if you don't tell me whatever it is I told you, I'm not seeing you again. And I don't mind what you do or say about it."

"You think you can do without me," he said.

"I'll find a way."

"You love me," he said.

"Not you—your body."

"But bodies are more powerful than minds."

"We will see," she said, and this time on a long swing he reached her legs and did not hesitate to grapple with her until she collapsed on the carpet and he was ruthlessly kissing her and her body flamed at him and what she fought was her own lust which slowly overwhelmed all resistance as it rose with furnace intensity to burn her will away. She no more remembered the scream than she remembered what it was she had told him, but afterwards all the way back toward her apartment the echo of the scream was still on the air.

And then she found that she had left her flat keys in the embassy. She redirected the taxi to the embassy and ten minutes later Ambleforth unlocked the main gate with sardonic remarks about day staff who wanted to join the night shift.

She hurried down the corridor, up the stairs to the first floor, and into the private office. There were her keys carefully laid out on her desk before she went, in order not to be forgotten, beside the wilting daffodils Schneisler had sent her. Suddenly she felt the exhaustion of drink, anxiety, and love-making and flung herself momentarily into her chair. She could have slept there and then, but she pulled herself together and staggered out into the corridor to come to a sudden horrified halt as she saw Robinsohn loping uncertainly toward her. She turned in the opposite direction at once but he called softly: "Miss Masters—just a minute— do you have a cigarette?" She hesitated and in that moment he overtook her and they stood close to each other while he lit a cigarette for her and he was talking fast about the isolation of the embassy at three in the morning, the subtlety of the scent she wore, it being Saturday tomorrow, and the excellent brandy he had in his room for a last nightcap.

The wild idea leaped to her mind from what source she never knew. Perhaps it was that she had torn herself away from Schneisler with her appetite still unsatisfied; perhaps the crazy notion that she should test the satisfaction of a substitute lover in case she was driven to give up Schneisler. She stood there leaning against the wall and even when he said: "You have no alternative—you must come and drink my brandy," she did not move away.

It was when he innocently took her arm to guide her toward the stairs that she recoiled extravagantly.

80

"I thought," he began to say, but she cut him short.

"You thought you could get me on the cheap, didn't you? You're just like the rest of them. Crude! Crude! God, how I loathe men."

And then she went storming away down the corridor, but as she went she knew that her pulse was mounting again and against all her code, somewhere at the far back of her mind it was reassuring to know that someone quite different from Schneisler was also capable of stirring her just by holding her arm.

Robinsohn watched her disappear down the corridor and turned back toward his room. Gloomily kicking the carpet as he went, hands thrust deep in his trousers pockets, he wished for the twentieth time that he had never come knocking on the gate of this straitjacket hell of a godforsaken embassy. Now the damned bitch would tell them that he was free and prowling about the corridors half the night. Exaggeration came so easily to outraged females. It was ludicrous and dangerous to try to lock him into his room after eight o'clock. Ludicrous because ordinary locks yielded so easily to technical manipulation, and dangerous because nothing was more calculated to intensify his frustrations to a point of frenzy. Moving down the stairs, he walked along the main corridor and pulled the curtain aside to look out at the back door. The same silhouette leaning against the wall, the same sense of unrelenting vigilance.

He turned back along the corridor, tried the door of the information office and found it, as he expected, locked; he climbed the stairs to the second floor again and turned the handle of the chancery—locked; he moved along to the private office—locked. This was the new regulation carried out with total rigor: everything to be locked after office hours. Restricted to the corridors, to just blank walls and threadbare carpeting, he walked from one floor to the next, a terrible sense of traveling on compulsive rails through an infinite perspective of narrowing tunnels making him feel faintly giddy so that he shut his eyes as he went. It reminded him too powerfully of the ruthless forces driving his own life.

Only the radio room left to try. He almost ran up the three flights of stairs but softly with his fleeting touch, and grasped the old-fashioned iron hoop handle. It gave to his twist, but the door again was locked. Then he remembered the library—surely that must be open and free—what could printed books give away to anyone? He hurried down to the big parquet-floored room with the double doors, but again the lock did not yield to him.

Slowly he shambled up once more to the third floor, turned away to the west wing and slid almost soundlessly past the ambassador's bedroom.

Back inside his own room everything was in chaos. Books and magazines were scattered over the floor, shirts protruded from half-open drawers, the old-fashioned fireplace was studded with cigarette ends, and ash ran down the pillow on the bed with scarred burn marks at the edges of the bedside table. He went over to the chest of drawers, pushed aside the brandy, eau de cologne, sleeping pills, and aspirin, switched on the table lamp, and stared at his reflection in the mirror.

Thinner, much thinner was the first impression, but how could it be otherwise. His appetite had gone. The gray in his eyebrows more pronounced and a new lackluster look in his eye, which made his face dull. When the time came it might all be helpful. He needed a new persona. But now . . . Slowly, painfully, he lowered himself onto the bed and lay there hands behind his head, staring at the beautifully molded ceiling, trying not to think and thinking more. He began at the beginning and it seemed that he went over half his life in half an hour.

He was preparing to follow the same routine the next evening when he was surprised to hear a timid tap on his door. Annabel Harding had made a pretense of working late, waited carefully until the night-lights appeared, climbed the stairs, and there she was outside his door.

"Could I talk—t-to y-you a minute?" she said full of a terrible nervousness, and he saw at once that she had dressed and scented herself—to kill. Everything about her was immaculate, from the glossy shoes to the frilly white blouse, and the scent came over in powerful waves.

"Of course," he said. "Come in—sit over here, will you—I'm sorry everything is in such a mess."

He gathered together a heap of newspapers, which swamped the big armchair, and stacked them on the bed. She saw then that the bed was unmade and winced because her dislike of dirty linen had for her an association with dirty sex. As she sat down, the big armchair engulfed her and her short chubby legs swung two inches off the ground.

"I've only got brandy," he said. "I hope you like it."

The quick wave of courage that had carried her up to his room evaporated rapidly and she heard the nervousness in her voice as she said Yes, she liked brandy. While he poured the drinks, he said nothing and she used the two phrases she had carefully prepared for just such a gap in the conversation. "I hope you don't mind my coming."

"Not at all," he said.

"It must be very exciting to do what you do," she said.

Pouring the brandy with his back toward her, he felt a sudden weariness overcome him. Oh, God, was he to be subjected to the hero-worship of a typist whose knowledge of espionage had come from the Hollywood films and a few pulp thrillers, and should he at once plead pressure of work, give her a very small brandy, and politely excuse himself after five minutes. It was intolerable to have to face uninformed admiration like some third-rate pop star confronting a teenage hysteric. Or should he make the brandy large and lethal, prepare a swift assault,

82

and provide her with what she obviously needed—an act of sex redeemed by simulated love? It would be pleasant to strip her and at least an hour could be spent in those secondary sensualities which pleased him more than any final climax, but then would come the inevitable complications on his side and hers.

As she took the brandy, her hand shook a little and he realized what a tiny apprehensive bundle of female allure was curled up so defensively in the big crimson armchair, but there were echoes in himself of her uneasiness. She had released the same old conflict between what he knew to be a cheap desire to indulge his lust, fear of revealing his weakness, and a commonsense recoil from situations of this kind. Somehow it was more humiliating to reveal the hidden place of his personality to someone who earned a living from typing than it would have been to a more complex, deeply aware person, but he resented the implications of the thought immediately it occurred to him. She was no less a human being because of what she did for a living, she had no part in molding her own prettily empty face and pin brain, and she certainly knew enough to complain to the Christian God for loading the dice against her from the start. Why should he, whose dice were loaded too, affect to patronize her?

The unaccustomed brandy burned her throat and made her cough, and—against his will—he was at her side with a handkerchief to dab the tears from her eyes and then there arose from her presence a distillation of young flesh, scent, and the faintest hint of fresh sweat, which threatened to overwhelm all caution. What if he had to meet her in the corridor tomorrow? What if she knew his secret and carried it publicly in her face as she passed him? What if she spread gossip in the typing pool and he saw the girls nudge each other and giggle as he passed?

When she had finished the second large brandy, she was very high, her face flushed, one leg crossed over the other, swinging vigorously as if her body demanded some satiation even if it were her own. His eye watched fascinated the pendulum of her glossy black foot—to and fro—to and fro—and he thought how absurd it was that someone should publicly exhibit sexual desire without being aware of it.

Conversationally he drew her out then with subtle questioning and as he probed into the small shallows of her mind, almost without thinking he gave her the third brandy. Presently she began to talk compulsively, the self-confessional pouring easily away because control of her tongue was never her strong point and now she was nearly drunk. Once she began to talk about herself she could not stop. Intimacies were thrown away casually. She spoke of the men who had used her, the guilt after every weekend sleeping with a new man, the slowly dawning awareness of abuse, and the intolerable snobbery of the embassy, where only one other typist condescended to be her friend.

For him it became a kind of safeguard. If he knew so much about her he could hold it all in hostage against any breach of confidence she might attempt with him.

"I swore I wouldn't again," she said. "I swore I'd stop sleeping around—but I couldn't, I couldn't, and it makes me so miserable."

The tears were running down her cheeks now but she made no sound of crying.

"That's all they ever want. It's terrible really. It doesn't work for me, whatever I do. If I sleep with them they leave me. If I don't sleep with them they leave me. What am I to do?"

She was sobbing gently and he thought, Oh, Lord, she's going to collapse on me. He went over to her again, took her head in his hands and kissed the salt tears running down her cheeks, a mixture of sex and sadness giving his caresses a kind of tenderness. He was alarmed when she responded, all his defenses went up again as her hot lips and open mouth fastened on his and such a surge of passion came thrusting through her tongue it drove him to respond.

But even as he picked her up and carried her to the bed, even as he kissed her brow, cheeks, eyes, and lips, even as he slipped off her blouse, and she buried his face in her breasts he knew it would not do. He remained there feeling the glow of her young skin, the elastic pressure of her breasts and her whole body tossed and turned but he made no move. He wanted to rip the skirt off, he wanted to bury himself between her legs, but there was no real response in his own body, nothing to offer her but his hands and lips. And what would the embassy make of all this if it permeated through to the old witch Miss Hallows, to Thompson, Hargreaves, Caroline, and finally the ambassador himself.

It was then that he restrained her passionate lips, pushed her hands gently aside and said, "Wait a minute—just be patient a minute."

When he was naked he came back to the bed and as he removed the remainder of her garments he kissed her gently on each newly naked spot. Then he lay beside her, took her gently in his arms and, kissing her soft shoulders, said, "Just lie with me—lie with me."

She did not understand the motive because she knew nothing of the mother's image which haunted every woman he had ever touched. She was quite unaware of a dead woman's jealousy which crippled him as a man and she had absolutely no idea that she had the power to humiliate him. Because for the first time in her life a man was holding her with what she mistook for respect and kissing her with what she translated into tenderness, and when violation did not break open her body or animal cries remind her of beasts of prey tearing like hyenas at still-living flesh, she felt happy. She sank down and down into sensual enchantment and for a whole long hour they lay without speaking, their lips mapping the sensual surfaces of cheek and shoulder, breast and back, and she never

84

knew that it was another body that inspired him and another woman, age-less and yet old enough for Annabel to be her daughter, who took her place on the bed.

And then at last he gently withdrew and said, "You must go now."

"But why . . ." she began.

"You must go now or it will all go sour," he said.

She cried again then, very gently, and a sudden fear shook him that he had gone too far and stirred her raw emotions to a response that could be dangerous. Dear Christ—if she started clinging. If she expected to re-peat this experience. No—it must be made very clear.

As she shyly dressed, he said, "I can trust you not to talk?"

She nodded. "It would spoil everything," she said.

"Yes, it would."

"I'm glad you understand," she said.

"Yes," he said, "but I do not know when we can meet again." He said it because he knew they would never meet again.

CHAPTER 10

When they discovered at ten o'clock the following morning that the cipher safe would not open, no one took it seriously at first. Hargreaves examined his key closely and came to the conclusion that by some means one of the teeth had been twisted out of alignment. He rang the ambassador but Caroline was in the middle of recounting what had happened in the embassy the previous night and listened with some impatience. Then she said: "Can we ring you back in five minutes?" Hargreaves agreed and she turned to the ambassador again.

"You mean to say," the ambassador said, "he was wandering the corridors at that hour?"

"Yes."

"Doing anything suspicious."

"Not suspicious, no. But I think he was drunk."

"Nothing else?"

"Well—he made a pass at me."

She knew it was a vicious extension of the truth but she felt vicious this morning. She had a terrible hangover, Hargreaves had asked to see her for security reasons, and she realized in the clear light of this spring morning how powerful was the sexual tie which held her to Leon.

The harshness in her voice as she spoke made the ambassador say, "You don't like Robinsohn."

"Not particularly. You did ask us to report anything, didn't you?"

"I did, yes."

"I must say," Caroline added before she could stop it, "I don't particularly like playing the spy."

The ambassador frowned and moved uncomfortably in his chair. "I couldn't agree with you more," he said, "but spying of course is the last thing I want to encourage. The whole idea is abhorrent to me. I simply want anything suspicious reported." Even as he said it there was an ambiguity in his words that troubled him.

86

"That man is changing this place," Caroline said.

"There's some truth in that."

"He's bringing out the nastiness in all of us."

"Well, I hope he won't be here much longer."

"He's leaving?"

"I can't tell you when, Caroline."

She changed the subject then and repeated Hargreaves's report on the cipher safe. "They say it won't open."

"What absolute nonsense."

"Mr. Hargreaves has asked to borrow your key."

"I don't understand." He unlocked the middle drawer of his desk, unhooked a small steel key from a ring full of keys and said: "Tell them I must know the contents of that last batch of telegrams by twelve o'clock at the latest."

But still when Hargreaves used the ambassador's key, the safe would not open and all the twisting and turning did not produce a quiver on the bland iron face. One hour later the repercussions were felt through one section after another and the total block on decoding incoming telegrams slowly spread its paralysis into the private office, the registry, the chancery, and typing pool.

It was then that Paul Rostand decided on some drastic action. "Don't you think we should rent a drill and drill our way in?" he said. "Otherwise this place will come to a standstill."

"Can you handle a drill?" Hargreaves said.

"No—but we could hire a driller too."

Hargreaves kicked the iron frame: "Goddam and blast the brute. Let's have one last go."

As he manipulated the key for the hundredth time he muttered: "You know, I'm wondering whether someone hasn't been tampering with this. Some odd things have been happening in this place since our refugee arrived. I wouldn't put it past him to have interfered with this as he has interfered with everything else."

"Better get the drill," Rostand said, but the brutal intervention of a drill from an alien land cut across the fine grain of Hargreaves's whole concept of the embassy. The cipher safe was a symbol and violating it with a drill a kind of blasphemy. No such symbol existed in Rostand's mind. Efficiency had priority over everything and this paralysis must be stopped from widening its grip even if it meant literally breaking open the cipher safe.

A long chain of urgent telephone inquiries began with Hargreaves's secretary desperately trying to wrest the necessary details of drills and drillers from a highly resistant minion in the Ministry of Works.

At that point Robinsohn came loping along the corridor, put his pale face round the door, and said, "I hear you have some trouble with the safe."

Rostand, now left in charge of operations by Hargreaves, nodded curtly.

"Can I help?"

"Not," Rostand said sourly, "unless you know how it jammed in the first place."

Robinsohn smiled. "You think I have tampered with your safe," he said.

Rostand didn't answer.

"I hear you've ordered an electric drill," Robinsohn said.

"You don't miss a trick, do you?" Rostand said.

"It won't work, you know," Robinsohn said. "An electric drill will simply skid off that surface."

"You must have tried it many times."

"No, but frontal assault is a waste of time." Robinsohn thereupon turned abruptly on his heel and left the room.

Twenty minutes later a man wearing blue overalls arrived with a boy assistant, plugged in an electric drill and scarred the door of the safe with one assault after another. It did not yield. Neither he nor his assistant spoke English and further communication was reduced to a series of extravagant gestures varying from the rude to the despairing. Once again Rostand decided on a change of tactics. "Get Robinsohn," he said to one of the two cipher clerks who had stood around gaping for half an hour, but Robinsohn was nowhere to be found. When they at last traced him it was to the ambassador's office. Robinsohn had just survived a final dressing down about violating the privacy of the embassy at three in the morning. He had taken it without saying a word, and a terrible sense of impotence with this man had driven the ambassador to use the strongest possible terms.

Hargreaves arrived back in the cipher office before Robinsohn and at once expostulated with Rostand. "We don't want him tampering with it," he said, "I simply do not trust the man."

"There's no choice."

"It's not the correct procedure."

"According to correct procedure the safe should be open."

"You say H.E. approved."

"He didn't disapprove."

Robinsohn was halfway through the door with his soft loping tread before they became aware of his presence. Rostand said: "You seemed to know something about safe breaking just now. We still can't get it open. Do you have any ideas?"

Robinsohn nodded and walked over to examine the safe. Fingering the scars on the safe, he took up and handled the drill, put it down again, and said, "Does anyone have a screwdriver?"

"Are you joking?" Hargreaves said. "We've got no time for joking."

Robinsohn stared at Hargreaves disdainfully. "I said does anyone have a screwdriver?"

Rostand communicated by extravagant gestures with the man in the blue overalls who finally opened his kit of tools. Robinsohn selected a big screwdriver, stepped over to the safe and began turning the screws which held the brackets by which the safe was fastened to the wall.

"What on earth are you doing?" Hargreaves snapped.

Robinsohn stopped with the screwdriver leveled at Hargreaves like a machine gun. "Do you want me to open your safe or don't you?" he said. When Hargreaves smothered a quick riposte there was a long silence. In that silence Robinsohn set to work again.

He unscrewed the two big brackets holding the safe flush against the wall and then asked for help to heave the safe round until its back was easily available. It took the combined efforts of Hargreaves, Rostand, the driller, his boy, and Robinsohn to swivel the massive safe on its pedestal table. "This," Robinsohn said tapping the back panel with the screwdriver, "is made of thinner metal—the rest is solid iron. Now if you—"

He broke into fluent Veralian, instructing the driller to make a series of holes outlining a triangle, each hole touching the other. The triangle of tin fell with a clatter on the floor leaving a gap just sufficient to take Robinsohn's hand, but now a row of tightly packed code books on one shelf still blocked his passage. He pushed them forward until they fell into the well of the safe.

"Do you have a flashlight?" he said in Veralian.

The driller gave him a pencil flashlight.

"And a finer screwdriver."

Keeping the light at the mouth of the triangle he peered in and reached the first screw holding the back plate of the jammed lock. One by one, without a word, patiently, he removed the four screws and the lock fell away.

In all it took twenty minutes, and as the safe door opened, still without saying a word he thrust his hands deep in his trouser pockets and shambled off.

Wandering the corridors that morning Robinsohn found the commercial attaché's office bursting with life. Huge posters for Scotch whisky adorned the walls, innumerable models of Scotch whisky bottles crowded the general office, and a number of calculating machines were being tested by local Veralian clerks stabbing away with flashing fingers. The commercial attaché's woman assistant, Miss Burrows, sporting a Highland skirt, explained: "We're having a Scotch whisky week—we hope to be drunk the whole week."

"Do you have any spare samples?" Robinsohn said.

"Not unless I will do," she said pertly.

"Just how intoxicating are you?"

"Men have been known to pass out under my influence," she said, but before he could pursue it she grabbed up some plywood models and hurried away.

Caroline's typist, Miss Fairweather, came hurrying down the corridor. "Mr. Hargreaves would like to see you in his office," she said.

"Okay."

The man was a terrible bore but as a means of passing another hour in this place . . .

He climbed slowly up to the second floor and without knocking entered the outer office of chancery to confront a middle-aged woman with a craggy face who said expressionlessly, "It's usual to knock before entering."

"Mr. Hargreaves asked to see me."

"I'll just check," she said. When she reemerged from Hargreaves's office she said with relish, "He can't see you immediately."

"But I understood . . ." Robinsohn began.

"He won't be long," she interrupted. He began pacing steadily round the room and as he did so, took out and lit a cigarette.

"No smoking," she said stonily, but he did not seem to hear her.

"I said there's no smoking in this office," she said.

"Yes, of course," he said and went on smoking and pacing.

"I must ask you to put that out at once," she said.

"It's my breakfast," he said. "A man has to eat."

A flood of crimson colored her ashen cheeks. "If you don't put that out at once," she began and he stopped in his pacing and stood over her, looking down at her, his face concentrating malevolence. "What terrible thing will you do to me?" he said.

Before she could answer, the inner door opened and Hargreaves said, "Come in, Robinsohn, will you?"

Robinsohn entered, refused the chair which Hargreaves offered him, and walked over to the window, standing with his back to the room, looking down on the green of the garden and the drearily familiar figure of the ABVO man.

"Thanks for cracking the safe," Hargreaves said. "I suppose it's all part of the game to you."

Robinsohn cut abruptly across the question and said, "What did you want to see me about?"

"Well, it's a delicate matter, but you are in a sense more fully aware of it than any of us."

"You want to know who gave me away to the ABVO," Robinsohn said.

"Not only that. Someone is leaking information from this place."

90

"Doesn't it happen to any embassy?"

"Well—no. I don't think so. I wanted to ask you," Hargreaves went on. "You're in this trade—where would you begin if you were looking for a leak in a place like this?"

"I'd begin with me."

Hargreaves smiled.

"Why would you do that?"

"For the very simple reason that you suspect me of being the leak."

"Would you give yourself away to the ABVO and defeat your own escape?"

"As a piece of double bluff it could be admirable."

"Am I supposed to take you seriously?"

"You're not denying that you don't trust me."

"No, I'm not."

"In that case you'd better keep your bloodhound Thompson watching me."

"It's not only Thompson."

"I'm fully aware of that."

"I believe there's a new plan to get you out of here."

"Yes—perhaps that will put me in the clear. If the leak goes on when I'm out, I can hardly be the culprit."

"There's nothing else you have to tell me?"

"Only that this conversation is pointless. Nothing can be proved one way or the other."

"In that case we'll have to take your word for it and go on suspecting you."

"There's only one snag."

"What's that?"

"If I carry my double bluff much further I'm liable to have a breakdown."

"I don't believe you're the type that has breakdowns."

In the next few days Hargreaves made what was for him a surprising discovery. In almost every person he interviewed there were small areas of uneasiness revealing an inbuilt guilt which even the least persistent inquisition could easily reactivate. A terrible sense of ambiguity also made his questioning seem more and more pointless because in the final analysis he knew that even his own life was not entirely free from the same disturbance. It was his wife Pamela who had introduced that old piece of diplomatic trickery—guilt by association. In turn his wife's lover created the situation where guilt flourished. If only he had had the courage to tell her—either you give him up or I divorce you—but she was too deeply interwoven into his sense of security for him to take the risk of a divorce. It humiliated him that he did not have the moral courage to challenge and outface her, but it was better than being left alone to cope with his profession, the children, the isolation, and a special sense of failure. Better to go on pretending he was not one of those classic cases of the failure of success. Certainly he had been successful professionally, but any satisfaction it brought him was wrecked by his inescapable attachment to the wrong woman.

The second person he interviewed came as a volunteer saying, "I heard on the bush telegraph you were investigating a leak."

"Who told you that?"

"It's all over the office."

"For God's sake," Hargreaves said, "nothing is confidential in this place anymore."

Mr. Godfrey Forman was a bald gnome of a man who had been invalided out of the navy where he served on H.M.S. destroyer *Phantom* as a wireless operator during a damaging torpedo attack. Trained in the services, he made an ideal diplomatic wireless operator, but now there was no diplomacy in his manner. He plunged straight in.

"I came because I wanted to tell you. Someone has been messing about in the radio room."

"Messing about—what does that mean?"

"Well, the dials register differently from when I left them, and I found this on the floor the other night."

It was a small fragment of heavily scented handkerchief.

"There are only two keys to the radio room? Is that correct?" Hargreaves said.

"Yes. Mine and H.E.'s."

"When did you find this?" Hargreaves held the handkerchief at the end of his fingertips and dropped it on his desk.

"On Wednesday, very late. I discovered I'd left my lighter in the radio room on my way back from Thompson's place. We passed the embassy and I came in to get it. It was about one o'clock in the morning. I had an odd feeling as I got to the top floor that someone was watching me. But I didn't actually see anyone. Then when I unlocked the door I smelled the scent at once—and there was this handkerchief."

"Is that all?"

"Not quite—no. Would you mind smelling that again?"

Hargreaves did so.

"Do you recognize that scent?"

Hargreaves thought a moment. "It could," he said, "be the classic Chanel No. 5."

"That's it," Forman said. "And do you know who uses that scent in this office?"

Hargreaves realized at once.

"Impossible," he said, "what on earth would she be doing in the radio room at one in the morning?"

"That's what I'd like to know," Forman said.

"You're not seriously suggesting that Caroline . . ."

"I'm not suggesting anything," Forman interrupted. "I'm just telling you what I found."

But he did not tell Hargreaves the rest of the story and as he sat there his mind went off into the past. He carefully avoided describing to Hargreaves his love for Caroline, the weeks of admiring her and following her but always from a distance because he dared not tell her what he felt, until the desire to kiss her—just once—became overwhelming and he planned to follow her home one night.

In all his long forty-two years Forman had only twice seen a woman naked and that was in a brothel in Barbados. Women recoiled from him. He concentrated every mediocrity with his small stature, bald head, drooping moustache, and weak mouth. Afraid of dentists, he neglected his teeth and his bad breath had once succeeded in repelling even a prostitute. But when he first set eyes on Caroline as she came out of the private office she suddenly crystallized into the perfect, unattainable woman who could change his life if only he could spend one evening in her arms and have the memory of it for the rest of his life. He knew it was impossible but his mind contorted itself in an effort to find a way. He spoke to her in the office about radio telegrams and she replied with businesslike brusqueness, he invited her to coffee and she refused, he sent her flowers—anonymously, and he invented office reasons to speak to her on the telephone.

And then on the fateful evening as he walked ten yards behind her in the semidarkness, following her home, he kept reformulating the words he had worked out and learned by heart: "If you would just have a single cup of coffee with me, it would change my life."

Suddenly she became aware of someone following her and swung on him half in fear, but when she saw who it was she said: "Oh, it's you—what the hell do you mean by following me?"

For a moment he was speechless but then the words came out flatly like an automaton repeating a programmed message: "If you would just have a single cup of coffee with me it would change my life."

They were muttered words and they dumbfounded Caroline. "What!" she said with the deeply indrawn breath of incredulity. He repeated the message then in the same flat voice and he was trembling as he said it. He never forgot her answer. It seared itself into his brain and spirit: "For God's sake, you little rat—have a sense of proportion!" She stormed into her apartment then, the door crashed to, and he was left alone with the ghost of the words still on his lips.

"Are you all right?" Hargreaves was saying.

Forman pulled himself back to the present. "I'm sorry," he said. "What did you say?"

"I asked you whether you've said anything to anyone else about this?"

"No—no one."

"Well, I hope I can rely on one person not to go spreading confidential information."

"Certainly you can."

When Hargreaves rang Caroline, her assistant, Joanna Fairweather, said she was very busy with His Excellency and wouldn't be free until three o'clock. It was four o'clock when she at last came into his office and at once he was aware of the same almost undetectable hint of uneasiness.

She professed not to know what the interview was about and when he tactfully explained and hinted that he simply wanted any suspicious detail she might have encountered in other members of the staff she said she had no such information. Then she added snappily: "I don't go about spying on people—although since that man arrived he's converted us all to his profession."

"Yes," Hargreaves said, "it's most unfortunate—he's certainly changed the atmosphere of this place. But there's one other routine question I am forced to ask you. Do you have any personal contacts with anyone outside the embassy?"

"Well, of course I do," Caroline expostulated. "You can't live in a town like this for two years without getting to know a few people."

"The last thing we want to do," Hargreaves said, "is to pry into the private lives of the staff but—"

"Isn't that exactly what you are doing?" Caroline said aggressively, and Hargreaves thought of the age-old strategy about someone on the defensive being better advised to attack.

"No," he said, "we're not. Let me put it this way to you—have you any reason to believe that any of your contacts knows more about the inner workings of this embassy than he or she should?"

She made a pretense then of thinking for a few minutes and said, lightly, almost casually, "No, I don't think so."

The lie came out very convincingly.

Hargreaves picked up the handkerchief on his desk.

"Perhaps I can be just a little more direct," he said, "but you've no need to answer if you don't want to. Has anyone ever approached you for information of any kind?"

She must be very skillful here. To deny it flatly was easy, to get angry at the possible implications easier still. Instead she half-smiled and said, "There was an idiotic journalist who thought he could get something out of me by getting me drunk."

"And did this journalist get anything?"

"No."

"May I ask his name?"

"Look, this is very personal to me." She did not know how it struck straight home into Hargreaves's guilt, but she noticed him stiffen at his desk, and wondered why the remark should carry such an impact. He could remember all too plainly the evening his wife Pamela had come back drunk from the arms of the young Veralian lawyer and revealed that he was in Veralian intelligence.

"We'll leave it for the moment. This handkerchief," he said to Caroline, pushing it across his desk. "Do you recognize it in any way?"

She picked it up, examined and sniffed it.

"My scent," she said, "but not my handkerchief."

"Have you any idea whose it might be?"

She picked it up again and reexamined it.

"Why, yes," she said at last. "I have. I think it probably belongs to H.E.'s wife."

"Why do you say that?"

"I've seen her handkerchiefs. That closely resembles one of them."

My God, he thought, not Penelope too. Why on earth would she be prowling about the radio room at one in the morning, or was Caroline simply trying to cover her own tracks?

"Does she use Chanel No. 5?"

"Everyone knows she does."

Hargreaves appreciated the implied criticism in the remark.

"Well, thank you," he said at last, "for being so cooperative." As he escorted her to the door he added: "If any whisper of anything does come your way, I'm sure you'll tell me."

"Of course."

When she was at last outside in the corridor again she became aware of the sweat between her breasts and running down from her armpits.

While he waited for Major Rivers to arrive, Hargreaves reflected how impossible this assignment had so quickly become. Unless one knew the details of the private lives of the staff, how could one possibly discover where the hidden motive for leaking information would lie and it was absolutely against his or His Excellency's grain to start probing deeply into anyone's private life.

It might be all right for someone from security to do that sort of thing but not Hargreaves. It was absurd, of course. The very nature of his assignment should cancel out all niceties, but did he shrivel away from pressing home his inquiries because he knew that someone might turn the searchlight on him and finally reach into the hidden places of Pamela's affair with a Veralian intelligence officer or was it a genuine belief in principle? Both of course. Old-world values were in his blood, but so were doubts about Pamela. Dammit—this was already becoming too much. Why did he ever allow himself to undertake such an inquiry? He should have left it to Rostand. He was much more ruthless and detached; much better equipped to cause offense without worrying, but then he, Hargreaves, might also find himself forced into the position where he had to mention Pamela's lover, whereas if he himself continued to control the inquiries, that need might never arise. Was it hypocrisy not to admit that he had taken on this distasteful job for self-protection?

As soon as Rivers entered the room, Hargreaves thought there was something almost farcical in the consistency with which the same tremor of anxiety came across to him from a man whose external persona spoke of almost complete confidence. As he rose to greet him and offer him a cigarette, Hargreaves detected alcohol on his breath, and he reflected that it was pretty early in the day to start drinking. He went swiftly through the preliminaries once more and then he said, "You know this place pretty well—where would you look for a leak?"

"What's the current estimate of Robinsohn?" Rivers said.

"Ambivalent."

"Isn't it worth wiring the F.O. again?"

"We've done that. They repeated clearance."

"What about his girl friend?"

"Girl friend? Does he have one?"

"A week ago I saw Miss Harding going up to his room."

Hargreaves made a note on his pad. "Yes," he said. "I remember now. He said he used Miss Harding as a decoy to delay Ambleforth ar-riving. But I didn't know she was his girl friend."

"Nor did I, but she seems to have been the only other person in on the boot business."

"I must try her," Hargreaves said. "You're absolutely certain you yourself didn't breathe a word to anyone else?"

"Absolutely. But we're coming up for another test now, aren't we?"

"Test?"

"The second attempt to smuggle him out."

"I for one hope it succeeds," Hargreaves said. "How many people know about it this time?"

"You, me, Robinsohn, and H.E."

"That sharpens the focus, doesn't it. By the way, didn't I see you at the Habana Club last Wednesday?"

"Yes."

"What do you make of that place?"

"First-class trap. Anything available from booze to blue films."

"You think it's run by the government?"

"Certainly. They try out everyone they can."

"Looking for weak spots?"

"Or weak people."

"Ever seen anyone else from the embassy there?"

"The Icicle once."

"Did you now!"

"Does that surprise you?"

"No. She gets around. Was she alone?"

"That so-called journalist, Leon Schneisler, was with her."

"So-called?"

"He's in intelligence."

Hargreaves sat back in his chair and sighed. "Oh, Lord," he said, "I'm hopelessly out of my depth in all this. Everything's a cover for something else. Everyone seems to have shreds of suspicion clinging everywhere."

"That's embassy life," Rivers said sententiously.

The next question was so delicate Hargreaves made a long oblique approach to it, and then at last he said, "I suppose I simply have to ask you one more routine question. I'm sure you'll take it as a sheer formality."

"What is it?"

"Have they ever, so to say—tried you out—at the Habana?"

"Of course," Rivers replied. "It was a bit of a farce. They're so bloody naïve. It's like their propaganda. They still haven't learned the meaning of the word sophistication."

"If Robinsohn's a double agent, they're sophisticated all right."

"But not in the Habana Club. The baits are all so obvious."

"I must say the night I was there no one tried to get at me."

"They wouldn't with you."

"Am I so incorruptible?"

"They don't go for first secretaries. They go for lesser fry. It's a waste of time with a man who will one day be an ambassador."

"I wish I had your confidence in the matter."

Ten minutes later Annabel came shyly into the room, her face tense from nerves. There was no ambiguity here. The girl clearly felt and showed her uneasiness because she lacked the equipment necessary to conceal it. For the first time Hargreaves felt sorry for one of his—the word victims occurred to him, but he had already begun to feel vaguely like a victim himself.

She answered his first few questions in muttered monosyllables which he could hardly hear. He leaned forward across his desk. "I'm sorry, but can you speak up a bit?"

When he put the crucial question to her at last he framed it as tactfully as possible and once again he was very aware of his shortcomings as an inquisitor.

"I understand, Miss Harding," he said, "that Mr. Robinsohn asked you to telephone Mr. Ambleforth about a week ago."

She burst into tears then. She simply released the tensions which had built up in ten short minutes and cried, leaving Hargreaves bewildered. How the hell could one press home questions to a simple crying exploited piece of female fluff like Miss Harding?

"Now you mustn't get upset," he said rather lamely. "There's nothing to get upset about."

She blurted out the words then. "He's been talking, hasn't he—but I didn't—I didn't."

"Didn't what?" Hargreaves said.

"I didn't sleep with him."

Hargreaves thought—oh, my God, I must get out of all this. Patiently he said: "Mr. Robinsohn has not in any way suggested that you have slept with him."

She tried to open her handbag but the clasp refused to answer her clumsy fingers and Hargreaves had a wild impulse to offer her his own handkerchief, but he suddenly imagined the lipstick from her lips staining it and said instead: "There's no need to get upset, Miss Harding—what you do in your private life is your affair. Now—dry your eyes and let's get this over with."

She had reached her handkerchief and out of the cavern of the big handbag came a wave of scent that swept across Hargreaves's desk and revealed itself as remote from Chanel No. 5. As she dabbed her eyes he said, "We simply want to know whether you told anyone else about that telephone call."

She shook her head.

"Now think a moment, Miss Harding. Remember all the people in the office—and the typing pool. Are you still quite sure you didn't say a word to anyone?"

"Quite sure," she said chokily.

"And Mr. Robinsohn did not tell you why he wanted that telephone call made?"

"No."

"But you are on friendly terms with him?"

She shook her head vigorously.

Hargreaves had to steel himself to ask the next obvious question because it was certain to upset her all over again.

"I must tell you," he said. "You were on one occasion seen going to his room."

"I didn't sleep with him," she repeated and now her voice was loud and the tears came flooding back into her eyes.

"All right," Hargreaves said. "Let's forget about that. There's only one last question—are you still on friendly terms with him?"

She shook her head.

"I don't want to see him again," she said.

"You feel hostile toward him?"

"Yes, I do."

"In that case you won't mind telling us if he does approach you again."

"I want nothing more to do with him," she said.

"Perhaps you're wise," he said. He felt relieved at her reaction and he suddenly realized that here was a possible stooge who could worm her way into Robinsohn's confidence and report back everything he said, but the whole idea of deliberately using a relationship between two members of the staff as a means of spying repelled him.

Much later that evening as he was about to leave the embassy he met the ambassador coming out of the private office.

"Can you spare ten minutes?" H.E. said, and led him back into his office.

"I just wondered how it went today," he said.

Hargreaves gave him a short account of the interviews and added: "It's farcical, but the Chanel No. 5 thing brought up, of all people— I hope you won't mind the reference—it's too absurd to mention, but it might clear the air—if it isn't too—"

"Oh, for God's sake, Franklin, get it out—what is it?"

"Well—it brought up your wife."

"Penelope?" the ambassador said. "How on earth could that be?"

"Well, besides Caroline, she's the only other woman who uses No. 5."

The ambassador smiled. "Did someone suggest she's been prying into classified?"

"Of course not," Hargreaves said.

"I think I can clear up the radio room," His Excellency said. "She did ask me for my key last Thursday. Her radio battery had run out— they keep a store up there—she went up and got one."

"But," Hargreaves said, "there's still a discrepancy, isn't there? Or could it possibly be that she went at three A.M. in the morning?"

"I might have been asleep. But it sounds unlikely. Anyway, I'll ask her *when* she went. I must go now. I wish we could devise a means of stopping this wining and dining among embassies. It's completely incestuous and totally exhausting."

As he drove away from the embassy in the battered old Skoda, Hargreaves felt unutterably weary. The routine of embassy life, his inquisitorial inadequacies, and the knowledge that he must now have another scene with Pamela depressed him.

It was Wednesday and he did not know whether she would be waiting at the flat to greet him. Wednesday was the day—or afternoon—of understood unfaithfulness. A situation he would have regarded as monstrous ten years ago he now accepted *faute de mieux*. She went to her lover on Wednesday afternoons and she usually came back in a much better mood, which simply underlined an ancient truism. She treated him better—much better—since he had at last, with the knowledge that there was no alternative, forced himself to face up to and in some way assimilate her need.

The Veralian housekeeper opened the door and he knew at once that Pamela had not returned. Tosca, as they called the big calm peasant woman, had a face as impassive and wrinkled as the trunk of a tree, but her eyes were alive in the dead face. Now they did not give him the usual welcoming smile and he had grown accustomed to the signal—the mistress was out. Without speaking more than broken English, Tosca had made it plain that in her view a wife who failed to be waiting when her husband came home from his work was guilty of the worst form of dereliction of duty.

He went upstairs at once and immersed himself in reading Sarah, the youngest child, to sleep. Toby, her older brother, was made of sterner stuff and scorned the idea of anyone reading to him. He could read himself. Living for three years in Washington—with his father as second secretary —he had acquired the toughness of the American child and regarded it as sissy to need encouragement to sleep. Hargreaves always regretted the American influence on his son and much preferred the soft, gentle, dreamy Sarah who didn't seem to have much of a brain but had an unexpected response to music and words.

By eight o'clock there was still no sign of Pamela. Tosca indicated that the food would be overcooked, and at eight fifteen he sat down to begin eating alone. By eight thirty he felt angry. By nine anger was replaced with anxiety. After all, how much did he or Pamela know about this Slav lover with his half Russian blood and his lavish expense account. Hargreaves simply did not believe he was an independent lawyer. No lawyer in Veralia could claim independence. "How much blood does he have on his hands?" he had once said in a vituperative outburst to Pamela.

Now he glanced at his watch again. Nine fifteen. Could anything have happened? He didn't put it past these bastards to kidnap her and use her as a pawn in their political games, since kidnapping had become so fashionable. He finished reading the previous day's *Times* and plunged into one of his favorite books, *Memoirs of a Midget,* by Walter de la Mare. And then at last he heard her key in the door, went out to greet her, and saw at once that she was high. She put her arms round him and kissed him, almost flaunting her glowing cheeks, but as he recoiled from this display, her high spirits collapsed, she frowned and said, "I'm sorry."

She raced up the stairs then, found both the children sound asleep and came slowly down again.

"The dinner's burned," he said.

She pulled off her gloves and sank into a chair. "I'm not hungry," she said. "Give me a drink, will you?"

"Don't you think you've drunk enough?"

"No," she said firmly. "Brandy, please."

As he poured it and took the glass over to her, she caught him by the

100

arm and said: "I'm sorry I'm so late, Frank. He was late, you see. Something had happened . . ."

He shrugged his shoulders as she continued to explain.

"Oh, don't look so miserable, Frank darling. After all, we're going on leave in a couple of months, aren't we?"

He didn't answer. He was studying her face and all over again it occurred to him that she was one of those lucky women whose touch of gray in the hair and slightly haggard features made her more attractive. Why had the good God given him the wrong set of gonads, why couldn't he satisfy her sexually, and why had she grown away from him as he grew closer to her. Because, he told himself for the hundredth time, that so often was simply the story of another stalemated marriage. There must be thousands of couples in the same situation, but how many were there who openly admitted the necessity of a lover, and why hadn't he slept with one of those voluptuous pieces in the information section himself as an act of sheer compensation? Did sex bore him? Sometimes. But that was only half the truth. Sexual excitement followed by nothing to say left a void worse than any form of frustration or loneliness, and beyond that he did not believe in balancing equations for the sake of—symmetry?—justice?—revenge? One afternoon a week in Pamela's life was really a cheap price to pay for preserving their harmony when so much else remained between them. The children, books, music, argument, and above all the simple element of companionship, of being together even in silence, an experience so utterly different from the same silence when one was alone. A small price to pay? But now the price had taken a different twist, because now he had a new anxiety.

"Pamela, there's something I've got to talk to you about."

"For God's sake, don't get all earnest. I don't feel like talking about anything."

"It's important."

"Can't it wait?"

"No, I'm afraid it can't."

"Give me a cigarette." He lit the cigarette for her and said: "I want what I'm going to say to be in absolute confidence."

"You couldn't make your mistrust plainer, could you?" she said, blowing smoke. "Am I to swear on the Bible?"

"This is serious."

"So's the Bible."

"Not to you."

She sighed. "Okay," she said, "what is it?"

"Especially," he said, "I don't want your lover to hear a word."

"He never does."

"I wonder."

"What does that mean?"

"Listen, Pamela—someone's leaking information from the embassy."

"Who to?"

"We don't precisely know—but the leaks are unquestionable."

"And you think I've been busy selling secrets I don't possess for fabulous prices to—"

"Of course I don't," he interrupted.

"What *do* you think?"

"I want you to go back over your last half a dozen meetings with your lover and ask yourself whether at any time you might by accident have let drop any sort of indiscretion?"

"Why, of course I have," she said smiling. "As you know, you can rely on me to be completely indiscreet."

"Be serious, Pamela. This is very important to me. The fact of the matter is I've been asked to investigate these leaks."

"So you're grilling me."

"I want to be sure," he said, "that there's no possibility of your having let drop any classified information."

"I don't know any classified information."

"You've heard me discuss the chromium deal—and Robinsohn."

"He should be certified not classified."

"Look, darling—for the sake of my peace of mind—let's approach it another way. Has Volenski ever tried to get information out of you?"

She laughed then outright.

"But, of course," she said.

He frowned.

"I remember," he said, "one night six weeks ago telling you that we had to get that chromium deal through at any cost. Is there the slightest possibility you might have mentioned that in any way to Volenski?"

"I do seem to remember the chromium deal."

She sucked at her cigarette and sat back thinking.

"And . . ." Hargreaves prompted her at last.

"I can't remember. I simply can't remember," she said.

"Are you trying to tell me you may have repeated what I said?"

"I simply don't remember."

"But—"

She interrupted him. "After all, no one ever told me the chromium deal was classified."

"You knew very well."

"I knew nothing. And it's been in all the papers."

"But no one knows what I told you about it."

She stubbed out her cigarette and swallowed her brandy.

"Oh, Lord—what a bore it all is."

"It may be a bore to you—it's something much more than that to me."

"Why is it?"

102

"Pamela! Don't be so bloody indifferent. What do you think would happen if H.E. discovered that my wife had passed classified information to a foreign lover in a hostile country? The fact that you have a lover at all is outrageous enough."

"Shall I go to the gallows?"

"Not you, Pamela—me. I would go to the gallows."

"Don't be absurd."

"It would certainly be the end of any chance of getting the American job."

"You really think you're in line for it?"

"Yes, I do."

"First secretary to the United States Embassy. I suppose it is a big prize. Give me another drink, will you?"

He went over to fill her glass again and stood looking down at her. "Search your memory, darling—search it detail by detail for my sake—search it for twenty-four hours—and then tell me what you find."

She curled herself up in the big armchair and tucked her legs under her.

"I do nothing but cause you distress and trouble, Frank—why do you go on tolerating me?"

"You know damn well why," he said, "I have no choice."

It was a game she frequently played. She needed to know that in spite of all her authorized infidelity, some remnant of his love for her still remained, and she prompted him to protestations he no longer wanted to make because she converted them into emotional reassurances.

"But there's one thing," he went on, "you could do for me to make it all more tolerable."

She looked a question.

"Stop seeing Volenski—until all this has blown over."

She said at once, "That's going to be very difficult."

"I know it's difficult—but in the circumstances it's not much to ask."

"We already have a date next week," she said.

"Then cancel it," he said, his voice becoming stronger.

"I've never heard so much nonsense in my life," she said. "Some ridiculous detail about an absurd chromium deal leaks out and you want to let it interfere with everything."

"Of course it's got to interfere," he said vehemently. "It's bad enough that—"

"And if I refuse?" she interrupted.

"Then I shall insist," he said. "It's got to be done. There's no choice."

"And if I still refuse?"

He swung on her then and his voice was cold. "I should divorce you," he said. "I know I've said it twice before but this time I really mean it—because now there's more than enough evidence." He knew it was the last thing she wanted. He knew that in his dull, stable, lame way he was more important to her in the long run than her lover and he didn't hesitate to exploit that knowledge to the full. He also knew how many times he had been on the verge of breaking his marriage without telling her, and he was glad now he had used the threat sparingly. It carried much more force.

"So I'm just a pawn in your professional life," Pamela said. "If I am a threat to your career you sack me."

"God dammit," he said. "Don't talk like that. After all, you're sleeping with another man and almost flaunting it."

"I do *not* flaunt. That's the last thing I want to do." But he knew that he too was bluffing hopelessly, because in the final analysis he would never be able to face losing her.

They wrangled on and it was nearly midnight before she at last surrendered. She would cancel her date with Volenski and stop seeing him for one whole month.

As they climbed the stairs he was very aware of her slender legs and swinging hips and he felt the first sexual stirring in months of easy abstinence. Immediately a picture flashed across his mind that crushed the impulse almost before he realized its presence. It was the picture of his wife naked being possessed by a man he had never met whose passion so wrought upon her sensuality that she revealed to him a hidden person that he, her husband, had never been able to evoke.

She stood in the doorway of her bedroom and reached up to give him a gentle kiss. All passion had been drained from the kiss by another man but even so Franklin hesitated in the doorway.

"Do you think," he said and stopped.

She smiled her slow sensual smile and said, "What is it?"

"If we have a whole month—wouldn't it be worth . . ."

He stopped once more.

"Trying again," she said. "I don't know. I simply don't know. It's late now, Frank—let's talk about it again tomorrow."

He went slowly to the small room at the end of the corridor with the narrow old-fashioned creaking bed, and it was a long time before he slept because he knew that talking about things tomorrow was always her way of saying no.

CHAPTER 11

On the morning of the Queen's birthday the embassy became a place of pageantry flaunting the superiority of an unassailable monarchy. The Union Jack floated proudly from the courtyard flagpost, bunting decorated the railings, a long awning stretched from the gate to the main entrance, and carpenters were busy rolling out the inevitable crimson carpet, tacking loose canvas, and pushing the flower tubs into fresh patterns. His Excellency sat in his office running his finger down the invitation list of two hundred people, with ironic asides about some of their shortcomings. Caroline never left the telephone checking last minute details, Rostand consulted with Thompson on security, and Penelope rearranged the pattern of buffet tables and bars. The big double doors between the general office and the library were folded back to give a wide vista of parquet flooring moving toward the open iron gates and the back garden gay with blooms planted not twenty-four hours before. A small marquee was slowly inflating itself at the center of the garden and freshly hired scroll iron chairs were being put in position. The pomp and circumstance pleased some and infuriated others.

His Excellency always drew on his private purse to supplement the Old Firm's grant for the Queen's birthday party, a fact that annoyed lower-paid members of the staff. To him it was one of those rare occasions when one could recover the past with official approval.

That morning as Rostand greeted Hargreaves at the main entrance, he said: "To quote Disraeli, everyone likes flattery but when you're dealing with royalty you should lay it on with a trowel."

"I suppose you prefer republics?" Hargreaves said.

"Not the de Gaulle kind—nor the Nixon—I'm against personality cults generally."

"Which removes Stalin, Kosygin, Brezhnev, Chairman Mao, and Kalogh."

"You're pro-pageant, of course."

"A little color in the proletariat's drab life."

"If you think Kalogh's a member of the proletariat . . ."

"Whatever else he is he'll certainly drink us all under the table. What are you wearing today? H.E.'s read the riot act."

"I know—but I'm damned if you'll see me in morning dress."

"If I were you, I'd think again."

"But then you're never likely to be me, are you?"

"If I said—thank goodness—you wouldn't be insulted?"

"On the contrary. No other embassy I ever encountered overplays Her Majestic Majesty's Majesty to such a ludicrous pitch as this one. After all, she's a pleasant enough young woman who might have got a Cambridge degree and become a research assistant—but all this for a research assistant elevated above her station."

Hargreaves stared stonily at Rostand for some seconds. "If you enjoy insulting Her Majesty," he said, "perhaps you could do it out of my presence."

Rostand laughed. "Oh, come on, old man—surely you don't take all this dead seriously?"

"Not dead—but seriously."

With that Hargreaves turned on his heel and walked away.

At four P.M. the crimson-jacketed master of ceremonies took up position at the main entrance and at four fifteen his voice began booming the names of the guests. The first to arrive were the German ambassador, Doctor August von Wieldmann, and his enormous wife looking like a female wrestler dressed in the wrong clothes. Various lesser mortals from different embassies followed until Monsieur François Picard, the French ambassador, made a stir with his fine attenuated presence accompanied—like an aristocratic poodle—by his tiny, high-stepping wife.

The hexagonal reception room had been transformed by red carpet and masses of flowers and there at the entrance stood the most commanding figure of all dressed in the pale blue uniform, crimson sash, and gold facings, His Excellency Minister Plenipotentiary Henry Gilroy Malvern.

It was substitute royalty to Rostand. The immensely dignified bearing, the great skill with which he transferred handshakes to his wife's white-gloved greeting, the slight bow, and even—could it be—the vaguest touch of imperial condescension all hinted to Rostand at a solid gold throne hovering mystically in the background. He found himself very much in the background, partly by choice and partly from nerves because it had cost him a heroic effort not to wear the correct clothing for the occasion. It should have been simple. He should have come naturally into the room in his brand-new lounge suit, wearing the air of one who expects to be taken for granted, but he found himself, to his immense annoyance, edgy, nervy, feeling—quite falsely—everyone's eye upon him and waiting particularly for the moment when the ambassador saw him. He hovered in the background, taking the spin-off after the ambassador and Penelope had passed the guests to Hargreaves and Hargreaves had begun to distribute them to various escorts through the main corridor to the garden. Two long trestle tables with spotless white cloths were dominated by Veralian substitutes for tea urns and loaded with smoked salmon sandwiches, petits fours, and a number of local delicacies. Four pretty girls, wearing peasant costumes of many bright colors from their different localities, were busy turning taps and filling cups, and Rostand had to admire this gesture of coexistence devised by Penelope and put through against considerable resistance.

She herself looked the part of substitute royalty not because of the splendid confection of pale blue silk wound like a snake-hat around her high coiffure, or because of the simple black throat band with the big pearl at its center. The close-fitting elegance of her dress was a shade too close for sexless royalty and her lace gloves just a little too fussy, but it was her bearing that carried the day. She could stand graciously and smile a smile that stopped just short of being mechanical, and she went flawlessly through the motions of—was it patronage? It occurred to Rostand watching her that she would have made a much better queen than the reigning monarch. She gave the impression that her most satisfactory activity was the gracious running of other people's lives. And then a little stir at the main door was followed by the bald, thick-set figure of Joseph Kalogh, who was already talking with quicksilver speed, surrounded by a small entourage, two of whom Rostand identified at once. One was Ivan Dabrowski, intelligence officer in the political branch of the army, and the other a man whose face seemed eaten away with emaciation—the secretary of the Party, Istvan Kostovik.

As the first formulas in the elaborate charade filled the ground floor with guests, Hargreaves, Rostand, and Major Rivers all moved easily from group to group, keeping the machinery alive and watching for any sign of a real response from any of the Veralian guests. Carefully briefed by H.E., they knew what they were looking for. An innocent birthday party sometimes yielded fragments of information that, fitted together, had as much significance as a long private audience with Kalogh himself. There were always mystery areas that needed clarification, and sometimes the clue to the mystery was dropped by a careless word at a relaxed official function. The process would be developed at a much later stage when they moved out of the garden into the library, and certain selected persons would be invited upstairs to the dining room where the drinks included champagne to improve the very remote chance of penetrating those defenses Veralian politicians had so perfected. Above all, one must not be outwitted at the game of calculated indiscretion, and Rostand knew his own preoccupation with wit did not help him. Where one intended to feed a piece of false information deliberately to mislead, the temptation to do it wittily might reveal its fraudulence.

As he saw Dabrowski suddenly isolated, uncomfortably trying to drink tea, he moved over toward him, but Caroline bore down on him and reached Dabrowski first. As Rostand turned away, he came directly in the path of His Excellency escorting Kalogh to the smoked salmon sandwiches. He saw the slightest hesitation in H.E.'s step as his eye encountered Rostand's lounge suit. In a flashing moment his face froze and unfroze and as he offered the sandwiches which Kalogh refused, he said, "You know Mr. Rostand, of course."

"Of course," Kalogh said and pumped Rostand's hand. "Tell me," he said, "how is the Labour Party doing in England these days?" Rostand was known to the ministry for his Labour Party sympathies.

"Reasonably well," Rostand said.

"Socialists are our worst enemy," Kalogh said, beaming at him.

"And the Liberals?" the ambassador said.

"The Liberals?" Kalogh laughed. "I thought the species was extinct."

"You have such perfect English," His Excellency said.

"The first step to misunderstanding," Kalogh said.

"You must explain that to me," the ambassador said.

"Well, take the double meaning of so many words."

"The English hypocrisy?"

"Not quite—no. But the words, there are so many two-meanings."

"Do you have an example?" the ambassador said as he handed Kalogh a plate of smoked salmon.

"Of course," Kalogh said, beaming. "I always have examples. This word, for instance—leak—you say, how is it?—you *have* a leak, or you *take* a leak. Now which is, say you, vulgar, and which not?"

"At the moment," His Excellency said with a benign smile, "it has no demonstrable application." No one would have known he was shaken by the remark.

"That is good," Kalogh said, laughing, "very good. I am glad." His face was alight with intelligence, amusement, and shrewdness, and Rostand thought how perfectly he married the appearance of Lenin with the ebullience of Khrushchev, and what total flattery such a description rendered him.

The ambassador changed the subject, but five minutes later Kalogh said, "I was rereading a favorite author of mine the other night, H. L. Mencken."

"A very trenchant writer," His Excellency said.

"Trenchant? How is trenchant?"

"Sharp and penetrating."

"Good—yes—that is so. He has some unpleasant things to say about ambassadors."

108

"Yes, I remember," His Excellency said.

"You remember? That is good. Would you quote, please?"

"If you insist."

"Why if I insist?"

"It's hardly flattering."

"Ah, yes, I know what you mean—but I have such a bad memory and yours must be good. What was the phrase?"

"It is very cynical."

"But also witty."

"Yes. And also, perhaps unconsciously, stolen from Wotton, who said the same thing three hundred years earlier."

"I like wit, stolen or not—what was the phrase?"

" 'An ambassador is an honest man who is sent abroad to lie for his country.' "

Kalogh seemed almost on the point of putting his arm around the ambassador as his laughter echoed through the garden. "That is vairy good," he said. "Vairy good. But we, of course, believe that our ambassadors are sometimes liars who are sent abroad to be honest men."

He clapped Rostand on the shoulder then and added, "What is the word? *Touché! Touché!*"

The swirling patterns of people, forming and re-forming carried Rostand away to talk to Istvan Kostovik, the party secretary. A very different person from Kalogh, his face reflected a minimum of expression and his eyes were coldly watchful. As they talked, Rostand wondered what could have eaten his face away in all those minute ravages, because it might so confusingly have nothing to do with experience and simply be a disease. His English was far less fluent than Kalogh's and after a few stumbling attempts he fell back on Veralian. Rostand had not yet perfected his Veralian and every so often Kostovik summoned one of his aides to translate a technical phrase or two.

"I do not understand your English socialism," he said at one point. "How can socialism be democratic?" Oh, God, Rostand thought—not that dreary old gambit again. "You must know all the stock answers by now," he said.

"Tell me again," Kostovik said.

"Well—here's one. It becomes democratic simply by allowing an opposition to differ."

"We allow people to differ too."

The way they went on hammering these naïve arguments bordered on the offensive. How could anyone with a mind repeat the obvious so frequently, but Rostand knew the formula reply in the ritual dance and gave it with just a hint of boredom. "To differ—but within the framework of the Communist Party."

"And you within the framework of capitalism."

One cliché after another, Rostand thought, and gave the next pre-arranged reply: "If we change capitalism into socialism, it will be done democratically."

Kostovik's small quivering expression of irony indicated that he thought this a pious hope.

"How can you have socialism within capitalism? It is a contradiction in terms."

"It's a different form of socialism."

"But you are in the power of the swing."

"The swing?" Rostand said. "What is the swing?"

"Your Labour party comes to power and alters things—then the Conservatives come to power and put it all back again. What is the good of that? As fast as one party reforms your country another party pushes it back again. If I may say so—you, the British, are slaves to the past."

"And you, the Veralians," Rostand riposted, smiling broadly, "are slaves to the future."

In Kalogh it would have produced a wave of laughter. In Kostovik it resulted in the slightest flicker of his lips which could have been distaste or amusement.

Over Kostovik's shoulder Rostand saw and heard the American ambassador making a late arrival with his daughter standing in for his sick wife. The cheerful young WASP was talking brightly and unceasingly in her frank American way with only an occasional throaty intervention from the gravel voice of her father.

"Do you think," Rostand asked, "we shall have any difficulty about the terms of the loan?"

"The loan? What loan?" Kostovik looked suitably surprised.

"I understood your ministry had approached us to negotiate a loan."

"Ah—not a loan. A trading agreement."

"But we are to put up a certain sum at the usual capitalist rates of interest."

"We hope," Kostovik said, "you will stimulate trade between the two countries by granting us the usual credit facilities."

"Of course," Rostand said, "forgive me for misunderstanding."

The French ambassador was bearing down on them and Rostand half turned to greet him. Kostovik knew M. de la Picard reasonably well and conversation automatically switched into French with Kostovik hanging on the speed of their words. Presently Kostovik said: "At least the French are realistic—they call a spade a spade and have a Communist Party within a capitalist system."

"Does it make any difference?" Rostand said.

"No," M. Picard said urbanely, "none at all. The French Communist Party has assimilated some of our best bourgeois virtues."

110

Caroline was signaling subtly to Rostand from across the room and he excused himself to thread his way to her.

"H.E. says can you bring Kostovik to the dining room at six o'clock. He's bringing Kalogh."

At that moment a very tall Veralian with prematurely graying hair came up and greeted Caroline. Rostand was surprised and interested in the immediate effect. Her color changed and the cool poise of The Icicle showed signs of disturbance. "Oh," she said after an uneasy pause. "Let me introduce you. This is Mr. Rostand—as you know, our Second Secretary—and this is Mr. Schneisler."

"Are you in the Ministry?" Rostand said.

"No—I'm just another journalist."

"Which of the two papers?"

"Three, Mr. Rostand. Three papers. And I write for all of them."

"Saying something different in each."

"Saying the same thing differently."

"That could be difficult."

"It is sometimes."

"And do you never find it tedious?"

"No. It's too important to be tedious."

Within a few minutes Rostand deliberately excused himself on the pretext of giving a message to Hargreaves but as he moved away he hesitated behind one of the library pillars, just near enough to continue observing and listening. He had the strongest feeling that Caroline would react very differently alone with this man—and she did.

"What the hell do you mean by coming here?" she half whispered.

"I was invited."

"Well, keep away from me."

She strode off without another word.

Rostand walked over to Hargreaves, who was busy trying to communicate with the Veralian commercial secretary. Rostand wanted to get Hargreaves alone for a moment to repeat Caroline's words. Someone obviously ought to keep check on this so-called journalist, but nothing would break into the commercial secretary's determined attempt to try out his bad English.

Pamela stood next to her husband, chain-smoking, without saying a word, but suddenly her face changed and Hargreaves, following the direction of her gaze, saw a man he had never seen before, with big poetic eyes in a pallid face. Turning back to his wife's face something told him at once that this was her lover, Volenski.

Pamela said, "Excuse me," and the next minute she was gone. Hargreaves saw her striding determinedly out of the garden toward the main corridor and a moment later the pallid man went straight past the group, following her. Hargreaves excused himself, passed the commercial secretary over to Rostand, and went in what was literally pursuit. At the main entrance to the embassy he overtook the man and they stood side by side to see Pamela driving furiously away in the family car. Hargreaves turned then and scrutinized him closely. He was a big, soft, catlike creature without any external appearance of virility, and why he should have sexual powers over Pamela, which he, Hargreaves, lacked, he found impossible on first sight to imagine. But sex to Pamela, he knew, was a complicated process and many factors of mood and temperament combined to produce what she had once called a process of refraction.

Jealousy? Did he feel it? Yes. It had lost the knife edge he had felt in the early days of his marriage and its ability to twist in the wound was gone forever, but if what he felt now was modified by the sheer usage of their marriage, the pain had not vanished. It was simply dulled.

Suddenly their eyes met and each studied the other afresh with expressionless faces. Volenski started to say, "Excuse me—are you . . ." But Hargreaves could not face it. He must remain completely himself in the complicated rituals of the birthday party and he could not allow personal problems to intrude. He saw immediately that this was partly a defense against the real truth. Seeing this man in the flesh had disturbed him much more than he expected.

Brushing past him, Hargreaves made his way back through the throng of guests toward the garden, and as he went, he wondered what the lesser staff of the embassy would say if they had seen Pamela rush away like that so early. Had His Excellency or Rostand noticed? Coming out into the blinding sunshine of the garden again, he blinked and hesitated. Then he saw across the road from the back gate the same ABVO man leaning against the wall. Even on this august occasion the so incongruous bloodhounds were still there—back and front, waiting for Robinsohn. One had to admire their relentless persistence and once again the question came to his mind: Why was Robinsohn so important to them?

In the garden as his eye traveled around searching for isolated stragglers, everyone seemed happily engaged in small talk, so Hargreaves turned back once more into the library. It was then that he saw Major Rivers standing in one of the alcoves in close conversation with Dabrowski. Rivers had his back toward the room and Hargreaves walked slowly past him searching now for a different kind of person—any Veralian V.I.P. who might be isolated and need attention. The words he heard as he passed were completely innocent but something in the way they were delivered made him hesitate. "No—I don't think we should do that." It was Dabrowski speaking and his voice gave the words a special emphasis. Did the "we" apply to Veralian or to Dabrowski and Rivers? As Hargreaves paused and stood there hovering a few feet from the alcove he became aware that they had stopped talking. When they began again it was all innocuous enough once more.

He walked over and joined them in the alcove. Dabrowski clicked heels and shook hands. Hargreaves was at once aware of tremendous controlled pressures in this man that gave an almost visible vibrancy to his personality. They spoke of army matters first, and became involved in a semitechnical discussion. Broken English and mutilated Veralian combined to produce misunderstandings, but there were phrases in Dabrowski's English that made Hargreaves wonder whether he wasn't concealing a much greater familiarity with the language.

"Nothing like a common profession to bring people together," Hargreaves said at last.

"I first met Dabrowski at the Habana Club," Rivers said.

"Did Marx gamble?" Hargreaves asked Dabrowski in Veralian.

"Certainly," Dabrowski replied.

"With other people's lives?" Hargreaves said.

"No—his own."

"I thought gambling was a capitalist's vice."

"We don't gamble on stock exchanges," Dabrowski said.

"I suppose we all gamble with something or other."

Dabrowski nodded.

"Even with words," Hargreaves said.

Above the murmur of voices and glasses, above the background emanation from a group of people all being desperately sociable, the stentorian voice of the red-jacketed majordomo rang out: "Ladies and gentlemen. Ladies and gentlemen. Pray, silence—ladies and gentlemen."

Obediently conversation hesitated and died away, but when laughter persisted in one small group, the majordomo repeated, "Silence, please— silence, everybody."

At last the silence flowed in and now this undistinguished man in his scarlet trappings appeared to blow himself up like a bullfrog and his voice took on a tremendous authority: "Pray charge your glasses—ladies and gentlemen. On behalf of His Excellency . . ."

He paused and waited . . . "I give you the toast—Her Majesty the Queen."

The murmur ran through the garden into the library as the English led the way with a half-chanted "The Queen! The Queen." The Veralians said nothing but simply drank, as the strains of the British National Anthem came from a record player concealed in a library alcove and picked up by amplifiers.

Rostand had emptied his glass with the half-muttered words: "To the Republic—God bless her!" But when he heard "God save our gracious Queen," coming from the record player it was almost too much for him.

113

If they could no longer afford the full panoply of a uniformed band of the Scots Guards, why invoke a dead mechanism from another and totally contradicting world? And why didn't they anticipate the amused cynicism of people like Kalogh, why didn't they realize that tactically to make a gross showing of royalty was to emphasize alienation? But even as he thought it, he knew the tomb of Lenin, the great posters carrying Kalogh's profile, and the Veralian National Anthem played the same emotional tricks with a different set of trappings.

And then it began. As the British National Anthem died away, the martial strains of Veralia's anthem rose with a much more direct and strident note because it was an old converted revolutionary song and still carried some of its fervor. The Veralians stiffened in almost travestied imitation of the English and their group now seemed to repeat the very behavior they had despised in the British. Inevitable, of course, Rostand knew—as Kalogh knew—that the principle of mystical unification had to be symbolized by music that sought to overwhelm fratricidal strife in both countries, even a strife so vociferous as the young in far-off England and the counterrevolutionaries in Veralia.

Everyone visibly relaxed in the next few minutes and the groups slowly repatterned themselves as people made excuses to escape bores, tried to reach their selected contacts, exchanged information, and made social dates, and a few specialists from the Ministry of the Interior and the embassy occasionally attempted to sound out the deeper reverberations of a gathering of people concentrating pages of classified information.

It occurred to Hargreaves as he talked to Dabrowski that this man probably held the key to many questions which troubled His Excellency. In the next ten minutes he tried many gambits, asides, and innuendoes, but they were all skillfully converted into uninformative cul-de-sacs.

As the appointed time for shepherding Kostovik to the dining room approached, Hargreaves kept wondering what it was between Dabrowski and Rivers that continued to puzzle him. Then he remembered Caroline and Schneisler and reflected that the whole thing was getting out of hand. People were not what they seemed, shadows became the substance, relationships belied their surface appearance.

Meanwhile it was Dabrowski's turn to begin his probing. He did it with subtle obliquity. Hargreaves found himself encountering a mind much more complicated than usually went with a military training, but most of Dabrowski's camouflaged curiosity was directed at Rivers.

At precisely five minutes to six Hargreaves excused himself and went in search of Kostovik. He found him standing aloof in a far corner of the garden talking to a saturnine member of his own staff. At first Kostovik resisted the idea of retiring to the dining room and Hargreaves had to explain that it was at the special request of His Excellency. Clearly reluctant and bored with social flummery, Kostovik sighed and implied—all right if you insist.

All over again the splendid figure of His Excellency in his pale blue uniform and crimson sash welcomed the selected elite into the oblong room with the two big chandeliers. Women were excluded except—momentarily—for Penelope. Not more than half a dozen from the one hundred guests were selected to drink the champagne, and Kalogh quickly dominated the group. By now his natural ebullience was reinforced by some very serious drinking, and ten minutes later he said, beaming with completely convincing tolerance, "Tell me, Your Excellency, in the West I used to hear the word boredom frequently used. We don't have an exact equivalent. In fact, we don't have the same word at all. What do you make of that?"

"You are very lucky people," His Excellency said.

"You don't like boredom?"

"Nor being bored."

"But don't you find that there's something wrong with a society where so many people are bored?"

"I don't think too many are bored."

"Personally," Rostand said with a cool smile, "I can forgive those who bore me, but I cannot forgive those whom I bore." Kalogh burst into a prolonged chuckle.

"That is vairy, vairy nice, Mr. Rostand," he said. "Vairy—vairy nice. Tell me, have you ever heard the story of Solzhenitsyn Conrad?"

"Solzhenitsyn Conrad," the ambassador repeated, "I don't understand."

"You remember the famous Russian author Solzhenitsyn—the one the West said was wrongfully jailed and sent to Siberia?"

"Ah—yes," the ambassador said. "But why Conrad?"

"Well, it was like this. You see, according to the story, when Conrad was a very young man and wanted to write his first novel, he met an English publisher. The publisher told him he could not sell the kind of novel Conrad wanted to write, but there was another kind which he could sell. Very reluctantly Conrad agreed to write that kind of novel and completed it. Then, what your English publishers call the editorial director went to work on it and insisted that it was far too long and must be cut by a third. He also insisted that certain passages were likely to offend good taste and must be removed. Still other passages were not correct in style and must be changed.

"The edited book was then sent to the lawyers, who went to work on it—and said that six passages about living people were libelous and must be removed.

"It was then pointed out that there were passages of quotations for which—what you English call copyright permission—was necessary, but the private enterprise copyright owners would not give permission so they had to be removed too.

"Now when all these cuts and removals were added together Conrad found he only had half a book left, just like Solzhenitsyn when his book was censored by the Russians.

"But the reason why the Russians now call him Solzhenitsyn Conrad was because the lawyers had missed a very nasty bit in the novel about a famous living politician, which said he was corrupt. And the well-known politician sued Conrad for libel, and being a poor man he couldn't pay the damages—and had to go to jail. And that's why we call him Solzhenitsyn Conrad!"

Kalogh burst into a prolonged chuckle as the ambassador said: "Much though I appreciate your wit, we all know that this never in fact happened to Conrad."

"Ah!" said Kalogh, wagging a knowing finger. "But Your Excellency, if I may say so, you misunderstand. It is—how you say?—the story is a parable. It is only a *parable* about Conrad, but true about a great *living* English novelist. . . . I cannot tell you his name because I might become a victim too and be sued for slander. But the novelist could be Graham Greene, or Anthony Burgess, or Iris Murdoch, or Agatha Christie—take your choice."

"Yes," the ambassador said, "but the two forms of censorship are very different."

"Censorship is censorship."

"One protects the private individual—and one protects the state."

"Your Excellency, in this country the private individual is the state. It was a simple adjustment made by the Revolution. By the way, I understand you have a new story circulating about the Revolution."

"You are very well informed about our little community," His Excellency said.

"Yes," Kalogh said, "but what is this story?"

"There are several," His Excellency said. "Mr. Hargreaves, I believe, knows one."

Hargreaves immediately wondered whether Kalogh could take it and how furious His Excellency might be if he went ahead and told the story. The cleverness of Kalogh's parable had driven him into a mood of retaliation.

"It is one, I believe, about the vodka," Kalogh said. "I know so many stories about the vodka."

"In that case you must know this one and I won't bore you by repeating—" Hargreaves began.

"I like stories about the vodka," Kalogh interrupted. "Please tell us."

116

"On reflection," Hargreaves said uncomfortably, "it is a story that could be misunderstood."

"Misunderstood!" Kalogh beamed, "but our relationship is made up of misunderstanding. Please!" He gestured with his stubby hand for Hargreaves to continue.

"If you'll excuse me," Hargreaves said, now fully embarrassed. "I think perhaps—"

Kalogh frowned. "You are not suggesting, Mr. Hargreaves, we cannot, as you English say, take a joke?"

"Of course not," Hargreaves said and looked swiftly for some sign of approval at His Excellency. When it was not forthcoming, Hargreaves said, "As a matter of fact I heard it from Mr. Rostand."

"Yes," Rostand said, "I remember the story. It's quite an innocent little joke—but jokes sometimes go wrong, Mr. Kalogh." As he spoke he looked sharply back at Hargreaves saying with his eyes—damn you for passing the buck. He was also very aware that he had drunk too much. His threshold of anger increased rapidly when he was high and as a surge of hostility toward Kalogh arose, he read the danger signal.

"Ah, but we are being too serious," Kalogh said. "Just tell us your little story, Mr. Rostand, and have done with it."

In turn Rostand glanced at His Excellency and received a shrug of the shoulders in reply. It then became a challenge to him. In the old diplomacy such a story as he had to tell would have been impossible, but the new atmosphere of frankness, the new direct approach in which he believed, demanded that the cobwebs of deviousness confusing the diplomatic scene should be blown away.

"It is, of course," he began, "just a story and is no reflection on Veralia. In fact, it is not about Veralia at all."

"Oh, come, Mr. Rostand," Kalogh said. "Why all these preliminaries? You're so much on the defensive." He took him by the arm and looked closely at him. "Let me tell you, Mr. Rostand. After thirty years in politics I am quite—how shall I say it?—incapable of insult."

"In that case," Rostand said, "there is no risk, is there? Well, it goes like this. A student from Eastern Europe was visiting Paris when he met one of the old Russian emigrés, then a man of seventy. The emigré asked many questions. Is Mother Russia still a great country, he said, and got the answer—Yes, still a great country. And does she still have a great army?—Yes, a great army. And Mother Church is still alive in Russia? —Yes, still alive. And the secret police still exist?—Well, yes—there are secret police. And writers are still sent to jail for writing what they believe in?—Some who would undermine the state. And tell me—the vodka, young man—how is the vodka, is that still the same too? And the student replied: No, the vodka is much improved. It's eighty proof instead of seventy. Whereupon the old emigré sighed. Ah, he said, I love Mother

Russia as I love the vodka, but tell me, young man, why does it need a revolution to improve the vodka by ten?"

There was a moment's stunned silence among the group and in that moment a swift look of such concentrated malevolence went across Kalogh's face as would have shriveled a forest in its path. As swiftly as it came, it was smothered by an incandescent smile and now Kalogh's laughter followed fast on the smile.

"Vairy good," he said, "vairy good," and he began pumping Rostand's hand. A thousand experiences of discomfiture made it easy for the ambassador to mask what he felt as he came in rapidly to change the subject.

"Mr. Kalogh, there are two matters I thought we might discuss in confidence while we are here."

"Of course. Of course," Kalogh said.

The ambassador tried to move swiftly away from the tensions Rostand's story had left. With the briefest possible preliminaries His Excellency came straight to the point.

"Your anti-British propaganda, Mr. Kalogh—we do not quite understand why it should have intensified recently."

Kalogh's face changed completely.

"Surely the reason is clear."

"Not to us."

"But you still have in this embassy a man called Robinsohn."

"And does that also explain the delay in the chromium deal?"

"Yes."

"And also—I can hardly credit it—the stalemate about the loan?"

"The credit, Your Excellency—the trade credit."

"But are you seriously asking us to believe that the whole of our relations have—as it seems to me—worsened—because we harbor an English subject who asked for asylum?"

"Yes, I am."

The ambassador said swiftly: "A very obvious question follows from that, doesn't it, Mr. Kalogh?"

"What question?"

"Why is this man so important to you?"

Kalogh blew out his breath and his cheeks and almost smacked his rubbery lips. "I thought we had dealt with that question thoroughly before."

"Your explanation didn't seem to us to justify what has happened since. It seems out of all proportion."

"It's very much in proportion."

"Unless, of course, there's a totally different explanation."

Kalogh's face emptied of expression and he spoke reflectively. "Come now, Mr. Ambassador—you know it all—we both know it all. Underneath this little incident there is a fundamental reason, isn't there?—a funda-

118

mental difference between us. As you English say, at root it is a question of the relative importance of the individual and the state. We cannot see the point of allowing one man's freedom to endanger international relations. And you—well, it's quite clear that you encourage such antisocial attitudes."

"We try to get a balance," the ambassador said.

"The happy old English compromise."

"Not compromise—balance."

"The oldest problem in the world—where do state rights end and individual rights begin?"

"We solve the problem differently."

"But, Your Excellency, I always understood that in a democracy the majority should prevail. And here you allow one man—" Kalogh gestured.

"Sophisticated democracies are not quite so simple as that. Three of England's most revolutionary reforms were put through against the will of the majority."

"What were they?"

"Legalizing homosexuality, widening the range of legal abortion, and the removal of capital punishment."

"So after all it turns out that you're not a democracy any more than we are."

"In some areas specialist opinion prevails."

"Precisely as here."

"Perhaps—with you—in all areas."

Kalogh turned to stare directly at the ambassador, his eyes absent with thought. All his mercurial vitality had gone, and the planes of his face without their animation fell into austere lines. There was dedication in the face.

"If it doesn't sound too pompous, let me ask you a basic question, Mr. Ambassador," he said slowly, heavily, almost wearily. "What seems to you to be the purpose of life?"

"If by life you mean human beings—to realize their potential to the full, thus enriching themselves and contributing something to society in the process."

"You are not a religious man, Your Excellency?"

"Yes, I am."

"But you make no mention of it."

"Because it would be irrelevant to you."

"Well, I half agree with your definition," Kalogh said, "except that serving society comes first instead of second. Have you read Jacques Monod?"

"The French geneticist?"

"Yes."

"No, I'm afraid I haven't."

Rostand intervened. "I've just finished *Hazard and Necessity*."

"Vairy good, young man. Vairy good," Kalogh said. "And you would agree with me that Monod is a typical example of bourgeois science trying to justify a capitalist society?"

Rostand said quietly: "No, I couldn't agree with that."

"What did you understand M. Monod to be saying then?"

"It becomes very technical," Rostand said.

The ambassador turned to Rostand: "Is it possible to put us in the picture without being too technical?"

"I could try. It will be very journalistic."

"Risk it."

"I could spell out his title—*Hazard and Necessity*."

"Do that," Kalogh said.

"Well, in the first place, Monod believes that the statistical chances of life ever having occurred at all are 100,000 to 1 against. The constant flux of chemical recombinations which by accident crystalized into the required formula for life was a very, very lucky—or unlucky—shot, much more likely never to have happened. So life not only began as a sheer accident—we human beings might easily never have been. Homo sapiens might easily never have existed. That was the Hazard part of the title. The Necessity came from the shaping influence of natural selection in the evolutionary process. We were made into what we are by the inevitability of natural selection."

"And what conclusions, Mr. Kalogh, do you draw from this book?" the ambassador said.

"I agree with the facts in the book, but I do not agree with their interpretation. Monod says that if life is an accident there can be no natural authority for any political code. Nature has no ethics, no politics. Nature is an accidental vacuum. Hence Marxism, capitalism, Maoism, anarchism all lack any authority from, so to say, the nature of nature. I agree of course that nature has no ethics, but I do not agree that it is without a predictable process. That process is the dialectical principle which we employ in materialism and it can easily be shown in history."

His lecture ran on for a full five minutes, precise, lucid, and persuasive, and everyone listened politely. No one noticed as he talked that the big heavy door of the dining room had swung silently open and there slipping soundlessly into the room to stand leaning against the wall watching and listening, was Robinsohn.

"I do not think," Rostand was saying, "that M. Monod would accept your interpretation."

"Isn't it characteristic of all political philosophies," the ambassador said, "that they claim to be superior to any other political philosophy? History can be made to justify any one of them."

"Yes," Kalogh said, "it depends in the end on what criteria you

120

measure results with. That is why I asked you what you thought the purpose of being alive might be."

"Much though I appreciate philosophic discussion," the ambassador said, "could we come back, for the moment anyway, to more earthy matters?"

"Certainly," Kalogh said. "But what could be more earthy than dialectical materialism?"

It was at this point in the conversation that a curious fact became apparent to Rostand. As the small group accepted fresh drinks and moved imperceptibly from one part of the room to another, Kalogh always seemed to return to one spot in the big dining room, directly under the chandelier farthest from the door. It was almost as if he felt happier beneath the multiple refracted light with its soft diffused glow.

"You see," the ambassador said, still unaware of Robinsohn's presence, "without knowing why Mr. Robinsohn is so important to you—we are not in possession of the full facts—and without knowing the full facts, we have no reason to modify our position."

Kalogh slowly looked from one to the other of the assembled company. "Perhaps," he said to the ambassador, "if we could continue this discussion together—in private?"

"There is no need for that." It was Robinsohn's voice and it stunned everyone to silence. They all swung round to stare at him. The ambassador visibly became a monument of ice. Rostand drew breath sharply. Penelope looked utterly horrified, Hargreaves drew himself up as if to receive a blow, and Kalogh went very still, his stare fixing with basilisk intensity the apparition lounging by the door.

In a flash the ambassador strode toward Robinsohn. "You go too far," he hissed and then Kalogh's voice broke across his.

"Ah, Mr. Robinsohn, how vairy nice to meet you again." His face alight once more with a beaming smile, Kalogh walked straight toward Robinsohn, his hand outstretched.

Robinsohn met and shook the hand and the two men stood there confronting each other, known adversaries put to the test.

"You must," Kalogh continued smoothly, "have heard our little philosophic discussion. Perhaps you'd tell us—what in your view is the purpose of life?" As he spoke he had Robinsohn by the elbow and was guiding him back once more to the same spot under the chandelier.

"To accommodate death," Robinsohn said. "I'd like a drink."

Penelope poured a glass of champagne and handed it to him as Kalogh said, momentarily malevolent again: "Yes, but the question is— whose death, Mr. Robinsohn? That is the vital question, is it not?"

"I agree," Robinsohn said. His eyes never left Kalogh's face and his own was waxen with tiredness and nerves. He drank the champagne straight down and held out the glass to be refilled. Abruptly, with a hint of truculence, he changed the conversation: "Will you tell them why I am so important to you or shall I?" he said as Penelope filled the glass again.

"Well, well," Kalogh replied, his smile becoming icy, "we are in the confessional, are we? I would warn Your Excellency that this man's word is not to be relied upon."

The glass in Robinsohn's hand shook and just for a moment it looked as though he were about to throw it in Kalogh's face.

The ambassador began: "Now look, Mr. Robinsohn, I think we have had just about enough from you. Mr. Hargreaves, perhaps you'd get Thompson to escort him back to—"

"There are three reasons why I am important to the Ministry of the Security," Robinsohn broke in with a cold certainty. "Whether he admits it or not, there has been serious trouble in the south. The Grundel cell organized it, and I know more about the Grundel cell than he does. It is counterrevolutionary, it includes some surprising names, and the real evidence lies in the document for which we are both searching: Mr. Kalogh and myself. I know where to find that document and he does not."

Kalogh's smile was completely unshakable. "If you care to believe all this, Your Excellency, you are welcome to it, but your Mr. Robinsohn belongs to a category of people very common throughout the world."

The ambassador no longer wanted to remove Robinsohn as quickly as possible. "What category is that?" he said.

"Those who know so many things that are not so."

"There is one even more vital point in Mr. Kalogh's mind," Robinsohn continued. "I have reason to believe one of the names in this document would be a big surprise if it—"

"I think," Kalogh interrupted, "if you will excuse us, Mr. Ambassador, we will leave you to enjoy the romantic stories of this gentleman whose name as you know is not Mr. Robinsohn. I think I ought to warn you that I have completely convincing evidence of a previous set of so-called secrets he sold to your government which were purely his own invention. He is well known and highly skilled at manufacturing secrets. And now, Mrs. Malvern." He took Penelope's white-gloved hand and bent to kiss it. "Good-bye and thank you. And you, Your Excellency, thank you for a most entertaining afternoon—with such a wonderfully well-contrived—how do the English say it?—twist in the end. I do admire your skill, Mr. Ambassador."

"Mr. Robinsohn's appearance here has absolutely nothing to do with me," the ambassador said stonily. "Isn't that so, Robinsohn?"

"Yes," Robinsohn said, "nothing whatever."

Kalogh nodded coldly and striding straight past Robinsohn ushered Kostovik toward the door, with Dabrowski following. As Hargreaves hurried to play escort and the door at last closed behind them the ambassador said with carefully controlled fury, "You have gone too far this time, Robinsohn."

"There is just one other point I have to make," Robinsohn said imperturbably. "A very important point, but I think . . ." Then he began to behave in what seemed a most theatrical manner. He put his finger across his lips as if to motion everyone to silence and said, "Can I see you outside alone a moment, Your Excellency?"

"You certainly cannot," the ambassador snapped. "I must ask you to go back to your room at once." Robinsohn then took a small notebook from his pocket, scribbled on a single sheet, and handed it to the ambassador.

"This room is bugged," the ambassador read. "Good God!" he said.

"Now will you come outside?"

"All right."

Excusing himself, the ambassador left the room with Robinsohn. "What on earth do you mean?" he demanded immediately they were outside the door.

"I cannot be sure," Robinsohn said, "but I would guess it's in the chandelier. If we had a ladder . . ."

"Are you seriously suggesting," the ambassador began.

"Yes, I am," Robinsohn interrupted. "Didn't you notice the way Kalogh dragged you all back to position you under the chandelier every time you moved away?"

"Now you come to mention it," the ambassador began and stopped. "It's crazy," he said. "Is that your only evidence?"

"There are the leaks."

"It's very little to go on."

"Why not check?"

The ambassador hesitated. "All right," he said. He opened the door. "Penelope," he said, "could I speak to you a moment?" When she came out he said: "Look, don't ask any questions at the moment—I'll tell you later—but there are two things I would like you to do for me. One is to get everyone out of the dining room, and the other—now I know it'll sound crazy to you but explanations later—can you get someone to bring the steps or small ladder up from the basement."

"My God," she said. "Is there a fire?"

"Perhaps you could use the telephone in my office," he said.

She half turned mockingly, "Always your unquestioning servant."

While they waited, Robinsohn said, "Kalogh now has a perfect recording of my voice, which is a disadvantage except that I can—"

"Wait a minute," the ambassador interrupted. "You say he has a recording. Are you suggesting the chandelier is connected with—"

"I suspect," Robinsohn said, "that somewhere it connects with the telephone, and the telephone with the exchange."

"And you base all this on the way Kalogh positioned himself?"

"Plus the leaks—plus experience."

"What experience?"

"I once attended a bugging class where we were given detailed instructions on how to bug lampshades—electric bulbs—the whole lighting equipment of any room. As you know, the mechanism is so minute it may take time to trace it—it could be concealed on any one of the hundred glass beads on the chandelier. Have you had this room decorated recently?"

"Six months ago, but I thought we kept the closest watch on everyone."

"Were there any new fitments?"

"My God—yes. They did say some wiring needed replacing. I remember now."

"A skillful wiretap placed by an expert is reckoned nowadays to be impossible to detect without a complete physical check on the line back to the central exchange. It's even possible that bounced-back short-wave radio transmissions to an ABVO receiver across the road could come off that chandelier."

The dining room door opened and Hargreaves led the rest of the company out of the room to file past the ambassador down the stairs. Penelope had evidently put his request by telephone.

When the stepladder at last arrived, the ambassador and Robinsohn maneuvered it into the dining room under the chandelier. Robinsohn mounted the steps and began a minute examination. It was long and tedious. After fifteen minutes the ambassador became impatient but restrained himself from commenting.

And then at last Robinsohn gave a small exclamation and indicated that the ambassador should mount the steps in his place. There it was— a minute crystal almost mingled with the crystal of the chandelier, but clinging like an infinitesimal crab with invisible teeth.

The ambassador came thoughtfully down the ladder again. As he descended, he recalled in a few flashing seconds some of the highly personal as well as classified matters which had been discussed in this room. My God—it was not only dangerous but highly embarrassing. All over again what troubled him at the deepest level was the sense of outrage to his values. How could diplomacy have ever descended to such degraded techniques as mechanical eavesdropping. It put in sordid pawn the whole dignity of the profession. What use were all those skills, all those protocols, all those years of training and understood codes of honor if it led to a mechanical device confounding the very ethics on which they were based.

Outside the door again, dusting his hands, he said: "Well, Mr. Robinsohn, once more I suppose you have partly redeemed your conduct. Now tell me—from what you know of these matters, what do you recommend we do now?"

"The usual technique is to leave it there—and feed it false information."

"Yes, I thought of that but it would make our dinner parties highly theatrical affairs."

"Isn't it worth it?"

"Perhaps—we will see."

Thompson came striding up the stairs two at a time. "Oh," the ambassador said, "I'm sorry to bring you all the way up—but I shan't be wanting you after all."

When he had gone the ambassador said to Robinsohn, "It's useless trying to control you anyway—but I'm glad to be able to tell you we've got everything ready for the second attempt to smuggle you out. It will be another test on the leaks, apart from—if I may be very frank—removing a thorn from our side. Perhaps you will come down to my office now and talk about all this in detail."

Seated in his office with a last brandy the ambassador was about to speak when Robinsohn said, "I'd like to check first." He then carried out a bugging check with enormous speed and facility.

At last the ambassador began: "Have I got this quite clear? You are in possession of information about revolutionary elements in this country which Kalogh doesn't possess and which he desperately wants— hence he wants you."

"Yes."

"Does anyone else have this information?"

"I sent a report to Control."

"Control being M.I.5?"

"Yes."

"They would of course pass it to the Foreign Office?"

"I should think so."

"Yet nothing has reached us."

"I can't be responsible for the Foreign Office."

"What is the real reason for refusing to pass this information over to me?"

"I have my brief."

"To report to Control only?"

"Correct."

"How long ago did you turn in your report?"

"Six weeks."

"Perhaps they're checking. I should hear soon. If I don't, I intend coming back to you again."

The ambassador paused and emptied his brandy glass. Then he said: "You are ready for the second attempt to get you out of here?"

"Just tell me when."

CHAPTER 12

The ambassador awoke at four A.M. and reached out his hand for the sleeping pill and glass of water. As he swallowed the pill he wondered for the tenth time whether he should completely trust Robinsohn and tell him the contents of that last telegram from the Foreign Office, but did it matter any longer? Given a run of luck they should get rid of him within forty-eight hours.

The question of trust had exercised him now for two whole weeks. Despite Robinsohn's infuriating habit of breaking every regulation and causing one outrage after another, the ambassador believed his role was consistently straightforward, but trust—that was another matter. The man was far too complex to read easily. The last telegrams from the F.O. had aroused the suspicion in the ambassador's mind that they were about to use Robinsohn as a pawn in their relations with Veralia. Well, once again—what did it matter? It was part of Robinsohn's professional hazard to be used as a pawn. Thank goodness he would be out of the embassy by the time matters came to a head; and no responsibility, moral or otherwise, devolved on His Excellency. When he first joined the Foreign Service the Old Firm did try to maintain fine scruples and live according to a code similar to his own, but now with the new policies anything seemed possible—or was that quite true? He ·reflected on the question of Foreign Office ethics for half an hour, conceding that it wasn't as simple as all that. So many conflicting principles clashed according to specific situations. But he had been deeply troubled for years now by a growing awareness of the erosion of traditional diplomatic behavior.

Once more he fell asleep, to come sharply awake one hour later on the edge of a painful dream. It was seven o'clock when he rose, but the urgent need to study that last telegram in detail again did not influence the great care with which he resurrected his public image. The silver hair tint carefully applied, the cheek and gum massage, the inner cummerbund of white cotton elastic before the silk shirt, the silk tie, the cuff links, and

Kilgour jacket. As he adjusted and readjusted the triangle of silk hand-kerchief exposed at his breast pocket, Penelope stirred in the bed and murmured, "You're up early."

"I'm going down to the office. Breakfast later."

Taking a last look in the mirror, he saw three things as he checked his appearance detail by detail: the slightest suspicion of an increase in the waistline despite the cummerbund, a thickening of the pouches under his eyes, and a pastiness in his face. Robinsohn had made life much more difficult in the embassy and that strain, added to his sense of increasing failure in Veralian relations, had taken its toll. Frowning, he turned to leave the bedroom and glanced out the window. The clouds were thicken-ing and rain beginning to fall. If it became one of those gray, misty days, perhaps he'd better give the word for Robinsohn's second escape attempt, but before the man went he must make one last effort to extract more in-formation from him.

He took the lift to the ground floor and his passkey carried him through chancery, to the registry, and into the strong room. A new safe with a combination lock now took the place of the old damaged one. He unlocked it, took out blue file No. 4 and hurried along to his office. Lighting his morning cigar, he opened the file at the red marker.

"In reopening negotiations with the Veralian Government about their intensified propaganda, the chromium deal, and the loan, we feel an entirely new approach is now required. Since, as you know, these preliminary negotiations are intended in the long run to lead into much more serious matters (the question of a nonaggression treaty first and the possibility of another Yugoslavian situation second), you are instructed to remove the conditions formerly imposed for the chromium deal and to offer it without strings. There are two reasons why this course of action seems to us necessary at this juncture. First, in the hope that this may release the deadlock in which we at the moment appear to be involved and improve our bad relations with Veralia; second, because a report we have received from M.I.5 suggests that there are forces at work within the southern areas of Veralia which would indicate the possibility of a change of government by other than peaceful means in the foreseeable future. Clearly, if the chromium deal has actually come into operation we shall have a strong bargaining counter with any new government that may emerge. . . ."

The telegram ran on for several more long paragraphs. Then came this: "There remains the question of Mr. Robinsohn. In the light of new information, which we have not yet been able to confirm, the whole ques-tion of Mr. Robinsohn's position may come under revision, but we instruct you for the time being to proceed with the policy as originally formulated in our telegram of the 9th inst. It is possible that at this complicated stage you yourself might think it wise to visit London to reappraise our strategy

127

personally in detail and this would seem to us advisable." The ambassador underlined in green pencil you yourself might think it wise. That was as good as saying—isn't it time you came to the Foreign Office to get these tangles straightened out?

Rereading the telegram he added another green line under the words: the whole question of Robinsohn's position may come under revision. As he did so, he wondered why he should bother any more about Robinsohn's fate. If they smuggled him out this evening, he hoped that that would be the end of Robinsohn so far as they were concerned and the embassy would quickly return to its normal harmony. Normal harmony? No embassy had any kind of harmony that could be described as normal. Some were even claustrophobic hells concentrating vendettas as intense as a small town in Mafia-ridden southern Italy. At least this embassy had so far escaped the worst.

The whole question of the leaks had now taken a new turn. If the leaks ceased with the discovery of the bugging device in the chandelier that would certainly clear the air, but would Robinsohn's disappearance within forty-eight hours of that discovery also remain suspiciously coincidental? Whether or not Robinsohn had tampered with the files was impossible to prove, but he certainly knew so much about the inner workings of the embassy that he could represent a formidable ally to an enemy. However, none of their suspicions had any real substance, London had given him clearance, and to start revising routines and locks, file locations and codes was clearly not only premature but unnecessary.

Twelve hours later the evening came down, dank, misty with drizzling rain, the perfect cover for the new attempt. Beyond the main gate the lounging figure of the ABVO man stood out sharply for unexpected reasons. A white macintosh had replaced the gray raincoat and—comically —the figure held an umbrella over its head. Somehow a secret policeman with an umbrella had elements of slapstick comedy. Instead of the blurred ghost in nondescript gray merging anonymously with any landscape he now stood out as an open warning reinforced by the white macintosh and the positively domestic umbrella.

Only two members of the staff—apart from Rivers—knew how the plan would unfold, Penelope and Thompson. In Robinsohn's room Penelope went to work on him with her makeup materials, thickening the thin eyebrows with eyeblack, blurring the edges of the black wig where it met his cheekbones. The distinct beginnings of a paunch were evident with Thompson and had to be reproduced with extra clothing on Robinsohn. Then came the change of suits—with the uniform trousers needing to be turned up and shortened. The shoes were large and required padding, but the navy blue raincoat sat well on Robinsohn's shoulders and the peaked cap with the lining padded almost fitted. Thompson finally went out into the corridor and gave a last demonstration of his quick military gait with its slightly bouncing effect. While Penelope watched, Robinsohn took over and mimicked him. "Perfect," Penelope said as he caught the exact rhythm.

"Well, we are all set," Robinsohn said.

"Amazing," Penelope commented. "You show no sign of nerves."

Robinsohn shrugged his shoulders.

"This place is much more nerve-racking." The neurotic, chain-smoking person who could not sit still for more than a few minutes had become a controlled, disciplined man, his movements light, precise. While Thompson waited awkwardly in the chaos of the room Robinsohn nodded distantly to both of them and strode over to the door. He would have gone then without another word but Penelope said, "Aren't you going to say good-bye?"

Robinsohn came back stiffly and took her outstretched hand. "Good-bye," he said abruptly.

"Good luck," she replied.

He went carefully down the stairs to the reception room and took his seat behind the desk. Ostentatiously moving before the lighted window he opened it and deliberately crashed the heavy key book down on the desk. The figure outside moved in response, but took no other action. Robinsohn selected a cigarette in readiness. No smoking for the staff was the rule in the reception room but Thompson always paused outside the main door as he left, to light a cigarette with a windproof lighter.

At seven thirty-five there was still no sign of Ambleforth. Goddam and blast the bastard. Late again. Even with all this planning drummed into him and all the threats if he failed to turn up on time, he still could not distinguish between seven thirty and seven forty-five. The familiar scene flashed through Robinsohn's mind as he walked round the reception room quickly, nervously. The sudden discovery, the chase, the shots and the hideous small scream of a metal bullet passing through the brain, the eyes, the stomach. . . . It was the sound which always remained with him. A kind of metallic hysteria as if a mad anger drove the bullet on to find its target. He had been hit once and it was the sound of the impact before the pain that echoed in his memory.

Ambleforth's footsteps at last and Robinsohn's stomach tightening as he saw the shambling figure trying to hurry and almost falling over his own clumsy feet. Ambleforth burst in at the door, talking fast—no taxis —everyone using them in the rain—the first night of a new opera—but Robinsohn ignored him. Waiting a long tense minute in silence he said aloud, "Good-night," pulled the raincoat collar far up over his ears and moved just outside the door. There as the rain blew in he made elaborate attempts at lighting the cigarette. Once, twice, three times. When it was glowing he opened Thompson's big umbrella and went striding toward the iron gate with Thompson's slight bounce perfectly reproduced.

The figure against the wall straightened and peered at the man now opening the gate. From the window of her bedroom Penelope held her breath, her fingers digging into her palms.

He was through the gate walking away with a fair imitation of casualness down the road when Penelope felt her heart jump. The white-coated figure had detached itself from the wall and begun to follow Robin-sohn.

Within seconds Robinsohn knew. It was useless running. They would cordon off the area in a few minutes. What had happened. Had someone given him away again or was this just a suspicious checkup? Only two courses of action were left in any case.

Or were there? Out here in the sweet fresh air of the street, walking freely with no wall to check him he felt light, buoyant, and ready for anything to preserve his freedom. He walked steadily on until he heard the pace of the footsteps behind him increasing. The man was about to overtake him. There had to be a confrontation. Run for it? Take a risk and run for it? But they wanted him dead or alive. Better alive for them but dead if it had to be. He heard the old familiar scream of the bullet. If not run, then lure this man close and deal with him. Was that possible? Both equally trained. Both capable of canceling the other's mode of attack. A stalemated struggle with the odds all on the other side because of the gun and the ruthless willingness to use it. Sweat, a parched mouth, and a sudden shiver of fear. The first impact last time had been curiously de-tached, but two minutes later there was a pain which reduced him to a screaming ball of flesh. He did not want that pain again. He did not want the loss of control. Above all he did not want the animal humiliation.

Yet this might be his last chance. To incarcerate himself all over again in that embassy prison? No. A smell like rotting cheese rose in his nostrils, filled his lungs, and made him cough. A kind of asthma momen-tarily seized him. Coughing, he cleared his lungs and took a long deep breath of the sweet free air. The farther he walked without challenging the ABVO man the less chance he had of retreating to his base.

Deal with him now. That was it. Deliberately he stopped and ground the cigarette into the pavement. The man was almost behind him. He counted his steps now. One, two, three . . . The voice was saying some-thing immediately behind him as Robinsohn stepped back a pace, without turning around, grabbed the man's waist with one arm and locked his second arm over the right wrist, bent swiftly down to lift and hurl the white figure clean over his head to crash on the pavement. From the way he fell Robinsohn knew his training had reacted at once—sprawling on all fours, taking the shock with four different supports, the arms and legs unrigid, giving way to the impact of the pavement. Every move had its inbuilt answer. Both knew the rules of check and countercheck. To break the rules and do something original was the only chance of getting the upper hand. In this flashing moment of advantage Robinsohn could leap on him or run. But if he ran, the gun would come into play. He must get the gun.

His foot went into its kick automatically from long training straight into the man's groin and as he groaned he leaped on him, his hands snaking over his body in swift spasms to find the gun. Even as he reached it the man brought his fist round in a half successful uppercut. Simultaneously his boot kicked the gun clean out of Robinsohn's hand. Both made a leap toward it and then they were rolling over and over, clawing, kicking, trying to stab each other's eyes with thumbs and fingers.

There was blood in Robinsohn's mouth, his jaw stabbed pain, his hands were torn, and the gun had vanished. This man was very strong. Much stronger than Robinsohn. Only total thuggery would master him. Robinsohn launched another tremendous kick at his groin. It was parried. His thumbs clawed toward the man's eyes and were torn away.

Just one technique left. Thrusting his full weight downward as if to pinion him to the ground, Robinsohn suddenly leaped up and straight down again on the man's groin with both feet.

Then he ran in a mad, sweat-ridden zigzag, waiting for the hysterical bullet which would race, overtake, and fell him. But as the gun began to fire he reached the embassy gate, flung himself sideways through—fell— bullets zipping past—stumbled up and burst into the entrance where Penelope, white and shivering, almost took him in her arms.

CHAPTER 13

The following day Robinsohn had a stormy interview with Hargreaves. He stated as a cold and furious fact that someone on the embassy staff had once again tipped off the ABVO. He refused to believe that their microscopic eyes had penetrated his disguise, and he also managed to convince Hargreaves—such was his controlled anger—that he certainly had not brought about his own unmasking. He insisted that every member of the staff be ruthlessly grilled in a process of elimination, because he could not go on like this. Nerves were likely to break if he anticipated discovery before any new escape attempt, and his threshold of tolerance of embassy life and its system of informers had dwindled away to nothing.

As Robinsohn left his office, Hargreaves wearily picked up a bunch of files and set off toward the private office for a last briefing before the ambassador set out for London. He found His Excellency trying to cope with every kind of pressure, but he pulled out of the interviews and telephone calls to listen patiently to a new and disturbing piece of intelligence. Hargreaves had lunched the previous day with Dabrowski and to Hargreaves's surprise he seemed fully familiar with the date and some of the details of the ambassador's visit to London. Quite clearly the bugging device was not alone responsible for the leaks from the embassy. Someone was still busy passing confidential information to the Ministry of the Interior.

"It looks, doesn't it," His Excellency said, "as if we shall have to go on with the inquiry—I can't tell you how distasteful I find it."

"That's what I wanted to talk about," Hargreaves said. "I would very much like to be relieved of the whole business. It's temperamentally alien."

"But who can take over?"

"Well, I don't wish to appear to saddle Paul with a nasty job I don't want, but he is a much more cool and detached person than I am."

Later that afternoon the ambassador discussed the possibility with

Rostand and he was relieved when he seemed prepared to continue the inquiry.

There were some difficult moments in the last few hours before His Excellency left. He knew that he was leaving a disturbed embassy charged with every kind of tension and suspicion. Penelope, too, always hated these moments before her husband set off on such journeys alone. She disliked her husband flying on his own and laughingly admitted that deep down inside herself she still had not quite overcome the idea that heavier-than-air flying machines were unnatural—especially when serviced by Veralian personnel.

There was not only a gap when he had at last gone: minor feuds sharpened at every level of embassy life. Substitute heads of mission never quite worked in this embassy. Without an unquestioned final arbiter, internal tensions tended to break into localized in-fighting. Annabel became openly hostile to Miss Hallows, Caroline found Hargreaves intolerable as a substitute for His Excellency, an uneasy alliance between Rostand and Hargreaves quickly showed signs of strain, and the change in Robinsohn became dramatic. Shutting himself up in his room he asked to be provided with a record player and carefully named a dozen records. Only three were immediately available but equipped with these, he took to squatting on the floor of his room, playing and replaying the records, sipping brandy and chain-smoking: meals were taken up to him and often left untouched: visitors were shunned, and his room slowly deteriorated from the messy and untidy into the plainly sordid.

At last, on the third day, Penelope was driven to go up and protest. As she entered the room, the thick fug almost made her cough.

"Mr. Robinsohn," she said with her hand on the open door, "you really must let the maids come and clear up this mess. It's becoming intolerable."

The slow and beautiful strains of *Pavane for a Dead Princess* were pouring scratchily away from the old record player and he did not look up or answer. Penelope strode over to the window and threw it up.

"Phew! You simply must get some air in here."

He came to his feet then, went over to the window and shut it again. They stood beside the window, confronting each other.

"You agree this is my room?"

"But part of the embassy."

"I am no part of the embassy."

"While you're here, you are."

He went over and switched off the record.

"Sit down," he said, "and have a drink."

"I don't drink at this time of day."

His face had remained expressionless while he spoke, but now a kind of melancholy amusement relieved the hollow cheeks.

"Relax, Mrs. Malvern," he said. "Relax."

"I should have thought that injunction would apply more to you," she said. "After all, what's happened to that wonderful philosophy of yours—learn to cooperate with the inevitable?"

"This," he said slowly—and his voice croaked now—"is my way of cooperating."

"I should have thought it was surrendering," she said.

"Which is part of cooperating," he replied.

Over the next two days he seemed to eat less and less and became more withdrawn. Under heavy pressure, he allowed the maid into his room once a day for half an hour, but after two visits she said she was afraid to go in again because she could not stand the way his unblinking eyes followed her round the room. They found another and tougher maid of peasant extraction, but Robinsohn in turn complained that she was unsympathetic.

By the sixth day, Penelope persuaded herself that she was becoming worried about his mental state: persuaded because she had to admit that a whole complex of motives now sometimes drove her, after dinner, to knock on his door and keep him company for half an hour. There were times when he failed to respond to her knock and did not hear her enter the room. On those occasions her first words brought absolutely no response, but when on the third visit she said, "Would you like to see a doctor?" he snapped back, "Good God—no! A Veralian doctor?"

Something very odd slowly became apparent to Penelope. This man appeared to be steeped in the very music that she herself appreciated. Instead of feeling like a health visitor trying to break down the resistance of a recalcitrant patient, she began to respond to the odd half hour when she relaxed from her social duties, sipped brandy, and listened to Mozart, Bach, and Scarlatti with him.

And then one evening, lying back on the bed, his hands behind his head, staring at the ceiling, he said: "When I was a young man, I did manage to learn just two quotations by heart. As a very old-young man one of them appealed to me. It put romantically what life then seemed to me to be all about. I wonder if you know it—you're so well read you probably do. 'There is an end of time and an end of the evil thereof; when delight is gone out of thee and desire is dead thy mourning shall not be for long. . . . Yet the adventure of life was glorious and the moments of love, and pity, and understanding beyond description or thanks.'"

She was astonished. He delivered the words with a biblical sonority.

"I like that," she said.

"Unfortunately," he said, "it is all romantic nonsense. I got past that stage at sixteen. The second quotation is much more accurate. It puts life in real perspective. 'Even in laughter the heart is sad and the end of mirth is—heaviness.'"

134

He dropped his voice until the last word fell like a weight into the room.

"Yes," she said, "that's good too." The incongruity of a man in his trade quoting literature was swiftly overcome by the memory of the chauffeur she had once had who read philosophy in his spare time. Incongruity after that had become a commonplace.

Over the next few evenings, from music and literature they moved toward more personal matters. Slowly, delicately she began to inquire about his early life and family. At first she could extract nothing from him, but suddenly one evening he said:

"You must be about the same age as my mother when she died."

Mrs. Malvern said forthrightly: "I'm forty-seven. Do you think I'm due to die?"

He sat up then as if startled.

"*Exactly* her age," he said.

"Well," she said, "after what you've said about her, I hope I don't remind you of her."

His eye ran over her with such a fierce scrutiny she shrank a little. "Not physically," he said, "but in other ways."

"Wasn't she a laundrywoman?"

"Yes—it makes no difference."

"Perhaps we should change the subject," she said.

They did then, but on the following evening when she called again, he was high once more and the personal note persisted.

"You drink too much," she said.

"What would you like tonight?" he said.

"I've brought you some new records."

"Good."

"A little Purcell—some Stravinsky—even Schoenberg—a very mixed bag."

"What would you like?"

"You decide."

"How's your mood?"

"Perhaps the Purcell."

"Excellent," he said.

Before it was over, he lay back on the bed in his favorite position staring at the ceiling and began what slowly became almost a soliloquy. At first it was disjointed and strange, or was it the music overwhelming the words and producing a slightly surrealistic effect? Then, as the music stopped, his voice went on and she realized that he was drunk and half talking to himself. A group of phrases became sharp and clear:

"I realize now why you remind me of my mother—it's because you totally misunderstand me in the same kind of way. You think I'm a civilized human being interested in music, literature, conversation, food—

135

all those boring prerequisites of bourgeois culture." He gave a throaty croak in place of laughter. "If only you knew . . ."

"Don't be absurd," she said.

"You know me about as well as my mother knew me—which was not at all."

Again his eye went over her. She had taken trouble—for reasons she would not fully admit to herself—to dress carefully tonight. The brassiere disguised her drooping breasts, the throatband the wrinkles in her throat, and the frock clung to her still slender hips and thighs. She also carried an aura of scent just above the level which good taste permitted.

"And how well," she said, "do *you* think you know *me?*"

"A dull marriage—a bored wife—a sexless middle age—wishing you had married someone—more—exciting."

The accuracy of some of his points was telling.

"Have you ever been married?"

"Once," he said.

"Did it work?"

"I drove her away."

"How?"

"A little discreet violence."

"You don't strike me as a violent man."

"Shall I tell you the—inner—impression I get of you?" he said.

"If you like."

"You are someone who desires to be dominated and never has been."

"Don't be absurd, Mr. Robinsohn. How can you tell that?"

He came to his feet and she was uneasy as he began pacing round her. She tried to change the subject abruptly.

"You look ill—you must get out into the garden and get some exercise—"

"You have never been unfaithful, I suppose?"

"Outrageous!"

"And how long is it, I wonder, since sex ceased?"

She came to her feet and moved toward the door.

"You go too far," she said, and then he was across the room standing in front of the door. His voice and manner changed. They were now soft and gentle.

"Don't go," he said. "I like your company."

"Unfortunately I don't like yours," she said.

"But you must stay—have one more drink?"

"I've drunk too much already."

As she tried to walk round him to the door he blocked her path again and the two maneuvers brought them very close. She stood her ground then, standing in front of him, staring straight into his eyes. "Will

136

you please," she began and stopped. That was too humble an approach. Her voice and manner changed. "Get out of my way, Mr. Robinsohn," she said coldly, and even as she said it she knew it was a double challenge. If he meekly surrendered and stood aside he would not have met one of those challenges.

He stood there a moment confronting her, and then he rapidly reached out his hands and rested them lightly on her shoulders.

She shook them off and fell back a pace. "How dare you," she said and at once he replied, "That's exactly what you want me to do."

She made a noise then of disgust, anger, distaste. "Are you going to stand aside?" she said.

"In my own good time," he said.

"You'll regret this, Mr. Robinsohn," she was saying.

"I'll stand aside," he said, "if you'll agree that you won't allow this absurd little skirmish to stop you from visiting me again."

"It certainly will," she said.

"Then we may have a long vigil," he said.

They stood there staring at each other for a whole long minute, and then—so abruptly once more that she had no time to stop him—he took her in his arms. She went rigid, her cheeks flushed, and she raised her hand to slap his face, but her hand fell away again, and they stood there gently embraced without a word. She released her indrawn breath in a sigh. "My God," she said, and she could feel the slow, very slow thawing of her blood and he, too, became aware that for the first time a woman of advanced middle age with a decaying body had resurrected the dead core with a certainty it had not shown for ten years.

Another minute they remained like that and as he looked into her face he searched long and carefully but he could see no resemblance whatever in her features to the woman he sought.

Then he released her gently, and without a word she walked to the door and left.

She did not return to the room the following night.

In his office Rostand scrutinized the list of names on his memo pad and thought that he no less than Hargreaves disliked playing the role of detective. So far he resembled Hargreaves, but once committed to any job, Rostand did not allow fine scruples to interfere with its proper and efficient execution. He went down the list again with his pencil. "Caroline —Thompson—Rivers—Robinsohn." Only one could be removed with any certainty from connection with the last escape—Caroline, but she was fully conversant with the dates and details of the ambassador's trip to London. The remaining three *did* know about the escape plan before it was tried. Robinsohn—could there still be any shadow of doubt about him? A startling thought had recently occurred to Rostand. Supposing the

137

real Robinsohn had been murdered by the ABVO and his papers given to this new and false substitute. Had anyone ever thought to ask the Foreign Office for an English photograph taken while Robinsohn was living in London, a precaution so elementary it seemed automatic. As far as he knew no such check had been made. He picked up the receiver and dialed registry: "Can I have the current telegram file, please?"

While he waited he carefully reexamined the record of each person on his list. If Robinsohn was a substitute double agent it would be consistent with his alibi to keep repeating the escape attempts. It would also be necessary to frustrate his escape to keep him safely in the embassy. Did he really discover the presence of the bugging device simply by the maneuvers of Kalogh and his party? It seemed very farfetched. If he had placed the bugging device himself it made much greater sense, and what a marvelous final mask for his own role to uncover such a device—while he placed another one elsewhere. Following the chandelier episode Thompson had spent a whole week testing every room but Rostand knew that Veralian electronics were in a different class from their English equivalent and could easily outwit a man like Thompson. Thompson—foursquare, solid, quite incapable of the degree of subtlety required to carry off this complex series of interlocking deceptions. Why would he do it anyway? His record was that of plodding loyal minor service and he had no apparent motive.

Rivers—there had been that moment at the birthday party with Dabrowski when they seemed to communicate like old friends, but two military men shared technical responses that could easily be misunderstood. What sort of place was this Habana Club? He had only been there once, briefly, himself. Perhaps he should go again and check in greater detail, although he hated gambling in any form.

What of the remainder of the staff? There was Hargreaves, of course, who knew most of what went on, but no one could ever question his integrity. It would be madness to ruin a career clearly leading toward head of mission, after years of immaculately correct service. Crazy to even consider Hargreaves, crazy to think up reasons why he could conceivably be involved but right in the context of a totally detached inquiry. The Foreign Office was after all these years still smarting from the humiliation of discovering the prolonged high-level deceptions of Guy Burgess and Harold Philby. But Hargreaves—an undercover Communist? Just as impossible as it had seemed with Philby, of course. His pencil moved down the list again to Caroline. As far as he knew she had no warning whatever of the last escape attempt and only the smallest suspicion arose from the scene at the birthday party when she recoiled from the Veralian journalist in that dramatic manner. Obviously something lay hidden in her private life of which the embassy appeared to know nothing, but then every private life concealed something.

Private life? H.E. had said "Be very careful about intruding," but that was clearly nonsense in a situation like this. Someone had to get results and get them quickly or the embassy would become an open book to one half of the Ministry of the Interior and a laughingstock to the other.

Inevitably, among the papers that Hargreaves had passed over to Rostand was one in which he recorded the uneasiness of certain people in the course of interviews. Caroline appeared among them.

He dialed Caroline's extension and she said yes, she was under no great pressure—she could come if he liked—right now. As she entered his office Rostand marveled again at the bandbox freshness of her appearance. The immaculate frock in vivid pink, with every hair of the silver blond coiffure in place, the starched and spotless lace at her wrists, and the long nails flawlessly lacquered.

In his most relaxed manner Rostand pulled a bunch of periodicals off the visitor's chair and said: "Have a pew, Caroline—still not smoking?"

"Still not smoking," she said, and he noticed at once the slightest tension.

"I'm sorry to drag you over all this again," he said, "but you know we've been having this crazy inquiry into security—and I just wanted to ask a few more questions."

"Have you taken over?" she said.

"Yes. I should have told you that in the first place. Now, as I understand it, when Hargreaves first spoke to you about this a week ago, you said that a journalist had once tried to get some information out of you?"

"Yes," she said.

"Did you ever drink with him?"

"Yes."

"Forgive my pressing the point, but all of us are in the same boat here. It is so easily possible to let drop an indiscreet remark. You can't recall any such minor indiscretion?"

"No."

"I hope you'll take the next question as it's meant—just a straight-forward inquiry. Did you drink much?"

For God's sake, she thought, this bastard is on the ball too quickly.

"I don't think so."

"You're not sure?"

"I can take quite a lot of drink."

"I see. Now it has become a purely routine question with every woman involved, and I hope, being a woman of the world, you will see it in the right perspective. Is he by any chance your lover?"

She exploded then.

"You go too far, Mr. Rostand. What's that got to do with you?"

"Perhaps," he began, but she interrupted him. Snatching up her handbag she snapped, "I'm not prepared to answer such questions. You have no right to ask them," and she stormed out of the room.

The violence of her reaction gave Rostand the answer to his question and as he sat tapping his notes with a pencil he read over the details of what was known about Caroline. Age thirty-five (she claimed thirty), father a navy officer, educated at Roedean, unmarried, puritan, aloof, not popular with the staff, previously employed as personal assistant to a Conservative M.P.

The door opened abruptly again and Caroline reentered the room, looking pale and determined. She sat down in the visitor's chair once more and said, "I've decided to tell you the whole story."

She then gave a cool, admirably precise account of what had happened between Schneisler and herself. "So you see," she concluded, "he claims I let drop something, but he may be bluffing. I simply do not know. I realize I've been a fool. I should have reported this before."

She rose from her chair. "If that's all," she said.

"Not quite," Rostand said. "I admire your courage in telling me all this. Thank you. But there is one remaining question."

"What's that?"

"Are you still seeing him?"

"Not at the moment."

Rostand sat back in his chair reflectively. "Supposing," he said, "you offered to give him a new piece of information—which we can falsify to fit certain confidential facts—in exchange for details of what you are supposed to have told him."

"I don't want to play the spy."

"But it's not quite the spy, is it? It's trying to get at the facts. Once we have these, you can drop him." He realized at once he had made a mistake.

"Good Lord, Mr. Rostand—is that the way you see human relations —something to be picked up and dropped at anyone's convenience?"

Rostand stared down at his desk and said softly: "I'm sorry—I apologize—but you speak almost as if you might be in love with him."

"I am not in love with him."

"Then why should my remark trouble you?"

"He happens to make life tolerable in this gray, boring, shit-house country." The word surprised Rostand but he said smoothly: "I suppose it is a choice between continuing to see him to find the facts or dropping him?"

"What sort of status do you give that remark?" Caroline said.

"Status?"

"Is it a suggestion—an order—or what?"

"Certainly not an order."

"Then what is it?"

"I'm simply suggesting two alternative courses of action."

"And if I take neither?"

"We should then have to look at the whole situation afresh."

140

Once more she was angry but this time she went very pale and controlled it. As she rose, saying, "I'll think about it," Rostand saw again why the general office called her The Icicle. All of her attenuated six feet had frozen into a long line of ice.

It worked out very differently with Robinsohn. Within a few minutes of entering Rostand's office he interrupted the introductory questions and said bluntly: "Let's proceed on the assumption that you think I'm a double agent planted here by the Veralians—then you can stop masking your questions and go straight to the point."

Rostand smiled. "It's nice," he said, "to meet someone who's completely frank. All right. Question number one—do you have a photograph of yourself taken in London before you joined M.I.5?"

"Of course," Robinsohn said. He pulled out his wallet, selected a small opaque envelope and threw down on the desk a photograph, passport size, of a very much younger Robinsohn, a face clearly showing an attempt to control suffering.

"Splendid," Rostand said, turning it over. There was nothing on the back.

"Do you mind if I keep this?"

"I certainly do."

"Does it have some sentimental value?"

"In a way, yes."

"That's unexpected."

"Why?"

"I wouldn't have expected you to admit sentimentality."

"I'm a sucker for tear-jerker films."

"I don't believe it."

"But that's characteristic of you, Mr. Rostand—you don't believe anything I say."

"Do you smoke?"

"Thanks."

He took one of Rostand's cigarettes, scrutinized it, and said: "Perhaps I'll stick to these." He handed back the cigarette and lit a Gauloise from his own blue packet.

"You lived for years off the Southampton Row area of London?"

"Correct."

"You know Queen Square?"

"Yes."

"It's one of the few where the Queen Anne houses remain untouched."

Robinsohn smiled sardonically as he leaned forward, put his arms on Rostand's desk and stared straight into his face. Confronted with the concentrated ruthlessness of Robinsohn's expression, Rostand felt out of his depth. Even diplomacy did not work in the dehumanized iciness conveyed by that look. It was a world devoid of atmosphere, a vacuum where normal human breathing could not take place.

"You are not very well trained in this business, are you?" Robinsohn said.

"Why do you say that?"

"Even if I did not know that all the houses in Queen Square have been pulled down, the way you frame the question would make me suspect that that was the case."

"Yes," Rostand said showing no discomfiture. "And what would you say about Lamb's Conduit Street?"

"I would say it is rapidly losing its old character."

"Like Great Ormond Street?"

"Great Ormond Street is a mixture—but it has the advantage of The Society for the Protection of Ancient Buildings—plumb in the middle."

"I thought you were brought up in poor circumstances."

"Correct."

"But that area is, as the English say, classy—well-to-do."

"Not all of it—not Rugby Court, which was still a bug-infested slum."

So it went on.

Robinsohn performed flawlessly. Quite clearly he must have lived a long time in that corner of Bloomsbury to know so much detailed topography. It still did not completely remove one possibility. There need be no inconsistency in Robinsohn, having a London photograph, knowing his topography with scholarly accuracy, and yet being a substitute agent for a murdered man. The embassy had no independent photograph from London to check against his features.

When it came to Major Rivers, Rostand noticed at once as he entered the room that his breath smelled of drink at eleven thirty in the morning, and his claret face had developed a patch of pure purple on one cheek. Within a few minutes Rivers said: "You see, I don't think there's any question of the ABVO knowing about the escape this time. They simply saw through Robinsohn's disguise."

"What's your evidence for that?"

"You didn't see Robinsohn in his get-up, did you?"

"No."

"He looked—uneasy—like a woman wearing a man's clothes."

"They all do that nowadays."

"But any ABVO agent worth his salt would have noticed something different."

"Then why let him take the risk?"

"He insisted. Nobody could have stopped him."

"Tell me—this Habana Club—do you go there very often?"

"No, not often."

142

"I'd like to come along one night."

"You'd find it an awful bore."

"I must say I'm not a great gambler. Do you play?"

"Occasional small flutters."

When Rivers had gone Rostand picked out his card again and read: "Born Great Berkhampstead to Brigadier John Felix Rivers and Mary Grace Adams, April 4, 1915. Educated Eton: Sandhurst Second Class. Served Second World War as Major in Artillery. Wounded at Ardennes. Married Patricia Bent. Two children. Entered Foreign Office 1948. Military Attaché 1950. Seconded Veralia 1951." The typed entries ceased at that point but someone had scribbled in pencil at the bottom of the card, "Arrested London—intoxicated—1956." Rostand tried to identify the handwriting, failed, and rang through to Hargreaves, but his line was engaged.

The following evening Rivers escorted Rostand to the Habana Club and the whole experience became a series of surprises. The club might have been a very exclusive Mayfair gambling establishment where a well-bred hush was the first prerequisite of membership and service. The dim lighting reduced all faces to shadowed blurs, the furniture was period, and the staff self-effacing ghosts who hovered and smiled but never intervened without an invitation. Very soft, very sophisticated French dance music came from hidden speakers in every part of the multiple rooms but it was never loud enough to interrupt conversation and never too quiet for dancing. One room lined with mirrors was packed with people —many from the French, British, German, and American embassies— dancing in a kind of trancelike demimonde close-up. The bartenders were, without exception, pretty girls or—and the word could not be avoided— beautiful young men. The central oblong room reproduced a complete travesty of Monte Carlo with two roulette wheels on green baize tables, croupiers in evening dress with eyeshades, and circles of light picked out in white concentration.

Everyone appeared to know Rivers, from the balding, bland manager with his searching eyes to the pretty girls behind the bar. As they retired to an alcove with two double whiskies, Rivers said:

"This place combines the naïve with the cunning."

"Very skillful—how does it work?"

"Well, they've picked on one big Western vice and reproduced its physical circumstances with naïve accuracy. The cunning can only be detected when you've been here a few times. Even then it's not easy."

Rostand glanced round. "I suppose the male bartenders are homosexual and the females call girls?" he said.

"No," Rivers said, "but if you want introductions to either, they will fix it. Much more sophisticated tastes are also catered to."

"Boys?"

"Drugs, nymphets—they don't miss a trick."

"Isn't the blackmail bit overdone these days? I mean everyone expects it, so why should they fall for it?"

"If a man's tastes are powerful enough." Rivers gestured.

"Were you screened for all this?"

"Heavily. Homosexual—no, drugs—no, pederast—no, drink—a little too much."

Rostand stared straight into Rivers's shadowed eyes. The dim lighting had changed his face into a gray relief of plasticine irregularities, and he wondered whether a superficial show of straightforwardness might not cover deeper deception. He was about to say, "How often do you gamble?" when it occurred to him that he might get a clearer picture by suggesting that they try their luck at the tables.

Rivers crinkled his nose in distaste at the idea. "Not tonight," he said. "I have some congenial company—why waste it on the tables?"

Fragment by fragment the picture fell into place perfectly all over again. A transparently open man with nothing to hide who could admit his minor weaknesses and regret his fondness for drink while demonstrating perfect control over the hypnotic power which the spinning wheel sometimes exercised on other people.

It was when Rivers left to go to the Gents that Earle Hawkins, the American naval attaché, came swinging past the alcove, paused, and said: "Goddam it, Paul—who would ever expect to find you in a place like this?"

"Sit down a minute," Rostand said. "And what are *you* doing here?"

"Drinking and whoring."

"Is it worth it?"

"The drink, not the whores. Say—that's quite a guy you've got for a military attaché."

"You think so."

"Drink anyone under the table. I thought Americans knew how to drink. I wouldn't like to challenge him."

"Do you come here often?"

"Once a week."

"I gather it's the great spy-homosexual-pickup-blackmail joint—exclusive free membership to those with the right vices."

"Dead right. It's all a bit of a joke at our place."

"Does it really pay off?"

"This is where they found Carstairs."

"What did he do?"

"Sold the blueprint of a new gunsight for a boy."

"I suppose the boy got the Stalin Medal?"

"Sure thing. Do you gamble?"

Rostand shook his head.

144

The American leaned forward. "Say, what the hell are you doing here? You don't drink—don't gamble—and sex is surely a bit of a bore to a man like you."

"You think so?" Rostand said.

"Why not stick your neck out and risk a couple of bucks on the red or black?"

"I have in fact just been trying to persuade Rivers to do just that."

"Don't tell me he refused?"

"He did."

"You never know with that guy, do you? I've seen him play pretty intensely."

Rostand fastened on the words. "Could you be a bit more explicit?"

"Explicit? Why?"

"Gambling habits interest me."

"What exactly do you want to know?"

"Does he make a habit of it?"

"No, I don't think so."

Rivers came striding toward the table as the American naval attaché ordered fresh drinks for all three of them, and said:

"What about a flutter, Theodore?"

"Not tonight," Rivers said.

"Well, if you won't play, supposing you tell me what's cooking in this benighted town. You guys down at the B.E. get sympathetic treatment. We get the rough ride. Now why in the hell is that? Right now we're practically sleeping with Mother Russia—so why should we be left out in the cold?"

They discussed the question at some length and then the naval attaché changed the subject with a question addressed to Rivers. "Have you left that wife of yours yet?"

"Divorce is too expensive."

"Less than alimony."

"That's the joke—not much."

"So you stay with her to save money?"

"There is another reason."

"And that?"

"I quite like her still."

"But you never see her?"

"When I go on leave. There's also the kids."

"How old are they now?"

"Patricia's ten and Jonathan's six."

Another hour went by before they left the club and by then Rostand felt quite high, but there was no sign of the drink taking effect on Rivers.

CHAPTER 14

Over several days, as Rostand pressed home his inquiry, the results revealed a general laxness in embassy regulations and behavior patterns which disturbed his sense of efficiency. When he first drew Hargreaves's attention to one shortcoming after another, Hargreaves said: "We're not machines, old man. For God's sake let's preserve a few human weaknesses." But the evidence steadily accumulated and became more and more irritating to a mind geared to removing all obstacles from the path of an efficiency he knew could never be perfect. All unaware, over the next ten days, he began to act from an inner compulsion to see this mission through. It took charge of him and became obsessive. It assumed characteristics beyond those of an inquiry into a leak. At the end of ten days he was driven to dictate a long and detailed memo, which reached Hargreaves's desk the following day.

There were ten points in the memo, ranging from the arrival of the lesser staff fifteen or twenty minutes late every morning to the prolonged tea and coffee breaks which often ran on for half an hour. The public telephone boxes in the reception room were never used by the staff for private calls, and some places frequented by staff after office hours were considered undesirable. In the higher echelons of the embassy, telegrams which could have been dealt with the same day seldom were, the Habana Club was frequented too much and should certainly be put out of bounds, and liaisons of a dangerous kind had developed between some members of the staff and external persons.

The situation with scores of classified and unclassified keys was very unsatisfactory, and Thompson's habit of using the safe to secrete them in during the day was open to abuse because, in the constant locking and unlocking, it sometimes by accident remained unlocked. Some members of the staff had actually taken classified keys home with them in the evenings, claiming that this was partly accident and partly to avoid the tedium of constantly reapplying for them every day. The cumulative effect was to throw suspicion on people at every level of embassy life and to make it possible for the lowest underling to become a threat to security. Thompson bore the brunt of the blame for certain shortcomings because he had failed to tighten regulations sufficiently when the news of the first leak reached him. It was advisable to clean up all minor deviations from embassy schedules, but something much more drastic was required in view of the leaks. Thus, all locks on the chancery, code room, strong room, and registry should be changed at once and the Foreign Office asked for code replacements as quickly as possible. As for Robinsohn, he should be kept under much closer surveillance.

Hargreaves read through this memo with growing astonishment, which slowly grew into something akin to anger. Damnation and hell, the memo read as if Rostand had been given a mandate to clean up the embassy instead of merely carrying out a discreet inquiry. The fellow had become a private detective and neither he nor H.E. could stand that type of animal. He was about to dictate a long acid reply to the memo when the words "short-circuit circumlocutions of communications" caught his eye on the second page. All right, he would short-circuit them. Picking up the memo he went striding along to Rostand's office, entered, and throwing it down on his desk said, "You don't expect me to take all this seriously, do you?"

Rostand shrugged his shoulders. "It's up to you," he said. "I have no authority in the matter."

"You don't exactly give that impression," Hargreaves said.

"I'm sorry," Rostand said. "I merely meant to set out the facts."

"Half the stuff you've dealt with there is really Bruce's province."

"It would be a fatuous exercise in the obvious to tell you he's away sick."

Bruce Canning was the resident security officer who had been absent for three months.

"Do you realize what would happen to the morale of this place if we tried to subject it to these—er—recommendations?"

"It's pretty demoralized already."

"That's Robinsohn's fault—once he's out of here everything will be all right again."

"You're very optimistic."

"I think we're making altogether too much fuss about what really amounts to two minor leaks."

Rostand interrupted: "And two escape attempts wrecked—are they minor?"

"The ABVO could easily have seen through them."

"And the liaisons with members of the intelligence?"

For a moment Hargreaves's heart stopped. That was a reasonable description of Pamela's relationship with Volenski.

"What liaisons?" he said quietly.

Rostand stood up, went to the door, opened it, and looked round his secretary's office. It was empty. Closing the door he came back and said, "I had a sort of confession yesterday from Caroline."

"A confession—from Caroline?"

Rostand told Hargreaves the bare facts of what she had revealed to him and as the story fell into place, Hargreaves felt his blood freezing because this was much too close to Pamela's story for anyone's comfort. In fact it looked uncommonly like a carbon copy.

When Rostand had finished he said: "If you apply a big enough microscope to the smallest detail you're bound to come up with suspicion. After all, any of us in recollection could probably remember a meeting where some indiscretion *might* have slipped out. It all becomes pretty silly if—"

"Can you yourself recall such an occasion?" Rostand interrupted.

"No," Hargreaves said slowly, and now he found himself on the rack. If he concealed the details of his wife's unfaithfulness, under these circumstances, he would be guilty of dereliction of duty, but if he came out now with the facts without consulting her first, she would not only be furious; such a breach of confidence might drive her—with her temperament—into much more dramatic reactions. Since she was no longer seeing Volenski, why should he bother to disclose her previous meetings. No one would ever know about the past.

There was a long pause and then he said, "Have you thought what H.E. would reply to a memo of that kind?"

"Yes. He wouldn't like it."

"More than that—he would loathe it."

"I suppose he would."

"So you don't expect to get anywhere?"

"I'm not so sure," Rostand said. "I think there's one way I might."

"What is that?"

"If I had your support."

"Out of the question. I'm flatly against any interference with the private lives of the staff, even more against reducing them to factory hands who clock in and out, have their tea breaks counted down to the last minute, dare not allow themselves to fall in love, and even get around to spying on one another."

"That's a gross exaggeration. Anyway they've been spying on one another for at least six weeks."

"Through no fault of mine."

"Couldn't you be a bit more rational about this?"

Suddenly a tremendous surge of guilt seized and inflated Hargreaves's uneasiness into flaring anger.

"Rational," he said walking toward the door. "If you really want to know what I think—the whole memo's an outrage."

148

Ten minutes later, back in his office, he brought his guilt-anger under control, paced up and down for several more minutes and then dialed Rostand's extension. "Look," he said, "I'm sorry about the outburst. Can we meet for a drink this evening to talk it all over again?"

"You wouldn't," Rostand said, "like to go to the Habana Club, would you?"

"In order to qualify for your list of suspects?"

Rostand laughed. "You're about the only one, *a fortiori*, I would be prepared to give a clean bill."

In the Habana Club, Rostand made for the same alcove where he had sat with Rivers and for nearly an hour the two men drank double whiskies, gradually softening up their automatic dislike of each other. The conversation became steadily more frank. At last, replying to one of Rostand's cynical analyses of diplomatic motives, Hargreaves said, "You don't believe in scruples, do you?"

"It's simply that my scruples are different from yours."

"Explain that to me."

"You are scrupulous about every individual. I am scrupulous about the collective organism."

"That's exactly the line Kalogh's lot take."

"And you take the line Queen Victoria took."

"I take the line H.E. takes," Hargreaves said. "I wonder what you really think of the Old Man at the back of that socialist brain of yours."

"A very kind, charming, considerate man."

"Read for kind—milksop, read for charming—evasive, read for considerate—weak."

"And for that matter read for diplomacy—double-talk. According to you I'm merely practicing the trade."

"You really do regard it as a trade, don't you?"

"It's like any other. Riddled with small corruptions."

"In your case too."

"According to you."

"If I tried to spell out what you really think of H.E.," Hargreaves interrupted, "would you tell me whether I'm right or wrong?"

"Try me," Rostand said.

"The image that comes to my mind is of a big overbred bloodhound. The bloodhound is supercilious, slightly degenerate from too much breeding, incapable of biting anyone, and content to play a decorative role, occasionally allowing a well-bred sniff to express its disdain for economics, nuclear fission, democracy, the proletariat, and all the encumbrances of the modern world."

Rostand laughed. "You should have been a writer."

"You accept the description?"

"Of course I don't."

"And me—I wonder how you *really* see *me.*"

"I think it's time we were going."

In order to get to the cloakroom they had to make their way through the oblong room with the roulette tables and suddenly Rostand caught Hargreaves's arm and drew him into the shadow of the wall.

"Look," he said, "there's Rivers. Let's watch a moment."

The brilliant circle of light made a sharp white edge of Rivers's profile and it was difficult at that distance to distinguish between a certain fixed concentration and an expression of—was it boredom, or misery? "I need a better view," Rostand said and moved very quietly toward the tables. Hargreaves followed him. They stood almost beside Rivers but he remained quite unaware of their presence and now it seemed to Rostand that the need to concentrate was stronger than the boredom or the misery in his face. For almost five minutes Rivers's expression did not change and when a blue-rinsed middle-aged woman sitting next to him spoke to him, she had to repeat her words because he did not hear. Hargreaves quickly lost interest in watching and was about to say something to Rivers when Rostand motioned him to silence. Taking him by the arm he guided him over to the gilded cage of the cashier's desk. "What," he said to the bladder-of-lard visage peering through the grille, "do the green chips cost?" Translating the Veralian currency into English it worked out at £1 each. "Not exactly ruinous," Rostand said. "Did you notice Rivers was playing with green chips?"

Hargreaves nodded impatiently. "Let's go," he said. "I don't like the feel of this place."

Once outside in the wet, deserted street, Rostand gave Hargreaves a brief résumé of the details he had collected about Rivers. "No one escapes you, do they?" Hargreaves said.

"So far I haven't covered much ground."

"So far! You're not going on grilling people, are you?"

"There's no question of grilling. But tell me—Frank—you've been at the embassy longer than I have. You know everyone much better—is there anyone not on my list you think I should talk to?"

At once the name Pamela leaped into Hargreaves's mind and the small shock brought a hesitation into his walk. They had drawn level with a wide concrete coping built to prevent people falling over a steep declivity that ran down to the river, giving a wonderful view of the industrial area spread out beyond—a forest of concrete towers and chimneys, pulsing with a fierce glow from two gigantic kilns. It was so obviously a moment for truth, but Hargreaves stood there staring across at the symbols of modern man's alienation and tried to avoid taking the decision by saying to Rostand:

"You, of course, believe in alienation."

150

"Yes—but not the Marxist brand."

"What's your brand?"

"Alienation of the mind."

"I don't understand."

"The more extreme ideologies deny the detailed use of the mind. They force you to think in a straitjacket. People become ideologue fanatics."

Hargreaves turned to Rostand and studied his face in the half-light from a streetlamp.

"My God," he said, "don't talk like that—or I'll begin to believe we have something in common."

"Could you," Rostand said with a deliberate show of patience, "abandon for a moment lofty philosophic flights. As I said before, do you know anyone else you think I should talk to?"

It was as if the words took charge then and a plan that had formulated itself in Hargreaves's unconscious suddenly broke surface and began to spell itself out.

"Look, Rostand," he said. "Can I speak to you in the highest confidence?"

"Of course."

"Perhaps I mean something more sharply focused than generalized confidence."

"I don't follow."

"Well, can we have it completely understood that if I add some information of my own to your terrifying dossier that, above all, it will never be repeated to H.E. or reach his ears from any other direction?"

"Until I know what the information is, how can I tell? I am under an obligation to prepare a report."

"In that case I shall have to stay silent."

"And what if I included this conversation in my report?"

"H.E. would respect my silence."

"I believe he would."

They walked slowly on without speaking. "Do you regard this information as important?" Rostand said at last.

"I suppose it could just possibly be."

The dreariness in his voice made Rostand comment, "You sound depressed."

"Look," Rostand said. "I'll surrender. I'll agree to keep the information confidential but with one reservation. If it leads to the culprit I shall obviously have to name him."

"Yes, I suppose you would."

Again Hargreaves hesitated and then at last he began: "I find myself in a highly embarrassing situation which I didn't want to talk about, but since Caroline has come forward with her story, I see no escape." He then gave Rostand a brief account of his wife's possible indiscretions with her lawyer lover.

"My God," Rostand commented at the end. "You certainly stick to your principles, don't you? In your situation I should have stayed quiet."

"You think I'm a fool?"

"No. I admire you."

"But you see the dangers with H.E., don't you?"

"I do indeed. One whisper of this to him and I doubt if he could bring himself to give a completely clear recommendation for the American job."

"So I can rely upon you."

"Certainly. And I sympathize."

"Professionally or personally?"

"Both. It must be very difficult with your wife."

"I've grown used to it: I simply don't want it to wreck my chances."

"Then you should have stayed silent. After all, if I found the culprit elsewhere, there would have been no need to implicate your wife at all."

"And if you didn't find the culprit and I was forced *then* to tell you later, what would H.E. say about my conspiracy of silence?"

"Christ!" Rostand said. "Add your two integrities together and you get—God."

"I suppose," Hargreaves said, "everyone's ambitious."

"Yes," Rostand said.

"And you see me going to America soon and you getting the first secretaryship?"

"Yes."

"Conducting this inquiry successfully will carry you another step forward."

"Maybe."

"Hence the ruthlessness."

"I don't see it that way."

"The youngest first secretary of a generation."

"Possibly."

"But that means there's a reason for your staying quiet about what I have said."

"You mean that if I talk you won't get what you want, and neither will I?"

"Exactly."

"So I shall find myself in your situation?"

"Yes. Which way would you jump?"

"I'd have to think long and hard."

"And H.E.? What's his future?"

"I think he may be driven to resign."

"Resign! Driven! I don't know what you're talking about."

152

"Just a hunch."

"I certainly don't see anything like that happening. If ever he goes they'll have to sack him, and his record is much too good for that."

"Not recently."

"Over the years it's distinguished."

"But this latest summons to the Foreign Office."

"Just a routine refresher."

"I hope you're right."

"This is where I turn off."

"See you in the morning."

Before he went to bed Rostand made a few notes from Hargreaves's "confession" and put them carefully in his private wallet.

Walking the last two hundred yards to his flat Hargreaves tried over in his mind various ways of breaking the news to Pamela. At first heavily on the defensive, the liquor began to take full effect and a certain bravado overwhelmed his gloom. By the time he reached the house he felt in much better form and a false sense of renewed virility urged him to a course of action from which he normally shrank. He strode into the bedroom to find Pamela lying in a transparent black nightdress on the bed listening to a Beatles record, smoking, and half-reading a Ngaio Marsh detective story.

She did not move or sit up as he came into the room and he began almost at once to throw off his clothes in what was for him a very abandoned manner.

"Good heavens," she muttered, "what's hit you?"

Before she had time to turn away or defend herself he came straight at her, snatched the cigarette, stubbed it out, removed the book and fell on the bed beside her, kissing her cheeks, eyes, lips, pushing the nightdress down over her shoulders and smothering her breasts with every caress his lips and hands could devise.

She fought him then, she struggled and kicked, and tried to slap his face. "You're mad! Mad! Stop—you lunatic! For God's sake, what are you trying to do?"

It did not deter him. He embraced her passionately, he kissed her deeply in the mouth, he moved between her legs and desperately tried to enter her as she slowly went limp not with the sensuality of surrender but with a sudden and much more powerful form of defense, indifference. That was the worst moment of all. She lay there like a corpse while he made love to her and no necrophilic impulse could carry him through the defensive *boredom* of her body. The artificial fire quickly went out of him and within a few minutes he quietened, relaxed and as he lay beside her again, confused and defeated, it was to him as if he literally sank down into an endless black pit. Her voice, when it reached him, seemed to echo, "You've been drinking—I'm sorry—I'm just not in the mood. And I've got my period anyway—"

He lay there inert for a long time, until the Beatles record ground to a halt. She swung up from the bed to switch off the arm and as she came back, he said, "I've something to tell you."

His voice was half smothered by the pillow and she said: "I can't hear—it's late—let's go to sleep."

He sat up then. "Listen," he said, "I've had to tell them."

"Tell what?"

"The leak—the inquiry—I had to tell them about you and—" he stopped.

She stiffened and her face was fixed in horrified astonishment.

"Do you mean to say—" she began.

"Now listen. There was no escape. I had to."

"You bastard!"

She grabbed another cigarette, and went storming round the room holding it unlit in her fingers. "You talk about discretion—you talk about confidences—taste—all those bloody principles you're so proud of—and then you go and undress me in public."

"No one's undressed you," he said coldly. "If you'll listen a minute, perhaps you'll understand."

"Understand! I understand all right. The whole bloody embassy will be sniggering behind its hand and talking about Hargreaves's whore. You know what that lot can do with a little gossip. My God! You! You with all your fine pretensions—"

He stood up then, went over to her, grasped her by the arms and said, "Stand still and listen!"

"Don't bellow at me."

"Let me tell you what happened."

He repeated the first part of the story and as the details developed she slowly relaxed, went back to the bed, and lay at full length on it, listening carefully. When he had finished, she remained silent while he climbed uneasily into his pajamas, moving round her, staring at her. Suddenly she sat up.

"You're a child," she said. "A naïve milksop child. There was absolutely no need to tell anyone anything. Why in God's name didn't you stay quiet. Who gives a fuck about their goddam leak? You're like a bloody boy scout, with a boy scout's sense of honor. Now I'll be the butt of every dirty mind in the embassy . . ."

"It's worth more than Paul's job to repeat anything."

"Which is precisely the reason why *you* repeated it all to him."

"What do you mean?"

"You saved your job—*your* chances of promotion."

"Don't be absurd."

154

"Absurd! Without a word of consultation you go and give away my private sex life and I—"

He interrupted her fiercely.

"If you didn't have an extra sex life, we shouldn't be in this bloody mess now."

"No—we should be in a worse one."

"What do you mean by that?"

"You know very well what I mean—I should have left you."

Momentarily it silenced him. Then he began trying to reason with her. "There's only one other person who may have to know the facts."

"H.E.?"

"Yes."

"And don't you think I'm already aware enough of his moralizing stare—his stuffed dummy values—his puffed-up, puritanical—"

"If you'd listen a moment you'd understand that he will never know," he interrupted.

He told her then of the bargain he had struck with Rostand and she blazed at him. "You go bargaining with my confidences, my private life, without consulting me, and all in order to save your bloody career, to make me something trodden into public dust on your way to head of mission. I think you'd convert me into a whore if getting to Washington made that necessary."

"I should have talked to you first. I'm sorry. But there was no alternative in the long run."

"Well, there is an alternative now," she said.

"And what's that?"

"Why do you keep on asking stupid damn questions? You know the answer."

She didn't mean it, of course. When she was furious she always resorted to blackmail. Threats out of all proportion to the given situation flowed away. But it always made him uneasy. Despite all the torments and humiliations she remained a necessary part of his *amour propre,* of his ambition, emotions, way of life, and something had grown between them over the years which would leave him bleeding if ever it were finally torn asunder.

Robinsohn lay at full length on the carpet, staring up vacantly at the ceiling while a Mozart violin concerto ran to its close on the record player. His hair had grown long, he wore no tie, and his pullover was stained. Rostand had replaced the supply of brandy with a much cheaper wine and Robinsohn reached out a hand to refill his glass. As the last notes died away he ignored the needle grinding on the margin and continued to stare at the ceiling. One new feature had appeared in the room, books, scattered at random over any convenient piece of furniture until they finally spilled onto the floor. Insomnia had driven him back to books, but a curious twist had become apparent in his taste. Not adventure, sex, detective stories, sport, or espionage characterized his reading—but science. *The Double Helix* by John Watson, the *D.N.A. Molecule* by Albert Rostoff, *Philosophy and the Physicists* by Susan Stebbing, *The A.B.C. of Relativity* by Bertrand Russell, *The Nature of Physical Reality* by Henry Margeman.

There was a tap on the door, but he did not hear it. The tap became a much louder rap, repeated three times, and without moving he croaked, "Come in."

Mrs. Malvern came slowly through the door and peered into the room. It was dusk of a November evening with rain drizzling outside and inside the accumulated residue of five hours of concentrated smoking and drinking.

"My God," she said, "it's worse than ever."

She switched on the light and his hand went over his eyes as if he had been struck by lightning. "Switch that off!" he almost commanded.

"Mr. Robinsohn," she said without touching the light switch, "you cannot go on like this."

"Why don't you leave me alone?" he said. He had not changed his position in any detail and continued to stare up at the ceiling from the carpet.

"They tell me you didn't eat lunch again."

"Your spies are not very reliable."

"So you have eaten."

"I've taken to eating books," he said.

She stepped into the room. "So I notice," she said and picked up off the carpet a book sprawling open on its face—*The Nature of Physical Reality*.

"Good heavens," she said spinning the pages, "it looks very indigestible. Do you understand this stuff?"

"No," he said.

"Then what's the point?"

"I get a glimpse or two of something different."

"Different from what?"

"Different from this place—different from you—me—"

"I don't understand."

"Did you know," he said, "we all came from carbon atoms?"

She put the book on the table and staring down at him said, "Supposing you make a gesture in the direction of commonplace politeness and get up off the floor."

He lay there unmoving, without saying a word for a whole long minute until she said, "In that case I'll go."

156

He came slowly to his feet.

"And the window," she said. "It's suffocating in here."

He did not protest when she opened it, and he offered her a chair and a drink. She took the chair and refused the drink.

"What are carbon atoms?" she asked.

"The stuff our guts are made of."

"My son studies microbiology at Cambridge—he keeps talking about something called D.N.A. molecules. He says *they* are the raw material of life."

"Yes," Robinsohn said. "Have you read *The Double Helix?* I recommend it—it's as good as a thriller—even I could understand it."

"I'm sure I wouldn't. I haven't the faintest clue why micro should belong to biology or the D.N.A. molecule take the place of the human soul. I thought in my fuddy-duddy way that life crystalized around souls, not carbon atoms."

"You are religious."

"In a desperately lazy way."

"You mean you don't go to church?"

"Once in a while I have to. My husband's a bit of a stickler."

"I used to envy religious people when I was young."

"Why?"

"They could explain away anything. A tortured child was part of the grand design. The ABVO and the Gestapo, intelligible experiments of the divine mind. Perhaps He had made one of those grandiose mistakes that reduce a million people to a prolonged agony and death, but all was for the best in the best of all possible worlds."

"That phrase sounds familiar."

"It is."

"Wasn't it Voltaire?"

"Somebody like that."

"Mr. Robinsohn, you astonish me. How does—well—to put it bluntly—a man in your profession come to be so well read?"

"First, I am not well read—second, an agent has long dreary spells of waiting, watching, doing nothing, and if he dislikes humanity as I do he turns to books. Why do you believe in God, Mrs. Malvern?"

"I don't think an Old Gentleman with a beard figures very large in the new religion. It's all talk of design—purpose, my husband says—a sort of Shavian life force pretty mixed up and brutal sometimes, but he sees it, unlike me, driving through everything to a good end."

"What's the evidence for that?"

"I long ago gave up evidence. I just believe."

"But the evidence on the other side is so much better."

"What evidence?"

"When you people talk about God—you are just speculating in words —it's an opinion. When science talks about D.N.A. molecules it can actually see and check their behavior."

"It's all over my head, but I do remember my son saying he wished he could in fact come face to face with a D.N.A. molecule because he would certainly give it a piece of his mind for being so bloody invisible. Doesn't that rather contradict what you say, Mr. Robinsohn?"

"What they see is not the actual molecule, but the shadow thrown by the electron microscope when it's trained on the molecule."

"Shadow! Mr. Robinsohn, shadow! But what about Socrates—or was it Plato?—I'm so badly read—wasn't he two thousand years ago talking about shadows on the wall of the cave?"

"Dead right. My God—think of it—all those clever scientists probing away for centuries and they come up with the same answer. But it's not like that in fact, is it? Plato—or was it Socrates?—dealt with *imaginative* shadows. These are *real* shadows."

"Shadows—real? Crazy!"

"One's in the imagination. The other literally there."

"Literally—what does that mean? If you move the light, the shadow vanishes—there's nothing you can touch—it's simply an optical illusion."

"Dammit, Mrs. Malvern, you're much too good at this. You sound like an intellectual."

"Please, not that."

"Did you go to university?"

"Roedean."

"What's Roedean?"

"A woman's public school."

"I didn't know there were such things."

"They teach you to think in certain grooves—one of which is the superiority of the male mind."

"Do you believe that?"

"Sometimes."

"And your husband?"

"He has a very special kind of mind, which I don't want to go into. And now can we get down from these heady heights? There's something much more important I've simply got to discuss with you—you cannot go on living this isolated life, shut up in here pacing around half the night, never getting any fresh air, half starving yourself. It's unhealthy."

"What's the alternative?"

"Isn't there some sort of work in the embassy you would like to do?"

"What do you have in mind?"

"Thompson's going off on holiday to England."

He smiled wryly and lit another cigarette.

"You try and sell that to your husband or Hargreaves or Rostand."

158

She looked at him then straight into his eyes, which were now blood-shot, and held his gaze for nearly a minute.

"Are you really what you say you are?" she said, her eyes unflinching as they watched every flicker of expression.

"Why should I lie to you?" he said. "I like you. No, I'm not."

She withdrew from him involuntarily for a second because the words came as a small shock.

"So you freely admit . . ." she began.

"That I'm a bloody bad agent to land myself up in prison like this," he interrupted.

She smiled a wan smile and said, "Couldn't you talk straight for once?"

"I *am* talking straight."

"But you're not answering my question."

"I am not," he said with quiet emphasis, "a double agent. Now shall we have some Scarlatti?"

"One day," she said reflectively, "I suppose we shall really know. In fact, when my husband comes back."

He had been walking toward the record player and turned sharply to look over his shoulder.

"When is he coming back?"

"Very soon now."

As he put on the record, he said: "I'll tell you something, Mrs. Malvern—I'm giving up this job when I've completed this mission."

"Why do you say that?"

"I've thought my way through it for days. I'm not a good agent. It's as simple as that."

"How long have you been one?"

"Ten years."

"If they kept you that long, you must be good."

"Most agents don't turn in more than one good mission in ten years."

"And you?"

"Yes, I did do one."

"So you're all right."

"Not in my eyes—no."

"What would you rather do?"

"I don't know. I simply don't know."

"Everyone covets somebody else's job."

Three days later when she knocked on the door again and received no answer she walked in to find Robinsohn sprawled half off the bed, his mouth wide open, his face yellow, and no movement in his whole body. Her heart jumped as she hurried over to him, called his name, and tried to heave him back on the bed. He rolled over without opening his eyes and she found herself staring down into a death-mask face. He smelled of wine, Gauloise cigarettes, and sweat as she thrust her hand inside his shirt. His heart beat uneasily. Nothing more than a drunken coma. Or had he taken something—and if barbiturates, should he be kept from deep coma? She suddenly saw and felt for the first time how smooth, white, and hairless his chest seemed. She took him by the shoulders and tried to shake him awake. His head flopped loosely like a puppet's, his eyes half opened, and he stared uncomprehending.

She hurried to the telephone and Thompson answered. She asked him to ring the medical emergency number provided by the Ministry of the Interior at once, and went back to Robinsohn. He was muttering to himself now, but she could not make out the words. Supposing it's a heart attack—loosen the clothing, put the feet up, let the blood flow back to the brain again.

At that moment his eyes opened and he croaked, "Leave me alone."

"What's happened? Tell me what's happened."

When he closed his eyes again and did not answer she said: "I've sent for a doctor."

At that he came bolt upright on the bed, sweat dripped from his forehead and he said, "No doctor!" Then he tried to shout: "Do you hear me?—no doctor. I don't want any damned doctor," but it came in a kind of hysterical croak.

He made a brave effort to stagger up off the bed but fell back, his hand reaching out for Mrs. Malvern's arm. His fingers gripped fiercely and he half dragged her toward him. Staring straight into her face with bloodshot eyes he snarled at her, "Cancel that doctor—or it'll be the worse for everyone."

There was such a concentration of malevolent ugliness in his face that she tore her arm away and recoiled from him in fear. She moved out of his reach and stood there looking down at him. His croak became shrill again, as his eyes blazed with fury. "I do not want a doctor—do you understand?"

Anger now worked like an electric shock, galvanizing his body into action. He sat up, swung himself off the bed and staggered over to the telephone. Picking up the receiver he mumbled into it and a bewildered Thompson could not understand a word until after three attempts the phrase came out with a degree of clarity, "Cancel doctor—Don't argue! Cancel."

He staggered back to the bed and lay down again as Mrs. Malvern said, "Are you going to tell me what happened?"

He seemed momentarily to have fallen back into his coma but then he muttered, "Nothing—nothing."

"Don't be absurd," she said. "You are ill. Now why don't you let me—"

160

"Leave me alone," he interrupted. She began to move round the room, tidying the books, the papers, emptying the ashtrays, and finally opening the window. She leaned out to draw a series of deep breaths, returned to the bed again, and sat at the foot patiently waiting. Her patience surprised her and she was astonished to realize that it arose from a genuine concern for Robinsohn's welfare. Common humanity demanded a minimum of medical action in situations of this kind, but not this Nurse Cavell vigil at the feet of a man who a moment ago had revealed a snarling viciousness in his character that horrified her.

Five minutes later he said, "Give me a drink!" She brought him a glass of water which he immediately rejected, and when she found the wine bottle it was empty.

Showing him the empty bottle she said again, "Tell me what happened?"

"Couldn't sleep," he said. "Haven't slept for days. Took too many pills."

Suicide would not have been possible with the brand of sleeping pills that she had provided six weeks before and they were too mild to produce even his present condition. She moved round the room searching for the Mogodon box and found instead a small empty bottle with a Veralian label. She took it back to the bed and said: "Barbiturates?"

"Who cares?" he said and involuntarily she replied, "I do."

His eyes widened on the remark and he said: "Now don't, for God's sake, start pretending—what I most admired about you was your lack of pretense. God. I've got one helluva head."

"Would you like some black coffee?" she said.

"No," he said, and then he added. "Any minute now I'm going to be nastily sick."

He obviously expected that to drive her away, but she remained sitting there at the foot of the bed.

"It's useless waiting," he said. He closed his eyes once more and five minutes later his breathing became even, then deeper, and finally reverberated into snores. She watched him for a few more minutes and in those minutes revulsion mixed with pity and pity with bewilderment. What tormented forces drove this strange man into such violent reactions against his incarceration, what brought such wild contradiction into his behavior, and had he in fact attempted suicide and if so, wasn't it dangerous to let him slump back to sleep again because that preceded the deep and final coma?

She bent over him to scrutinize him closely. The yellow had faded from his cheeks and they now looked more healthy but she saw how sunken they had become in a few short weeks. Sweat stood out on his brow and the chin was unshaven but what should have been the collapsed ruin of a face held together with some distinction because of the bold nose and determined jaw. The chaos in the room and the hideous snores combined to produce an aura of sordidness that finally drove her out, down the corridor, and back to the spacious, spotless, richly furnished dining room. There she wrote a careful note: "I shall call again in the morning. We must find a different *modus vivendi* for you. I am sending your clothes to the laundry. The cleaner will call tomorrow to do your room."

She hesitated whether to sign it Penelope or Mrs. Malvern and then simply added 'P.M.' She returned to his room, put the note on his bedside table and left again.

He was still sleeping soundly when she returned at eight thirty the next morning. She instructed one of the daily maids to take him breakfast an hour later and hurried off to fulfill a long round of social engagements. By seven o'clock in the evening she returned to the embassy exhausted, sank back into a bath, and remained there fully half an hour trying to relax and overcome the strong impulse to visit his room again. She made a compromise with herself. Instead of going before dinner she would go after dinner, but when she had eaten a cold chicken salad and drunk half a bottle of 1956 Veralian vintage hock, drowsiness overcame her and she almost fell asleep.

It was the distant sound of a Mozart violin concerto—which must have been playing at full blast to reach her ears—that finally took her along the corridor toward his room again. Immediately she knocked, he opened the door as if he had been waiting behind it for her, and she was at once aware of a complete change in him. He had shaved, made some attempt to rehabilitate himself. The maid had cleared the room and the window was open. By silent agreement they heard the remainder of Mozart played to its end and then she said, "I'm glad to see you looking so much better."

He said, "I've been trying to think why you go on coming to see me."

"And what conclusion did you reach?"

"Will you have a drink?"

"No thanks."

She noticed that he did not drink either, but his hands trembled as he lit a cigarette and all the new external smartness could not conceal the terrible weariness in his face.

"I should have to be very frank to answer your question," he said.

"I've never known you short on frankness."

"Did you say the other day that you have some new guests coming this week?"

"Yes—there's the first secretary from Washington and Lord Calford from the United Nations."

"Do they interest you?"

"Moderately."

"And today you did the social rounds?"

"Yes."

"It bores you—all of it—doesn't it?"

"Not exactly."

"I think you are interested in me because you are bored with your social round."

"You could be right."

"But you're also bored with something else."

"What is that?"

"Your whole way of life."

"You think so?"

"And it even goes beyond that."

"In what way?"

"Well—there's your husband."

"What about my husband?"

"Isn't there boredom there too?"

Somehow after all these visits, seeing him in so many moods and knowing him so much better, the words no longer seemed an impertinence and she did not interrupt him as he went on.

"You need the stimulation of a different way of life. Years of posing and functions and playing the hostess to people all stamped out to pattern has left you dead. You need something new. You want something real and full of red blood for once. I'm supposed to represent these things— God knows why."

She smiled ironically. "You sound like a psychoanalyst," she said, "and I cannot bear the breed."

"But there's one more—much more—important element in it all, isn't there?"

"What's that?"

"You won't like this."

"Try me."

"The sexual element."

She stood up at once and said: "Mr. Robinsohn. I did not come here to discuss my private life with you and I do not want to listen to your amateur attempts at psychoanalysis. I came here to help you. If you insist on talking about my private life, I shall leave at once."

"Take it easy," he said. "Now just sit down again and listen a moment. You see, the fact is—you may be surprised to hear—I don't want you to go on coming to see me—for reasons I'll try and explain."

She hesitated a moment and then as she sank back onto the chair, she was astonished to find that his words produced a twinge of disappointment in her, which she carefully masked. "As a matter of fact, I shall be far too busy with what you call my boring social round to come and see you next week," she said.

"Good," he said. "That is good."

"But you really must get out of here. You simply can't go on shutting yourself away like this."

"What do you recommend?"

"There's the garden in the day—the canteen—the library—and you must come and dine with us again."

"But I have to get away from you."

"Get away—why?"

"This is going to sound to you like the worst head-shrinker's jargon," he said, "but what you unfortunately do is reactivate my past."

"Good God!" she said, "what on earth does that mean?"

"There is another reason why I must stop seeing you. You see—I destroy people, and I might even end up destroying you."

"Don't be ridiculous."

"Let me try and give you a few details."

It came out hesitantly at first. He circled round the early facts trying to touch them in with a delicacy that surprised her in a man who could be so ruthless. As he talked she realized that there must be a constant struggle between the ugly, ruthless side of his nature and the person who could come with such sensitivity to personal revelations. He paced round the room, he smoked incessantly, and if the words at first were chaotic, slowly they began to cohere into a recognizable shape. He told her then so much of his story that she began to understand how she had become the resurrected ghost of his mother who had the power to reach back into the most sensitive areas of his past even when her words were completely different. He had neglected his mother, abused her, and let her rot—utterly alone—even in her coffin—and she, Mrs. Malvern, had come back to haunt him in her—likeness? No. In disguise, in heavily deceptive middle-aged disguise.

"Guilt is cheap—guilt is bourgeois—guilt is absurdity. I want nothing to do with it—but you stand for it—you are a pointing finger—because something far worse than you could ever credit is hidden underneath all this."

He tried to tell her then about his brother, skirting round him first, refusing to come to the core, but slowly the words took charge and a trancelike element came into his utterance as if she, Mrs. Malvern, were no longer there, until at last he was so carried away with the necessity of pouring it all out that the facts became confused.

Was it his mother, his brother, or his wife? Did one produce the loathing of the other, were they so interlocked he did not know which one he had pushed from the windowsill and whether the scream on the air—which still echoed in this room—was his brother's scream or his mother's. But beyond all that there was something else, something he had never told another human being, something so deeply locked away in his unconcious, it took a woman like Mrs. Malvern, a second incarnation in the likeness of his wife, Valerie, to split open all his defenses and expose his soft, pulsing brain to a ruthless probing finger until the agony produced a sound from his own lips that had in it elements of a scream.

He was leaning over Mrs. Malvern, his eyes staring straight through her into the image of his late wife's face, his finger jabbing within an inch of her eyes and the words pouring out of him in a white-hot torrent, and his wife rose from the chair just as she had risen all those years ago and fear was written deeply on her face and she just managed to reach the door as the last crescendo of abuse burst and she slipped through and fled down the corridor with the words, "Get out! Get out!" ringing in her ears.

He collapsed on the bed when Penelope had gone and the scenes rushed in mad kaleidoscope through his mind, obliterating the room, the embassy, Veralia, and reason. They moved without sequence in a wild disorder of their own.

Valerie leering over him naked and whipping with words the lifeless penis, in total scorn at his inadequacies; Valerie mocking his lack of social graces; Valerie tearing open the insecurities under the masks; Valerie daring him to be a man, to hold down a job, find a stable way of life, stop pretending to be an actor, and acting the pretense and failing to provide a living—and failing—failing. "You even fail to retaliate! You dare not even retaliate—"

Until he did and took her throat in his strong hands and squeezed until her face was blue and he just stopped in time before she ran terrified out of the flat.

Destroying people. That was the inbuilt mechanism he could not control. His brother, mother, wife. A sick man clearly, but not so sick that he could not enjoy the exercise of his destructive powers, and not so sick that it stopped the scream of his conscience tearing the nights apart. Until neither wishing to die nor wishing to live, what was there left to do but seek redemption in some way of life that became a prolonged search for death as retribution. Which was why he went one day to the highly confidential interview where they warned him all too clearly that death—nasty mutilating death—was the occupational hazard of their trade. Control guaranteed that no one would ever attend or even hear of his funeral.

CHAPTER 15

t was on the morning of the day preceding His Excellency's return from London that Rostand, hurrying back from a minor interview at the Ministry of the Interior, almost collided with Earle Hawkins, the American naval attaché.

"Off the record," he said falling in step with Rostand, "what's cooking?"

"You suspect something special?"

"I certainly do. Our intelligence boys have gone quiet enough to make me suspect the worst."

"What would the worst be?"

"Kalogh assassinated."

"Is that the line they take?"

"They don't take any line. By the way, I saw Major Rivers at the tables again last night."

Rostand fastened on the remark. "Playing high?"

"Too high for me."

They walked on in silence for a minute and then Hawkins added, "He tried to borrow some money."

"And you lent him some?"

"The only thing I have to lend is an overdraft high as Rockefeller Center . . . This is where I turn off. Shall I see you at the reception tonight?"

"No. Hargreaves is standing in for H.E."

"Well—see you soon. Ciao."

Back in his office Rostand began a rapid series of very oblique telephone inquiries from two contacts in the Ministry of the Interior into the possibility of gambling debts at the Habana Club. When they asked for more details, he had none, but the assistant press secretary gave him the name of the undermanager of the Habana whose number was not listed in the telephone book. Franz Schultze turned out to be elaborately evasive, but Rostand emerged from a long series of exchanges with the feeling that gambling debts were not unknown at the Habana Club.

Overcome with an urgent desire to pinpoint the possible leak before His Excellency returned, Rostand paid a rapid visit to Major Rivers on the pretext of checking some naval intelligence. He found him looking very fit and confident in his office. Gradually he led the conversation away from technical matters and said: "By the way—where would you go in the Habana Club to check on gambling debts?" He said it abruptly without any warning and just the slightest stiffening of Rivers's very upright back and a sudden mask over his face seemed significant to Rostand.

"Debts are not possible."

"They give no credit?"

"No." Rostand knew from Schultze that they did.

"Well, that clears up one point."

"What point?"

"It looks as though someone has run up big gambling debts."

Rivers shook his head. "Can't be done," he said, and added smoothly, "Otherwise I might be in trouble." That was daring, Rostand thought.

"Why in trouble?"

"If I could afford to play for high stakes, I might, but on my salary I can't."

"Well, thanks," Rostand said and left the office believing that Rivers was in fact in some sort of trouble.

On the same morning Mrs. Malvern sat over coffee in the dining room, rereading a letter from her daughter Vanessa.

"Dear Mummy,

"Everything is going splendidly with me. Ronald is very nice to me. We've run into a bit of debt but we study hard and there's another year before the exams. Now I know you'll take this in your stride, but the fact of the matter is we do need a bit of money for a very special purpose. I expect you can guess it's the same old dreary daughter trouble although how I came to get pregnant when the student doctor put me on the pill, only science could explain.

"We've checked everything pretty thoroughly. We waited until six weeks and the new litmus paper technique converted my urine into a definite yes. Very much off the record, the student doctor let drop a hint about a reliable man in Golders Green and we can cope quite well—but we don't have any money.

"Now I know I arranged to come back with Daddy when he returns—and I am coming with him—but you know how difficult he may be so I thought I'd dash off this letter to reach you before we come, hoping you'll soften him up for me. I shall only be able to stay about a week but please work on him for me while I'm there, Mummy—and let's get this all over without too much fuss.

"I respect you because I know you belong to a different generation and yet you've adjusted. I admire that. It must be very difficult for you. I also love you because, despite all my emancipation, I feel like running to you with my troubles still and I expect I shall have a good cry before this is all over. I send you a big hug and lots of love.

"Vanessa."

There was for Penelope a kind of humiliation in the letter. Other people's teenage daughters had every right to get pregnant because no concessions had been made to the modern outlook in their upbringing, but Vanessa. . . . All that enlightenment, all that gracious giving way to student values, all that acceptance of a contrivance called the pill had led to exactly the same disaster. On a second reading of the letter the first shock diminished and a plan began to form in Penelope's mind. It was all very distasteful, disturbing, and liable to cause terrible trouble with her husband, but one of them at least had better try and grasp the nettle with a quick practical hand. Her aristocratic nose wrinkled in fresh distaste at the deception it would involve but . . .

She would not tell her husband. She would simply put up the money from her own small private income and get the whole thing over and done with in two short weeks. He need never know what had happened. But should she wire Vanessa at once—keep it completely confidential—or would her daughter have the sense not to break the news to her father herself? He had resisted every emancipated step in Vanessa's upbringing and did not even know that she was on the pill. When Penelope first learned that her daughter at the age of sixteen had already slept with three young students, the pill—*force majeure*—seemed the only possible solution but she had to keep it from her husband. Multiple sex at any age was, to her, cheapening, but for a girl in her teens it seemed like the beginnings of prostitution, and it took great moral courage to wrench herself out of her traditional mold to try and see it in the modern perspective. In the end the most she could do was to suspend judgment, shrug her shoulders, and say: "Darling—it's *fait accompli,* isn't it, and I'm not going to say, 'Don't come running to me when you're in trouble.' I hope you will. I suppose in your code as in mine we have one meeting point—*don't get pregnant.*"

"That," Vanessa had said with as much youthful bravado as determination, "is the whole object of emancipation."

And now, twelve months later, without a word of apology or any sense of a failed philosophy, she had written this letter admitting she was

168

pregnant. Penelope read the last paragraph through for the third time, savoring it because there seemed to her a good deal of hope in the way it was phrased: "despite all my emancipation, I feel like running to you with my troubles still and I expect I shall have a good cry before this is all over. I send you a big hug and lots of love."

On the day before the ambassador's return his chauffeur, Richards, picked up the Veralian bug and ran such a high temperature that Penelope herself drove the old Rolls out to the airport at midnight to meet her husband. She found him looking so gray and tired she thought he must be ill, but on the way back he explained that the Foreign Office consultation had been much more intense and disturbing than he expected. Then he added, "I also have some bad news about Raoul."

Oh, my God, no—Penelope thought—not Raoul as well—and immediately she knew that if her daughter had paid what she regarded as one of the penalties of the modern style of living, there was no reason why her son should escape similar hazards.

"He's given up his degree. Hasn't read a book for months. Says books are full of dead ideas."

"That's certainly bad news. Is he still living on his grant?"

"No—it's run out. You won't believe it—he's driving the mini-van of a pop group, called The Escalators, for a living."

"Oh, my God! All we need now is a little drug addiction."

"I don't think the hard stuff —but pot is obligatory."

"And how does he look?"

"His hair is longer, his shirts wilder, his trousers dirtier."

"They're all so damned conformist really."

"Worse than that—they elevate every detail of what they do to a philosophy. My God, in my day we wore Oxford bags instead of dirty jeans, played the ukulele instead of electric guitars, and drank endless cocktails instead of taking drugs, but we didn't try to pretend we had found the one true absolute answer to life or that we were opting out of a totally evil society."

She slipped her hand over his. "It's a phase—don't worry too much—they grow out of it."

"That's just the trouble—he may grow out of long hair, fancy shirts, and pot, but I doubt whether they'll take him back at St. Anthony's."

"Many a distinguished man has managed without a degree," she said, thinking—thank God, Vanessa had the sense to keep quiet about her pregnancy. How would he have taken the double blow? It was a necessary part of his code that you might be forced to flinch in the face of adversity, but you tried to convert it into ironic acceptance and you must not go down before anything except certain death.

"Something much bigger happened at the Foreign Office," he said, but when she tried to discover the details, he simply muttered heavily: "Later—later," and leaned across to kiss her on the cheek.

Slowly over the next few days His Excellency picked up the threads of embassy life again, but it was not until the third day that he at last found time to read Rostand's report and recommendations on the leak.

". . . a series of very prolonged tea and coffee breaks . . . private calls on official lines. . . . undesirable places frequented. . . . the Habana Club should be out of bounds . . . at least one woman emotionally involved with a Veralian intelligence officer. . . . classified keys at large . . . some actually taken home . . . office hours regularly broken . . . signing in and out desirable . . . replace all locks and code books. . . . private lives no longer inviolate. . . . widespread laxity . . . security in need of severe tightening."

As the ambassador read on, astonishment gave place first to distaste and then to controlled anger. Halfway through the memo he deflected his house microphone and said to Caroline, "If Mr. Rostand is free, can you ask him to come and see me."

Rostand knew at once what it was about and braced himself for the shock. His memo had failed to observe one basic rule of traditional diplomacy, which required diffidence when the second secretary addressed the head of mission. The necessary qualifications, the circumlocutions, not to say a dash of—was it servility?—were all missing from a crisp and direct document, but he was determined not to surrender too easily. The new diplomacy would never get off the ground if it constantly gave way to pressures from the past.

The preliminary greetings between the two men revealed nothing of what they were thinking and then the ambassador said, offering Rostand a cigarette, "I see you have been very busy while I've been away."

"You did ask me to—" Rostand began and was annoyed that the remark sounded defensive.

"Carry out a preliminary inquiry," the ambassador said tapping the long memo with his blue pencil. "But this is much more than that, isn't it? After all, it's pretty full-scale—indeed, comprehensive, I should say. Now you have been very direct in your memo, so I take it you won't mind if I'm blunt in reply?"

"Not at all."

"Well then," the ambassador said, "let me not waste words. Frankly, I think you have overstepped your brief. It seems to me you have made an investigation, not a preliminary inquiry. I realize, of course, that you sometimes work on the principle that ends may justify the means—but where the private life of the embassy staff is concerned I flatly disagree with that. You seem to me to have probed too deeply into people's private lives. That's not our job. It doesn't come within our competence, thank goodness. If it's anyone's job, it's the job of the security men. A real security man is coming out from London in one week's time. He could have done what I fear I can only describe as the dirty work. And I must say I don't think we should have got mixed up in all this—"

"But, sir—"

The word burst out against all intent. Sir! Dear God, he was playing into their hands, but he obviously meant it as a sop to the Old Man's vanity and a means of softening him up. Was it any more justified for those reasons?

"As for your recommendations," the ambassador was saying, "personally I find them—I can find only one word—distasteful."

"Surely not all of them, sir?"

"Well—no—obviously too much laxity has crept in at certain points. But do you realize what would happen if we put into effect your major recommendations?"

"Oh, I know they would cause a certain amount of bad feeling."

"What they would cause is first a very well-founded resentment—then serious bad feeling and finally disruption."

"May I say," Rostand said, "I think that is somewhat exaggerated."

"You may certainly say it, but I think I know the staff here better than you do."

Rostand was thinking—I could have forecast all this word perfect, and it was certainly a risk not to change the tone of the memo, but if I am right about Rivers being the leak, then subtle questions of tone will disappear when I finally play that trump card. Combined with his past record, the Foreign Office wouldn't hesitate to back his application for the first secretaryship if he turned out to be the man who settled the embassy's worst trouble.

"I have one new piece of information which does not appear in the memo," Rostand said.

"What is that?"

"One person has come under fresh suspicion."

"Who is that?"

"Major Rivers."

It broke His Excellency's mask of urbanity and he looked startled.

"Are you really suggesting that a man with Rivers's record, who has been in the service all these years, would put his whole career at risk by leaking—or do you go so far as to say—selling information to—well—the enemy? I know it's useless these days talking about a man being an officer and a gentleman, but—" His Excellency did not trouble to finish his sentence.

"I'm not suggesting in any way that he is guilty," Rostand said hastily, "but let me just tell you the details."

When Rostand had almost finished his short sharp account His

Excellency broke in and said: "So it is all based on the suspicion that Major Rivers has gambling debts with the Habana Club."

"There is one extra piece of information. I have also found that Major Rivers is being threatened with bankruptcy by a number of creditors."

His Excellency sat a long moment in silence, staring at Rostand. Then he took out his morning cigar and trimmed and lit it.

"Still not smoking?"

"No, thank you."

"There's something I would dearly like at this stage to tell you," His Excellency began, "but it remains so confidential that until we have complete evidence it would be highly indiscreet. I will just say this. When I was in London I read a long, complicated, highly technical dossier which has accumulated about our friend Mr. Robinsohn. According to that dossier new evidence has come to light. Whether the evidence is true or false will presently appear but, if it is true, then there is more than one suspect in this case."

Rostand felt a small shudder go down his spine. Supposing after all his work, all the resistance he had aroused in H.E., it turned out that he was suspecting the wrong man. He decided to cover his tracks as far as possible.

"I can only repeat," he said, "that I have never said that Rivers *is* the man. I, too, like you, trust him. It would come as a shock if what is vaguely implied by this evidence turned out to be true. But there is one point on which I should appreciate your help."

"And that is?"

"Would you yourself interview Major Rivers. It is possible that confronted with you in person he might easily tell you more than me and clear up these suspicions."

"Certainly not," His Excellency said. "I simply do not want to get involved. Moreover, I think the obvious course of action now is to wait until the new security man arrives—and hand over to him—your—" he hesitated on the word to give it the right note of distaste—"dossier."

Late that night a weary ambassador left his study, took the lift to the top floor, and as he walked past Robinsohn's door saw the light still showing underneath. Three steps later he stopped and turned back. He had not seen Robinsohn since his return, and now with the new briefing from the Foreign Office the man had assumed a quite different significance. He glanced at his watch but could not make out the time in the dim nightlight of the corridor. Perhaps it was too late. He listened outside Robinsohn's door for a moment and hearing no sound walked on to his own bedroom to find Penelope already in bed reading Proust's *À la Recherche du Temps Perdu*.

"I wish you wouldn't overdo it," she said, as he came in the door. "It's nearly eleven o'clock."

As he went slowly through the ritual of dismantling his official image, he said: "Have you seen much of Robinsohn?"

"Yes," she said, "quite a bit."

"How is he?"

"Not very well."

The ambassador found the process of removing the tie, the handkerchief, the shirt, and cummerbund more depressing than the early morning resurrection. Tiredness came down much more easily these days, and stripping away the protective camouflage late at night emphasized the inroads of age. Staring very closely into the mirror without his reading glasses he saw every crevice of his face enlarged by the paradox of short sight, and when he moved from the bathroom back to the bedroom, his vision blurred and he could not find his watch.

"It's on the dressing table—by the Chanel," she said, watching him. "We really must get you to bed earlier—you look dreadfully tired."

He turned out the main light and she put her book aside. "Talk to me," he said. "I'm too tired to sleep."

"You've had your Doriden?"

"Yes, but it's always so damned slow in acting. I gather there's been no more trouble from Robinsohn?"

"Not really—no. In fact, I've come to like him."

It was odd the way she did not immediately admit the frequent visits to his room, but she began a slow description of his withdrawal, depression, record playing, and talk, which made the ambassador say:

"You seem to have got pretty close to him."

"I suppose in a way I have."

"Do you respect him?"

"Yes, I do."

"You don't think he's double-dealing?"

"No. I think he's a very brave man. What's more, he's a most complex character full of unexpected depths. To my astonishment I found him reading books right out of my depth. And there's one other thing—I'm not sure he didn't try to commit suicide." She gave him then a short account of the morning she had found him apparently unconscious.

"My God," the ambassador said, "that makes it all the worse."

"*What* all the worse?"

"In London Sir Richard tried to make me see him as just another adventurer very useful to M.I.5 but prepared to use thuggery to earn a living, and glamorizing his own life as a secret agent."

"He's the very opposite of all that."

"Perhaps I had better tell you," the ambassador said. "He's now under the highest suspicion in the Foreign Office. I understand that evidence has been placed in the hands of M.I.5 to show that he is in fact a double agent."

"I simply don't believe it."

"Let me put it another way—the evidence indicates that he's a double agent. M.I.5 is checking—but here's the really appalling thing. I think Sir Richard is so driven by the foreign secretary to improve our relations with Veralia, get the chromium deal through, and be ready for any upheaval that he is hoping against hope Robinsohn will turn out to be a double agent —in which case he can simply use him as a pawn to get what he wants."

"How would that work?"

"If we turn Robinsohn over to Kalogh, we could probably get at least two—and maybe three—concessions."

"But you can't do that."

"Why not?"

"He's not a double agent."

"You know better than M.I.5?"

"Yes—I do."

It was crazy, of course. She had no authority for such a statement, but that absurd conviction—I feel it in my bones—drove her to defend him.

"If it came to the point," the ambassador said, "I don't know what I would do. On principle I'm against using Robinsohn as a pawn."

"Things sound very different in the Old Firm."

"Sir Richard is a nominee of the Labour Government—he wants to step up the changes in the old traditions. You know it all better than I do —there have already been some pretty drastic revisions—they are putting the pressure on. I like it all less and less. It's no longer the old Foreign Office I used to know."

Vanessa arrived three days later and brought a kind of sparkle into the jaded atmosphere of the embassy. She was dark, petite, mini-skirted, and conveyed an external zest for living that deceived everyone except her father. He saw at once that she had to work hard to sustain her cheerfulness, but it was at least forty-eight hours before he said to her: "Something's worrying you." Automatically she denied it and immediately despised herself for being such a coward.

The first secretary from Washington, accompanied by Lord Calford from the United Nations, arrived an hour later, both en route to Russia and needing close briefing about Veralia. In the course of a normal year many guests came and went. There were times when the embassy resembled a hotel with meals, drinks, and sometimes accommodations provided for scores of people. Since Robinsohn's arrival, internal entertainment had been relatively small and Penelope relaxed, but Vanessa found herself drawn into her mother's external social life. At first the social round was

174

a glittering relief from the austerities of studying, but on the third night she realized that this represented nothing more than a painful relic of a way of life that all her university friends despised.

An official lunch and dinner for the first secretary and Lord Calford followed. At the dinner Vanessa first encountered Robinsohn. Fresh pressure from Penelope had persuaded him to try a last experiment with one more dinner party under the chandeliers in the old-fashioned dining room.

It was a still warm evening with the tall windows wide open on the night sky and the same silhouetted figure outside the main gate. Sitting between her daughter and Robinsohn, Penelope quickly became aware that he fascinated Vanessa. Robinsohn looked slightly less tired and gray, but his mood was withdrawn and he answered questions in monosyllables. Vanessa found herself apologizing for leaning across her mother to talk to him.

After dinner Lord Calford and the first secretary left for a reception at the Ministry of the Interior and the ambassador retired to his study with Hargreaves and Rostand. In the rush of picking up the backlog of work and stepping into the social round once more, this was his first chance to give them a breakdown of the new briefing he had received from London.

He made it as short and succinct as possible. One common theme ran through the details—concessions would have to be made to establish better relations with Veralia. Intelligence indicated a worsening of relations between Russia and this particular satellite, and every diplomatic stop was to be pulled to take advantage of the situation. Long-term strategy included encouraging Veralia's defection from the bloc. M.I.5 intelligence also suggested that Robinsohn's reports about Veralia were substantially accurate. Ominous reverberations had now been detected in the inner circles of the present government.

The first details of a grand design to be coordinated by all Western embassies in Veralia began with clinching at any cost the chromium deal, finding and cultivating those elements that might come to the top in any upheaval, and making the requested credits certain if a Yugoslavian situation did develop. The long-term final goal was to facilitate in every way any possible new defection from the Eastern bloc. And Robinsohn—what was his position in all these remotely splendid diplomatic structures? Much more, it appeared, than His Excellency could really credit.

"It seems," he explained to Hargreaves and Rostand, "that they suspect him of being a double agent. I was instructed to refrain from organizing any further escape attempts on his behalf until M.I.5 has confirmed or denied a number of reports. But in some prolonged interviews with Sir Richard it seemed to me that if a situation arose in which the evidence was fifty percent for and fifty percent against—and that from all the details seemed very likely—then they did not intend to give him the benefit of the doubt. Sir Richard constantly quoted from an M.I.5 memo which said, roughly, 'We cannot afford to have any serious doubts about any one of our agents. Dubious agents must be suspended or abandoned.'

"Now—here comes the really highly confidential—and to me surprising—part. I felt very strongly that Sir Richard did in fact actively hope that such a situation would arise because then he would be justified in handing Robinsohn over to Veralia—and this would prime the pump for all future negotiations. So Robinsohn ceases to be a human being or an agent and becomes a diplomatic pump primer. How do you react to that, Franklin?"

Hargreaves shifted uneasily in his chair. "I think, Your Excellency," he said, "we would probably see eye to eye on this. I wouldn't like to be responsible for handing him over to the tender mercies of the ABVO unless we had conclusive evidence that he was a double agent. On the other hand, an instruction is an instruction."

His Excellency nodded and turned to Rostand.

"Personally," Rostand said, "I would agree with that, but professionally—if the possibility of shifting the balance of power really depends on surrendering a highly suspect Robinsohn—"

"But does it?" His Excellency interrupted. "Doesn't that strike you as a pretty extravagant suggestion?"

"It certainly does. Even as a sweetener to reopen negotiations there are, after all, other possible sweeteners."

"Exactly," His Excellency said. "Why is there so much insistence on exaggerating Robinsohn's importance everywhere?"

"Perhaps," Rostand said, "we are being used by M.I.5 to do their dirty work for them—and get rid of him."

"That's one possibility. There are others."

His Excellency refused to be drawn on to other possibilities until twenty minutes later Rostand excused himself and left. Then at last His Excellency turned to Hargreaves and said: "I didn't want to speak in front of Paul—he's a good fellow, but I know he sympathizes with Sir Richard's view. You see—the fact of the matter is, I did pick up a rumor in London that Sir Richard is thinking of abandoning the Foreign Service and going into politics. He obviously needs a safe seat at his time of life. Perhaps if he fulfills the foreign secretary's ambition to drive another wedge into the Warsaw Pact, he might be offered it. After all, the foreign secretary could persuade the Parliamentary Labour Party, the P.L.P. could persuade the secretary of the Party, and the secretary, the local selection committee."

"So Robinsohn is to be sacrificed to Sir Richard's safe seat?" Hargreaves said.

"Who can say?" His Excellency said. "Who can ever say where the chain of cause and effect begins and ends? It becomes a major philosophic problem. But I quite frankly do not want to be a party to giving Sir

176

Richard a safe seat—at such a price—if that is in fact what really lies behind all this."

"I've had a bit of a shock," Penelope said to Vanessa. "I didn't realize what the Bahamas trip cost—and Raoul's illness—and my contribution to the birthday party—and that ghastly American associate professor in London absconding with six months' rent owing. I've got a huge overdraft, darling."

"Oh, dear, Mummy—does that mean—"

"Now don't let's panic. There are two ways of handling this—either I must get a loan elsewhere or we had better tell your father."

"Not that. It wouldn't work. Now I'm here and see him again I realize it simply wouldn't work. I don't feel up to a fight—I was sick again this morning."

Vanessa sat in her nightdress on the bed of the third guest room looking suddenly very young and helpless, all her sophistication drained away.

Penelope went over to her and put her arm round her. "I'm sorry, darling," she said, "you're having a nasty time. But don't worry—we'll cope."

Robinsohn lay naked on his bed, trying to read the *A.B.C. of Relativity* by Bertrand Russell, but his attention constantly wandered and at last he was driven to give free rein to the same persistent question which never really left his mind—how could he break out of this slowly suffocating mausoleum and escape the inevitable daily encounters with a woman whose presence he both desired and feared.

Ten minutes later, slipping on the borrowed dressing gown, he went into the corridor and moved toward the second bathroom. As he approached it he heard sounds of someone—retching and retching—and paused with his hand on the handle. The sounds came from the lavatory next door to the bathroom and he slipped into the bathroom as the retching continued—long agonized upheavals followed by spewing sickness. Was it a man or a woman? Could it be Mrs. Malvern?—was she ill—or was it her daughter, and if so, didn't such persistent retching indicate one possibility among several others?

As he came out of the bathroom to return to his room, Vanessa emerged from the lavatory. She looked gray green and deeply miserable.

"Are you all right?" he said.

"Don't come near me," she said, "I smell," and with that she dashed into the bathroom and locked the door.

He returned to his room, lay back on the bed again, and wondered what a man like His Excellency would do with a pregnant teenage daughter.

177

Ten minutes later, fully clothed, he set off down the corridor again only to confront Vanessa just leaving the bathroom.

"Is there anything I can do?" he said.

"I don't think so," she said, "unless you have some aspirins."

"Of course," he said and led the way back to his room. As she hesitated in the doorway and saw the chaos that had once more overwhelmed the room, unexpectedly she laughed.

"Why do you laugh?" he said, entering and rummaging through one of the bureau drawers.

"It reminds me so much of our room," she said.

"Our room?"

"Ronald's and mine."

"Who's Ronald?"

"My boy friend."

"So you live in chaos too."

"Some people would call it chaos. I like it."

"Your mother doesn't."

"I know too well."

He came over to her with a tape of aspirins. "There you are," he said. "You have some trouble?"

"Yes, I do," she said.

"In that case," he said, "both of us can be said to be in trouble."

"Oh, mine's nothing like yours."

"If I read the signs aright," he said, "it would be pretty remarkable if it were."

She smiled wanly. "You know—don't you? But please, please don't say anything to Father."

"Young lady," Robinsohn said, "Your father has a bedroom at the end of this corridor. If he doesn't know by now, I'd be amazed."

"I suppose so," she said glumly.

"Are you going to marry him?"

"Good God—no!"

The vehemence did not surprise him.

"Of course marriage is a major crime in your calendar?"

"We're certainly not so daft as to get married for the sake of some damn silly thing called respectability."

"You look pretty respectable."

"Our set regards that word as an insult."

"I didn't mean it that way."

"We think the family as an institution is doomed."

She said it like a parrot repeating the first of ten commandments.

"Are you in favor of women's liberation?"

"Very much."

"I too believe," he said, "that all women should have the right to go down the mines."

She colored and bridled.

"It's not funny. We've been second-class citizens for centuries," she said, repeating the second commandment.

"I'm a male feminist," he said. "There's a beautiful young woman trying to break out from inside me."

She strode to the door saying, "You're making fun of me." She left him then, slamming the door behind her.

Over breakfast the next morning Mrs. Malvern said to her husband: "There's something I have to tell you about Vanessa."

His Excellency groaned audibly and said, "Don't worry—I know."

"Did she tell you?"

"Not in so many words. I guessed. How many months is it?"

"Two."

"And of course she has come here to persuade me to pay for an abortion?"

"Not quite, darling. No, she's come to try to explain to you—"

"That she doesn't believe in marriage, she doesn't want children, she doesn't believe in bourgeois values, the family is a tiresome anachronism, and everything will go up in smoke as soon as she gets a chance to apply the match. Meanwhile will I please sign the check to pay a capitalist abortionist to break the law because of her principles."

"It's not like that at all. Underneath all this lofty protest stuff she's just a frightened young girl asking for help out of an age-old difficulty."

"Penelope—you know what I feel—I don't have to repeat it all to you. I will not be a party to an abortion on my own daughter."

"So you want a seventeen-year-old child to be converted into an unmarried mother because of your principles?"

"She should have the child and get it adopted—that's the obvious way out."

"Go through nine months of pregnancy, give birth to an unwanted human being, find herself too attached to it to part with it, and be ruined for the rest of her life—that's what your principle means in practice."

"If the adoption is arranged before the birth, the problem doesn't arise."

"Think of all those months of pregnancy—think what will happen to her studies—think what scars it will leave."

"Scars come from *having* abortions, not avoiding them."

"So it is commonly assumed—but so many crazy things are commonly assumed. Think of the child itself. Illegitimacy still matters, and who knows whose hands it will fall into. If she keeps it, the child will be brought up fatherless under conditions of terrible strain. If it's adopted, the whole question of identity is put in pawn. I don't think we should be a party to allowing a child to be born in such circumstances."

"And I will not be a party to destroying a human being."

"At this stage it's an accumulation of cells without identity."

"At two months the heart is already beating. Think what havoc the abortionist's dilators would wreak with that—think of piercing an embryo heart and exploding it—think of—"

Penelope put her hands over her ears. "Oh, for God's sake, stop," she said. "You make a perfectly sensible miscarriage sound like butchery."

"Because it is not a miscarriage."

"Nature spontaneously miscarries one child in four in the first two months—"

"Because they are deformed."

"Not all of them."

He sighed heavily and fell silent. Then he said: "Let's talk later. I have to go down to the office now, but you can tell Vanessa from me I want nothing to do with abortions."

"You know what you're suffering from?" Penelope said.

"Yes, I know."

"Hardening of the mental arteries."

"Spiritual, not mental."

He had half risen to leave the table but suddenly he slumped back into his chair again and sat there silent for a long minute. When he spoke again his voice was heavily reflective: "Does it occur to you, Penelope, that what I am really suffering from is a combination of attacks on my way of life such as threaten to bring it down in ruins? My son has abandoned his studies and become a drifter, my daughter is pregnant by a boy she doesn't want to marry, my wife is an advocate of indiscriminate abortion, Sir Richard in the Foreign Office is expecting me to sell a man because it is expedient for his career, and the very foundations of diplomatic ethics have been so eroded that it is a world in which I no longer have a place."

She came to her feet at once and went round to kiss his cheek. "I'm sorry, darling. I didn't mean to upset you—and you are having a terrible time—one way and another—and I do not believe in abortion on principle —it's simply that in this situation it seems—"

"Expedient," he interrupted. "That's the ethic everyone lives by nowadays. Expediency."

He came to his feet and brushed past his wife. "You're the last person I expected to adopt that creed," he said and left the dining room.

"So you've got rid of Christianity?"

"Well, it's obviously outdated, isn't it?"

"And Christian marriage?"

180

"That's breaking down too."

"And the family?"

"Doesn't really work any longer."

"What is to take its place?"

"We shall have communes."

"Group marriage in fact."

"Not marriage—just group."

"And the children will have five fathers and five mothers."

"No—but they will be shared."

"Shouldn't you in that case *join* one of these communes?"

"We are thinking of it."

"Well, it had better be pretty quick, hadn't it?"

"Why do you say that?"

"Well, there is your own child to consider."

She said stonily, "I'm not going to have it."

"Vanessa, let me make an appeal to you. I will help you all along the line—I will arrange the nursing home, the doctor, the adoption, pay for everything—and even continue loving you if—"

"It's not on," she interrupted. "I do not want the child."

"And how do you propose paying for the abortion?"

"I shall go to the back streets if necessary."

"Is that a threat?"

"No—it may become a fact."

"You are trying to blackmail me."

"If that is the only way to get the money—I don't think I should mind."

His Excellency came to his six feet one inch, towering over his petite daughter and snapped: "You go too far. It's bad enough to get pregnant, and talk of abortion—but to openly embrace blackmail. . . . Now I have a very busy day ahead of me. I must ask you to leave."

"Well, darling, that was pretty mad, wasn't it. Even I wouldn't use blackmail to get my way."

"But it wasn't blackmail, Mummy. It's the simple truth. I shall have to get it done somewhere whatever happens."

Her voice became shrill with emotion. "I've got to get rid of this damned parasite."

"Good God—I don't think you should speak of it like that."

"It—it—that's all *it* is, isn't it. Why get all sentimental about it?"

"Now listen, darling, if you go on talking that way you'll just about alienate everyone—including me."

"I don't care. I don't care anymore."

She was suddenly stamping about her bedroom, her face all puckered up, tears desperately held back in her eyes.

"I've got to get something done—now. It's growing every day. I feel it." The tears ran down her cheeks and Mrs. Malvern walked over to her and tried to take her in her arms but she tore herself away, stamped her foot again, and said: "Don't get all sentimental with me—I must stop crying."

"All right, darling. I'll speak to him again. Don't worry, I'll persuade him. Now just relax—and sit down."

"What's the use of relaxing? No one seems to understand me."

"A few days won't make any difference."

"But they will—they will. Oh, God, I'll go and see Mr. Robinsohn—it's easier to talk to strangers."

". . . So what would you do?"

"Borrow the money elsewhere."

"There isn't any elsewhere."

"When do you get the next chunk of grant?"

"In about a month."

"Buy the abortion with it—and go on public relief."

"But another—month—you don't understand—at three months it's dangerous."

"It's not that much different from two."

"You believe I should have this abortion, don't you?"

"Of course."

"Perhaps Daddy would listen to you."

Robinsohn laughed wryly. "I shouldn't mention my name in that connection if I were you."

"This is where men have the advantage. They never have to face an abortion."

"Doesn't that undermine unisex?"

"A woman can still have a masculine mind."

"And a man a feminine one."

"If you stick to the old-fashioned meanings of the words. We've washed them out. Your *sex* doesn't give you one or the other. Did you know that male and female hormones don't enter the brain?"

"My God—you talk like a doctor."

"We've read it all up. We have to know our stuff."

"I must say I've known some dangerously strong-minded women."

"Why dangerously?"

"They get themselves into such a fix."

"I don't understand."

"If you think the equality bargain through—doesn't it mean you start filling in the tax forms—fighting wars—paying alimony—paying for lunch? Would you like all that?"

182

"We wouldn't have to pay *for* anyone—we'd simply pay for our-selves."

"Like now," he said, and she was so furious at being outwitted that tears came into her eyes and she was on the point of storming out of the room again, when he stopped her.

They talked on then at length and she found this man steadily more sympathetic. The anarchist vacuum of values in which he lived had meeting points with the "philosophy" of her student friends: men and women to him were not members of different sexes with characteristics conditioned by their sex but simply individuals to be judged by their behavior. He shared her disillusion with "society," and was one of the few adults she had ever met who had broken out of a job, a family, and just about every convention to follow his own lead. It was when she learned that he too believed that certain extreme situations justified the use of violence that she eagerly asked him whether he had in fact ever used it. He watched the flushed face and the glowing eyes and evaded the question, but she came back to it again and again. He reflected on the absurd anomaly as he talked. Vicariously the idea of using violence produced an almost sexual excitement in this young woman, but he knew quite well that the sight of a broken head gushing blood would horrify her.

"You have never seen what bullet wounds do to a man," he said.

"No," she said breathlessly.

"Perhaps you'd have a different view of violence if you had."

"When did you see that?" she pressed him, undismayed.

"I once shot a man myself."

A new wave of excitement went across her face. "You actually shot a man?"

"Yes."

"And did he—"

"For God's sake," he interrupted, "either you're a very morbid young woman or you're a sadist."

"I'm neither," she snapped, and then out came the third commandment, word perfect: "I simply believe that the worst forms of oppression can only be overthrown by violence."

"Like your father's oppression."

"His is not worth worrying about."

She was still breathlessly hanging on the thrill of his ability to shoot a man and now with an indrawn breath she said huskily, "Have you ever killed a man?"

"I think," Robinsohn said, "this conversation has gone far enough. Why don't you try talking to your father yourself again. He's a civilized man. He'll relent in the end."

"What makes you think that?"

"He's got no choice, has he? He can't let you go to a back-street abortionist."

"Would *you* allow it?"

"You're not my daughter."

"And if I were?"

He went over to where she sat, took her by the hand, and made a gesture of pulling her to her feet. "I really must ask you to go now," he said.

"Can I come back?" she said.

"Not today—some other day."

CHAPTER 16

The following morning at nine o'clock, one of the cipher clerks gave Caroline the decoded telegram marked Top Priority and she took it through the green baize door and placed it on top of a pile of documents at the center of His Excellency's desk. Five minutes later he came striding into his office, sat down and began reading the telegram:

"A confidential report received from M.I.5 this morning (May 21st 43562 [1] [A.2]) now makes necessary a reversal of our policy with Mr. Robinsohn on the grounds that sufficient evidence has accumulated to question his integrity as an agent in the service of H.M. Intelligence. It appears that two corroborative witnesses have come forward with statements that compromise his position and suggest that contacts with underground movements in Veralia originally assumed to be the result of clever infiltration by Mr. Robinsohn can now be read as reaching beyond infiltration toward cooperation with those movements. We have to bear in mind that on one previous occasion information filed by Robinsohn in his Dec. 1956 report (456 [S] r2) turned out to be information deliberately planted by the Russian Government. On that occasion we gave him the benefit of the doubt and assumed that he had been the innocent victim of such planting, but in the light of one corroborative witness whose testimony was recent (May 10) we now realize that he could once again easily have been the willing tool of the Russian Government. We have also to take into account the fact that the leaks from the embassy, which coincided with his arrival in the embassy, have continued despite the discovery and removal of the bugging device and no satisfactory explanation has yet been found.

"Moreover, we have new evidence to show that the civil charges that the Veralian Government desires to bring against him could in fact be sustained in a court of law and our international legal advisers find this new evidence highly embarrassing."

185

The telegram ran on for two more complicated paragraphs interlocking and interpreting the vital new evidence. Then came the phrase which His Excellency had anticipated from the outset but hoped against hope would not occur: "In the circumstances we have no alternative but to rescind the asylum granted to Mr. Robinsohn and to instruct you to release him to face the civil charges which the Veralian Government desires to bring against him. . . ."

His Excellency lit his morning cigar and turned mechanically through the remaining pile of documents. Then he came back to the telegram and read certain phrases with concentrated care. . . .

"It *appears* that . . . *can now be read as* . . . *could easily have been* . . . never found a *satisfactory explanation* . . . ." Every one of those phrases had an inbuilt uncertainty which qualified everything preceding and following it. Rescrutinizing the whole memo, His Excellency searched for a clear-cut indictment of Robinsohn in vain, but the aura of suspicion created was thick. The question remained—if suspicion and repeated suspicion justified M.I.5 in dealing ruthlessly with him, did it also give the same mandate to the Foreign Office, or were they acting as executioners for M.I.5?

Executioners . . . the word might sound extravagant but came close to the literal truth. What would happen to Robinsohn if he came under Kalogh's—care—was as predictable as placing a Jew in the hands of the Gestapo.

So here it was at last—the final confrontation. The whole telegram smelled of Machiavellian expediency, but what real evidence had he to show that their suspicions were false and the main burden of the telegram an ingenious political maneuver? Nothing more than familiarity with the man over many weeks, Robinsohn's own evidence, and the opinion of three highly discerning people who had been thrown into contact with him —not least Penelope. That was the factual side of the question. As to the moral. . . . Objecting to this instruction on moral grounds led into a forest of complexities. Was this man in the position of someone brought before the civil courts who should be given the benefit of any doubt that existed, or did the whole code change when the security of the state was at stake, no actual charge had been brought, and the person involved was an espionage agent? Was the sacrifice of one individual in the interests of a network of diplomacy justified or did the accumulation of suspicion, no matter how massive, remain simply suspicion on which no such action could be justified? Sitting back in his chair His Excellency drew heavily on his cigar and the image recurred to him of a man he had once had to interrogate during the war, a man just released from Dachau. The ghoulish death's-head with its missing teeth and hoarse voice, the scarecrow figure and halting speech was the extreme end of a line that began in those concrete dungeons below the Ministry of Security where less extreme

186

methods reduced political criminals to waxwork puppets mouthing false confessions with their will to resist broken. . . . Did anything justify exposing a man to such a fate? Could even the worst suspicion, if it remained simply suspicion, condemn Robinsohn to the ABVO? The answer was obvious. If leaving him at large exposed a series of agents and revolutionaries to the same fate that now threatened him, the answer was clear —but that omitted the special dimensions distinguishing this particular case. The Foreign Office desperately needed a scapegoat to set negotiations moving again with Kalogh, and Sir Richard needed a safe political seat.

His Excellency just checked an impulse to tear the telegram in two. Momentarily it all smelled of more than expediency. It stank of corruption.

Robinsohn came loping into His Excellency's office, quiet and watchful, shook hands distantly, took the proferred chair, and refused a cigarette. When H.E. inquired after his health, he simply shrugged his shoulders. His Excellency noticed how different he was from the man who had come clamoring on the gate all those weeks—it must be months—ago. The body thinner, the clothes hanging loosely, the eyes dulled, but above all a new cadaverous quality in the face from which a small shock came because it was almost as if the early stages of Dachau emaciation had begun to overtake him. The face, to His Excellency, already had an inbuilt accusation. It looked out from its waxen pallor, one year ahead in time. Presently His Excellency said: "I have received a telegram this morning—I thought I should talk to you about it."

Robinsohn said nothing.

"These suspicions over your precise role and activities seem to persist."

Robinsohn remained silent.

"You say nothing," His Excellency said. "Would you be prepared to comment?"

"It's all been said before. Repeating it becomes boring."

"Unfortunately," His Excellency said, "the situation has now taken a different turn."

Robinsohn said nothing.

"Supposing," His Excellency said, "I asked you what proof you could give us that your activities have been solely in the interests of—so to say —H.M. Government?"

"But they haven't," Robinsohn said.

His Excellency was disconcerted. "You mean," he began.

Robinsohn interrupted, "They have been in my interests too."

"Of course," His Excellency said, "but I need something more than your own asseverations to reply to this telegram."

"The man they shot down would have given it to you."

"There must be others you contacted in the Grundel cell."

"Yes, but I am locked up here."

"Let me elaborate a little. It seems that two corroborative witnesses have reaffirmed the suspicions which Control has developed about your integrity."

"Suspicion is our occupational hazard."

"You see nothing unusual in this?"

"Nothing."

"I didn't quite realize," His Excellency said, "that the situation was so commonplace."

Another detail stressing exploitation seemed to fall into place. If it were so commonplace, what was all the fuss about?

"I simply felt I would be in a better position to rebut these—er—witnesses if we could put forward some independent witnesses of our own," the ambassador continued.

"They would never respond."

"Even if you wrote a note in your own hand?"

"They don't know my own hand. . . . But tell me, why are you taking all this trouble about me?"

His Excellency tapped the ash from his cigar. "A quite new instruction was conveyed in this telegram." He picked up the telegram and read: "In the circumstances we have no alternative but to rescind the asylum granted to Mr. Robinsohn and to instruct you to release him to face the civil charges which the Veralian Government desires to bring against him."

Robinsohn showed no reaction whatever.

"Have you nothing to say to that?" His Excellency said.

"What's the use? I knew I would become expendable. Everyone does. It's just a bit sooner than I expected."

"You still deny being a double agent."

"Of course."

"And you have no means of proving that?"

"No."

"You have nothing else to say?"

Robinsohn stirred and leaned forward, staring straight across the desk into His Excellency's eyes. "Yes—there is something else—I think your conscience will never let you carry out that instruction."

"Why do you say that?"

"Because you believe what I say. You believe I'm a genuine agent. And you *know* you would be passing an innocent man into the hands of the ABVO. You also know—too well—what that would mean."

It was His Excellency's turn to fall silent. He moved uneasily in his chair and found himself looking over Robinsohn's shoulder. "As you know, it isn't a straight question of shooting," Robinsohn continued. "You know the means they would use to extract all the information I possess and a great deal more that I don't. I know you. I have come to respect you. You are different from the men who run M.I.5. I don't think you would be able to live down sacrificing another human being to that kind of death."

His Excellency remained silent.

"There's one other thing—a big thing," Robinsohn went on. "Do you really believe that my arrival here—asking for asylum—two attempts to escape—the way they were discovered—the imprisonment in here—and consistent denials are all part of a plot laid on by the ABVO? It's crazy. You clearly don't believe that. And nor does Control or the Foreign Office or any of those bureaucratic bastards. There must be factors hidden behind this that I don't know about. But *you* must know. Don't you think you have a responsibility to tell me what those factors are?"

His Excellency stirred himself. "It is not within my competence," he said.

"So you admit there are other factors?"

"I have no comment."

"If I'm a double agent why does Kalogh scream to get his hands on me?"

"You might not be a double agent for Veralia."

"Who else?"

"I don't know."

"Perhaps you think it's Russia."

"Why is Kalogh—as you put it—screaming to get his hands on you?"

"Because he's afraid I shall jump the gun on a piece of information about him which could ruin him."

'What piece of information?"

"I can't tell you—yet."

Robinsohn swung to his feet and now a concentrated malevolence distorted his face again as he strode over to the door. "Don't imagine," he said as he opened it, "that I intend to fall into the hands of the ABVO. No one is going to hand me over. I shall make my own arrangements."

"What do you mean by that?" His Excellency said.

"You know damn well what I mean," Robinsohn said, and swung through the door.

Yes—it was obvious what he meant and equally obvious that it of-fered a solution to H.E.'s dilemma. He could literally take no more notice of him: turn a·blind eye to anything that happened for the next forty-eight hours, plead that he knew nothing of Robinsohn's intention to escape. But wasn't that committing the very crime of which he complained? Wasn't that making the end justify the means? Didn't that involve deceiving Sir Richard, the Foreign Office, and M.I.5 by the very method they themselves used—expediency? What did that matter if it preserved another human being from slow death by—could it possibly be anything so extreme as torture?—or was that just the melodramatic rhetoric of an oversensitive conscience? What place, in any case, did all these fine scruples have in the modern world of modern diplomacy?

Even more complicated, under torture Robinsohn might—if he were nothing more than a British agent—reveal damaging information to Kalogh—which was yet another reason for not voluntarily surrendering him.

And supposing among all these complexities Sir Richard's suspicions proved to be true and Robinsohn did turn out to be a double agent.

Working steadily through the routine of the day, the complexities of the problem persisted at the back of His Excellency's mind but ten hours later as he uneasily took the lift to his bedroom, the clash became more intense.

As he entered, Penelope was sitting at her dressing table trying to deal with a minute pimple on one nostril. Still with her nose twisted between thumb and forefinger she saw his reflection in the mirror and said very nasally: "You look worse than ever. What on earth has happened?"

As he slowly took the image to pieces, he gave her a quick résumé of his talk with Robinsohn.

"Well, that's simple, isn't it?" she said. "There's no question about it."

"Why do you say that?"

"You must give Robinsohn a chance."

"And supposing he is a very clever double agent who has deceived us all in here—think what havoc he might cause—and think how much he knows about the working of this place now."

It was on the tip of her tongue to say, I don't think this place matters much, but instead she said: "They admit they don't really know—they admit reasonable doubt—no English court of law would convict him. You must give him the benefit of the doubt."

"Must?"

"Yes—must."

"You seem very determined to help him."

"I am. I've come to know him much better. I respect him. He's a worthwhile person, and you simply can't just hand over a man like that to the ABVO."

"And my principles?"

She wanted to say, I hate you when you sound so smug, but instead she said, "A temporary compromise."

"You believe in expediency—just like Sir Richard. He's using it at one end—you want me to use it at the other."

"I believe that every principle is open to qualification in special cases."

"Which constitutes expediency."

"Or diplomacy. Think of all those broken treaties—think of our undertaking to Czechoslovakia before the war—think of Russia and the Hitler pact—think of England and the Asian passports—it permeates the whole world of diplomacy. How can you go on talking as if Boy Scouts' honor prevailed in a world like that?"

"You put their case word perfect."

"Their case—whose?"

"Sir Richard's—M.I.5's. Don't you see the savagely ironic mess we're in?"

She put down her hand mirror and powder puff, swung round on the gilt stool and said: "Really—after all these years you still confuse private and professional ethics—you still refuse to adjust—you are part of the modern world—and refuse to accept it. Why go on tormenting yourself?"

"I cannot escape as easily as you can."

"Well, let me tell you something. If you hand that man over to the ABVO I can't be responsible for what it will do to my opinion of you."

"What on earth does that mean?"

"I mean that I shall lose my respect for you."

"You make it sound as if—"

"I couldn't forgive you if you sacrificed him," she interrupted.

"Sacrificed! What an extravagant word. My God— there's no end to this man, is there? He disturbs the whole embassy, he upsets half the staff, he causes a conspiracy in London—and now he's coming between us."

As Penelope stripped off her dressing gown and put on a flimsy night-dress she said, "Do you remember the argument we had six months ago about values?"

"Which argument?"

"When you admitted the case for plural values."

"Yes—I remember."

"You also admitted that no *one* code was absolutely better than *all* the others."

"Not quite. I said every man must stick to his own code and that made his absolute for him."

"So Sir Richard is right in sticking to his?"

"It may be right for him. It's not for me."

"Now you're in danger of contradicting yourself. If it's right for you to stick to your code in a world of plural values, why shouldn't Sir Richard be equally right to stick to his?"

"Some codes have more moral content than others."

"There's no means of measuring morals."

"You're too clever for me, Penelope. But there's a point where this kind of Jesuitry has to stop. One has to make a choice—an irrational choice—an act of faith. It becomes a simple matter in the end. And clearly my choice is different from yours."

"Meaning mine is inferior."

"I did not say that."

"Well, let me be quite clear about this. Whether it's an act of faith or whatever you like to call it—if you hand Robinsohn over to the ABVO, I shall—what's the use of boggling at the word?—despise you."

They were silent after that and when they finally went to bed both found it very difficult to sleep.

The telephone rang sharply, and as a startled H.E. reached out a fumbling hand in the darkness, he wondered who in heaven's name would have the audacity to disturb him at that hour of night. Thompson's voice said: "I'm terribly sorry to disturb you, sir, but Mr. Hargreaves said I should ring you because something terrible has happened."

His Excellency was awake and alert at once. "Well—what is it, Thompson?"

"Major Rivers, sir—he's shot himself."

"Shot himself?"

"Yes, sir."

"Good God! All right, Thompson, I'll be down in five minutes."

"What is it?" Penelope said, coming out of a deep sleep.

"Nothing," His Excellency said. "You go on sleeping—I'll be back."

"Don't treat me like a child," she muttered, only half awake.

"I'll be back," he said, and pulling on dressing gown and slippers, he was about to hurry down the corridor to the lift when he stopped in front of the mirror. Switching on the dressing table light, he glanced first at his watch—three A.M.—and then peered into the mirror. Taking up his brush, he brushed his hair back, tidied his pajama jacket, and took out his glasses. What in God's name could this mean? Shot himself? Rivers, of all people—a stable, rather dull, well-adjusted man. Was it serious? An accident—a flesh wound—or—

Thompson met him on the ground floor at the lift gate. "I'm sorry," he began again, but His Excellency cut him short. "Where is he?"

"In his office, sir."

They hurried down the corridor and a tense, white-faced Hargreaves opened the door of Rivers's office as they approached. "It's very messy, I'm afraid," he said and looked as if he were about to vomit.

Rivers was still sitting in his chair but his head flopped back as if the neck were broken, with part of the back of the head torn away and blood and brains still seeping down his neck, collar, shoulders, and chair to make a steadily widening pool on the floor.

"I've phoned for a doctor," Hargreaves said, "but he's dead."

A service revolver lay underneath the chair where it had fallen as death released his grasp on it—or so H.E. at once assumed.

"There's a letter," Hargreaves said, handing His Excellency an envelope. "It's addressed to you."

"Perhaps we had better try and clean things up a bit," Hargreaves added to Thompson.

192

"I'll get some towels from the lavatory," Thompson said as the ambassador tore open the envelope and read swiftly:

"Dear H.E.,

"I cannot go on any longer carrying this nightmare load of fear and guilt and above all this despising myself and all that I am. It's been seven years now and the strain has grown every year.

"You see, I am the guilty man, I am the leak from the embassy. I have been guilty of selling information to Dabrowski, but I never sold him much. Most of it was trivial, worthless stuff, except perhaps for the time when I told him the details of Robinsohn's escape attempt. That was unforgivable, that might have led to Robinsohn's death and I can't tell you how glad I was when he came safely back into the embassy. But let me try and explain and then perhaps you might—if not understand—see things in a different light. I cannot hope to justify myself—no one could do that in my position—but let me try to explain.

"My life has been one long inadequacy. I was inadequate at school and just crept by. I was inadequate at Sandhurst and just scraped through. I was inadequate at marriage and it collapsed. I was inadequate at sex—and for a reason which no one knew—I have fought a homosexual impulse all my life and am proud at least that I never succumbed to that. But at what a cost. I took to drink first of all and then to gambling. I constantly deluded myself with the idea that I would win a fortune and get myself out of reach of any of these troubles. I became a compulsive gambler, and that is where Dabrowski trapped me. He offered me gambling facilities and credit on a scale I had never been able to get in England.

"I got so heavily into debt that they not only threatened to disclose everything to you but swore that they could prove homosexual acts which I had unwittingly carried out while drunk. All I had to do was to feed them an occasional piece of confidential information and nothing would happen. In the beginning I fed them trivialities to stall them off, but the pressure slowly increased for bigger and better information and then at last, after a whole year, I gave them something more worthwhile. I owed them £8,000. It was overwhelming. They showed me photographs of myself in compromising situations. Those photographs were faked. They never happened. But in the last few weeks the pressures have increased for more and better information. I could not go on. I drank and drank. There were times in the middle of the night of near collapse.

"But now it's all over. Now the shame of everything I've done overwhelms me and I want to destroy the dirty little cringing traitor

193

I have become. Don't worry about my wife and children—I wrote to them yesterday.

"It remains to say—perhaps you might have it in your heart to find some extenuating evidence in all this. I was glad to serve under you in your embassy. You seemed to me a fine man. It made more horrible everything I did. But it will all be destroyed by the time you read this and I am glad it will be dead—dead—dead. How is it with the happy dead?

"Theodore Jackson Rivers"

Suddenly H.E. broke away from the letter. "Cancel the doctor," he said. "I don't want it known we've had a suicide. And if he comes, stall him off. Now I wonder if we can try to deal with—" he hesitated on the word and left the sentence unfinished. It took them a whole hour to clean up the room and lay out Rivers's body, and almost as they finished, Hargreaves stuffed his handkerchief into his mouth, muttering, "It's the smell —the smell—" and just prevented himself from being sick.

One hour later he discovered an incongruous element of relief far back in his mind. As he tried to sleep, he at last identified it. Rivers's death would at least free Pamela from any complicity in the leaks, and that brought the first secretaryship in Washington closer.

Rivers's body was locked away in one of the men's cloakrooms, but rumor ran swiftly around the embassy the next morning despite all attempts to stop it.

One man alone had a heavily qualified sense of guilt at what had happened—Rostand—and he carefully avoided meeting H.E. for the greater part of the day. A deep-laid sense that his inquiries might have played an insidious part in hounding this man to suicide troubled him so much that he invented excuses to be out of the embassy the whole morning and walked the streets trying to readjust himself to the thought of Rivers—dead.

Late in the afternoon H.E. issued an official memo through Caroline which said that Major Rivers had suffered a heart attack and died, but even after that the presence of a body subdued the normal noise and bustle of the embassy.

At four o'clock, behind the green baize door of his office, H.E. wrestled with the second draft of a top-priority telegram to London, the first one of which he had dictated to Caroline.

"Almost simultaneously with receiving your telegram of the 14 inst. (No. 43236) a tragic event occurred in the embassy that had

194

such direct relevance to its contents that we have for the immediate future suspended any action on your instruction.

"Major Rivers shot himself through the head in an unmistakable suicide and left a note which clearly identified him as the source of the many leaks which have troubled the embassy over the past few months. All the documents relating to his death are being forwarded immediately for your consideration and for the information of his next of kin.

"A brief résumé of his evidence includes the basic fact that his gambling debts amounted to £8,000 and he was under blackmailing pressure to disclose more and more information to prevent this fact from being reported to this office. Far more complicated matters were the early breeding ground of the unfortunate position in which Major Rivers found himself. . . ."

Two more paragraphs recapitulating details from Rivers's letter were followed by a crucial paragraph, the formulation of which H.E. now revised. The final version read:

"In the circumstances, one of the main counts which has given rise to so much suspicion around the person of Mr. Robinsohn is now shown to have no connection whatever with his case. Since he is thus completely cleared of any complicity in the leaks that have occurred, I felt justified in suspending further action until this new and very important fact was considered by you and your colleagues. I await your instructions in the light of the new evidence. . . ."

Within twenty-four hours an unequivocal answer came back from London which simply intensified H.E.'s dilemma:

"We deeply regret the incident that has taken place and await the full details before communicating with Major Rivers's next-of-kin, but we feel you overemphasize the importance of his 'confession' in relation to Mr. Robinsohn. There is no evidence to show that the several very different kinds of leaks all emanated exclusively from Major Rivers and it does not in any way qualify the independent report of M.I.5 which concerns far more compromising matters external to the special area of the embassy itself.

"We therefore consider that any qualification of the instruction given in our telegram of 14th instant is not justified and we would ask you to proceed with that instruction."

"Don't you think you are seeing rather too much of Mr. Robinsohn," Penelope said.

"I like him," Vanessa said.

"So do I—but he's a very strange man and I must warn you—"

"Warn me? There's no need to warn me. He understands my language. I can talk to him better than I can talk to—"

She stopped and Penelope added quietly, "Your mother."

"No. I meant Daddy."

"But you can still talk to me."

"Yes, but I cannot wait much longer. If Daddy doesn't agree to lend me the money I'm going back to London. I've got to get something done—at once—now."

As she went along the corridor to the bathroom again at one o'clock that morning Vanessa saw a light under Robinsohn's door and hesitated momentarily. He had heard her mules flapping down the carpet and he knew that she had stopped outside his door. Before she had time to walk on, he strode over to the door and opened it.

"Not sleeping?" he said.

"No. I have to pee," she said with her adolescent determination to be frank about everything.

"Drop in on the way back," he said. "Do you drink brandy?"

She nodded.

"I have some news for you," he said.

When she returned she found his room in even worse chaos and he had to remove a pile of newspapers, books, matches, and an ashtray from the single visitor's chair.

She sank deeply into it, clutching her dressing gown round her, desperately trying not to show—was it fear or just apprehension?—at being alone in the middle of the night with such a man as this. Their talk rambled inconsequentially from one subject to another, but Vanessa had the feeling that he was probing deeply into her views with a purpose. As they talked she thought that what she wanted above all things was to be an outsider in this society, but he actually *was* one. What she theorized about he had put into practice. A man born in a far-off country to an alien culture with an education and upbringing remote from her own revealed more rapport with what she regarded as her flowering spirit than her own flesh and blood parents.

She found herself saying, "A woman also has a right to do what she likes with her own body."

"Up to a point," he said.

"Why only up to a point?"

"Well—if you became a drug addict, it would change the lives of at least three people other than yourself."

"My father, mother, and brother."

"Yes."

196

"But why should that stop me?"

"Well, it's very simple, isn't it? When you damage your own body, it isn't any longer only your own body, it's other people's lives too."

"So I can only live by permission of their opinions."

"I wouldn't put it quite like that."

"In that case you must be against my abortion?"

He leaned forward with a renewed interest. "On the contrary—not only am I for your abortion—and your right to have it—but I now think I can help you."

"You—but how?"

"By lending—or rather giving you the money."

"I don't understand. I thought you had no money."

"I shall have in forty-eight hours from now. What time is your plane?"

"The late night plane—eleven o'clock."

"I'm not pretending there's anything lofty about this. If I get you the money, I want you to do something—rather difficult—for me."

"How difficult?"

"Very."

"Tell me."

"You may find it all too horrible."

"I like horrors."

"I wonder whether you will this one. You see, it's like this—your father is about to turn me over to the nonexistent mercies of the Veralian ABVO and—"

"My father!"

"Yes."

"I don't believe it."

"I thought you regarded him as a political pawn."

"But he wouldn't do a thing like that."

"Well, there's a very big danger that he may, and as I know the habits of the ABVO, I'm out to avoid it at any cost."

"I simply can't believe . . ."

"Listen," he interrupted. "Will you swear by—now I wonder what you believe in enough to swear by—not God—not queen and country—*not* Jesus Christ—not capitalism."

"Sex," she said. "I swear by Almighty Sex . . ."

"That you will not on pain of death say one word of what follows to any person inside or outside this embassy."

"I swear."

"How reliable are you?"

"With you, completely."

"I'm suitably flattered. Now I need your help to carry out a plan. . . ."

He then revealed to her young, astonished ears a scheme so macabre, daring, and dangerous that it sent a sexual thrill to the roots of her still-adolescent being. Hargreaves had arranged for Major Rivers's body to be removed at dawn to the garage in the garden, where the undertaker would prepare it for a traditional burial in a wooden coffin. Robinsohn explained that he intended to burgle his way into the garage at midnight, unscrew the coffin, drag out Major Rivers's body, conceal it under the old tarpaulins in the dark recesses of the garage, and lightly rescrew the coffin lid before returning to his room. The funeral ceremony had been arranged for eleven A.M. the following morning and this was where Vanessa came in. Together they would hang around the garage, wait until no one was about, and slip inside. Robinsohn would immediately climb into the coffin and Vanessa would rescrew the lid so that it could easily be pushed open again from the inside. Robinsohn knew that funerals in the embassy area always proceeded to the crematorium on St. Kevion Street, where the coffin remained for ten minutes in a side room before being lifted onto the rollers to disappear into the furnace. He had attended the funeral of a Veralian agent once—out of sympathy for one of his own kind he had learned to respect—and knew the general geography and procedures of the crematorium. He also knew that a small variation in timing might either consign him to the literally living hell of the crematorium furnace or lead to his discovery, but matters were desperate now, and this idea appealed to him for two reasons—one of which was simply its daring. This reason he explained to Vanessa, but he did not tell her that at a much deeper level he knew he was flirting in a quite new way with the death he half desired, and this time what a death!—to be roasted alive—the kind of redemption only saints could countenance.

Vanessa's excitement mounted as he unfolded the plan. "Couldn't I help you at midnight tonight," she said eagerly.

"I don't think so."

"But why not?"

"Do you think you could face handling a dead man?" Robinsohn said.

Vanessa shriveled into herself and said, "I could always try."

"It might be fatal if you fainted or did something absurd like being sick."

"I can't guarantee not to be sick."

"I'll handle the body myself," Robinsohn said decisively. "All you need to do is to rescrew the lid the following morning leaving two screws loose."

"Supposing they aren't loose enough?"

"I'll show you. But are you sure you want to go through with this?"

"Yes," Vanessa said with a kind of passion. "At least I shall have done one useful thing in my life."

198

"I doubt whether your father would agree with you."

"I think it's absolutely disgusting that he should even think of giving you up."

"The most important thing is that no one shall get the faintest whisper of a warning about this—especially your father. Can I really rely on you?"

"Absolutely." By now her eyes were shining with pure dedication.

"Fine," he said, "fine," and went over to take her hand and pull her up from the chair. "You must go now," he said, and her almost naked body quivered toward him. Just for a moment his arms rested lightly round her and he could feel the pressure of her breasts but he kissed her quickly on the cheek, held her back at arm's length, and said: "Swear by Almighty Sex you won't fail me."

"I swear," she said in a choky voice. Then he escorted her to the door.

It surprised and worried Robinsohn when His Excellency summoned him to his office at nine o'clock the following morning. There was always the danger that an adolescent girl had already unintentionally given something away, but he had been forced to choose her because no one else would dare to cooperate. As he entered the room, Robinsohn noticed how very careworn the ambassador looked, but he did not know the long struggle with conscience which had kept him awake half the night, nor did he dream what subtleties of moral analysis had reduced him to a state of total confusion by the time dawn broke.

After the briefest preliminaries consistent with good manners, His Excellency asked for an undertaking of absolute confidence and then said he was about to commit what some might consider a breach of the Official Secrets Act.

"But I have no choice left," he added. "If you are to understand my position—and I am for reasons I do not wish to discuss very anxious that you should understand—you must know the background." There followed a quick résumé of his exchanges with London.

"So you see," he concluded, "they *still* feel—and from their point of view quite rightly—that the revelations about Major Rivers do not clear you of suspicion. But after prolonged examination of all the evidence I cannot reconcile myself to that point of view.

"I feel very strongly—from knowing you, from what you have told me, from the reports of my staff and especially my wife—and of course from all the other evidence in my hands—that you should be given the benefit of the doubt. Now the only way I can do that without directly disobeying my instructions from London is to turn a blind eye to any escape attempt you may organize in the next few days. I dislike doing this. It is a counsel of expediency, and expediency is not a method I would willingly

199

use *for my own benefit*. It does benefit me in this case. It saves me from a head-on clash with London. So now you know the position. It does not give you much time, and I cannot directly help you, but I shall take no action to stop any plan you may be able to devise."

There was so much more he would have liked to tell Robinsohn, but any further exploration of motive might have involved too much personal revelation and complexities which Robinsohn would regard as trivial. There remained the equally disturbing fact that this situation had forced him to reexamine his own code of conduct in such detail that he had come to doubt its unassailable authority. Years of self-satisfied conviction had carried him over unexamined events with ready-made answers, but now the code itself had revealed ominous cracks, and that was the most disturbing factor of all. Or nearly the most disturbing, because one other new decision overwhelmed the importance of Robinsohn and his fate. He had decided that there would be only one thing left for him to do after this was all over—resign. Clearly Robinsohn alone had not driven him to this conclusion. Robinsohn was the climax to a long history of growing disillusion with the new diplomacy. Deeper still, he had gradually discovered inadequacies in his own career and character that he found difficult to face. What had once seemed satisfactory now seemed trivial. Achievements of which he had been proud had lost their significance. What had once appeared unquestionable was now full of doubts. And every development in this current situation had served to highlight self-doubt and professional disillusion. Somewhere interwoven with it all was a sense of failure, even with his own children.

Robinsohn was saying: "I appreciate what you suggest—and—believe me—" he rose from his chair and came forward to H.E.'s desk with his hand outstretched, "you are not mistaken about me."

As H.E. took his hand and they remained for a moment like that, looking straight at each other, both were embarrassed by the gesture. Dropping his hand, Robinsohn added, "I like the English, and you of course justify liking them."

A growing uneasiness with all these lofty protestations coming from a man like Robinsohn, whose trade—whatever integrity he himself might have—could so easily and ruthlessly encompass murder, made His Excellency desire to get the interview over and done with.

"Well," he said standing up, "in case I do not see you again—the very best of luck."

"You do not need luck," Robinsohn said, "but I hope everything goes well with you too."

"We all," said His Excellency, "need luck." And with that he showed him to the green baize door.

After he had gone, almost at once, on the spur of the moment, ignoring the pressure of many urgent telegrams, letters, and duties, His Excellency sat down and began to draft a letter of resignation. Halfway through the third sentence he tore up the sheet of paper and threw it into the wastepaper basket. A moment later, with unusual thoroughness, he collected the torn pieces from the basket, made a small pile in the empty, old-fashioned fire grate and set a match to it.

CHAPTER 17

Wandering down toward Stalin Square from the back streets of the industrial quarter, Rostand was shaken out of his preoccupation with Rivers's suicide by a sound like the distant baying of a thousand wild animals. He quickened his pace as he moved away from the factory belt into the twisted Gothic catacombs of the old city with its narrow streets, nodding houses, and small squares surrounded by mustard-colored villas where a few old-fashioned people still tried to live out the last of their traditional lives in penury behind massive iron gates. Beyond the squares the tightly packed quarter with its narrow chasms opening on the sky deadened the roar of what Rostand knew must be a huge crowd, and one narrow lane gave on another, twisting off in such confusion that he almost lost his way. The old city had yielded so many of its inhabitants to the new that it seemed reluctant to lose Rostand today, but now there was the wide, six-laned sweep of Stalin Boulevard cutting across at right angles and alive with traffic. As he came out of the claustrophobic maze, he saw the gleaming river running parallel to Stalin Boulevard and the sound hit his ears afresh—a great rhythmic roaring of many thousands of voices chanting slogans.

He realized now that people—everyday people—were still hurrying out of their workplaces, some running, some walking swiftly toward Stalin Square. Within minutes he joined a group of three students and they rushed him breathlessly along, telling him their story in snatches.

Twenty students arrested and imprisoned in the dungeons of the Ministry of the Interior without trial . . . Russian interference creaming off the rewards of industrial recovery . . . lack of any participation in running factories . . . too many people simply disappearing . . . food prices doubling in two years . . . and then the ban on all demonstrations that the students were—today—ignoring. It was a very old, repetitive, familiar story.

As they hurried along, Stalin Square opened out in front of them and most of its familiar landmarks were black with people. A great mass of people swayed and drifted in waves, throwing up bolder spirits who climbed the great iron statue to Lenin, and others who swarmed over the huge tank sculpture commemorating the Veralian dead of World War II. It seemed to Rostand that this was no party political stunt but a spontaneous uprising from the ordinary citizens of the capital city, and as he felt himself sucked into the swirling outer currents he remembered Hungary.

It was so like the famous first demonstrations on Parliament Square in Budapest and yet so different—different because so far there was no sign of the army—just a double row of black-coated ABVO men in front of the Ministry of the Interior with revolvers drawn facing the mob, and the windows of the Ministry crowded with civil servants plainly visible staring out, and somewhere high up on the fourteenth floor Kalogh's office, the biggest window of all, with no one visible.

Then Rostand realized that he was trapped. People had massed behind and around him and his arms and hands were crushed so tightly against his sides he could not move them. Two young girls were struggling to keep their feet as a wave went through the mass and nearly trampled them to the ground. It was one great living organism with independent tides racing across its surface to produce whirlpools and convulsions that threatened to dash people to death. Rostand felt the undertow of one such wave and only just kept his feet and now fear tore at him as the baying of the crowd broke out again and he knew he had lost control of any independent means of escape.

"Out with the Soviets!"

"Down with the Ministry!"

"Disband the ABVO!"

"We want our students!"

One slogan after another taken up, chanted to full pitch and discarded for another, and then a hundred voices giving a scattered cry of "Look!" and a great gasp going up from the massed ranks. There, high up on the slender ridge surrounding the shoulders of Lenin's statue, two students were clinging perilously and hammering at the Soviet Star on his breast below. The clang of metal on metal echoed across the square and the crowd fell silent—waiting. Pigeons wheeled across the vast mosaic of upturned faces and the only other sound came from the breeze ruffling the trees and newspapers. The ABVO men made no move to interfere because it would have been impossible to force a way through the massed ranks to the statue. And then a deep-throated murmur began in one corner of the crowd—"The star! The star!"—to be caught up by thousands as the students with a few final blows sent it crashing down to fall in the thick of one part of the crowd and send up screams as two people were hit. Inhumanly—everyone was laughing and jeering, and close to the star they trampled, kicked, tore at it, fighting for possession, almost ignoring their injured comrades.

"Look!" Once again the great cry was taken up and now Rostand saw four more students climbing the plinth of the Lenin statue with a huge Veralian flag, but a different flag. A gaping hole appeared in the middle, where the hammer and sickle had been cut out with ruthless scissors.

Another chant began again:

"Avénijon Veralia! Avénijon Veralia!" Long live Veralia! Long live Veralia! From another part of the crowd a deep-throated hymn came slowly up to dominate all other cries as everyone doffed his hat, men and women ceased to laugh and jeer, tears came into some eyes, and the melody swelled out with organ notes to crash against the Ministry of Security and reverberate back—a vast, overwhelming diapason of sound, of people profoundly moved to surrender all differences to the Veralian National Anthem. Afterwards there was silence and for a long time no one broke it.

It was seven o'clock before a disheveled Rostand at last returned to the safety of the embassy. Trying to telephone, he had found the lines out of order. Footsore, thirsty, dirty, he burst in on an astonished Thompson and said: "Is H.E. in?"

"He's still in the private office," Thompson said, "but he didn't want anyone to disturb him."

Ignoring the remark, Rostand limped up to the first floor, burst through Caroline's office and tapped on the green baize door. "Who is it?" His Excellency said, but his voice was so muffled by the double doors, Rostand strode through them and immediately apologized for breaking in. When His Excellency saw his disturbed state, he said, "What on earth's happened?"

Sinking into the yellow brocaded chair, Rostand gave a quick account of the demonstration and his final escape from it.

"Believe me," he finished, "this is something much more than just another demonstration. Some of those people really mean business."

"I think you're right," His Excellency said. "For a time this afternoon no one could get through to the ministry. All those twenty lines out of order. We heard rumors the main cable had been sabotaged."

"What happens next?" Rostand said.

"I can't believe they will let it get out of hand. The ABVO is ruthless enough but the army's the next step—and they wouldn't hesitate to mow them down."

"Remember Hungary," Rostand said. "It took ten days to reach a climax."

"Then they called in the Russians."

204

"It should be possible to predict from Hungary, shouldn't it?"

"Demonstrations—violence—the army called in and defecting—and then the Russians."

"Perhaps we should stock up for a siege."

"That's a bit premature."

"In Hungary it was six weeks before normal supplies came in again."

"Perhaps you're right. Can you dictate a wire to London?"

"I'll do it now."

"Wait a minute—you look all in. Leave it to me."

Rostand glanced at his watch. "The Veralian news should be on," he said and His Excellency went over to the window ledge and switched on the radio set. The Minister of Information's vibrant voice was mouthing the classic phrases. ". . . and now these student demonstrations are a deliberate attempt to undermine the power of the working class . . . Without any sense of responsibility to our great ally they heap false slanders on the head of the Soviet Union. Beware of impudent lies . . . Do not trust that small section of our youth who are deliberately fomenting trouble . . . Their propaganda is lying propaganda . . . and the rest —the majority—the great majority of our young citizens—know it for what it is. . . ."

They listened for the hard news at the end of the bulletin but there was no hard news. In classic Veralian fashion the Ministry of Information was busy burying the public's head in the sand.

As he switched off, His Excellency turned back to Rostand and said: "An odd little thing has happened here too. Someone's rifled the petty cash. And not so petty either. The cashier persuaded me this morning it was wise to have some ready money to hand. He drew out £300. It's all gone."

"That's a tidy sum. First piece of pilfering I've heard of in this place."

"I get the uncomfortable feeling the ghost is still at work."

"Whose ghost?"

"Major Rivers's. . . . By the way, you'll be coming to the funeral?"

"Of course."

One hour later the ambassador took the lift to the third floor, walked down the corridor, and tapped on Vanessa's door. "Come in," she said, and the ambassador walked in to find her lying on her bed reading and smoking, wearing nothing but her pants.

"For heaven's sake, Vanessa—supposing it had been someone else."

"I knew it was you," she said. "No one can mistake your tread."

The ambassador sniffed the air. "That's an odd cigarette you're smoking," he said.

"It's a new brand from France," she said.

"A brand called POT, I suppose?"

"No—it's better than POT."

"And what, pray, is better than POT?"

As she threw her book down on the bedcover he read its title, *The Female Eunuch* by Germaine Greer.

"Look, Daddy," she said. "You've refused to help me out of my trouble and I don't see you have any right to interfere with my life after that . . ."

"So you've got everything under control, have you?"

"Yes," she said calmly, "as a matter of fact, I have."

As he began walking round her room, automatically he picked up items of underwear and moved over to the bureau to pack them into a drawer. Opening the drawer he saw three copies of a paper he had never heard of called *SHREW*.

"Look, darling," he said with his back toward her. "You are very important to me—you may not think so—but I would rather give up my principles than see you ruin your life."

"So you agree," she said sharply, "that having the child would ruin my life?"

"No," he said, "I do not. But your mother has put your case so strongly to me that I have come to see the force of it."

She came up off the bed then and half naked as she was went to him and put her arms round him.

"That's very sweet of you, Daddy," she said, "and terribly—terribly broadminded."

"I still haven't finally made up my mind," he said, "but I wanted to ask you this. If I do what you want—give you the money for the abortion —will you take another look at your whole—what I believe you young people now call—your life style? After all, I notice this has caused you great anguish and upset everyone. Isn't that proof enough there may be something wrong with it?"

She drew away from him frowning.

"I don't want anything with strings attached," she said. "I have thought my way through it all. I think our values are the right values. No one is going to sell me conventional morality. It's a sham and a fraud."

As she talked on, he was saddened to see how hard her face and manner became.

"And in any case," she concluded, and by now her voice was stony, "it's too late."

"What do you mean—too late?"

"I have made other arrangements."

"What other arrangements?"

Still childlike in her mercurial changes of mood, she softened again and said: "I'm going to be all right, Daddy—don't worry, everything's going to be all right. I *do* appreciate what you said just now. I know how

206

important your values are to you, and you were ready to give them up for me. That's really lovely and sweet of you. After all, I'm not prepared to do the same thing. But please don't press me anymore. Please leave me alone now. I'm going to be all right."

Half an hour later, when her father had gone, Vanessa slipped on her dressing gown, surveyed the empty corridor, and hurried soundlessly in slippers along to Robinsohn's room. He received her with a carefully preserved distance and almost at once said, "I've got the money."

He went over to the bureau, opened a drawer and took out an envelope. Tearing off the flap he divided the money into halves saying, "Fair shares, half to you, half to me." As the envelope fluttered to the floor she noticed that it carried the General Office stamp.

"You stole it," she said, and she could not conceal the admiration in her voice.

"Never mind how I got it. There, that's the equivalent of £150— enough for the best abortionist. Now are you ready—the day after tomorrow, ten A.M. at the garage door?"

"Yes," she said stiffening with the thrill of the approaching moment. "More than ready."

"Here's the screwdriver," he said, pulling it out from under the mattress. "And here're some screws. I stole this stuff from the basement. You'd be surprised what they've got down there. Now I want you to show me what you can do with this—" he dived under the mattress again and pulled out a piece of wood.

For nearly fifteen minutes they worked away together and time and again Vanessa drew breath sharply as their hands and bodies brushed, but he seemed totally oblivious of any physical attraction she might have. All Vanessa had to do once he was inside would be to replace the screws —lightly—into three specially prepared holes.

Minute by minute, detail by detail, he went over their precise routine once again, from the moment they descended into the garden and entered the garage and he climbed into the coffin.

"But how will you breathe?" she said.

"I went down last night and bored some discreet holes."

"My God," she said, "you're wonderful."

"Well, that's that," he said at last and escorted her to the door. There she paused and turned to look up into his face with that kind of admiration that has in it something more than admiration. She stayed like that very close to him, her mouth half open in expectation of the kiss, but he withdrew from her, kissed her hand, and said, "That would ruin everything." Then gently, he urged her through the door. As she climbed into bed again, a sense of sexual humiliation, thrilled expectancy, and sudden spasms of fear that she might fail in her appointed task kept her tossing and turning half the night until at four in the morning she rushed to the bathroom to be violently sick.

The city was quiet the following day until dusk and then once again the distant sounds of roaring crowds, the rush of lorries with policemen, and the confusion of the telephone service sent Rostand off on a mission for the ambassador in the battered old general-purpose Skoda. The uproar drew him in a different direction this time—away from Stalin Square —and he found that he was heading for the radio station. Police barriers stopped him within half a mile of the station, but even there tear gas hung on the air and a mess of mud and water from hoses rushed down the gutters. Leaving the car he turned down the back streets, and five minutes later found all traffic at a standstill. The narrower streets giving onto Lenin Boulevard were choked with cheering people, all trying to edge toward the far end of the boulevard where, at the intersection with the Konstanza Boulevard, the huge glass-faced Radio and Television Center reared its glossy cliff high above the river. The black mass of people in front of the building and the flexing tentacles reaching out into all the neighboring streets looked like a gigantic human octopus with the pulsing eyes of two overturned buses at the center. The sheer magnitude of the beast seen from the higher level of a steep side street stopped Rostand's breath as he leaned over a concrete balustrade trying to estimate its size. Sixty thousand—eighty thousand—even a hundred thousand people were all stamping their feet in unison. On the cobblestones it made a great thunder that crashed against the cliff face of the center and came reverberating back. Those feet in all their multiplied might sounded as if they could trample down and out of existence any obstacle that stood in their way.

As he watched, the chanting began again:

"Down with Kalogh!"

"Out with the Soviets!"

"Death to the ABVO!"

Death to the ABVO. That was new and much more daring. Dusk merged into darkness but the great black building remained unlit, in silence, with only the two standard lamps flanking the entrance illumining the thick cluster of ABVO men waiting with revolvers drawn once more. The front waves of the crowd pushed in and out like a tide, but immediately confronting them now was a double line of barbed wire and behind that a row of Veralian soldiers, the dark blue of their uniforms studded by red Soviet stars on each shoulder. The complete lack of any response from the black buildings drove the crowd into another single-word slogan:

"Light! Light! Light!" they chanted and then, "We want light!"

Rostand knew what was happening inside. The broadcasting studios were at the back and these offices were deliberately used as a protective front to prevent any intruder from easily taking over cameras or transmitters. Administrative staff normally occupied the front offices but it was too late for them to be on duty, and the back entrances to the building could only be approached through a maze of flats occupied by trusted party members with no main gate through the network of narrow streets.

"Light! We want light!" The phrase became a gigantic wave of sound crashing against the silent impassive façade.

Suddenly and unexpectedly two giant chandeliers—ice-cold, glittering, magnificent—burst to life on the third floor, the big windows rolled slowly upward and a figure stepped forward on the steel and concrete balcony. It was Istvan Bolsover, Secretary of the Central Committee.

Through a hastily dragged-out microphone his vibrant voice echoed round the square: "Comrades! Comrades! Listen to me, Comrades. Quiet, please! We know why you are here, Comrades. We know you are dissatisfied with certain aspects of the current industrial and political situation. We know the remedies you propose. Do not imagine that we have ignored either your dissatisfaction or your remedies. We are considering them. It takes time. At nine o'clock tonight I shall be appearing on television to explain to the nation new reforms that will end some of your dissatisfactions. This open space and this balcony are not suitable places to convey the somewhat complicated measures we propose taking. So I would urge you all to disperse quietly, return to your homes, switch on your televisions and radios—and look and listen. A satisfactory answer will be given. Rest assured of that—a satisfactory answer. Thank you, Comrades, for your very lively interest in the affairs of state."

The figure was about to withdraw when a man supported on the shoulders of two others called up at the balcony through a big bullhorn: "Now it's your turn to listen, Comrade," he said. "We want our charter televised. We want our six points broadcast. We want real workers' participation."

As he made each separate point, a great roar came up from the crowd underlining it in thunder. It was like a black preacher playing his congregation.

". . . A national policy independent of Russia" (*roar*). "A national policy on a socialist basis" (*roar*). "Participation in everything" (*roar*). "The ABVO disbanded" (*the biggest roar of all*).

Suddenly the two big chandeliers went out, the silhouetted figure of the minister remained a moment in darkness and then disappeared through the big window, which slowly rolled down again. What began as a groan from the crowd became a snarl and from a snarl it grew into the angry baying of thousands of frustrated animals. Rostand shrank into himself at the sound and was glad he had not pressed forward deeper into the jungle where the biggest wild beast he had ever seen was now on the prowl for revenge, baying on the air with a single voice that obliterated reason, circumstance, everything.

Vast surges ran through the crowd that pushed a score of people into the barbed-wire defenses. Screaming, they tried to disentangle trapped clothing and skin from the sadistic claws. Another bullhorn from the main entrance carried the loud voice of an ABVO officer, full of menace: "This is to warn anyone who enters the barbed wire. He or she will be shot. . . . This is to warn. . . ."

A woman's voice screamed out an obscene phrase describing the ABVO as something one should wipe one's arse with and the crowd again pushed another group into the teeth of the wire.

Now a short sharp command and Rostand felt himself freeze as a deafening volley of shots rang out. He strained his eyes but in the dim light thrown by the streetlamps he could not see whether anyone had fallen. There were no screams, no cries, but a great generalized gasp of disbelief went up from the crowd until it became evident that this first volley had been fired over their heads. It silenced them. The baying ceased and the only sound was the soft whirring of pigeon wings as they circled, baffled, above this mass of immobile human beings. And then one by one the street-lights along the boulevard went out and almost total darkness threw a fresh blanket over the waiting multitude, waiting now like a peasant crowd —patient and enduring—mass upon mass of ghost faces in a great black pit, uneasy, aware of the power they finally confronted, of the brutal repression they had challenged, and uncertain, wondering what to do next, half afraid to further incite the mutilation of bullets. But still they remained —just standing.

Suddenly someone struck a match and set fire to his rolled copy of the Veralian paper, *Jus Kugeren*. The action was caught up and repeated by hundreds of people. A chain of fire crossed and crisscrossed the crowd until twenty thousand newspaper torches, held high, threw their eerie light over the faces, and clouds of smoke collected as pieces broke away like flaming birds to dash themselves out against the black impassive wall. The tableau of the ABVO men crouching together for safety, bristling with revolvers, became yellow, then red, then ghoulish gray. As the torches faded and the shadows swept back into blackness, from a far corner of the crowd came a murmur of singing, and slowly the Veralian National Anthem rose on the air, sung like a dirge, slowly, painfully, a deep-throated protest which reached a deafening crescendo.

As the silence flowed in once more, a file of young men tore their way to the front rank of the crowd and confronted the ABVO officer at the main doors. One of them thrust a paper at him and shouted through a bullhorn, "We want that broadcast. We shall stay here until it is broadcast."

Now half a dozen army trucks screamed to a halt at the rear of the building and a hundred soldiers poured out to begin forcing their way through the network of streets to the main entrance.

Rostand, stiff from leaning over the concrete balcony, strained his eyes into the one remaining pool of light thrown by the single globe over the main door. The ABVO officer and the young man confronting him were picked out sharply as if in a spotlight. Something happened between them that he could not see or hear, but suddenly the ABVO man was tearing the sheet across as the young man closed with him, a single shot echoed and reechoed round the square and the young man fell screaming.

Simultaneously the battling file of soldiers reached the front entrance and their officer conferred swiftly with the ABVO officer. Far up on his balcony Rostand craned forward, his heart beating fast. The old-fashioned regular army with its patriotic tradition had never concealed its distaste for the new upstart ABVO. What was said Rostand never knew but a new cry now went up from the front ranks of the crowd:

"Veralian soldiers, be Veralians!

"Veralian soldiers, join us!

"Veralian soldiers, wear Veralian uniforms.

"Join us!

"Join us!

"Join us!"

On each new repetition the note swelled until the whole hundred thousand people were stamping their feet and chanting "Join us!"

What happened between the two pinpoint figures down at the main entrance? What was said? What horror of shooting down an ordinary student in a normal demonstration overpowered the restraint of the army officer? How much loathing of Soviet uniforms, how many years of hating the ABVO, and how much sympathy with the ever-widening demonstrations over the past six months simply seized this minor incident to trigger off an explosion out of all proportion?

Rostand never knew, but a short sharp order echoed up to him on his balcony and a second later the soldiers had trained their automatic rifles on the ABVO men. The crowd froze into absolute quiet and stillness and the seconds ticked away electrically. With almost theatrical slowness the army officer then unclipped the Soviet badge from his cap and threw it over his shoulder into the massed ranks of the crowd. A great cry broke the stillness—"The stars! The stars!" as the soldiers followed suit and one after another tore the red Soviet emblems from their caps and threw them to the waiting crowd. Swiftly the ABVO men were disarmed, the Veralian officer took over a loudspeaker and called: "You can send a delegation into the Center—we will protect them. . . ."

But the bloodlust of the crowd, momentarily suppressed by the arrival of the troops, burst out with cries of vengeance—vengeance on the ABVO officer who had shot down an innocent student—vengeance which dragged him away from the protecting soldiers, vengeance when a hundred hands tore him limb from limb.

Rostand did not stay for any more. He felt very sick and turned away to hurry off to the old Skoda, only to find his path barred by another crowd massed in every side street. It was four hours before he at last made his way back to the embassy, an exhausted and apprehensive man.

The ambassador listened carefully to his report and as he finished said: "Bigger things have happened. The demonstrators broke into the Stalin Barracks. Now they've got arms."

His manner had an expressionless calm.

"We've improvised beds," His Excellency said, "in case the staff need to stay in the embassy."

"And Rivers's funeral tomorrow?"

"It's in the opposite direction from the fighting—better to try and go through with it, I think."

Hargreaves came bursting into the private office at that moment, but English politeness checked him in the doorway. "I'm sorry," he said. "Am I interrupting?"

"Everything's interrupting now," the ambassador said.

"I've just heard from Reuter's correspondent," Hargreaves said, quietly adjusting his Rugby tie. "There's been quite a hullabaloo at the Stalin Barracks."

The account he gave was suave, detached as if he were reporting a court case, but its content was full of the frenzied savagery of a develop-ing civil war. . . . The big contingent of ABVO men sent to protect the Stalin Barracks from looting; the battle between army officers loyal to the government and those who had thrown in their lot with the demonstrators; the cry from the people pouring round the barracks—"Give us arms! Give us arms!" The first rush of defecting soldiers tearing rifles from the racks and hurling them down to the clamoring crowd; the few officers who saw the full consequences of what they were doing, trying to interfere: the struggle and shootings inside the barracks: the smell of blood, the sudden hail of rifles, revolvers, and hand grenades dropped to a mob who had no technical training in their use.

"This is all on the East Side?" the ambassador said.

"Yes—for the moment we're in the clear. But not for long," Har-greaves said, "unless I am very much mistaken."

"You think there will be more army defections?"

"I don't know. At least four different factions are fighting. National-ists—National Communists—Marxist-Leninists—Marxist-Catholics."

"I tried to get Kalogh an hour ago," the ambassador said. "He wasn't available."

At midnight the sound of gunfire continued to dominate the eastern sector of the city and the glare of two great fires reached the embassy,

212

but the radio poured out reassuring messages—the government had everything under control. Thompson kept an all-night vigil, but the Minister of Information's expected speech from the Television Center did not materialize. By three in the morning the gunfire had died away, the fires had dimmed to a smoky haze, and an expectant hush descended on the city, with nothing more than an occasional sniper's shot rattling from the rooftops.

Robinsohn paced his room half the night chain-smoking and trying to resolve the new situation. Extraordinarily, in all the disturbances, the white-coated men at the back and front of the embassy remained on duty. The bureaucracy had probably overlooked their existence by now and even if the worst slaughter broke out, they would remain like automatons, duly relieved by sequences of other white-coated men. If only the stupid bastards were called to what were obviously more important duties, he could simply walk out now. If only the riots spread to the western areas of the city he would easily be able to slip away in the total confusion. But by the dawn everything was quiet again and when he looked out of the window a new agent lounged opposite the main entrance once more.

Three hours later Robinsohn checked his money, passport, papers, food rations, basic clothes, and death pill, all packed into the small holdall. Precisely at five minutes to ten he walked along the corridor, gave the prearranged taps on Vanessa's door and went on down the stairs out into the garden. There he found the hired hearse already waiting but Richards, the chauffeur, seemed intent on cleaning His Excellency's Rolls in the garage. That was the first unexpected snag. Robinsohn went in and began talking to him, swiftly surveying the tarpaulins in the far corner. Nothing had been disturbed. It was a gray misty day and the small frosted-glass windows of the garage did not carry the light into the corners.

It had cost Robinsohn a considerable effort to heave Rivers's body into a half-sitting position consonant with the shape into which the tarpaulins fell, and everything looked very normal, but the presence of the body within a few feet of Richards forced Robinsohn to keep a highly trained control on his nerves. There was no reason why anyone should try to shift the coffin at this stage, but if anyone did and found it empty—

All at once Richards straightened from polishing the big brass headlamps, walked over to the coffin, tapped it, and said: "Who'd ever have thought old Rivers was a spy. Such an honest, upright chap. I had no idea. Came as a shock. I mean I'd as soon suspect me own mother as suspect him. Did you get to know him?"

Robinsohn stood beside the tarpaulins and he said very smoothly, "No, I didn't really know him." Moving to a position midway between the coffin and the car he took out his cigarette case. "Have a cigarette?" he said, extending the case.

"Thanks," Richards said and walked two paces away from the coffin to select one. At that moment Vanessa came in, saying to Richards: "I think Daddy's looking for you."

Her voice sounded so high and strained Richards looked sharply at her and said: "You don't look well, Miss."

"I'm all right," Vanessa almost snapped, desperately anxious not to allow a conversation to develop, and Robinsohn saw that she was tense to the breaking point. Richards had now turned his attention to the nose of the Rolls and was repolishing the already gleaming metal.

"My God—you treat the damned machine as if it were a woman," Robinsohn said as Richards held the flag fully extended and carefully dusted it.

"She is to me," Richards said laconically.

"And what about Daddy?" Vanessa said desperately.

"There's one thing I will always say about your father, Miss—he never believes in unnecessary rush." Richards now walked round the breadth and length of the Rolls scrutinizing it from all angles. Suddenly Vanessa went very white, her face twitched, and Robinsohn thought, Oh, my God, she's going to be sick. She put her hand in front of her mouth and retched and Richards stopped his survey. "Can I get you anything, Miss?"

"No," she choked, "but"—and he repeated with dumb persistence, "But what, Miss?"

She had stuffed her handkerchief into her mouth when Robinsohn said, "She's best left alone. Don't you think you should see what His Excellency wants?"

"I suppose so," Richards said, throwing his duster in the open boot of the Rolls.

He went at last and in one stride Robinsohn was at the coffin unscrewing the lid and saying to Vanessa: "Hang on—Just another minute —Hang on."

He worked with lightning speed but Vanessa gave a moan, rushed to the door of the garage, and was violently sick.

"Quick," Robinsohn said ruthlessly. "Screw me in—Be sick over the damned coffin if necessary, but screw me in."

He had slipped in and was lying flat as she returned and made a great effort, retching and screwing, retching and screwing. Coming to the loose screws she heard him call, "Don't forget—loosely—loosely."

Fumbling with nerves and sickness, it took Vanessa almost three minutes to get everything in position again and all the time Robinsohn talked softly, encouragingly.

Footsteps came down the paved path. Vanessa turned the last screw desperately as Richards returned and said: "I don't understand. Miss Caroline says there was no such message."

Vanessa still had the screwdriver in her hand and she muttered helplessly. "I must have misunderstood—he did say . . ." She stopped as she felt Richards's eye riveted on the screwdriver.

"Where did you find that?" he said. "I was looking for it all yesterday."

"It was under the car," she said.

"Under the car . . . but . . ." He looked round the garage. "Where's Mr. Robinsohn?"

Vanessa felt her body, blood, bowels flowing excrementally into the earth. She closed her eyes, her face went parchment white and she swayed and staggered. Richards strode over to her, put his arm round her and said: "You're ill, Miss—let me help you back in—I'll get your mother." He began to escort her to the door.

As the footsteps faded from the garage, inside the coffin Robinsohn at last dared to breathe again and immediately he became aware of the stuffiness. Deliberately he was lying face downward with his mouth close to the three holes he had bored at the lower seam of the coffin, and now he twisted his arm and wrist to get a glimpse of his luminous watch—ten thirty. A whole half hour to go. Could he stand it?

Five minutes later the echoes of the past began to reverberate inside the coffin. Five more minutes and he felt the sweat under his armpits as the claustrophobia intensified.

He saw a suburban road lined with identical red-brick houses and along the road came four jet black finely prancing horses drawing an ornate hearse which swung from side to side of the road in the rhythm of a waltz, and there he was in the driving seat with a great whip urging the horses to more abandoned behavior, gradually increasing their speed until on one of its biggest swerves the coffin slipped, shot off the hearse, turned over twice in the road, burst open and there was his mother's flesh-less cadaver, skull screaming, "You murderer! You murderer!" Richards came back into the garage at that moment and Robinsohn went rigid inside the coffin. Some slight sound caught Richards's attention and he muttered to himself and moved over to the coffin. Robinsohn tried to stifle his breathing. Richards rapped the coffin sharply and the sound bounced round inside the box. Then he put his ear to the lid and listened. Robinsohn clenched his fists, held every limb rigidly still and stopped breathing. "Damned funny," Richards said and his footsteps moved away.

A sudden wave of sweat burst out all over Robinsohn's body, soaking it, as he relaxed again. Five minutes later the fantasy, the remembrance of his mother's neglected funeral, the death he did not solemnize, came back to him with full force. He was trapped, in here, trapped in his mother's coffin, trapped with her haunting presence. Crazy nonsense. Imaginative idiocies, fantasies—not worth the stuff they were made of. Control them— Kick them all to pieces— To hell with his bloody mother— Concentrate on survival.

Breathe slowly, gently, relax, use every drop of air with care. Let the limbs lie loose. No need to fear suffocation.

The hearse again, the prancing horses, and now a crazy notion that his own coffin was slipping—slipping—and beginning to turn over and over—and his head, dizzy sickness threatening, and a sudden attempt to curl himself up in a ball. Richards strode over to the coffin again, listened a moment, and once more tapped the lid. The tap became a rap, a severe knocking, and Robinsohn tried to freeze in deathlike stillness.

For nearly a whole minute Richards stood beside the coffin, alternately rapping and putting his ear to the lid. Then at last he shrugged his shoulders, muttered: "Ghosts—don't believe in 'em," and walked out of the garage. Robinsohn heard his footsteps fade and took a great gulp of air, immediately regretting it because it was wasteful and carbon monoxide multiplied with breathing. But more than anything he feared the return of the fantasy.

The cortege proceeded solemnly enough for the first half mile with the coffin carried on an ornate prerevolutionary hearse and six people from the embassy sitting upright and silent in the Rolls. The black clothes, the snail's pace, the hearse driver with the insignia of a broad black tie, all acknowledged the past, but the two Veralian motorcycle police made a farce of mourning. Rostand had asked for permission to cremate Major Rivers and two policemen had been directed to keep check on the ceremony.

They were turning a slow bend in the road toward the industrial sector when the sound of firing began. Now down the middle of the road came careening a long line of transport lorries normally used for carrying heavy goods but now packed tight with factory workers all cheering and waving brand new arms of every variety—rifles, pistols, hand grenades. Within a hundred yards of the hearse fierce bursts of firing from either side of the road sent one lorry into the ditch to overturn, another drove wildly down the wrong side of the road, a third went madly into reverse as men leaped out, crouched, and fired back. The army had ambushed the Freedom Fighters.

Panic seized the hearse driver. Ignoring the police outriders he saw a side turning, accelerated wildly, and swung down it. As he gathered speed, half a mile later he came to a sharp bend, the coffin heaved, twisted, rolled over into the ditch and burst open. No one so much as glimpsed the badly shaken figure of Robinsohn trying to pull himself out of near concussion but having just enough of his wits left to crawl along the ditch as far away as possible from the burst coffin.

Back on the main road Richards had brought the Rolls to an abrupt halt as His Excellency said quietly into the mouthpiece, "Pull over on the path—and everyone take cover in the ditch." He was the last one out of the car and as he jumped down beside Penelope in the ditch she said something which the firing drowned out. Hargreaves and Rostand were crouching close to each other without a word, Caroline had her hands clasped tightly over her ears and her eyes were wide with fear as Richards said, "I hope they don't hit the car."

It was as if he had become so accustomed to the protection of diplomatic privilege that no stray bullet would ever dare to violate his own person. Then Caroline felt something highly embarrassing happening to her and with no regard for bullets she simply came to her feet and ran down the ditch, anxious only to escape the humiliation of its discovery by the others. His Excellency called something after her but she ignored him and ran on.

The skirmish was short and sharp. The Freedom Fighters retreated back the way they had come leaving one wrecked lorry and several sprawled figures. As the firing ceased Rostand limbered himself up from the ditch to survey the road. The army was pulling its motorcycles out of camouflage, mounting and roaring after the Freedom Fighters. Five minutes later the only sounds in the still air were the moans of the unattended wounded. The sound made them hesitate. Should they drive on and give what help they could—thus risking complicity—or should they race back into the center of the city and send out ambulances.

And what of the hearse with its coffin? His Excellency decided on a quick search for the hearse as the first step. When they had piled back into the Rolls they became aware that Caroline was still missing. They drove along the road back toward the embassy and presently sighted her figure walking swiftly and purposefully. When they overtook her, she at first refused to enter the car.

"I'll walk back," she said.

"It's too dangerous," His Excellency said, "Get in—"

"No," she said, "I'm walking."

"Get in—that's an order," His Excellency said.

"I have reason," she said coloring—"for God's sake don't press me."

Suddenly Penelope caught an acrid whiff on the air and said, "I think I understand—but this is no time for niceties—get in, girl, and let's have no more nonsense."

There was no doubt about the smell as she lay back in the corner of the car, her face turned away in shame. Nothing worse could have happened to the elegant, spotless, Chanel-scented Caroline. "The hearse next," His Excellency said, and Richards swiftly swung the Rolls round, drove back, took the side turning and there they came upon the coffin lying half in the ditch broken open—and empty. The search lasted for nearly ten minutes and they were bewildered when there was no sign of the body. Simultaneously the hearse came lumbering back down the road. The driver climbed out and stared in amazement when they explained that they had failed to find Major Rivers. They gave up the search when tanks came rushing down the main road and firing began again. As they drove swiftly back toward the embassy, the roar of gunfire broke out from the old quarter of the city and within minutes every kind of weapon seemed to be involved, including, from the decisive sound, mortar shells and tank guns.

A big, burly man with rubbery lips and a hoarse voice awaited His Excellency in embassy reception. The ambassador recognized him at once.

"All the lines are cut," he said. "I've come to ask a favor."

"I'm very busy," His Excellency said.

Thompson came across from the reception desk and handed His Excellency an envelope. It was addressed in Robinsohn's handwriting and spelled out in block capitals were the words CONFIDENTIAL. Automatically opening it His Excellency heard Andrew Cunningham, Reuter's correspondent say, "I must get this dispatch through—may I put it over your radio?"

"I'm sorry," the ambassador said automatically, "you know very well we cannot abuse diplomatic privilege."

"But have you heard the news?" Cunningham said.

"What news?"

"They've called in the Russian tanks."

"What's happened to Kalogh?"

"Vanished. No one knows where he is."

"Vanished—but—"

Cunningham interrupted: "I must get this through. Isn't it vital that the Foreign Office should know?"

"I shall keep them informed," His Excellency said.

"Why not the British people too?"

"That's your concern—"

Cunningham said, "Is your Telex still working?"

"Even if it were, I could not allow—"

"Oh, for Christ's sake," Cunningham interrupted, "this is civil war —this is death and disaster—what does a strip of red tape matter in such a situation?"

"I'm sorry," the ambassador said and turned to Thompson: "Will you try and get the ambulance people?" he said. "There are some casualties on the Virogrov Road urgently needing attention."

"You won't get through," Cunningham said. "All the lines are dead."

"If there's nothing else we can do for you—" His Excellency said. He had reason not to like this man. He had grossly exaggerated the story of the embassy leaks, built on information from a source which he refused to disclose.

"Yes, there is," Cunningham snapped. "I need some gas. The pumps are either closed, empty, or in the hands of the army. You have a dump here. Let me buy a couple of gallons."

"We haven't got what you call a dump, and if all the pumps are closed we're certainly going to need what we've got—but we'll spare you one gallon."

"Two—I must get to the border—to telegraph this. It'll take at least two."

"All right, two," His Excellency said, and now his mind was completely engaged with the letter as he walked slowly toward his office.

"Dear H.E.,

"With luck, by the time you read this I shall be well away from your embassy at last, but I could not go without trying to thank you for—I don't quite know what—trusting me, I suppose, which sounds a misplaced activity. I also wanted to apologize. I'm afraid I've had to handle poor old Rivers pretty roughly. You see I had to take him out of the coffin and put myself in. You will find him under the tarpaulins in the corner of the garage.

"I know you would regard this as the worst form of sacrilege and I did not tell you about it for that reason—but I had no choice. It was my best way of getting out. There was no time for fine scruples.

"There's one other hint I wanted to drop because it may be of some help to you. I know you will regard this as so crazy it isn't worth taking seriously. But I have just a suspicion—nothing more— that you might find Kalogh himself had something to do with the Grundel revolutionary cell. I know it sounds mad beyond belief. But it would—wouldn't it—make it even more vital for him to get me before I got at the fact—if that is a fact. If he were cooking up a conspiracy he wouldn't want me to jump the gun by uncovering and possibly revealing his name. He knew I was on the trail of that document and I believe the names of those concerned in counter-revolutionary activities would have been in it. Suppose *his* had been there. Anyway, I give you this hint for what it's worth. It's just an idea that fits certain facts I know.

"I haven't mentioned it before because I knew you simply wouldn't believe such a fantastic idea without some real evidence. I'm out to try and get that evidence now and if I do I'll be in touch again.

"Thank you for tolerating me so long. I learned to respect you while I lived with you. I'm hoping we may meet again when all this is over. But perhaps I'll be dead by then.

Robinsohn"

Sitting back in his familiar chair at the mahogany desk, His Excellency tried to adjust himself to the astonishing facts revealed in the note.

Carefully rereading it he came to the phrase about Major Rivers and frowned. As Robinsohn said, he found it highly distasteful that anyone should have so casually used the dead body of another human being in an escape conspiracy—"find him under the tarpaulins." The phrase carried a kind of blasphemy. But Kalogh? Cunningham had said he had vanished. Was Robinsohn right? Could it possibly be that all this time . . . ? It certainly looked a possibility now although twenty-four hours before he would have totally ridiculed Robinsohn's idea. His Excellency deflected the switch of his microphone and Caroline's assistant, Miss Fairweather, answered. "Is Caroline there?" the ambassador began and swiftly added, "No, of course she's not. Can you ask Mr. Thompson if he will come and see me, Miss Fairweather?"

"Certainly, sir."

Five minutes later Thompson entered his office and His Excellency said: "It seems that we are going to have to arrange a second burial."

When Vanessa heard that all flights to London were canceled because the airport was under gunfire she broke down and wept.

"Oh, God," she said. "Everything's against me. What am I going to do, Mummy? I can't just go on sitting here waiting while this—thing—grows and grows."

She was lying face downward on her bed and as she spoke, she pounded the pillow with her fist.

"The fighting will be over in a few days," Penelope said. They dare not let it get out of hand."

She knew she was lying. The gunfire, the smoke, the fires, the continuous battles, and the breakdown of all public services now indicated something much more serious than an easily suppressed uprising. She knew very well that civil war had broken out, and shuddered to think what that could mean.

Much later in the afternoon she went along to Robinsohn's room to check whether the maid had cleared it up. She found everything in perfect order with the bed freshly made, the phonograph records carefully replaced in their racks, and the books tidily arranged on the chest of drawers, the windowsill, and mantelpiece. She stood there full of a sudden uneasiness and found herself searching the room for some small personal memento that he might have overlooked and left behind. There was nothing. He had gone completely. She hurried out of the room again, more disturbed than she wanted to admit by an odd sense of—was it deprivation?

CHAPTER 18

Large areas of the city were now savage battlefields, the embassy was a place of refuge, and living-out staff had become living-in. Pamela, Toby, and Sarah were among the first to camp down in Hargreaves's office. At first the refugee rule was English only, but that rapidly broke down when a French engineer, an American businessman, and two Scandinavian students asked for asylum.

As the numbers increased, offices were converted into bedrooms with mattresses dragged from the third floor, food was rationed and large butts in the garden were filled with water as a precaution against burst water mains. Penelope took over the planning and ranged constantly round the embassy keeping everything moving despite the piled-up luggage and bedding and steadily multiplying population. She developed a rota system in the canteen for light meals and thought of making the male and female lavatories unisex.

All the typists were now living in, at least four extra women materialized from different parts of the city and proved themselves to be English citizens, married members of the staff brought in their wives, and the female population quickly outnumbered the male. Every available candle was commandeered because the electricity supply had become eccentric. Thompson was deputed to forage in the immediate locality for any kind of field cooking apparatus since the gas supply had lost its power and completely vanished after six o'clock in the evening.

In the background it was as if a steadily narrowing ring of skirmishes, battles, smoke, and fires closed in on this diplomatic oasis as ambulances rushed the more fortunate wounded past the main gate toward the hospital, and the less lucky stumbled along—unhelped—pleading for shelter. It was surprising how quickly some staff members became accustomed to the roar of artillery, the crackling machine guns, the great smoking glares in the night sky, and the sight of blood and bandages. It was a backcloth against which they had to live but a backcloth steadily encroaching on the peaceful areas of the city and steadily becoming more threatening. Hysteria overwhelmed one younger member, sleep became difficult, and everyone tended to cling closely to the embassy environs.

At first the injured stragglers passing the main gates were directed to the hospital half a mile away, but when, late on the evening of the sixth day, a young woman collapsed at the gate bleeding profusely from a wound in her breast, Penelope took her in. She wore the green armband of a Freedom Fighter over a man's gray macintosh and still clung to her Sten gun. Trained in first aid during World War II, Penelope applied what little skills she had and was astonished when the cool immaculate Caroline volunteered to help. As they stripped off the girl's macintosh, blouse, and bra the sight of a breast reduced to a bloody pulp and oozing blood merely produced in Caroline the remark, "Shall we use her slip for bandages?" Penelope agreed and Caroline went to work, swiftly pulling off what turned out to be a half slip and tearing it into four-inch strips.

"You know something about this?" Penelope said as Caroline bound up the wound with technical proficiency.

"I was once a sister in a hospital," Caroline said, and Penelope looked astonished.

"Good God," she said, "I would never have dreamed—that's going to be very useful."

Two hours later Rostand drove the old Skoda round to the front entrance, Thompson and Hargreaves carried the girl to the car, and they rushed her down to the Leningrad Hospital. On the way back Rostand said, "I think I'll see what's happening." Dropping Hargreaves, he drove on toward the old quarter of the city once more. Within five minutes he reached a double barbed-wire barricade across the road and there were two Russian officers, nursing rifles and demanding his papers, with rows of machine guns covering the approaches to the Kaganovitch Barracks.

The Russians advised him to return at once to the safety of the embassy but then firing began, three armored cars with rebel soldiers came furiously down the road, and everyone rushed for cover. As the Russians returned the fire, Rostand drove furiously away at right angles and managed to penetrate nearly a mile along the narrow Korut Street before furious firing and the deep snort of tank cannon again brought him to a standstill.

Turning into an even narrower side street, he drove the car up on the pavement, turned toward the firing, crossed two more streets and then an amazing sight opened before his eyes.

There was the vast Firozier Square giving onto the Volgarin Bridge with the big Café Condé collapsed in ruins, the metal chairs twisted up in a grotesque pyramid, and huge improvised barriers across the boulevard at his side of the bridge. Everything had been commandeered to build the barricades. Huge steel railway carriages from the neighboring yard had been manhandled across the square and toppled over by repair men with giant levers so that their metal floors presented a wall of steel across the road. The big slabs of concrete paving the square itself had been hacked up and piled behind the steel walls. Trees that had given years of shade to the square had been torn up by what must have been hundreds of fanatical hands and dragged behind concrete slabs. Protecting the flanks of the barricade were burned-out lorries and buses all turned on their sides with their wheels facing the bridge, like beetles forced over on their backs feeling the air helplessly. Twenty yards ahead the jagged teeth of torn-up railway tracks with a four-foot trench dug behind them and a mass of overhead cables twisting like jungle growths over everything formed a tank trap.

Crouched in every convenient crevice behind the barricades were scores of young men all wearing the green Freedom Fighters' armband but with little else in common—men Rostand judged to be students and workmen—all tense, watchful, waiting.

The night was now dead black with all the streetlights out of order and a faint mist hanging dankly on the air from the river. A moon came and went behind the clouds and in one moment of illumination, Rostand saw at the opposite end of the bridge a group of Russian tanks, their big snouts pointing in a semicircle to cover every approach across the bridge. He also glimpsed what the Russians could not see—three Freedom Fighters swinging their way under the blackness of the bridge between the network of supporting struts toward the tank ditch twenty yards away.

Five minutes later came a great roar of revved-up engines and the tanks charged across the bridge, followed by armored cars packed with infantrymen. Immediately the machine guns behind the barricades went into action but the Freedom Fighters must have known that their bullets were powerless to penetrate tank armor.

Rostand found himself trembling, cold and afraid, but some need not to squander the chance of seeing the realities of this historical moment stopped him from hurrying back to the car. Half hidden in a shop doorway, he watched as one shell from a tank tore into the overturned bus, broke its length wide open and spurted two Freedom Fighters into the air like splinters from its own explosion. One screamed as he crashed back among the wreckage and went on screaming. The other fell soundlessly. Two young women with Red Cross armbands immediately crawled over the barricade toward them and as the moon came out again the three figures under the bridge suddenly emerged and flung themselves into the tank ditch almost in the path of the first tank. A second later three flashes tore at the entrails of the tank as the men threw Molotov cocktails upward and forward to carry the explosion away from themselves with the motion of the tank. Riding roughshod across the ditch without injuring the Freedom Fighters, the tank hit the iron teeth five yards behind, the cocktails exploded in its entrails, the overhead wires choked the churning treads and the tank reared up like a huge beetle caught in a web and burst into flames. A great cheer went up from the barricade as the second tank slowed down, fired five rounds and went into reverse.

A lull followed and in that lull Rostand slipped out of his shelter to talk to three of the Freedom Fighters. The picture they drew seemed too optimistic.

They claimed that down in the old city the network of small streets was largely in their hands. Tremendous battles were raging at the Kosygin Barracks with army artillery battering the besieging Russians who were on the point of withdrawing.

In the industrial area the Red Workers Battalion fought from every housetop and when the Russians brought up tanks and simply pounded one block after another into powder, the Freedom Fighters melted away before the blocks collapsed and reappeared elsewhere.

There was no overall coordination. One group in the east of the city did not know how another group three streets away fared. They simply fought on in heroic ignorance of the general picture, but the general picture was, they claimed, very good.

As Rostand made his way back to the old Skoda and headed for the embassy, he felt that this could not go on much longer. Every other street had its dead bodies unattended; every few minutes he ran up on the pavement to avoid reinforcements rushing past in lorries; shops were torn open, buildings were shattered, streets were carpeted with broken glass, and gas mains were sending thirty-foot flames into the air at the junction of Forut Street and the main Konstanza Boulevard.

Every kind of person and vehicle seemed to be converging on the embassy, and in the short time he had been away it had changed again. Refugees, wounded, British and American citizens were all crowding round the main gate. As he attempted to force his way through the crowd the roar of a new tank bombardment so deafened his ears that it could not have been more than two streets away. A small panic went through part of the crowd and several people tried to push their way past Thompson. As they did, he slammed the gate shut and snapped, "One at a time or not at all."

Only the English and Americans understood what he said and a wail went up from other parts of the crowd. Waving wildly at Thompson, Rostand reached the gate and said, "What's the drill?"

"Wounded—British citizens—no room left for anyone else."

People were sitting in groups on the paved frontage of the embassy, and the corridors inside were crowded with people trampling to and fro. All the ground floor offices had been converted into bed-sitting-rooms, except for the private office, and reception was overwhelmed with heaps of personal belongings, each carefully labeled with a name. Caroline and Penelope came in through the swing doors, nodded cursorily at Rostand,

and pressed on to some urgent business in the basement. The secretarial staff had become hotel domestics; the executive staff, managers; and when Rostand found His Excellency, he was sitting in splendid isolation in the private office listening to the Veralian radio.

Rostand gave him a swift account of his expedition. "My God," His Excellency said, "it sounds terrible. But the picture is even worse at the political level. The city is split into four factions. The Freedom Fighters are divided against themselves. The National Communists against the Marxist-Leninists, the International Communists against the pure Nationalists."

Suddenly the Veralian National Anthem came blaring out of the radio at double its normal pitch and an excited voice said: "Stand by for an important announcement! Stand by!" The next words were delivered with almost a sob in the broadcaster's voice. "We have taken Army Headquarters—the Russians are retreating—the battle is practically won. Stand by for an important announcement. . . . Comrades! Comrades! We are now about to hear from a very unexpected person. Comrades! Our uprising, our success has all been engineered for the last two years by a man you all know well, a man many people thought was a faithful member of the Party dictatorship we have overthrown. But we know now it was he who organized its overthrow—he who, under cover of his work as Minister of the Interior, persuaded the army to defect when the uprising began. Comrades! Listen! I give you—Joseph Rekavik Constantine Kalogh—our great new Leader. . . ."

"This is no time for explanations but for action," Kalogh's voice began.

"My God," His Excellency muttered and Rostand looked at him in amazement.

"Kalogh," he said, "it can't be."

"It is," His Excellency said.

" . . . and now I have even greater news for you," Kalogh's voice was saying. "Comrades, we are in negotiation with the Russian High Command for the withdrawal of all Russian forces from our beloved capital. There is every chance we may succeed. I would therefore call upon everyone for a cease-fire during the next twelve hours. Listen carefully, comrades. The cease-fire is necessary to enable the negotiations to proceed without duress. Cease fire! That is the command for the moment: 'Cease fire!' Bulletins will be broadcast every five minutes. If necessary, the battle will be resumed. But—for the time being—cease fire and hold your positions—cease fire!"

"Unbelievable!" Rostand said as the announcer's voice took over again.

His Excellency opened the top side drawer of his desk and pushed Robinsohn's letter across to Rostand. "Read that," he said.

As he finished it, Rostand said: "For God's sake, that fellow had second sight!"

"I wonder what's happened to him in all this?" His Excellency said, and Rostand detected the note of genuine concern in his voice.

As Robinsohn entered the Café Grundel he saw her at once and withdrew. A hundred yards down the sidewalk he turned back again. What did it matter if Caroline saw and greeted him? Reentering the café he turned away from her table and recognize her companion as the Veralian lawyer he had seen at the embassy reception. Lovers—clearly lovers—and very dangerous.

Buried behind an outdated copy of *Vie Veralia* he automatically ordered coffee, and was told that there was no more coffee. Cognac or water were the available alternatives.

He was beginning to sip the cognac when a chunky man with a pointed beard sat down and spread a copy of *Vie Veralia* across the table. That was the first sign. Taking his cue Robinsohn said, "Is yours a later one than mine?" They compared newspapers and—as prearranged—exchanged them. Both carefully checked an interval of three minutes and on the third minute the bearded man said: "The service is bad here. I don't think I'll wait."

Again the coded phrase from Robinsohn: "What do you expect in the middle of a revolution?"

The man left the café without replying. Robinsohn swallowed his cognac, threw down some money, and followed him.

The pace was slow at first and keeping him in view not difficult. Uneasiness began when they entered an area unfamiliar to Robinsohn. Sporadic gunfire grew louder. This was not according to plan. Keep away from the fighting, he had said, and here they were.

Robinsohn increased his pace and tried to overtake him. The bearded man increased his pace too. Dangerous to run. Some overzealous Freedom Fighter might put the worst interpretation on a simple burst of speed. The gunfire increased. What the hell had happened to the cease-fire? Who could hope to control all those freedom fanatics given lethal weapons and a heady sense of victory within their grasp?

Suddenly he was gone. As if spirited away, the physical presence of the man had evaporated. Robinsohn hurried on and a voice said, "In here." Automatically Robinsohn ignored it. The voice came from a deep dark doorway, the perfect place to split a man's belly open with any convenient weapon. Robinsohn stopped, waited for a man and boy to overtake him, and turned back again. Near the entrance to the doorway he leaned casually against the wall and said, "Why not out here?"

"In here," the voice said urgently.

A soldier came running down the street, stopped, and challenged

226

him. As Robinsohn produced his flawless forged papers, the soldier nodded and hurried on.

"In here," the voice said.

"Out here," Robinsohn replied.

Nothing happened then. No words, no sound, no movement. Robinsohn flattened himself against the wall. Again he felt the flash of the bullet, the reeling impact, the delayed pain in his blood and bowels. Instead the man stepped out and said, "What the hell is this?"

Robinsohn stiffened as he saw the slight bulge in the pocket of the raincoat. Swerve, duck, and dive diagonally was the drill but he remained still and said, "Have you got it?"

"No, but I have a message: meet at Frankael's Café Wednesday—I'll have the photostat then."

He went at once, striding away with military precision.

Robinsohn lived in a lavatory cum bathroom. It was the only part of a gutted house where the roof remained intact. It had the triple advantages of total anonymity, immediate service for basic needs, and water that still ran freely. He had dragged a mattress onto the tiled floor and slept there for two nights.

He lay there now smoking and thinking. Gunfire echoed and reechoed from the center of the city. The cease-fire was a farce. His quest more farcical. What did it matter if the photostat proved him right, when he could no longer communicate with London and the identity of the man he sought must be revealed at any moment by forces much more powerful than anything he, Robinsohn, could deploy? Or would it? Supposing the Russians suppressed the revolution? Would *He* go underground again. Underground? Become anonymous once more? Wait for the next chance?

There was always the next chance. No dictatorship ever remained permanent. The farce repeated itself. The proletariat had *not* revolted to put this lot in power, but now it was revolting to throw them out, totally reversing the Marxist doctrine—always providing you didn't see it as a counterrevolution. Would the proletariat behave any better if they won? The most you could say of any *organized* form of society was that it might be less unsatisfactory than the next one. Choosing became a question of temperament as much as justice. Choice? He had a choice now.

Whether to trust the man with the beard and keep the rendezvous at Frankael's Café. The double double cross had become drearily familiar. Useless to examine the pros and cons or even the so-called facts. Nothing survived scrutiny. It was the old, old business of the calculated risk. Which risk seemed the most rewarding and which the most dangerous? They coincided, of course—the greater the risk the greater the reward. They coincided now.

He didn't trust or mistrust The Beard any more or less than any other agent. He declined with necessary cynicism to deal in words like trust. He had to keep this rendezvous. Six months' work would be clinched or destroyed. Whether it came too late did not matter. Carrying the job through to a successful conclusion gave the final satisfaction. There was a kind of elegance in a prolonged and tortured strategy falling at last into perfect shape and form. But a safeguard, always a necessary safeguard, had to be fixed. Try to change the meeting place at the last moment . . . anticipate the worst by simply . . . creating it.

He knew The Beard's name now. Costain Ferenczi. Supposed assistant director of Cipher Section, Counterespionage. Living with his mother in one of the pink villas up on the hills reserved for the Party cadres. Dandified down to a pair of glossy shoes different from Veralia's standard product. What a mistake for counterespionage to wear shoes like that in a country like this. Or was it? Nothing if not cleverness itself. Deft footwork came naturally to Ferenczi.

Two hours to the rendezvous. Telephone now. Change the venue. That was the first safeguard. The box brought back the public telephones in the embassy. Rigid undecorated steel—not even a coat of paint . . . H.E., Penelope . . . Caroline . . . All seemed remote . . . Penelope still mouthing her ridiculous formulas in that la-di-da voice . . . Wasted woman . . . In another society she had potential . . . Convert her into different material . . . No real resemblance to his mother . . . until she . . .

Isolation had been hard to take after the embassy. There, claustrophobia, now agoraphobia. . . . The streets full of people but echoing emptily . . . Avoiding eyes, faces, talk . . . The lavatory, silent, lonely, cold, with just the hissing in the pipes for conversation and the gush of the cistern answering back . . . Softness set in so quickly . . . Man was a social animal . . . Alone and hunted, he needed metal for bones, water for blood, a computer instead of a brain.

The voice came unexpectedly high over the telephone. "Ferenczi here!"

"Our meeting today . . . The fighting's still going on. Make it another area. Down by the Bruhm Statue on Station Square."

"Wait, will you." Muffled voices and then, cold and clear. "All right, two thirty." The line went dead.

Two o'clock now. Fifteen minutes from the Ministry of Defense to the Bruhm Statue. Ferenczi should leave the office at two fifteen. Wait outside and follow? Or watch from the shadow of the Bruhm Statue? Action again. Frozen blood flowing once more.

Black coffee, followed by black coffee. Two fifteen . . . Set out now . . . Two twenty-five . . . The iron grille with its sunken courtyard offered concealment. Ferenczi was a walking man but if he came by car. . . .

Presently he stepped swiftly down the street with his precise military gait . . . no car . . . no escort . . . no police.

Suddenly a tank appeared, followed by visored motorcyclists. Everyone flattened against the walls.

Firing came closer. A great roar, with debris falling. Somewhere ahead the tank had smashed away a barricade . . . That's all he needed . . . The fighting to engulf the Bruhm Statue and six months' work lost in a fusillade of bullets . . . To hell with counterrevolution or whatever it was . . . Completing the plan completed a work of art . . . All the pieces came together symmetrically, or smashed irretrievably. He saw it—simply—in his mind's eye—the perfect gleaming alabaster bowl with Document 435 casually lying at its center . . . an ancient parchment in keeping with the bowl . . . and all its parts slowly, painfully put together by the artist Robinsohn.

Ferenczi left the shelter of a doorway and walked on lighting a cigarette. Almost there now. Next to the Bruhm Statue was the concrete gun emplacement, a relic of the last war. Drag a man in and nobody knew if you cut his throat.

Sweat under the armpits, in the palm of the hands . . . The tic beginning in the eye . . . There he goes past the entrance . . . Back again now . . . Let him pace, three, four, five, six times until completely secure . . . No sign of police . . . No cars . . . But who was this? . . . Attenuated legs like stilts, head buried neckless between thick shoulders . . . The ABVO? . . . Ferenczi's bodyguard? . . . Plainclothes detective? . . . No . . . He was passing on . . . Beyond the Bruhm Statue away to the right.

The eighth turn would be enough—Ferenczi relit his cigarette, walked back, did not see the arm flash out, but fell into the emplacement, throat gurgling, eyes bulging, blood blinding, kicking straight and true between the legs as a second blow cut off consciousness. The flashlight. The search began. Every pocket, case, crevice, swiftly turned out . . . letters, money, photographs . . . but no photostat. Another dreary double cross . . . Beat it quickly.

Back in the bathroom Robinsohn lay on the mattress, sweat pouring away, the cigarette dead between his lips.

A mistake. Violence had been a mistake. Perhaps if he had waited . . . Gone on negotiating . . . But no . . . Ferenczi without the document meant one of two things. Either it was all a frame-up and he had no real access to 435 or he had come as a decoy to trap Robinsohn.

There remained one other source. Begin again tomorrow . . . if there was a tomorrow . . . The fighting had died away . . . The cease-fire might be effective—for a time. In that time he must work swiftly. But sleep first . . . sleep. Two hours later he took the pills. Heavy, sweating sleep obliterated consciousness.

Hunger and thirst drove him awake. Check outside . . . Christ . . . Who was that? . . . A man paced up and down, up and down . . . Nondescript, unremarkable, just another citizen . . . But he went on pacing . . . Six one way, six another. Why would anyone do that unless . . . No sign of a gun . . . No Freedom Fighter's armlet.

Ten minutes later he still paced. Unaware of mimicking him, Robinsohn began pacing in the room . . . The last cigarette sucked dry. Must find food, drink, cigarettes . . . No back door . . . Whole wall of building blown away. Just the one remaining twisted staircase, perilous under any weight, leading immutably straight to the one front exit and the pacing figure . . . Nonsense . . . A nobody . . . Go down boldly . . . Walk out, risk it . . . Intuition, fear, cunning, experience held him back . . . When the many voices conflicted violently as now . . . sit still and wait . . . Waiting was to this game what breathing was to the ordinary human being . . . Waiting, turned inward, desperately reexamining thoughts worn threadbare until the nightmare threatened again . . . The wolf mother baying back. . . .

Find another image . . . Fasten on it . . . H.E. There was a marvelous exorcist. Solid, decent, clean-living, everything that repelled evil . . . What was the crazy old bourgeois darling doing now? . . . How did his impossible pomposity and ridiculous sense of honor survive a civil war with no holds barred? . . .

The embassy . . . solidity and warmth . . . order and decency . . . The cold air came through the shattered window pressing round him like a winding-sheet . . . The death of loneliness . . . Only the inner voice ceaselessly talking . . . A man outside? . . . Ridiculous . . . There was always a man outside.

Corrupted by the embassy, softened up by the sheltered life, flabby, fearful . . . Get back there . . . get back to the warmth, safety, and immunity. Christ, the big joke . . . Craving the prison you've escaped from . . . The old lag who couldn't stand the world outside . . . It's cold outside . . . Christ, yes . . . It's murderously cold outside . . . But what a rip-roaring cliché. . . .

Drink, cigarettes . . . Must get both . . . Over to the window . . . The figure still pacing . . . But if Robinsohn was his target—why wait?— why not come and get him? . . .

The roar of machines, guns, screams, began at the end of the street and flowed over everything. Russian tanks and soldiers driving the Freedom Fighters down the street like sheep to the slaughter . . . Blood, violence, flame, smoke . . . Choking in the narrow roadway . . . Men mutilated and dying and it was all a remote film on some unrealistic screen until one man peeled off and ran for shelter into Robinsohn's hideout.

The tanks rolled on. The Freedom Fighters vanished. The man opposite peered out again from his doorway. Not even the Russians could obliterate him.

Footsteps. Stumbling, moaning footsteps. Robinsohn went to the stairhead. The man was dragging his shattered leg up the stairs, blood pumping away in jets. A final cry of agony, shrill as scalding steam, gigantically engulfing the whole ruined building . . . echoing on . . . and on.

Robinsohn leaped down the shaky stairs as someone leaped up . . . The agent from the doorway? Obviously. Robinsohn reached the automatic rifle first and tore it from the dying grasp . . . fired, fired, fired . . . Not death. Mutilation in glorious detail of brother, mother, guilt, memory, enemy . . . Pieces of flesh spattered the walls. The eyes blown out the back of the head. The jaw shot away . . . Robinsohn leaped over it all and raced down the street.

Blood on his shoes but no guilt . . . a wild exultancy . . . It would not last . . . Killing always brought sexual excitement. Pulses hammering, pores sweating . . . And then the sudden collapse. To leave an empty shell—shaking—unrealized . . . still looking for a satisfaction beyond the flesh.

Join this group of singing Freedom Fighters. Didn't matter where or why. Become anonymous. Above all anonymous. What the hell were they singing about?

The embassy . . . a violent snake of volition uncoiled deep inside him and struck . . . Back to the embassy. Back at any cost . . . Back to the safety, smugness, security, boredom . . . Were they going that way? . . . Luckily . . . Otherwise.

Keep with the group. Crazy to go back . . . Marching, singing, jubilant . . . except for the man on the fringe . . . eying Robinsohn, diagonally.

Christ. It was the man from the doorway—disguised like himself as a Freedom Fighter—armlet—automatic rifle—what the hell could it mean? . . . Must have shot someone else on the stairs . . . No time to identify . . . Another murder . . . and this man . . . The ABVO . . . No mistaking his eye swiveling to check every few seconds.

Abandon the embassy . . . walk past it . . . march on like these people, bravely . . . bide his time . . . no other choice.

"We have won!"

The voice from the radio echoed round the private office of the embassy bursting with jubilation. "The Russians are withdrawing from the city."

Outside in the streets there seemed living evidence to justify the statement. In the dusk of the misty evening long lines of Russian field guns, ammunition lorries, and tanks were pouring out of the city, all carrying the great Red Star, with their field kitchens marked by glowing fires in metal containers. Everyone crowded the windows of the embassy to watch the almost silent procession.

One hour later the last of the tanks disappeared as a great new hubbub arose—a hubbub of people linking arms to dance down the roads, into the squares, making for the Stalin Boulevard. Some sang, some embraced, some kissed in orgiastic release from horror into triumph; bunting and flags appeared, an accordionist began to play on the street, and a crowd of students formed a giant crocodile, heading for the center of the city, carrying two banners:

"We Are Going to Rule Us."

"Out with the Ruskies."

As His Excellency turned away from his window he said to Rostand: "It isn't going to last, you know. It isn't going to last."

Within three days his words proved all too true, but those three days were charged with every kind of drama, triumph, and despair. On the first day the city gave itself up to a festival of victory with music, dancing, drinking, and great crowds of people surging through the trafficless streets, some chanting, some drunk, some holding impromptu celebration ceremonies. The electric atmosphere broke down all convention, with young girls dancing wildly in the streets and strangers kissing strangers.

On the second day the saturnalia was qualified by mourning for the many dead, and here and there at intervals amid the uncollected rubbish, the smashed streetcars, the rubble, the burned-out machines of war and the stench of neglected trash cans, someone was weeping over a body dead but still unburied.

At Stalin Square the bodies were laid in rows with a scattering of flower tributes—the ordinary typist riddled by machine gun bullets, the student with a sheet over his dismembered body, and the young army lieutenant whose burns made him unrecognizable. People poured in and out of the great Gothic cathedral on the square, some sobbing, others bowed in public prayer.

On the third day the radio bulletins were still exultant and all calls to clear the city of rubble and rubbish, to set the traffic moving again and return to work were ignored in the last moments of intoxicated triumph.

But on the third day the new Russian forces that had been pouring across the border and massing tanks and artillery outside the city to join the remnants retreating from inside, slowly gathered their vast strength. On the fourth day at dawn the combined Russian forces of the old and new—now in overwhelming power—struck back again.

Within hours the city was converted into an exploding inferno, far worse than anything that had happened before, and among the battles, two came close to the embassy. At eight o'clock on the fourth day, the front windows crashed in, the lights went out, and His Excellency ordered everyone down to the cellars as shells came bursting closer and closer. The cellars were more extensive than the basement, each one opening into others to form a small catacomb. Following the pattern of London air raid shelters, Penelope appointed marshals and everyone was forced into an orderly single-file retreat into the damp, cold underground. There, huddled under what blankets were available, lit by an occasional candle, but reassured by the complete calm of H.E.'s burly figure directing operations, the women and children among the refugees sat, lay, or crouched, some crying, some very frightened, others just waiting with peasant resignation for the worst to happen. One section of the basement, with the steel riot-gate drawn across it, was given over to the staff, and there, by the light of two candles, Hargreaves and Rostand exchanged an occasional witticism. Penelope and Caroline remained ready to make forays up to the kitchen for coffee and food, and Miss Fairweather sat hunched up crying silently. The lesser staff members crowded close to one another, whispering apprehensively but much too English to express open fear. Thompson and Richards moved around keeping check on the external refugees, reporting back to H.E., who had set up a small office in one of the alcoves off the basement. Piled in one corner were the vital code books, the Top Classified and Current Telegram files taken from the strong room, and the registry.

By ten o'clock the crash of bombardment came much nearer, the earth shuddered every few minutes, and it seemed certain that the shells must presently begin the slow demolition of the embassy itself. Hastily, H.E. briefed key members of his staff on how to deal with any hysteria that might break out. The danger of someone creating panic and releasing a trampling mob was high. Two loudspeakers were given to Thompson and Rostand who remained within reach of the main entrance to the cellars.

By two o'clock in the morning the atmosphere grew foetid, the mass of refugees more uneasy and uncomfortable. Pamela showed a cynical coolness which Hargreaves had to admire and set an example by the way she controlled Toby and Sarah. Four babies in arms created a constant background of wailing and crying, and a young peasant woman who had come in to market that day discreetly slipped her nipple into the lips of her three-weeks'-old baby boy. Everyone had his or her chance to be escorted to the ground-floor lavatory, but greater risks had to be taken before very long. The simultaneous needs of several people quickly rendered one lavatory inadequate. Longer forays along the ground-floor corridor to the second lavatory now took everyone past smashed glass and twisted window frames. As the bombardment came even closer and the shuddering earth seemed—on occasion—to rock the embassy on its heels, H.E.'s movements became slower and even more measured, his words fewer but more authoritative. The suave diplomat was becoming the military commander. Returning to the staff section of the cellars after one of his rounds,

Rostand saw the brittle quality in several faces, the overbright talk, the readiness to laughter pitched too high, and knew from the constant coming and going to the lavatory reserved for the staff how frequently the bowels demanded retribution for all this very English external attempt at control.

It was when the shell hit the roof with a thundering roar, sending the slates crashing down, that hysteria swept through that section of the cellar directly under the explosion. H.E. had just begun his first personal round when the "incident," as he later referred to it, occurred. It sent a dozen people fighting for the exit. He grabbed the loudspeaker from Thompson and in a voice rich, resonant, and unruffled called: "There is no danger— stay where you are—remain calm. Stay where you are."

The effect of the voice, the words, and the solid, unmoved figure standing foursquare before them quickly took effect. The screams died away, the pushing and struggling ceased. When Rostand made a quick foray to the third floor to discover the extent of the damage he found it very superficial. The shell had exploded before hitting the roof.

It was the first of many dangerous moments successfully contained by sheer force of a small number of personalities, and when, two hours later, the bombardment subsided, everyone was shepherded back into the embassy proper. As they settled down once more, the embassy remained a crawling anthill of apprehensive, contending people. H.E. remarked to Rostand over a frugal dinner of bread, cheese, and coffee: "Sartre believed that hell was other people. I believe it's the enforced community of uncongenial spirits."

Certainly there were many uncongenial spirits and an occasional burst of open quarreling, and the one American journalist among them became very unpopular because of his brash comments. In order to reduce the tensions H.E. was forced to open the big period dining room to a dozen strangers who slept in their clothes on the floor. He and his wife also tried to sleep in their clothes but achieved nothing more than fitful dozing. Neither allowed their growing weariness to interfere with running what had now become a small refugee camp.

On the fourth day the battle seemed to veer away from the embassy and as he wearily climbed off his bed frame in the dawn—the mattress and eiderdown had been surrendered to refugees—H.E. said to Penelope, "We must get some of these people out of here and across the border."

"And how do you propose doing that?" she asked.

"We have *some* petrol—and we have the Rolls."

"That must be reserved for the staff," she said. "It looks very much to me as if we ourselves will be forced out of here at any minute."

"I shan't go until the place is falling down," H.E. said, "but since you've brought it up, I've been thinking we should get all the female staff away at once."

"Does that include me?"

234

"I think you and Vanessa should go."

"Vanessa—not me."

"What's the point in your staying here?"

"You're not suggesting I'm useless?"

"On the contrary—but why expose yourself to unnecessary danger?"

"And why, for that matter, should you?"

"Don't be absurd. It's my job."

"And so is it mine."

"I don't think we should have any false heroics."

"That applies to both of us. But I must get Vanessa out of all this—I think she's heading for a breakdown."

It was Rostand and Thompson who finally went to work on the abandoned army lorry with a flat tire and failed ignition, which stood, drunkenly, half on the pavement opposite the embassy. It took them three hours to get the machine in working order again and then they used two of the six precious petrol cans stored in the garage, half filled its tank, and felt a sense of triumph completely out of proportion, when the engine sputtered to life.

There were so many people clamoring to go when it came to the point that quite clearly the lorry could not take them all. First some old chairs were hauled up from the basement and ranged down either side of the lorry under its canvas hood to give some support to women and children, but the chairs had to be dragged out again to make more room. When everyone was piled in with luggage, there were two indiscriminate heaps—one of human beings and one of luggage. Two big Union Jacks were tied over the canvas hood and the radiator. Nearly forty people squashed together under almost concentration-camp conditions and when Vanessa—late as usual—came out with her suitcase and glanced at the mass of women and children, she quickly retreated back into the embassy.

"Why can't we use the Rolls?" she said to her father.

"So when it comes to the point you demand capitalist luxury, do you?" he said.

"I shall be sick all the way in the lorry." The tears were already rolling down her cheeks. Madame Beaucaire, the wife of the French commercial attaché, came up with her three-year-old girl dragging at her hand. His Excellency knew that one of the chance brutalities of this civil war had been to kill her husband when the French Legation had accidentally become the center of a battle between Russian tanks and guerillas. She looked yellow and exhausted and could not stop trembling.

"Pliss," she said . . . "would like—if you pliss. . . ." She could not find the words but gestured toward the lorry.

On the instant he made the decision. Rostand would drive the Rolls and take Vanessa, Madame Beaucaire, and another eight people who could not be crushed into the lorry. The car with its pennant, badge, and papers would provide the full panoply of diplomatic protection for what looked as if it was becoming a convoy. But now a series of minor accidents seemed to connive in a conspiracy to force the ambassador to become involved himself. Rostand's right hand had been badly cut by broken glass. That left Hargreaves, his chauffeur, or Thompson. Hargreaves, he knew, had not driven for years, his chauffeur had badly sprained his wrist moving beds and furniture, and Thompson, when approached, said he wasn't really capable. Finally there seemed to be no alternative, especially since his own daughter was involved. He would drive the Rolls himself. Kadar, a wizened Veralian tourist dragoman who had taken refuge in the embassy, agreed to drive the lorry but quickly showed impatience. Sitting in the driving seat he began honking his horn furiously.

"Tell him to wait five minutes," His Excellency said to Rostand and sent Caroline in search of Penelope. Swiftly eight people were selected from the remaining refugees, the seat arms of the Rolls were pressed back into their slots and everyone piled in with luggage protruding from the boot, overflowing the roof, and tied to the wings.

Hargreaves and Rostand both protested that H.E. should not expose himself to the dangers that—diplomatic privilege or no—undoubtedly lay ahead.

"I want to see my daughter safely across the border," H.E. said, but Rostand felt very strongly that that was not the only motive. For complicated reasons the Old Man would have insisted on taking the Rolls even if he believed that someone else could have driven it and it did not carry his daughter. Before he left, H.E. gave instructions to Hargreaves with a carefully coded message to be put over the radio as soon as the end of jamming and other interference made it possible.

"I'll be back in three hours," he said.

A third, very faded and tattered Union Jack was drawn over the Rolls's long bonnet and secured with rope, before the car finally drew—magisterially—out of the big iron gates and the lorry lumbered into position behind it.

Against the luxurious upholstery Vanessa was crushed between Madame Beaucaire with her baby daughter, and an elderly Englishwoman, once a devoted Communist who had joined the Veralian broadcasting services but who had seen enough in the last forty-eight hours to crave a quick return to England. A frightened businessman who continually mopped the sweat from his face was pressed against an injured nurse, and a Veralian nun had her arm round a white-faced typist who was trying not to cry. Pamela sat impassively in one corner trying to cuddle the Rivers children, Patricia and Jonathan.

In the lorry, everyone attempted to adjust to the savage bumps and

236

jolts as it crashed over potholes, but very soon the children were being sick and the lurching of the lorry threatened even the adults.

As the absurd little convoy with its grandiose leader drew out of the central area and into a working-class suburb the firing began again, and when tanks came tearing up the road, they pulled over onto the path, the lorry tilting dangerously as it came to a standstill. A Russian officer roared up on his motorcycle and demanded papers. He spoke no English, came from the Caucasus, and could not understand H.E.'s heavily accented Russian. Immensely dignified, splendidly imperturbable, H.E. beckoned Kadar, the Veralian driver of the lorry, who came up to interpret.

He rapidly translated the Russian officer's words: "*You* won't get through—you had better turn back." Ignoring the warning, H.E. waited until the tanks and motorcycles had screamed away again, gave the signal, and set off once more, carefully matching his speed to the maximum possible for the lorry. Inside the canvas cave, conditions quickly became so foetid and uncomfortable that quarreling broke out and the single nurse among them—suffering from an injured arm—shouted in pain and anger for the driver to slow down. Seeing the lorry dropping away behind him in his mirror H.E. reduced speed also.

Then came the first official Russian checkpoint with a barbed-wire barrier across the road. The clumsy three-cornered exchange among Kadar, H.E., and a fat, jolly Russian major led to some facetious remarks on his part. If you want to get killed, do you prefer tank cannon . . . or machine guns?

It was at this point that H.E. had reason to curse the Foreign Service afresh. Unlike any other country's ambassador, he—representing no less than Her Imperial Majesty of Great Britain—carried a blue and gold passport no different from that of the ordinary British citizen. One flimsy set of papers marked him out as an ambassador—his letters of credence with the Royal Coat of Arms. The Russian major stiffened when he presented these credentials as his irrefutable right to proceed. Sheer force of personality, allied to the belief that such credentials would open the gates of hell if His Excellency so desired, finally persuaded the Russian major to contact some remote superior by field telephone. Five minutes of wrangling in high-pitched Russian and he came back with the single word —"Proceed." He then added something that Kadar could not quite interpret—the lunatic Englishman prefers death to life.

Two minor skirmishes led to one devastating period of half an hour when they all crouched for shelter in a ditch as the convoy came under heavy fire. Afterward they found that parts of the lorry and Rolls had been pierced by bullet holes but nothing vital had been hit. Once the lorry broke down and had to be towed before the engine came to life again. Two big country towns were scenes of terrible devastation. In one the tanks had simply pumped shells indiscriminately into houses, offices, public buildings, wherever the slightest sign of resistance appeared until the buildings were systematically reduced to rubble from the top to the lower floors. In the second town, the dead and wounded lay on the sidewalk and battles still raged with at least three big fires burning fiercely and unattended. And then came the final confrontation.

They were called to a halt a hundred yards from a bigger heavily armed Russian post, the last before the border. Interrogation in considerable depth followed. His Excellency simply demanded diplomatic immunity and the Russian lieutenant, finding himself out of his depth, summoned a colonel.

The colonel, polished, suave, amused, acknowledged at once that he was dealing with a man of substance and became so interested in meeting personally for the first time such an august person as a British ambassador that he took the conversation into unnecessary bypaths. As if unaware of any danger, His Excellency became very forceful, brought the conversation back to immediate issues, and insisted on his rights. Whereupon the colonel indicated that if he, in his Rolls, had diplomatic immunity, the lorry and its occupants certainly had not. When H.E. asked him, through Kadar, what he proposed doing if they simply drove on down the road, he said, "We should be compelled to open fire."

"Would you," His Excellency said, "be prepared to take responsibility for shooting down in cold blood a British ambassador?"

"We should, of course, avoid that."

"And if I am driving the lorry?"

"You would be very foolish to drive the lorry."

"Why don't you interrogate everyone in the lorry—you will discover that they are innocent men and women who had nothing to do with the uprising."

"All right," the colonel said.

The interrogation was not only long and detailed but deliberately prolonged by the colonel for reasons which he refused to disclose.

Finally he drew His Excellency aside and said, "It is the same—you may proceed but not the lorry."

Without another word His Excellency walked over to the lorry, ordered Kadar to take over the Rolls, and climbed into the driver's seat. At first he found the gears unfamiliar and they ground away viciously. Then, as the lorry moved forward, the machine gunners a hundred yards away ostentatiously trained their weapons on him. The colonel stood for a moment in the path of the lorry ordering him to halt. At the last minute he stepped aside and turned with his arm raised toward the machine gunners.

In the driving seat His Excellency's foot hesitated on the accelerator. How far should he carry this bluff—how far should he really endanger his own life and the lives of the refugees? What had heroism to do with diplomacy? Why in heaven's name was he sitting here in the driving seat of this crude machine and why—above all—should he try to behave like a second-rate hero in a Hemingway novel? Simply because a man as intelligent as the colonel would not dare to open fire and kill in cold blood the British ambassador? That seemed true enough. And yet . . . He had closed to within fifty yards of the machine guns and, sitting rigid as an iron girder, he kept his almost paralyzed foot on the accelerator. Forty yards . . . thirty . . . They would not dare. But they were lifting the barrels slightly now and taking careful aim . . . Twenty yards . . . The figures were tense over their guns, waiting the final command. . . .

As a sudden spasm of fear bit deeply into His Excellency his hands shook on the wheel, the Russian colonel came rushing down the road shouting at him, and His Excellency's foot lifted from the accelerator. The colonel reached the lorry, peered upward into the cab, and indicated that he wanted Kadar the interpreter brought to him.

Two minutes later the colonel said through Kadar: "You are either a very brave man or just another mad Englishman. I am a soldier. I admire courage. Because I admire courage, you may go through."

At the border customs post, Vanessa turned back momentarily and fell into her father's arms. White, strained, miserable, she did not trust herself to say anything more than thank you. Then she hurried across the checkpoint desperately trying not to cry in public. It took nearly an hour for the remainder of the refugees to filter across in closely examined groups and by then the Rolls and the lorry were on their way back to the embassy.

Coming wearily into the city again, His Excellency was constantly stopped at one Russian checkpoint after another. Clouds of stone dust blew along the streets, the smell of cordite and fires permeated everything, and collapsed buildings, burned-out tanks, and bodies marked every other crossroad. A new bombardment of guns broke out as they entered Stalin Boulevard, and the Russians turned them back once again. From the old city the firing was still continuous and Kadar took the lead in the lorry to make a detour round the network of side streets. There they came upon one whole row of buildings which had been blown to pieces with great clouds of dust still rising on the air, half-buried people moaning under the debris, and rescue squads trying to reach them. Brought to a halt again by the mountain of rubble across the street, His Excellency had a glimpse of what looked like half a dozen suits hung on a railway bridge, drying in the wind. As they drew closer his breath stopped. They were men—hanged —their necks broken—their heads grotesquely hunched together like grapes. This was to be the fate of scores of Freedom Fighters. When the Rolls tried to pass under the bridge, they found the whole area sealed off.

For nearly half an hour they made different approaches to the embassy and at last found a way through. Dusty, weary, red-eyed, His Excellency stepped out of the Rolls in the forecourt to be embraced by Penelope, who simply said: "Thank God. We were sure something horrible had happened."

Pressure on beds and space had eased with thirty refugees safely spirited away across the frontier, and His Excellency was able to lie on his own bed in luxurious isolation but he found that he could not relax. His nerves still raw from the struggle to reach the border, pictures of the dead, the mutilated, and the hanged kept coming up at the back of his mind. With all the front windows blown out and a gaping hole in the roof, the smell of blood and carnage could not be excluded even from his own private bedroom. The door of the dining room was hanging lopsidedly on one hinge with thick dust on the chandeliers and furniture.

One hour later he gave up trying to relax and once more took charge of a still-besieged embassy. They were still eating bread and cheese and drinking dubious water that had to be boiled on the mobile stove somehow conjured out of the rubble by the ever-resourceful Thompson. The stove had a Russian trademark stamped on its iron frame and was so clearly part of army equipment that His Excellency wondered whether they might not very soon be arrested for looting, but without gas or electricity there seemed some justification.

No baths, no lighting, and minimum rations reduced living standards to basic necessities. Friction between certain groups of the remaining refugees created a tense atmosphere. Hargreaves and Rostand found their morale deteriorating by the sixth day. Caroline had a hysterical outburst on the seventh, and the most unexpected people revealed reserves of patience and adaptability. Miss Hallows, supervisor of the typing pool, remained plump and smiling, almost seeming to enjoy the situation, in part because the caste system had to relax under such conditions and everyone spoke to her without regard to status. She enjoyed a new sense of being a complete human being.

But the person who continued to behave as if everything were completely normal, the man whose imperturbability appeared to show no signs of cracking, the diplomat whose external calm reassured everyone, was His Excellency. Penelope bustled about ruthlessly insisting on observance of the new regulations, but it was His Excellency's unhurried walk, his benign presence, and extraordinary patience that gave a central core of strength amid the steadily growing hardships. One of the worst hit them on the eighth day. There was no more water to clear the lavatories and within twenty-four hours the stench began to seep down the corridors and into every room.

The bags under His Excellency's eyes grew steadily heavier, the eyes themselves duller, his nerves so raw it was like the minute stabbing of multiple knives, but the monumental weariness that weighed down every limb rarely interfered with routine duties. Penelope alone—in the recovered privacy of their bedroom—saw him collapse every evening on the bed and lie prostrate in total, nerve-wracked exhaustion; Penelope alone worried deeply whether the strain might not bring on a heart attack, or, even worse, a stroke; Penelope alone hoped that his rigid control would at last crack and he would be forced to surrender and stay in bed.

There was absolutely no warning. A man came running down the street, tires screamed in the distance, a fusillade of shots rang out, the man staggered, fell, began crawling toward the embassy gates, and collapsed. Standing in the front courtyard talking to Thompson, His Excellency cut off in mid-sentence. As the man stopped crawling, twisted convulsively, and a great moan came from his lips, something about his face and figure seemed familiar. His Excellency waited perhaps five seconds and when no more shots came he said, "Quick!" to Thompson and bending low they hurried out into the road. They reached the twisted but now still figure as two ABVO agents came roaring down the road on motorcycles. Lifting the figure between them, they hurried back toward the gate. Screaming to a standstill one agent raised his gun and shouted in Veralian, "Halt or I fire!" There was a split-second chance of death, a flashing moment when the agent could have shot them *outside* the gate but a second's hesitation allowed them to get inside. A huge Union Jack had been draped across the gate, with the words British Embassy in crudely sprawled letters spelled out on white cardboard. When the agents came rushing across the road, His Excellency simply confronted them, standing very foursquare, pointing to the sign. The two men went into brief conference, and spoke in rapid Veralian that His Excellency pretended not to understand. They wanted to know whether their victim was dead or alive, but they received no answer. They then made threatening gestures, and tried to push through the gate which Thompson promptly locked. Guns were waved, further threats made, and at last they roared away.

Instantly returning to Thompson, now kneeling beside the prone figure, His Excellency heard him say: "He *is* dead, I'm afraid."

Robinsohn lay there, his chest all shot away, his clothes soaked in blood, his eyes staring up at the sky.

Penelope appeared in the doorway.

His Excellency went over to her at once. "I shouldn't look if I were you," he said.

"It's Robinsohn, isn't it?"

"Yes."

"Is he? . . ."

"I'm afraid he is."

"My God," she said, "but you need some help. I'll get Caroline."

His Excellency went back to the body and stood a moment staring down at the face. It was thinner and yellowed, with the lines from the nostrils down either side of the mouth now cruelly etched. The brow was puckered above the nose in two deep and tormented furrows. In one short week the face had changed. What had happened to him since he escaped from the embassy to leave new and even crueler marks? They would never know. Nor did the ambassador know that one part of Robinsohn's mission was now accomplished. He had found the retribution he continually sought. Somehow this man had entered and changed His Excellency's life: somehow he had brought to a head the steadily growing conflicts that had been part of His Excellency's daily experiences over ten painful years, and now the ambassador felt close to him as with someone who had created a very special kind of not clearly understood bond.

He was worthy of a better death. To run like a frightened rabbit and be shot to pieces . . . there were sordid elements in that. . . . But no sadistic hand had delayed the black curtain. It had come down suddenly with a ruthless burst of metal in his body. One practical thing remained to be done—inform the ABVO or there would be no peace.

Slowly over the next forty-eight hours the fighting diminished, the fires were brought under control, the Freedom Fighters broken into smaller and smaller groups, and the Veralian Army overwhelmed by such massive Russian armor that nothing could stand against it. Slowly one refugee after another decided to take the risk and move out of the embassy. A few telephone lines began to work again with the outside world and a scattering of telegrams were exchanged once more with London. In his first outgoing telegram His Excellency gave a long report on the immediate situation.

At eight o'clock on the evening of the third day of peace he finished his first cooked meal in over a week and said to Penelope: "There's a rather special letter I wanted to write—I think I'll go down to the office again."

Ten minutes later sitting at his desk he began writing in longhand:

"Dear Sir Richard,
    "I think you have been aware that for a considerable number of years now I have had increasing difficulty in adapting to the chang-.ing values of the modern world and in particular the expression of those values in the new diplomacy. I did once believe that there was such a thing as a single code that could be justified above most, if not all, others—but I have long come to accept a world of plural values in which alternative credos are susceptible of almost equal justification. That is to me not only the modern triumph but also the modern tragedy.

242

"However, the theoretical acceptance of such a position does not in my case admit of too much erosion to my own chosen principles, and while I can understand that a certain arrogance is implied in my continuing to cling to them, I have found myself in recent years surrendering so many—so to say—points in those principles, that they were in danger of total dissolution.

"In a strange way, my growing dilemma has been crystalized, these past six weeks, by the arrival, lodgment, and treatment of Mr. Robinsohn. I think I made clear in our prolonged exchanges over his position that it brought the whole of my code into fresh question. It would be superfluous to repeat the arguments which led me to believe that the charges brought against him were not sufficiently proved, but I would emphasize that my persistent attempts to understand and accept the position adopted in your office were continually frustrated, by the evidence, my personal knowledge of him, a number of reliable witnesses in this office, and his general behavior. I readily admit, however, that against the far more detailed evidence available to you in London there might seem to be a romantic element in my persistent belief in the man, but I have always found, in the final analysis, that when rational inquiry is exhausted, temperamental inclination dominates my decisions. Perhaps that is why I have never been a very good ambassador, since the first prerequisite for such an office is to be able to accept instruction and carry it out with conviction, even though one does not believe in it.

"I feel now that I must, as a preliminary, admit to you that my interpretation of your last instruction about Robinsohn was deliberately Machiavellian and not in the tradition either of the Service or my own code. In fact I was forced once again into a very serious modification of that code."

The following two paragraphs were meticulously phrased to describe His Excellency's resolution of his own dilemma which led him into "deception by omission."

"Since then a terrible climax—which I almost see as retribution —has occurred. Mr. Robinsohn was shot down in front of this embassy three days ago and died a painful but mercifully quick death. In his particular profession it would be axiomatic to expect violent death, but—against all rational argument and common sense—I cannot free myself from a feeling of some sort of complicity in his—well —I can only call it murder.

"If I had had the courage of my convictions and simply refused to carry out your instruction, thus prolonging Mr. Robinsohn's

243

period of asylum in the embassy, he would still be alive, but such a reaction would, of course, have foreshadowed another inevitable step: that of my resignation.

"Instead, I chose the course I have sometimes been forced, in recent years, to accept in diplomacy but have always despised in my private life—expediency. As a result Mr. Robinsohn has died a particularly horrible death and I cannot rid myself of a disturbing sense of guilt in the matter.

"I know that for a sophisticated man of the world seasoned in the subtleties if not cynicisms of diplomacy, this may seem to you an overrefinement of moral responsibilities if not a farcical piece of ethical finesse, but it is, of course, merely the occasion for the final clash of a long struggle in my life to adapt to a modern world.

"I have now to confess failure. As Marx would say, I cannot escape the conditioning of my class or upbringing, and as I would say—very simply—I cannot escape my creaking, outdated, old-fashioned conscience. If I were a younger man, I would continue with the struggle but I am now fifty-seven and it seems to me that my habits and values are firmly set for whatever days remain to me.

"I hope, therefore, that you will not consider it in any way an implied criticism of the policy you have pursued, but rather the admission of failure of a rapidly aging man—if I now tender you, with the greatest regret, my resignation."

A heaviness came down on His Excellency as he slowly, ponderously read through that draft of the letter, making corrections as he went. Most of the early emendations were minor but when he came to the last sentence he added two words. ". . . now tender you, with the greatest regret *and respect,* my resignation." Frowning heavily he stared at the words—with respect. They were false words. He had no respect for Sir Richard. He despised him. Slowly he drew his pen through them. It would mean rewriting the whole letter but he settled down—laboriously—to begin all over again.

It was dusk when he slipped out of the embassy with a brief word to Thompson at reception, and at once became aware of an atmosphere so new it intruded almost more than the old. No gunfire, no bullets or machine guns, but a deep hush on the air as if the resources of sound had been so exhausted there was nothing left but the calm of total vacuum. The street lighting no longer functioned but as he crossed the road and picked his way through the carpet of splintered glass, he saw a glow in the near distance, and as he walked on to enter Fanon Square, he came upon a forest of candles poised on railings, on rough-and-ready graves, on window ledges, and on the green patch of grass before the Memorial. Passing beyond the square, as the dusk deepened he saw more candles spring to life, and then as he approached the Gothic church at the corner of Vilivocs Street, the steps running up to the entrance were lined on either side with still more candles sending their flickering patterns over the façade with the artistry of a thousand minute flames.

Crowds of people were pouring silently in and out of the church, and on the steps themselves, figures were crouched, some in prayer, some in tears, one at least openly sobbing. In the light from the candles, the big green square fronting the steps revealed a number of crude crosses over graves dug for Freedom Fighters where they fell, and every other grave had at least one black figure bowed before it.

All Souls' Day. His Excellency knew all too well what it meant. The day of the dead, and here in the Veralian capital, the day of mourning the dead was prolonged into all-night vigils. He walked slowly on, mounted the steps, and entered the church. A great blaze of lighted candles illumined the immediate area of the altar and the aisles, the candles constantly renewed as people came and went among scores of kneeling figures, the organ playing softly in the background and the murmur of prayers revealing the deeper levels of religious communication.

Under the shawls and the kerchiefs, young and old bore the unifying stamp of grief and suffering. Some few of the lifted faces were touched by a kind of grace as if they drew on some deeper place of the imagination or spirit to lift themselves above the indulgence of grief.

Silently, unobtrusively, His Excellency chose a place among the pews and knelt beside an old peasant woman. He had often tried to reach the benediction of that grace of which his religion spoke, and now, frowning, eyes shut, he attempted to surrender himself half in wordless prayer to the music, the beauty, the extra dimension he sought. Simple prayers were no longer possible; familiar phrases hopelessly outworn; appeals to a god in human shape useless. But whatever forces had culminated in this beautiful church and the poetry of these rituals should be capable, if he surrendered to them, of elevating his mind above the terrible sense of failure, inadequacy, guilt—and even a kind of death in himself. He was here grieving for something that had died too, but he could not clearly identify what: a way of life perhaps, but that was putting it too high—his own way of life, his ideals? Patiently he knelt, absorbing the atmosphere. Patiently he waited. But nothing happened: nothing came to his aid. No sense of grace or relief or elevation. He felt his moving lips without words ridiculous. His knees hurt him on the cold stone slabs. Heavily, wearily he came to his feet again, and walked slowly out into night air.